ORBIS

LORE OF TELLUS BOOK TWO

E A Purle

WHEN ALL SEEMS LOST, I WILL GUIDE THE WAY

Previous book in the series

LORE OF TELLUS
BOOK ONE

On the world of Tellus there are two ways of doing things: the Old Way and the New Way. In the city of Portis-Montis, these two ways and their worlds collide.

Hugh Geber is the alchemist at the University of Science and Progression. In a world where everyone follows the family career, he has found himself the last in line to carry the torch.

When a meeting with Chancellor Robert James Smithson leaves him with an impossible deadline and a mysterious package, Hugh is left with no choice but to try and save the family name along with his job. Fate, however, is not on his side, and his world is turned upside-down.

Now Hugh must not only fight for his place within the university, but also find out what lies behind the mysterious package before time runs out.

Orbis Editorial Review

The family ties grow stronger and wider, the spiritual journey deeper than ever before, the quest yet more dangerous.

We re-join Hugh Geber and his companions as their lives become even more exciting and their foes ever more evil. E A Purle takes us on another adventure to his mystical world, populated with characters who have grown in complexity since we left them in the falls cavern at the end of Firestone. As we learn more of the New World and the Old World, their origins and their conflicts, Purle's skilful balancing of challenge, triumph and disaster, relationships and emotions takes us on a journey into his imagination and into the midst of another rattling good tale!

Lynn Godson, The Digital Wordsmith

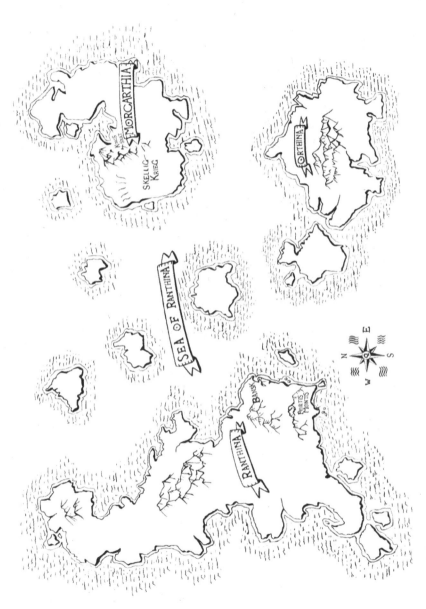

First paperback edition February 2022

978-1-7398965-1-5 (paperback)

978-1-7398965-0-8 (hardback)

978-1-7398965-2-2 (ebook)

Www.eapurle.co.uk

For my wife, Kay.
Team Ked all the way x

Chapter 1

So, this is what dying feels like, then? Kind of floaty, a bit dark, but bright at the same time. I still feel as though I'm moving …

Hugh looked around the semi-darkness, trying to figure out where he was or, more specifically, what he was. The last thing he remembered was being in the cavern behind the waterfall, consoling Barrington after they had just watched Thomas fall through the watery abyss. They were about to head back to the hotel when the cavern went dark. Hugh remembered someone talking to them, but for the life of him, he couldn't remember what they had said. It was all a bit of a blur now, but he was certain of one thing. He wasn't in his body. It felt cold, almost damp, and very peculiar. He had felt a falling motion, followed by a feeling of rising. There was now a new sensation coming through, something more tangible. His face was as cold as ice, and there were ridges, yes, definitely ridges, running along his face.

He opened his eyes.

The tiled floor was cold upon his cheek, but Hugh could not move. Something had paralysed him. It took him a moment for the rest of his senses to make their way back into his body, but when they arrived, he could hear someone talking. He knew he needed to listen, but it was taking all of his energy to stay in this room. Slowly but surely, he could focus on the voice, and it sounded pretty angry to Hugh.

"I can't believe you thought you could get away with that. You were lucky I was there to rescue you," said the voice of an angry man. "I've a good mind to throw you back, let the sprites deal with you. Do you have anything to say for yourself?"

The man waited for a response from whomever he was talking to, but it didn't sound as though he was having much luck.

"There's no use trying to use hand gestures with me. I'm not accustomed to parlour games. Just talk to me; use your voice like a normal servant."

Still silence, and then the man seemed to realise what was going on. Hugh moved slightly on the floor.

"Oh, I see. You don't wish to talk because of them, is that it? Well, once I'm finished with them, they will be no trouble to us anymore. Nobody messes with the King of Morcarthia, I can assure you of that."

Hugh felt a foot drive into his stomach, and the pain made stars appear in his eyes. The voice became distant, and he knew he was losing touch with reality once again, but he could just about make out the last part of the conversation.

"You move the bodies whilst I tidy up here. I can dispose of them once I'm done. We don't want people knowing we were here and —" There was a pause in his instructions. "Now, what are you waving your arms at? I expect my servants to speak to me, not flap their hands like a bird."

Suddenly, a bright light filled what remained of Hugh's blurred vision, followed by the sound of a struggle.

"What the devil? Who are you, and what are you doing here? Remove that hood at once, reveal yourself. This is an order from your King! No …it can't be …not you? Run boy, *RUN!*"

Hugh blacked out once again, unable to stay in the present anymore.

'Hugh, can you hear me?'

Everything was still dark, and Hugh was floating again, but the voice seemed familiar to him.

'Hugh, can you hear me?'

It couldn't be. But it seemed a plausible option to him that it may well be.

'Father?' The word sounded foolish as he spoke into the empty void.

'Ah, good. You can hear me at least,' said the voice of his father.

Hugh looked around, but he couldn't see him or anything else, for that matter. What he would do to see his father one more time.

'Father, where are you? I can't see you,' said Hugh into the darkness.

'It's alright, Hugh, I didn't expect you would be able to see me. Listen, we have little time ...'

'What do you mean, where are you? Where have you been all this time?'

Hugh tried to make out where the voice was coming from, but it seemed to be from everywhere and nowhere, as though it were in his head, if he had one that was.

'You are in the astral plane known as the sight, somewhere between worlds, but there's really no time to explain. You must complete the task you have started. It's vitally important that the Elf King does not get the book. Do you understand?'

'No, not really. What is going on, and where are you? Why can't I see you?'
Just one look, that's all Hugh wanted, but his father did not appear.

'You need to follow my instructions,' his father continued. *'The world as we know it is at stake, and you are the only one now to pick up the task in hand. I will come back to see you, I promise, but for now stay safe, and remember that I always love you.'*

Hugh could sense the connection disappearing. It was as though he was being pulled in a different direction.

'No, wait! I just want to see you!'

But it was no use. His father had gone once again. He looked into the dark, feeling sad but unable to cry. Hugh was aware of someone approaching, and to his amazement, it was Emily.

He couldn't see her, apart from a small glowing triangle, but he could definitely feel her presence next to him.

'Hello stranger,' she said in a calm voice. *'I've been looking for you everywhere. Come on, we need to get back. It doesn't do to dwell out here for too long. You might not find the way back.'*

Hugh sensed a force, drawing him away from where his father was.

'But my father, he's here. Please, I want to see him.'

It was no use. As hard as he tried to fight the sensation, Hugh could feel the overwhelming force getting stronger by the second. It was as though he were being squeezed through a gap two sizes smaller than he was, then he felt himself expand once more. The smell was familiar. Bed linen, mixed with a mustiness. He opened his eyes.

The morning sun shone brightly across his face, and the room of the Hotel Alpine slowly came into focus. He saw the blurred outlines of people surrounding him, but he struggled to make them out.

"Ah good, he's back with us."

The familiar but croaky voice belonged to Barrington, who was slowly coming back into clear vision, his beaming smile showing Hugh how pleased he was to see his friend back in the room once more. He could see Emily getting up from the bed next to his, taking her hand out of a glass of water, and he realised he was back in the Hotel Alpine.

"Hello stranger," said Emily with a knowing smile. "Fancy meeting you here." She was beaming from ear to ear with a smile as well. A warming sensation glowed on Hugh's chest where his firestone that Emily had made for him was, and she reached a hand up to hers, with her cheeks flushed.

"Well done, lassie, ye did it," said Hamish, who was at the end of Hugh's bed.

"Why is everyone so pleased to see me?" asked Hugh. It had only been a short while since he'd last seen them all.

Then he remembered the voice of his father. He leapt from the bed and started searching the room, whilst the rest stood bemused.

He soon regretted getting up so quickly, as his world spun from standing up too quickly.

"Whoa there, laddie," said Hamish, coming to his rescue. "What's the rush? We're all here, and yer safe." He gave Hugh a reassuring smile.

"Where is he?" asked Hugh. "My father, where is he?"

He was trying to fight off the man, but he was too weak and gave in, letting Hamish guide him back to his bed.

"Looks like they knocked ye up good, laddie," said Hamish. "Your father is not here. Yer in the Hotel Alpine in Dallum." He spoke in a slow and steady voice as if he were attempting to bring Hugh round to the real world.

"I know where I am, Hamish," said Hugh a bit too sharply. "Sorry, it's just that I know I heard my father." He looked at Emily pleadingly. "You were there. Surely you heard him speaking to me... hang on, what are you doing here?"

Everything was catching up with him now. The last he knew, Emily was in Skellig-Krieg.

Emily squatted down next to Hugh and held his hands. When she spoke, her tone was comforting.

"Hugh, you have been through a lot today, far more than I can explain right now. You were lucky I found you before I lost you for good. I know this will be hard to understand, but you have to believe me when I say that your father is dead, and there is nothing we can do to change that."

"But his voice, I heard it, you must have heard it, you were there."

Hugh looked into her eyes, pleading for her to back him up, but it was no use. He knew it was too good to be true, and the harsh realisation came back to bite him hard.

"So, it was all just a dream, then?" he said, searching the depths of Emily's eyes.

She looked deep into him, saying nothing, but Hugh distinctly hearer voice ring out *inside* his head.

'It's hard to explain just now, but I will someday and to the best of my ability, I promise. For now, all I can say is that you were in the place we call the sight, as your father's voice said. It's a complex place. You were neither dreaming nor imagining things. The voice of your father was indeed there, but I fear there something different behind it, a malevolent force wishing to appeal to your better nature. I ask you not to follow it until we have the time to look into it further. Do you understand?' She continued to look at Hugh until he nodded his assent.

Hugh looked to Barrington and realised how awful he looked.

"What happened to you?" He asked, his memory of the events in the cave still hazy.

"I'm alright," said Barrington. "Don't look in the mirror, you look exactly the same. We're both lucky to be here, and we have Emily to thank for it." He looked across at Emily with a look of gratitude on his face.

Hugh looked from Barrington to Emily, still unsure of what had taken place in the parts that he could not remember.

"I'm not sure what's been going on since we were in the cave?" he said. "The last thing that I can recall is talking to you, Barrington, then everything went dark. Then I think I was in a room with … but it couldn't have been, could it? I was surely imagining it?" Hugh looked around the room for someone to fill in the pieces of the puzzle, but no-one stepped forward. "If someone could please tell me what has happened, I would be most grateful," he said, attempting to bring forth an answer.

"Well, it's hard to explain," said Emily, shuffling on the spot. "I'm not sure that you would believe me if I told you."

"Try me," said Hugh, who was tiring of dancing around the subject.

"Alright," she rose and sat next to him on the bed, still holding his hands, and Hugh turned to her, looking into her eyes. "Well, you were ambushed in the cave behind the waterfall. Barrington has already informed us that Thomas turned up and threatened to kill you both. I'm sorry that it ended how it did," she said, looking towards Barrington.

He raised his hands as if to say that it was alright, but Hugh could see by the look on his friend's face that the incident still pained him.

"I know about Thomas, and I don't wish to recall those events again. I want to know what happened *after* that. Who was it that ambushed us, the second time, and why are you here?"

Emily turned back to Hugh. "Last night, I was in the Rangles Inn, and Smithson came in. He revealed too much to me, he even propositioned me." Hugh's eyes widened at this. "It's alright, I told him I didn't like him in that way, but still …." She shuddered.

"When I realised you were in danger and that I had to get to you as soon as possible, I left straight away. I can only apologise for it taking so long to reach you. A landslide on the track to get here delayed my arrival. By the time I reached the hotel, you had already left. The man in charge led me to believe you were dead, but luckily Hamish was there to explain all. We ran to find you but realised we had missed you at every stage.

"When we figured out what was going on, we ran for the falls and arrived in time to hear the gunshot. We feared the worst, thinking you were on the receiving end. Hamish and I were at the top of the falls, when we witnessed you being carried back up. We hid ourselves, then followed your captors. We watched as they took you and Barrington out of Dallum to a hut in the hills. We weren't willing to leave you in their hands."

Hugh could see this troubled her, as her eyes were welling up.

"It's alright, I'm fine, so you don't need to worry," he said.

"I know, but the thought of you being … dead …." Hugh held her hand tighter and wiped a tear from her cheek.

"Listen, let's not dwell on what could have been," he said.

"We're here now, and that's all that matters. So, who are the mysterious *they* you keep mentioning?"

"Sorry, yes, I was just getting to that part. We had to wait until the party of henchmen carrying you had left before I could enter the hut. You weren't imagining things, Hugh. It turned out to be the Elf King who was behind your second ambush."

Hugh's eyes widened. "So, it's true then? The Elf King exists?"

"Well, of course he does," said Emily. "You're going to have to stop interrupting me, otherwise I'll never get to the end. I held back and observed what was happening and saw that he had a servant with him still. By the looks of things, he had been for a swim in the river, got himself into trouble in the currents, and the king had to rescue him.

The servant was mute, whether it was from the shock of nearly drowning or an inability to speak, I don't know. One thing that stood out was his white hair. I don't think I have ever seen anyone looking like that before, at least not outside the University of Science and Progression in Portis-Montis.

"One thing I can say is they weren't expecting me. I took them by surprise, and he, the king that is, seemed to recognise me. I don't know how. I suppose, given the number of crows floating around Skellig-Krieg, they must have been following me for some time. I tried to stop them, but they fled before I could. They even took Hamish by surprise and stunned him on the way out. I helped him up, and he desperately wanted to give chase, but I needed him with me. I had to focus on saving you and Barrington and saw you were in great peril, just from the fact that you were so pale.

"Barrington came round, and we all worked together to get you back here. It was an effort, and we had to stop quite a few times. You are heavy for one so slight."

Barrington nodded at that.

"Anyway, by the time we arrived here," she said, "I knew we were running out of time. I had to retrieve you from the plane where you were wandering before you lost the connection to your body."

Hugh looked at Emily, confused.

"What do you mean, *retrieve* me? I know that sounds strange, but I really could hear my father. He said we were in *the sight*, whatever that is, and that he had little time to talk." The memories were all flooding back to Hugh now. The dark space and the sound of his father's voice, followed by Emily's arrival. "He told me I had to carry on with the task we have begun and stop the Elf King from getting the book. Then you came and brought me back here."

Emily looked at Hugh, intrigued, giving some thought to what he had just said to her.

"I cannot explain everything here, Hugh. I promise you I will explain to you when I can. I do believe you when you say that you heard your father's voice, but strange things happen when we disconnect from ourselves and wander within the sight unprotected. As I've already told you, the malevolent forces at play in that realm wish to exploit old memories connected with our desires and can cause us to see and hear things that are not actually there."

"But it really was my father. I know it was. You must believe me." He looked at Emily, who sat nodding sympathetically. He realised that everyone else was giving him with the same look. "I didn't imagine it, dammit, it really was him!"

"Hugh, nobody is saying that you imagined it," said Barrington. He took in a deep breath and sighed. "Look, I think it's probably a good idea to go out and grab a bit of fresh air before we look into any more messages, real or otherwise."

Hugh took in a deep yawn, patting his chest. Something crinkled under his hand, and he remembered the note from the cavern beyond the falls. He pulled it out so that they could all read it.

"This was in the chest instead of the book," he said, flattening it out on the bed next to him. Hugh recognised his father's handwriting, and a wave of emotion washed over him once again.

I have the book. I will keep it safe until the time is right to pass it over.

All you have to do is follow your instinct, and you will find it.

"What's that supposed to mean?" said Barrington. "*Follow your instinct, and you will find it?* It hasn't worked so far."

Hugh shrugged, wiping a tear from his face. "I don't know. I feel that if my father says the book is safe, then it will be. Now the question is, where did he hide it? I'm sure that, with more research, it'll become clearer. But right now, what I need most is a break from all of this, and I think your idea to get some fresh air and food before we try to decipher anything else is the best thing to do. I need to take my mind off everything for a while. Does that make sense?"

With the rest of the group in agreement, they headed out of the door. On his way out of the room, Hugh tripped over a loose floorboard and stumbled forwards, slamming shoulder-first into the wall. He cursed the floor before heading out the door. They grabbed some food from the hotel breakfast buffet, with Eric the Hotelier complaining that Emily wasn't a guest and could not just help herself.

"Seeing as you told me he was dead, I think you can afford to let me eat something," said Emily.

"Like I said before, madam, it was your misunderstanding, not my mistake." He went to waggle a finger in Emily's face before thinking better of it. He turned to look at Hugh and Barrington. "Goodness me, what on earth has happened to you two?"

"If it's all the same, I'd rather not say," said Hugh.

The idea of trying to explain everything to Eric overwhelmed him, so he kept quiet.

"Suit yourself. I was only asking. Don't leave too much dirt on me floors and save some food for the other guests, will you." He gestured to the empty room around them.

The group stood open-mouthed for a moment before diving into the buffet without dwelling on Eric's words. The hotelier walked off, muttering to himself about "not getting paid enough to deal with this level of rudeness."

After they had their fill, the group headed out into the morning air, surprised at how busy it was. The town was crammed with people wandering around, full of jovial spirit, and they followed the crowds heading towards the main street they'd walked down the day before.

The reason for the bunting now became apparent for people lined the street to prepare for an event, and Hugh noticed that most of the crowd were holding ratchet rattles. It was now that Hamish remembered it was Banishment Day. He explained how it was a tradition for a shaman to run down the street in a loincloth, wearing an animal head and carrying a spear. As the holy person ran down the street barefoot, he or she would holler at the top of their voice, spear held high, to ward off any evil spirits from the local area during the winter months.

Right on cue, the crowd fell silent as the shaman entered the top of the street, wearing the ceremonial dress. Hugh noticed they were daubing him with some sort of red paste, which Hamish explained was from the blood of a local animal given as a sacrifice. The excitement in the crowd was building as the shaman began chanting and running on the spot. Once again, Hamish explained the shaman was channelling his energies with the spirit world.

All along the street, Hugh saw people raise up their ratchet rattles and spin them. The noise was deafening as it spread like a wave through the crowd.

Then, with a loud shriek, the shaman began his run down the street to the raucous encouragement of the crowds. Whooping and shrieking, making noises that Hugh would not believe possible from any human, the shaman ran past them, looked in their direction, then skidded to a halt, nearly stumbling over.

The noise stopped instantly.

Everyone focussed their attention on the shaman, trying to see what had caused the pause in the ceremony. Still in character, he padded over warily to where Hugh was standing and sniffed him up and down.

He prodded Hugh painfully in the chest with his spear before uttering three words to the group.

"YOU ... WAIT ... HERE!"

With that, he turned and carried on with his run, hollering and shrieking, with the rattles coming to life once again. Hugh had hoped to keep a low profile, but it appeared a majority of the townsfolk were now watching them with interest. The crowds eventually dispersed around them, and Hugh wanted to head back to the hotel, just to be away from everyone's gaze.

"No laddie," said Hamish, placing a hand on Hugh's shoulder as he went to turn. "If the shaman has said to wait, then that is what we should do. Ye don't want to anger the spirits."

Hugh gave in and waited as instructed.

He now had the time to take in the surrounding street. Although the shops appeared to be similar in style to those back home, the names were completely foreign. They sold an entire manner of things that they could not sell in Portis-Montis. There was Jabir's Panaceas, for all your remedy needs, and Rangles Staffs, Sticks and Orbs. Next to that, Bertha's Beasts had a menagerie of animals known and unknown in the window. Across the road was Futharks, for all things Runes, and Fables books.

Further down the street were bigger shops. Flights – Carpets, Brooms and Kettles for all your enchanted needs and Dragon's Breath Tours, which promised to get you up close and personal with the Seven Sisters' Falls. At the end of all this was Eau – Healing Waters and Tonics, where people appeared from the shop door looking drenched.

Hugh was just wondering if the shop had a direct connection to the falls, when a man daubed in blood, minus the animal head and spear, approached him.

"Now then, young Hugh," he said in a raspy voice, the blood now dripping off him. "I've not seen you for a while."

Hugh stood agog, unable to believe who was standing in front of him.

"Jeb? I thought you went off to explore the world? What are you doing here in Dallum?"

Jebediah Hogwinkle was the Head of Shamanism at the university. His was one of the earlier subjects deemed unnecessary by Smithson. Hugh took in the sight of the man, who was all elbows and knees. His head appeared freshly shaven for the event, and he looked cold, covered from head to toe in goosebumps.

"Well, it's a funny story, really. After I left Portis-Montis, I went travelling, but I didn't get far. I met an old shaman, and it transpired that he's related to me on my father's side. My interest in the subject, which the rest of my family had long forgotten, has strong roots linked to this area.

"Anyway, the old man taught me a thing or two about the role, and it turns out that I have a knack for the shamanic way of life. It was all very and I could step into the role. I suppose blood connections are stronger than the New World's will to stamp out the old ways." He stopped talking to lick some of the blood that had dripped onto his fingers.

Hugh looked back in shock and disgust. "Do you really have to lick that off? Surely it's toxic?"

"What, this? Far from it, young Hugh. It's strawberry jam, diluted in water, and rather tasty. I'm not a fan of animal blood, but the people insist on keeping up with tradition. As long as the crowds think they have daubed me in blood, then everyone's happy. They need not know the ingredients." The town clock struck ten, and Jeb looked up. "I'm sorry, but I will need to cut our conversation short. I'm needed at another ceremony down the road, and I can't be late. Will you be staying in town long?"

"I'm afraid that won't be possible," said Hugh. "We need to get back to Portis-Montis. Barrington, here, has a shop that needs attending to, and Emily her greenhouse."

It was now that Jeb turned his attention to the rest of the group.

Barrington held out a hand to shake with Jeb's. "Barrington Delphin, at your service."

Jeb grasped it with his sticky, half licked palm.

"Ah, yes, I remember you. You were always hanging around with Hugh at the university. Jebediah Hogwinkle, at your service."

Barrington grimaced at the sticky residue left behind after Jeb released his grip, and attempted to wipe it away on his cloak. Jeb neither seemed to notice nor care, as he looked to Emily and Hamish.

"Goodness me, young Emily, is that you?"

"Yes, it is. You still remember me after all these years?"

"How could I forget a face like yours, my dear. You look so much like your mother, it's uncanny. And Hamish, what a lovely surprise!"

"Wee Willy Winkie!"

"Hmm, I see you haven't forgotten your old nickname for me."

"How could I forget a name like yers? I see yer keeping well."

"As well as can be, given all that's going on around here. Tell me, are you in town for long? It would be great to have a good catchup."

"I'm afraid not," said Hugh, looking at the passers-by, who were taking an interest in the newcomers to town. "No, like I said, I think it's time we were heading off, unfortunately. We really do have things to tend to in Portis-Montis, and your shop needs manning, Barrington. You can't leave it all to Wanda."

"Very True, Hugh. Maybe next time, Jeb."

"Ah, that's a shame," said Jeb. "Well, if you are heading through the area again, let me know. The town hall can contact me via the usual methods. For now, though, I'll bid you a good day. Stay safe. If the rumours are true, I think we are heading for turbulent times."

Jeb turned and walked away before Hugh could question him on this last statement, and he turned to the rest of the party.

"I don't like the sound of that," he said, looking concerned.

"I know what you mean," said Barrington. "Our task is growing by the day, but I think you are correct, we need to head home. I don't like the idea of the shop being left unattended."

Emily nodded.

"I also need to get back, but I think we will need to take the valley run. Looking at the weather up there, I don't think it will be passable until after winter."

They all turned to look up at the mountain above them. Sure enough, they saw it covered with cloud, with a fresh covering of snow below it.

"Well, that's four of us to get back home then," said Hamish. "If there's no other business here, then may I suggest we head back to the hotel? We need to get a moving if we're gonna to get to a decent camping spot tonight."

With nothing else left to do for now, they headed back to the hotel to prepare for the journey home. They were packed and on the road before lunch, this time settling the bill before they left. It was two days hard walk along the low valley pass, to head back to the trading city of Skellig-Krieg. They were all tired and in need of a rest. As they approached the gates to the city, Hamish suggested that he and Emily split from the group.

"I just think ye'll get through the area quicker without me. It's tricky enough for you two, without adding the extra factor of me and Em. I doubt my papers will get me past at this time of day; 'tis too quiet, and Em left the city without getting hers checked. If she comes with me, I can get her back into the city."

"How will you get back home?" asked Emily.

"Ah, 'tis alright, lassie, I have me ways of getting about. Now, Hugh and Barrington, ye have to get to the airdock. Don't be tempted to head to Alfred's. I need ye to get a message to Balinas. Tell him the chase is back on, and we're running out of time. He'll understand what I mean."

"Alright, I will do." Hugh didn't understand what the message meant, but his gut feeling was that he wouldn't like the answer. He turned to Emily. "So, this is where we part once more."

"Yes," she said, "but this time it won't be for as long. Plus, we can keep in touch with each other."

This seemed to jolt a memory from Hamish, and he patted himself down. "Ah, yes, here it is. Sorry, I meant to pass this to ye yesterday." He pulled out a crumpled letter and passed it to Hugh. "Sorry, it's in a wee bit of a state. The chap on reception gave it to me yesterday."

Hugh took the letter, looking at Barrington and Emily, who looked just as confused as he was. He went to open it, but Hamish stopped him. "Not here, laddie, there's too many people about."

Inside, Hugh was glad to have a reason not to open the letter. He'd had enough of secret letters and coded messages to last him a lifetime.

Hamish looked up the road, seeing more people coming their way.

"Em, I dinnae like to rush things, but we've to get a move on."

Emily gave Hugh and Barrington a big hug before Hamish led her quickly away from the path into the undergrowth. Hugh and Barrington turned their noses towards the gate. Hugh felt weary and missed the familiarity of home. It might be busy, smelly and squeezed into a small space, but he yearned for the hustle and bustle of Portis-Montis life.

They were finally heading home to the new reality of normal, wondering about what life in Portis-Montis would bring. The light hit the trees, which were showing signs of autumn in the evening light, as Hugh and Barrington headed through the gate to Skellig-Krieg, disappearing into the evening rush to get home.

Chapter 2

Winter had arrived early in Portis-Montis. It was rare for the city's streets to receive snowfall because of the tightly packed nature of the buildings and the heavy footfall, but Main Street – the widest street in the city – had become treacherous underfoot.

Though the snowfall here wasn't too bad, what had penetrated the lower levels had been compacted and turned to ice. This impacted all the city's residents, but none more so than the runners. Their routes had to be kept clear at all times, causing a headache for the city street cleaners. No matter how hard they tried, they could not keep up with the near constant task of salting the streets down. This caused a delay in the runner's programme, meaning that no sooner had they finished one run through the districts than the next was due to start.

The wind was coming straight down from the mountain and whistled through the city, causing the many shop signs to sway and creak ominously. It passed the front door of DELPHIN'S TRAVEL EMPORIUM, but even that couldn't mask the raised voices within.

They were fighting again. Hugh had woken up to a chill in the air. This wasn't down to the current cold weather outside, but more down to the living arrangements he was currently having to survive. It had been three months since the fire in the university alchemy laboratory, which destroyed not only the room, but wiped out generations of knowledge as well.

The trips going back and forth to Skellig-Krieg had indeed kept them busy for nearly two weeks, but on their return to Portis-Montis some two and a half months ago, Hugh had to face up to the reality of the situation. Barrington was true to his word, and let Hugh become a permanent resident at his shop. Not only did Hugh have to face the residents of the city talking in hushed whispers as he passed them in the street, but he was also called to Runners House to explain his actions in bringing the system to a halt outside Barrington's shop. Occasions such as this were rare in the city, as nobody dare break the cardinal rule of impeding the runners – the city's messaging system. It was reported in the papers, which caused Hugh more anguish and mocking on a near daily basis.

Barrington stood at his friend's side the entire time, even refusing to leave Hugh when he attended the inquiry at Runners House, insisting to those in charge that he be there as defence for his friend. When the issue was raised over what to do with the runner who was taken out by Hugh, which had left the poor man jobless, Barrington stepped up once again, pointing out that it was a journalist that caused his friend's fall. He agreed that, as long as the investigation against Hugh was dropped, then he would take the injured man on in return. This was agreed, with conditions that Barrington stuck to his word, otherwise Hugh would face further repercussions.

Now Hugh found himself living not only with his best friend but his recently appointed shop assistant, Jenkins, and it was a safe bet to say that their working relationship was not a harmonious one. The fact that Hugh was also living there, having to face the old Runner daily, didn't help matters.

He pulled on some clothes, and picked up an unopened letter from his nightstand. Even though he had received it from Hamish when they parted, he had been putting off opening it, always finding an excuse to do something else. He had a feeling that it would only lead to more trouble and another trip away from Portis-Montis, which he could not face at this point in time. The argument downstairs drew his attention once more, so he made his way down to see what today's fight was about.

"... and all I am saying is the fire must be lit in the hearth. There are overnight logs to the left, and daytime logs and coal to the right." Barrington was stating the formalities of the shop floor once again to an unwilling Jenkins. "If you need more supplies, then you will find them outside the back of the shop, and if they are running low, it is down to you to order more!"

"And what *I'm* saying," said Jenkins, not knowing when to stop, "is if *you* want a fire ready for the morning, then why don't *you* lay the bleeding thing yourself?"

"Mind your language! The reason *you* have these jobs to do, my dear fellow, is that it's part of the agreement under which *I* took you on. I have provided you with a job with free board and lodgings, and in return, you are to do whatever I ask of you. It's fairly simple to understand."

"Well, I ain't no skivvy!"

"Oh, Sprites help me. It's *your* job! You have some basic tasks set out by me to do throughout the day. As you progress and gain my trust, I will give you more to do. You have some big boots to fill, my dear boy."

"Yeah, you've mentioned that once or twice now. Anyway, I wouldn't be here if it wasn't for *him*," said Jenkins, pointing at Hugh, who had just entered the room at the wrong time. "If he hadn't bleeding well ran out in front of me whilst I was running, then maybe *I* would still have me old job!"

"Will you mind your language!" said Barrington. "I don't want to warn you again about cursing on the shop floor. It's not good for business nor for my reputation. I will not get drawn back into the argument of my dear friend here again. As I have said, frequently, he tripped over a journalist who was standing outside my door and fell into the road as you came past. It was not his fault that it happened. Now let that be the end of the subject."

"Yeah, well, the journalists wouldn't have been there if he hadn't set fire to the university," Jenkins muttered audibly.

"*That is enough, Jenkins!* We have already said, many times before, that Hugh here had nothing to do with the fire. They cleared him of all charges, and that's the last word on the matter."

"It's not what people are saying on the street," said Jenkins under his breath, before starting to turn away.

Barrington grabbed him by the arm. "What did you say, boy?"

"I said, it's not what people are saying on the street." He spoke slowly and loudly. "Cor, no wonder the old guy left here, no-one can hear a bleeding thing."

Barrington's grip increased around the wide bicep, and Jenkins attempted to throw him off, but Barrington was a strong opponent. His attention turned back to Hugh.

"Everyone knows it was him who started it and that he is only squirming out of it because he's with you, and you have a history of getting out of things."

This caught Barrington off guard, and he released his grip, staring open-mouthed at his assistant. Jenkins stumbled forward, glaring at him, whilst rubbing his arm.

"Yeah, we all know the truth. Word is that you've been hanging around with Old World people, getting up to no good and cavorting with the enemy—"

"*That's enough!*" Barrington's voice boomed through the shop, cutting Jenkins off mid flow. "Get out of my sight and make Hugh some breakfast."

Jenkins knew that he'd overstepped the mark and chose not to fight. He left the room, scowling and muttering under his breath.

Hugh was aware that people were talking about the pair behind their backs. They only had to step outside the shop these days for people to look at them and whisper with their neighbour. It was only down to the fortune of Barrington's close connections with Art Gustoffman, the Chief of the Guard for the City, that had kept them in the clear so far. He had worked tirelessly to defend the pair, time and time again, which wasn't going unnoticed.

The government of the New World had taken a greater interest in the original enquiry, putting pressure on Art to come up with more evidence. They began questioning his motives, calling out his close links with Barrington and Hugh, stating this may have skewed the results of his findings.

Tensions escalated further when a team of auditors arrived from the capital city of Bansk. They uncovered new evidence, which contradicted the original enquiry and cast the shadow of doubt over the entire outcome of the previous investigation. When Art raised his concerns that all this so-called new evidence was not as clear cut as it first appeared, it put him at loggerheads with his superiors.

On top of everything else, Hugh and Barrington were being followed by the city's press. Not a single day passed where Hugh didn't spot a keen-eyed journalist and photographer watching them from the distant shadows – the tell-tale flash giving their position away. All of this, mixed in with the local gossip and the daily paper's update on the pair, meant that Hugh and Barrington were feeling the pressure.

Barrington was calming down, busying himself by laying the fire for the day. Hugh joined him and sat down in the chair opposite his friend.

"I'm sorry you had to witness that, Hugh. It was totally out of order, and you should not have to face that sort of thing, especially not when you have just woken up."

The fire was now under way, and Barrington sat back in his seat, preparing his pipe. Jenkins appeared through the curtain at the back of the shop, carrying a tray of tea, which he set down heavily on the table in front of the pair, before turning swiftly and leaving to sort out the rest of the breakfast. Barrington scowled at him, put his pipe away and poured them both a cup of tea.

"The worst of it is, I couldn't get rid of him if I wanted to."

Hugh looked at his friend, feeling a pang of guilt.

"Barrington, I really didn't mean to cause all this trouble."

"It's alright, I don't blame you for all of this. I stepped up to the plate, and this is the outcome. I just miss Thomas."

Hugh looked at Barrington with a sympathetic eye. He knew all too well that his friend was still struggling with the loss of Thomas.

"I know it's difficult, Barrington, but the pain will ease with time. He meant a lot to you, and it's left a big hole in your life ...our lives. Thank you" Hugh took the drink from Barrington, taking a sip, knowing it would be too hot. It burnt as it made its way down his throat.

"Hugh, you really are the best friend a man could have," said Barrington. "Let us move forward from this conversation. I see that you have brought the letter down with you this morning. Is today the day you're going to face up to opening it?" Hugh looked at the letter in his hand and then back to Barrington, nodding.

"Yes, I have decided that I cannot put it off any longer. I know it will contain some clue to take us on another mission, and I cannot deny that I am weary of the current situation here, but ..." he tailed off, the words caught in his throat.

"I know this will be hard for you," said Barrington. "With all that's being said about us at the moment, anything else that could lead us into more trouble seems off-putting, but let's not jump the gun just yet. We must read what is in the letter first. It may contain nothing of importance." Hugh looked at his friend with raised eyebrows. "Well, alright, it undoubtedly will lead us into *something*; after all it is from your father."

Hugh nodded, looking down at the unopened letter as though it would explode if he touched it. Someone had left it for him behind the desk at the Hotel Alpine, and he knew from the handwriting that it must be another message from his deceased father. He also knew that it would contain some new information which would take them away from the safety of Portis-Montis, even if their days living within the protection of the city were numbered. With some trepidation, he opened the letter, pulled it out and read the page aloud.

Hugh,

If you are reading this, then I can assume that you have made it to the Hotel. First let me reassure you that I'm alright but not in a state that will leave me much time on this plane. As for Robert, well, sadly, he has passed over.

He gave his life for mine when someone ambushed us – a gesture I shall never forget. I tried to chase the offender, but I had to get back to Robert. Before he departed, he imparted some important information to me. I cannot write it down in this letter, but I will leave it somewhere safe for you to find it. The only clue I dare leave is this. I had a wonderful trip in my room. I hope you can figure that out. I will leave the room booked out in my name, and the hotelier has assured me that the room will remain unoccupied until Mr Geber returns, so I apologise for the bill.

Hugh looked over to Barrington, who sat rubbing the back of his head. His mind flicked back to the moment that Barrington offered to settle the bill on his behalf, only for him to pass out from the amount Eric asked him to pay. If only he had considered the exchange rate, then maybe he wouldn't have passed out. Hugh carried on reading.

As for the lore book of alchemy, all I can say is that you will not find it behind the waterfall, so please don't go looking for it. It will only lead to you becoming soaked for no reason. If you have already been there, then I apologise once more. I hope that the ride back up the fall wasn't a rough one.

You will find the book, I guarantee it, but first you must find out about something called 'the sight' and learn how to control it. I urge you to practice, so that one day you will be skilled enough to venture deep into that plane. You never know, you may find out more than you expect. I know our paths will cross again, but until that time comes, keep safe, watch out for the crows and be wary of who you trust. There are many people out there who will sell you for a cheap price.

Until such time we can meet again, I will bid you farewell.

Love always, F

The pair sat in silence. There was so much to take in that Hugh didn't know where to start. Barrington finally broke the silence.

"I wish you had received the letter before we set off for the falls. Then we wouldn't have had to go to all the trouble that we went through in that ghastly place."

"Now, come on, Barrington. If we put the obvious distress to one side, then I think you would still agree that we gained a lot from making it to the cavern," said Hugh. "You forget that I have links to that place, so please don't be so rude about it."

"I'm sorry, Hugh. I keep forgetting that the place holds important significance to you. All it reminds me of is the death of Thomas."

"I know, and I haven't forgotten that. In fact, I doubt we ever will forget the events of that day."

"And, of course, the resulting mess he left in his wake." Barrington looked through to the back of the shop, to where they could hear the conversation, and Barrington was not very subtle with his remarks.

"It's an awful faff to be trying to train up a new shop assistant, now that we have a new task to accomplish, especially when the replacement refuses to toe the line!"

The sound of something being placed heavily onto the side came through from the back of the shop, followed by the back door slamming. Hugh looked at his friend with raised eyebrows once more, shaking his head.

"*What?*"

"You know, you could attempt to be a little more understanding with him," said Hugh. "It's as difficult for him as it is for you."

"*Piffle!* He has it far easier than Thomas ever did."

"What do you mean?"

"Well, he's landed on his feet, got himself a decent job, with decent money. Like I've already said, I didn't have to take him on. Now that's enough of this talk. What are we going to do about this letter?"

Hugh realised there was no point in attempting to carry on arguing with his friend, so he turned his attention back to the letter in his hand.

"What about it?"

"Well, it's obvious that your father has left something important back at the hotel, something that he would like you to retrieve. And what is 'the sight'?"

Hugh looked back, shaking his head.

"It's really hard to explain, but I think I've been there before, when I was outside this very shop. It happened after Jenkins ran into me and knocked me out and then again when we were ambushed at the waterfall. I think it has something to do with being knocked unconscious, but until I figure it all out, I won't know for sure. Anyway, back to your previous question, we can't go off now. What about the shop? Jenkins is no way near ready to run this place. Then there's Wanda. She's still getting over the fact that Thomas is dead."

Wanda, Barrington's contact for all things relating to travel bookings, was the owner of TCD Travel. She looked after Barringotn's shop when he was out of town, and had taken a liking to Thomas – losing him had devastated her.

"I know," said Barrington. "In my wildest dreams, I didn't imagine that she was seeing him."

Hugh now looked away from Barrington. He had been well aware of the relationship taking place under Barrington's nose. It was a tough day when he had to reveal that he not only knew but also aided Wanda' escape when they returned unexpectedly in the middle of the night three months earlier. It led to a long, drawn out and heated conversation, which only added to the tension in the shop.

The death of Thomas had hit Wanda hard. They rarely saw her out of her shop these days, and when she was, she was always wearing black and looked dreadful with bags under her eyes and her hair hanging limp over her face. The spark had gone from her usual cheery persona, leaving an empty shell in its place.

"Wanda is a grown woman and more than capable of looking after her own affairs," said Barrington with a tone of finality.

The revelation of the relationship between Thomas and Wanda had ruffled Barrington's feathers. Hugh and Barrington had spent many evenings since the latter found out about it, discussing the subject at length by the firelight. Hugh didn't want to admit that the reason was probably down to the fact that they knew Barrington would react badly to the situation.

"Hugh? Are you listening to me?"

"Hmm?"

"You disappeared off into one of your daydreams again. You must start paying attention to what people are saying."

Hugh felt himself flush.

"Sorry, you were saying?"

Barrington let out a sigh.

"I said that we ought to take the letter to the Great Library at the university."

Hugh flinched at the mention of the place.

"It's alright," said Barrington, "we don't have to take a trip to what remains of your lab, though they are pressing on with the restoration works at a cracking pace."

Hugh had not visited his laboratory since their return to Portis-Montis.

He just couldn't face it. This also meant that he was yet to pay a visit to Balinas, despite the many letters he had sent to them requesting that they come for tea.

"Do we really have to visit Balinas? I don't feel up to it today."

"You never feel up to visiting him. There's always some excuse or reason not to go. We have to face up to it at some point, and now we have the letter from your father to decipher. Unless you have a better idea, or any clue what 'the sight' is, then I really see no other option but to take a trip there."

Hugh shrugged, keeping quiet.

"Well, that's settled then. If you collect your bag and cloak, we can head there now."

Reluctantly, Hugh got up from his chair and went to fetch his belongings from his room.

"Oh, I nearly forgot about this," said Barrington, picking up an object from the mantle above the fire. "It's the object I found in the chamber behind the fall, but I think the damp air may have affected its ability to show the way."

He tossed it to Hugh, who caught it and studied the object. It appeared to be a compass of sorts, with two needles, one in the centre, and one around the outside, neither of which stayed still for longer than a second. It was clear to Hugh that the object was far from useful. He turned it over and saw an inscription on the back.

When all seems lost, I will guide the way.

"What a peculiar object," he said, looking up at Barrington. "Is it a compass?"

"I think the word that you should use is '*was*'. Like I say, I think the damp air from the falls has got into it, so it's only a trinket now. The inscription on the back is interesting. It seems to ring a bell for me, but I am not sure why."

"Well, that's easy to answer. It's very similar to the one on the Firestone. Given that it came from a chamber where all the items related to each other, I guess they all linked with each other at some stage in the past."

"Anyway, I thought you would like to keep it, seeing that it came from somewhere linked to your family. I suppose you could call it an heirloom."

Hugh nodded as he pocketed the compass and went to fetch his bag and cloak.

When he returned, Barrington was already by the door, waiting to leave.

"We'd best lock up. Heaven knows when Jenkins will be back." The sound of the runners' horns sounded outside, and Barrington placed a hand in front of Hugh to prevent him going any further. "Whoa there! We don't want you running in front of anyone else now, do we?"

He stood smirking, and Hugh pushed him off.

"Thank you, Barrington," he said and stepped out into the fresh morning air.

Chapter 3

Barrington joined Hugh outside the shop, and they waited until the runners came past before making their way to the university. As they stood, Hugh couldn't help but notice the awaiting crowd staring at them. He thought he saw some of them talking to their neighbours, nudging each other and pointing in their direction.

Barrington sensed his friend's unease.

"Just ignore them. They only want to gossip, and we know the truth."

They heard the runners' horn sounding at the post down the road, signalling that the runners were about to arrive and collect their goods. It wasn't long before the onward call sounded, and everyone turned expectantly to cheer the party on.

"Watch out, Geber, they're coming!" called out a hidden voice.

"Yeah, watch your step!" said another. The surrounding crowd laughed, nobody standing up for Hugh.

"Who said that?" said Barrington, craning his neck, searching the crowd.

"Oh no, not the unsinkable Barrington Delphin. What are we going to do now?" someone retorted.

"Gonna burn anything else down, Geber?" said another lone voice, also met with laughter.

"Right, where are you?" said Barrington. "Come on, show yourselves, you worthless pieces of ..."

Whatever Barrington said next, Hugh didn't hear as the crowd erupted into applause and cheers as the runners came through. Hugh saw them look towards him with a scowl as they passed them, before returning to soak up the applause. He flushed as his heart thumped in his chest.

"Leave it, Barrington," he said as the crowd dispersed. "We already have enough attention being thrown our way. Let's not add any more fuel to the fire."

Barrington looked to Hugh.

"I know, I know. I can't tell you to ignore them, then not take my own advice. It just irks me to hear yours and my good name dragged through the mud."

"Thank you, it's very kind of you to stand up for me like that, but for now, can we head up to the university, drawing no more unwanted attention to us, if such a thing is possible?"

"Alright, but I fear that will be a hard task. Both of us together always draw the crowd's gaze. Come on then, let's get this walk over with." He set off down the street with Hugh following, looking down at his feet. He knew, as they walked through the streets, everyone would stare at them. He couldn't face looking into the faces of the gossipers.

The walk seemed endless, and Hugh was glad when they finally reached the gates to the university courtyard. His relief, however, was short-lived, when he saw the corner of the ongoing works where his lab once was. An access platform covered the entire side of the building, a void replacing where the rooms once stood.

A team from the guild of stonecutters were busy sorting out the mess from the fire and were indeed making good progress. The mullioned windows, which had been destroyed in the blaze, were well on the way to being restored. The workers all stopped to look at Hugh and Barrington walk across the open space. Hugh could tell that they wanted to say something but were being restrained on account of the fact there were members of the Collins family stood with them.

The Collins family ran the day-to-day life of the university, including overseeing the task at hand of rebuilding the remnants of the first floor. They could be recognised by their dark green velvet suits and blonde hair, tied back into a tight ponytail. They nodded to Hugh as a sign of respect, and he cringed inside. He hated the idea of anyone waiting on him or seeing themselves as below him. He always went out of the way to make them feel included where possible, but they always refused, carrying on with their job.

As they entered the university, Hugh was greeted with the familiar smell of home. For a moment, he could remember things as they were, before all the troubling events occurred. He returned to reality when more smells confronted him, tainted with the lime dust from the building works currently being undertaken. Anxiety and guilt coursed around his body, having a field day, as he thought of the amount of extra workload this would cause for the Collins family.

On the very edge of his perceivable smell was the lingering whiff of charred materials, threatening to churn his stomach. He ignored the door to the corridor where the destruction had happened. The pair made their way to the Great Library, a place older than the university itself.

Here the smell of the building works disappeared, replaced with that of parchment and leather-bound books. The room seemed different somehow, and Hugh couldn't understand why or how. It was as though the room had come to life. There were more Collinses moving books around, like they were preparing for something big.

The air was tingling with energy, making Hugh feel uneasy. It would be hard to spot Balinas amongst the many blond heads of the other family members. Hugh was about to express his concerns to Barrington when a voice spoke behind them, making them both jump. They turned around to see the warm face of Balinas.

"Hugh, Barrington! You've finally taken heed of one of the many letters I have sent and come to visit. Well, this is good news, for we have so much to talk about."

Hugh couldn't help but noting he was looking unusually tired.

"Hello, Balinas. It's great to see you again. I apologise for not coming to you sooner, it's just that, well …" He flushed and looked down to the floor.

"I understand completely. The fire is still fresh in your mind, and you couldn't face coming here as it only brings it all back to you once more. It's completely natural to have these feelings, Hugh, but what you must learn to do is conquer your fears. That is the only way in which you will move forward in life. You must learn you cannot change the past, and although the future may be laid out for us, how we get there is of our own making. You must learn to live in the here and now, for that is the one thing that we have control over. Anyway, listen to me babbling on. I take it you are both here to discuss something important?"

"Yes, can we go somewhere quiet?" asked Hugh.

"I think we can arrange that. Follow me."

Balinas led them through the library, and Hugh looked up at the ceiling. It seemed to have changed since the last time he saw it. The Great Library was known for adapting to the needs of the user, but the ceiling appeared to have an extra fresco added to it, and to his horror Hugh saw they had added the fire to the montage.

"The ceiling, like the room, is ever changing. The big events that happen to the university, and the world at large, are added as time moves forward. It also helps to predict what may come to pass. Of course, it does mean that some of the lesser events disappear, but there is a Collins family member assigned to logging the events as they show up. We can use it as a guide to what's happening within the world."

Balinas, like their good friend Emily, had the knack of getting inside other people's heads. This was good, as it meant for Hugh that he didn't need to speak aloud all that bothered him, but it also meant that he could keep nothing secret.

They climbed the grand staircase, its carpet soft underfoot. Hugh's hand glided up the handrail, polished by centuries of similar hands rubbing along its smooth surface. The room always had a calming effect, with its row upon row of bookshelves, seeming to go on forever. As they reached the top, Hugh wasn't watching where he was going, and he nearly took out one of the Collins family, who was carrying a pile of books.

"Hugh, be careful where you are walking, and try not to daydream," said Barrington. "Balinas, is there something happening that we're unaware of?"

"All in good time, Barrington. Let us be somewhere private before we delve into any discussions," said Balinas.

He turned down an aisle, searching for the correct book. With a quick look around, checking nobody was watching them, he pulled on the book to reveal a secret staircase, one that Hugh and Barrington knew led to the Chamber of Prophecy, hidden deep under the university. They descended the winding staircase, and Hugh struggled to keep his focus on the stairs, becoming dizzy with the constant winding. Eventually, they made it to the vast space, their footsteps echoing around as they entered.

"So, gentleman. As you've already noticed, there is a sense of urgency around the building. We have had news that the Elf King is active and searching for the lore book of alchemy."

Hugh nodded.

"Yes, we heard a lot about the Elf King whilst we were in Morcarthia. It seems we had a run in with him outside of Dallum."

"Really? I'm pleased to see that you made it out safe. It's rarely that happens with enemies to the king."

"If it weren't for Emily, I fear it would have been a different story," said Barrington. "She was in the right place at the right time, meaning she could rescue us."

"Ah, yes, just like her mother. You'll be needing more help from Emily over the coming months. I wish I could be of more use, but given the current situation, and considering that I am also duty bound to the library, well, there is not much I can do."

"So, what has the current situation got to do with everything that is happening upstairs?" asked Hugh.

"Well, the last time this happened, everything ended up getting messy, and they dragged us into a war that nobody wanted. Everyone was ill prepared last time, so this time around we wanted to be ahead of the game. As the ceiling in the library has been changing, it is, in effect, portending what may come, a lot further ahead than the *Book of Prophecy* ever has."

"So why don't you try to head it off early?" asked Barrington. "Surely if you have been forewarned, then you can prevent it from coming true?"

Balinas shook his head, a look of woe in his face.

"It's not as simple as that. Yes, it shows us the ultimate destination, but the where, when, and how we get there is not so easy. Like the *Book of Prophecy*, there is no way of changing the big events that are laid out in front of us, only how we travel to get there. We cannot change the future that is woven for us, for that requires a greater power, more than any living being can possess. You can trust me on that."

The room fell into silence whilst the words settled around them like dust.

"So, what is the reason for your visit here today?" asked Balinas. "I can assume that it is not a social occasion."

Hugh shuffled uneasily on the spot, unable to make eye contact with Balinas once more.

"Oh, it's alright, Hugh. I won't berate you for ignoring my letters. To be honest, I'm glad for a break from the never-ending task of running the library. All this constant preparation for what may come to pass really wears one down."

Hugh finally met his gaze. "I'm sorry, Balinas. I really should have attempted to come here before now, especially as you are all working so hard to prepare for everything. It was selfish of me to not answer your messages. The fire is not an excuse to forget about the important things in life. I have to face my fears head on if we're to get through this experience together."

Balinas looked at Hugh with surprise.

"My, my! It seems the trip to Skellig-Krieg has changed you since the last we met."

"How so?"

"Well, I'm pretty sure that the old Hugh would have done anything not to carry on the colossal tasks you are now facing. He would have wanted to shy away and focus on his work. This new Hugh seems ready for action."

Hugh shook his head quickly. He didn't want to get the old librarians hopes up. He was getting annoyed with the elf's ability to read people's minds, and longed for the chance to learn how to block him out.

"It is a most useful skill, when used appropriately, and responsibly. One day you will learn the many abilities associated with the sight, including the ability to look into others, and learn the skill to keep certain thoughts hidden. I feel Emily should be the mentor for that task, and I think you should enquire with her the next time you meet. I'm sure she'll be more than willing to help in the matter."

He looked at Hugh, who quickly looked to his feet. He could feel the firestone glowing gently under his shirt, and he knew Emily would experience the same with hers. Hugh couldn't be sure, but he could have sworn he felt a small pulse of energy vibrate against his chest, but no sooner had it happened than it disappeared once more. Balinas looked warmly at Hugh, before deciding that the time was right to continue.

"For now, we must focus on what you are here to discuss," he said, making Hugh jump.

Barrington looked on confused, before cottoning on with what was happening, shaking his head.

"Hugh, you must know by now that we can all read you like a book, some easier than others. Explain to Balinas about the note we found and the letter from your father, and the reasons you don't wish to act upon it?"

He stood looking knowingly at Hugh.

"What note, what letter?" asked Balinas, now looking concerned at

Hugh, who felt the pressure on him to speak up and explain everything.

"Thank you, Barrington. Well, it would seem that the cat is well and truly out of the bag."

He pulled out the note and the letter from his father and passed it to Balinas, who read it at a glance. He stood, with his hand over his mouth.

"Oh my! Oh my, oh my."

"What is it? What's wrong?" asked Hugh, not liking the way Balinas was reacting to the letter.

Balinas staggered backwards to his chair, falling into it.

"Well, if this letter is to be believed, then we have to assume the book of lore for alchemy is back out in the open. That means that anyone can get to it, access it, and wield its power. We must consult the *Book of Prophecy* once more, for that is our guide in these situations."

He leapt to his feet, scurrying off to a bookshelf, before returning to the large table in the middle of the room, placing it down hard on the wooden surface. It sent a plume of dust into the air, made visible by the light shining in, unseen from above, illuminating a revolving pyramid where the books of lore should be.

Balinas thumbed his way through the pages, searching for the end of the text. He found what he was looking for, and once again, Hugh and Barrington stood watching the strange symbols appear upon the page, just ahead of the librarian's finger. He moved fast and spoke words unknown to Hugh under his breath as he read. The text stopped appearing abruptly, and he looked up from the book.

"Well," said Hugh, his voice tight with anxiety, "what does the book say?"

Balinas took in a deep breath and let out a long sigh.

"The book confirms this very meeting, and the book of alchemy is definitely out of the safe place. But it also speaks of it *being* in a safe place, which is most curious. It is also alluding to another book, the one of the earth, that the seekers must find, for the Elf King has expanded his search to include this book as well."

"Another book?" said Barrington. "But we have yet to find the first one. Now you say that we are to go after a second? And what is the book of the earth?"

"I say nothing. I only relay what it says on the pages. It is not I that sent you after the book of lore of alchemy, nor am I the one speaking of this new quest. There are four books relating to the four elements. Fire for alchemy, earth for magic, water for the sprites and water magic, and air for the sylphs and air magic. I dispatched all four books from here, and all must return to guarantee their safety."

"So, forgive me if I am wrong, but we are looking for four books now?"

"Yes, Barrington, that is correct."

"Is it not bad enough that you expect us to find the one book, let alone *four!* I mean, the whole thing is getting out of control. And I take it you get to sit here, whilst we are out doing all the hard work?"

"Barrington, please go easy on him," said Hugh, wanting to diffuse the situation.

"It's alright Hugh, I've got this. The *Book of Prophecy* is our guide here, Barrington. All I can do is advise you of what I think is best until my role becomes more substantial. Of course, you don't have to do what the book is asking you to do. You could just ignore it and pretend it is not happening, but I advise you not to do that.

"It's a surprise to me. I can assure you, that you are being diverted from the original search, but the prophecy speaks of grave things that shall come to pass if we do not find the four books. If I'm being honest, I think you have no choice, but to take up the task that is stretching out in front of to you. Of course, as I have already said, you don't have to agree with the book, or take my advice. You could just ignore it, and hope the problem goes away." He looked at the pair in front of him with a grave look on his face.

Hugh stood, unable to take in all that he was hearing. It was looking like he and Barrington must take on another task.

"I really don't know what to do. I'm tired of all this running around, chasing after unseen books, and just want things to return to how they used to be!" He banged his fist on the table, sending more dust into the air. "Why is it down to me and Barrington to take on the roll to save the world?"

"I understand your feelings, Hugh. I too wish there was another way, but the fact still stands that if we do not act upon this, it could spell untold misery for us all. I have no control over this, and if I did, I would change it. We must follow what the book tells us, if we are to get through these troubling times."

"But that's the point, it's not *we*, is it? You can stay safe here, behind the protection of the university, the Great Library, and the mountain it's buried beneath!"

"I assure you, I am no safer here, than you are out there. For starters, there's the uprising that's happening over in Skellig-Krieg."

"What uprising?" asked Hugh with concern.

"Dear me, have you really been so ignorant these past few months? It's all kicking off. There have been attacks across the New World, with reports that the Elf King is behind them all. Innocent blood is being spilled again, and those who were in hiding are becoming brave once more. Villages are being attacked by those loyal to the Elf King as they make their way towards the old powerhouse of Kings Seat. The troll guards have also been recalled. Word is that they are preparing for the Elf King's arrival, but how true this is, I do not know."

"Troll guards?"

"Yes, trolls were best suited to the menial tasks, and took orders without questions. There were many horror stories to come out of that place, and it was said the numbers that entered the vast place, never matched what came out. Those who escaped spoke of horrors and of furnaces that were lit all day long. I believe there is a room of the lost souls, which locals were forcibly shown around, to remind them what would happen if they stepped out of line.

"Then you must factor in the resistance, that is, those who were against the world being calved up into Old and New all those years ago. They have bided their time, waiting for the right moment to strike. The return of the Elf king will give them perfect cover to carry out attacks and blame it on the king. These are some of the many things that makes the return of King Riddor so worrisome, and this is one thing which makes his return to power so dangerous."

"*Oh yes*, because it's *so dangerous* for you, in the safety of your underground cave!"

"Again, don't assume that because I am here that I'm not in danger. For all I know, the Elf King may well be within Portis-Montis right now. He may well have infiltrated the library itself. Who do you think he will seek first? One of the many under-librarians who keep the place running, or the one in control of the entire operation? It fills me with dread."

"Will you two stop bickering for one moment!" said Barrington, coming between the pair, looking towards the stairs.

"What? Don't tell me you're on his—"

"*Shhh!*" Balinas flapped his hands at Hugh to stop him.

"*What?*"

Hugh didn't need an answer. He, too, could hear the footsteps descending the spiral staircase.

Chapter 4

They all stood in silence, staring at the entrance to the staircase, listening to the footsteps getting louder.

"I thought you said that this was a *secret* room," said Barrington in a hushed voice, his eyes fixed on the doorway.

"It is, unless you know where it is," said Balinas.

Hugh's breathing was speeding up, along with the pace of the footsteps. "So, does that mean this person's a friend or a foe?" he asked.

The footsteps were getting closer.

"I don't know. It could be the Elf King has broken through the inner circle, has someone held to hostage and they've finally given in," said Balinas. "Or it could just be one of the secret keepers."

"I thought you once said that nobody comes back here a second time?" said Barrington, unable to hide the alarm in his voice.

"Well, you two have."

"Good point. So, is there another way out of here?"

"Well, no, that's the only way in."

"Oh, well, that's good. You designed a room that you can get trapped in! *Amazing* forward planning there, I must say."

"I didn't design this room! It was already here."

"Pack it in, you two," said Hugh. "This is not the time to fight. We need to think fast and prepare for whoever is about to come through that doorway."

"Good thinking, Hugh, that's what I like to see, someone presenting solutions, not problems," said Balinas (Barrington threw him a sideways glance). "Here, take this."

He passed Barrington a heavy book.

"Oh good, we can read them a bedtime story before they kill us. Won't that be nice?"

"Don't be silly, man. Use it to hit whoever is coming over the head."

"Oh ..." Barrington took the book, red faced.

Balinas passed Hugh a weighty book as well – *One Thousand Poisonous Plants and How to Spot Them* – but he was unsure if it would hold up to a sustained attack. It was already falling apart at the bindings, and the cover was worn under his hands.

They stood, each armed with their tome, waiting for the person to reach the bottom of the staircase. It felt like an age, and the book was making Hugh's arms ache. They could hear the person breathing heavy, puffed out from running down the winding stairs. They heard them lose their footing, slipping some steps, which turned into an all-out stumble. A torch preceded the mass of arms and legs that landed on the floor in front of the three defenders.

Balinas went screaming forward, a book over his head, ready to bring it down onto the crumpled body, unwilling to let them get a further footing into the room.

"*No, wait,*" Hugh began, but Barrington was already one step ahead of him. He pushed past Hugh, tackling Balinas to the floor, before he could cause any damage. Balinas was already pushing Barrington off him, and Hugh had to admit, he was stronger than he looked.

"What did you do that for? Quick, *get him*! He's standing up... Oh ... it's you?" Balinas stopped struggling as he looked into the face of

Art Gustoffman, the Chief of the Guard for the City of Portis-Montis. He was wrapped in his dark blue cloak and fought to untangle himself.

"Gentlemen, Balinas," said Art whilst getting back to his feet, his truncheon swinging by his side. "I apologise for catching you all unawares, and I applaud you for your caution on my unceremonious arrival. You can't be too careful in these uncertain times."

His hobnailed boots clicked on the floor as he moved. They covered most of his lower legs and were caked in the detritus of city life. Hugh could see that he must have rushed through the city, the signs on his navy-blue riding pants all too clear to see, where he had slipped in his haste. His jacket, with polished silver buttons, appeared to be dirty, from where he had wiped his dirty hands down it.

Being the Chief of the Guard, he got to wear the flat cap of office with goggles around the band, as opposed to the usual custodian helmet of the lower-ranking officers. He scooped it up from the floor and adjusted it on his head as he regained his composure.

Barrington got to his feet and headed over to his friend. "Art? This is a surprise. So, are you part of the Extended Geber Family too?" he said, rolling up his sleeve to reveal an EGF tattoo.

Art scowled at him.

"I am, and you shouldn't speak so freely of it. I may not have been a member, and then where would you have been?"

Barrington looked at his feet, unable to answer his friend's question.

"I can take it we have inducted you into the extended family?"

Hugh went to answer for Barrington, before Art waved him away.

"It's alright, Hugh, I know you will be a part of it."

Hugh shook his head. "I need to know. How can we trust you?"

Art pulled out his identity badge. He flipped the polished silver emblem of the city guard upwards, to reveal a secret symbol known only to those in the EGF.

"Well, that's good to see," said Hugh, revealing his tattoo.

Art raised an eyebrow but said nothing as he turned to Barrington.

"You should take notice of your friend here. Always ask before you reveal!" Barrington lifted his arm to reveal his tattoo. "That's good. At least I know I can trust you."

Barrington looked up in shock at Art. He was one of his oldest friends, only surpassed by Hugh, and the thought of him not trusting him took him by surprise. "But you know you can trust me?"

"Well, we cannot be too careful these days. Besides, the EGF is above all friendships and trust. You mustn't take offence, that I asked. This is a very serious business we're mixed up in."

"I too am pleased to see that you both bear the family mark upon you," said Balinas, "though cards and hidden marks are more the fashion these days, if we can talk of fashion in something so serious."

It was only three months ago that Hugh met up with an uncle he never knew existed. It was he who first introduced them to the Extended Geber Family and gave them an embossed card to show as proof. It was only when they met an old family friend, Hamish, that they realised others in the group had tattoos. It seemed a much better idea than carrying a card, so Hugh and Barrington got theirs done in Bansk, the capital city of Ranthina, whilst they had the time to get them.

"How do you know about this room, then?" Hugh asked with interest.

"That is easy to explain," said Balinas. "We needed someone on the ground in Portis-Montis, someone who could monitor what's happening within the guard, and Art was the perfect candidate. That way we can be ahead of any dangers coming our way."

"So, why the urgent arrival into the chamber, Art?" asked Balinas. "Is there something amiss?"

"I'm afraid so," he said, catching his breath. "I bring you some troubling news, which we must act upon immediately if you, Hugh and Barrington, are to be kept safe."

"What do you mean?" said Hugh. "What's going on?"

"Well, since the fire, we have had a warrant out for the arrest of Robert Smithson Jr and his assistant, Collins. We thought we were getting nowhere, when they turned up yesterday, out of the blue, and of their own free will. Sadly, I was not on duty when they arrived."

"Alright," said Barrington. "So that must be a good thing, right? I mean, they are now safely behind bars and awaiting trial ...they are, aren't they?" He looked at his friend with a look of worry.

Art shuffled on the spot.

"Well, that's where it all gets sticky. We had to let them go."

"What? Why? And what do you mean, *sticky?*" said Hugh.

"You must listen to me. They came back with the full support of the sitting government in Bansk and brought a couple of hangers-on with them. I don't know how they did it, but they must have friends in high places, that's all I can say."

"Well, I know Smithson is definitely on the side of the New World," said Hugh. "So it's no surprise to me he's made some important friends in Bansk. He studied there, after all. But how did they exonerate themselves from the fire situation?"

"Well, they have turned the investigation on its head. You are now the main suspect once more, Hugh."

Hugh looked aghast.

"But, what, how? You know it wasn't me. I was with Barrington, and there was the evidence that we gave to you on our return from Skellig-Krieg. We told you that Thomas admitted to setting fire to my laboratory, and you had the evidence to link Thomas and Smithson working together. You said it was clear as day?"

"Yes, well, I'm sorry to report that those papers have mysteriously disappeared, and as there weren't any witnesses, it will be your word against theirs."

"*What?*" said Barrington.

"I know, I know, but you must listen, as that's not the worst of it.

56

They've now dragged you into this as well, Barrington. The evidence currently points to you two working in cahoots in order to save your job, Hugh, and remove Robert Smithson from his seat of power."

"What? But that's not true," said Barrington. "You *know* we are innocent, and you're the Chief Guard. Surely, you can sort this out."

"I'm not the one accusing you. This is all coming from way above me, and I have no choice over the matter. That party which arrived yesterday? Well, it came with a replacement for me and, in my absence, took full control with little resistance. They have swept me aside, and there is currently a team on its way here to arrest you!"

"What? I don't understand?" said Hugh, his head spinning. "How do they know we are here? What are we to do, and how do we get out of this?"

He looked around the room, panicking, feeling like a trapped animal.

"Calm down Hugh," said Art. "They saw you leaving Barrington's shop this morning, and an agent followed you here. That is how they know where you are. I also have my own, trusted people working on this, people I've had following you and them both. Luckily, they reached me before the other team's tail returned. I could leave unseen and head here, leaving my chap to delay the rest of them finding you, but we don't have long. I fear they will already be on the way to come and arrest you."

"Alright," said Barrington. "Thank you for all the help you have given to us, but I feel we must leave *now!* Balinas, can you get us out of here?"

They all turned to Balinas.

"I'll have one of the Collins family make up two emergency backpacks right away." He paused, then disappeared with a …

–POP–

And returned to the room a scarce moment later with another …

-POP-

Hugh and Barrington looked at him in awe.

"We can use the sight for many things, Hugh. We are all trained within the gift, some better than others. There is already a message sent to get provisions for your trip. Now, you must listen carefully. The *Book of Prophecy* spoke of an object, something that will help you in your search for the books. I do not know where it is, or what it looks like. It goes by the name of Orbis. Find this and your search will be a lot easier. You must find the second book of lore. Get to it before the Elf King. When you find it, you must return it to me here, do you understand?"

Hugh and Barrington looked stunned.

"Balinas, we have to move, *now!*" said Art.

"I understand that, but this is critical. They must know how important this task is Hugh?"

"Yes, of course," said Hugh. "Bring the book to you. Alright. If you are sure that there is no other way to do this, then this is how it'll have to be. I'm not comfortable leaving here, especially so unprepared, but seeing as our friend here reports that we are no longer welcome, we'll have to go."

Hugh could feel his heart thumping against the wall of his chest. Just knowing they were back in the firing line once more made him feel sick.

"We must hurry if we are to get you out of here before everyone arrives," said Balinas, turning to run up the stairs.

With no time to dwell further on the situation, Hugh and the others followed, trying to keep up with Balinas. The higher and faster they climbed, the more out of breath and dizzy Hugh became. He was glad to reach the top, but still there was no time to wait. The Head Librarian was already running down the aisle, not even stopping to catch his breath.

"Has he got superhuman powers?" Barrington called out from behind Hugh, attempting to get his breath.

"No, Barrington," Balinas called out, without stopping to look back, "I'm an elf."

"Ah, yes, I forget. Apologies, I mean no offence."

"None taken."

They rounded the end of a bookcase and were now on a landing in the centre of the library itself. Hugh was pleased to see the library was being generous to them. The great room could change form, depending on the user's requirements. With today's urgency, the doors to the powerful room appeared closer than normal. They ran down the carpeted staircase, onto the library floor, but to Hugh's horror, he saw a lot of commotion in the atrium. Balinas was already on the case, whistling out a tune as they all stumble to a halt.

"Members of the Collins family, to your duties!"

His voice seemed to boom across the room, drawing out all noise from the atrium. To Hugh's astonishment, several more tuneful whistles followed. Many members of the family appeared on the library floor, seeming to flow out from hidden nooks and crannies all over the room.

All of them were carrying large piles of books and were now criss-crossing the main floor of the library. As if answering their call once more, the entrance to the room seemed to stretch far away from Hugh before his very eyes, so that the raiding party would have some distance to travel before they reached them.

Balinas changed his course, now running back up the impressive staircase once more, taking three steps at a time. Hugh dared not look back to see how close the city guards were. Art had already melted away into the background, ready to join at the back of the commotion now entering the room.

As they reached the top of the stairs, Balinas whistled another tune and a doorway appeared in the wall. Two members of the Collins family joined them as they passed through the small arched entrance, and Balinas came to a stop.

"Hugh, Barrington, this is where we leave you." He passed them both a bag each. "Here, these have enough supplies for your trip. I'm sorry it has to be like this, but given the circumstances, this will have to do. You will come out in the train tunnel. You need to turn left and watch your backs. With any luck, you will be out before the express train to

Bansk comes through."

Barrington looked alarmed. "And if we don't?"

"Well ... good luck anyway." Balinas patted him on the back. "Now *go* will you, I have urgent jobs to attend to."

"Where do we go once we are out?" asked Hugh.

"Leave that to me. It will be obvious what to do."

A crashing noise came from the direction of the library. Hugh caught sight of many books flying up in the air, somewhere close to the stairs.

"*GO!*"

There was something in the way Balinas ordered them to move that Hugh and Barrington could not resist. Their legs began moving before their brains had time to ask them to. Balinas and the other two members of the Collins family had already run back into the library to join the fray, and the doorway was sealing up once more. Hugh feared it would plunge them into darkness, but as they turned to run along the tunnel carved through the rock of the mountain, lamps automatically came to life. It was as if they sensed Hugh and Barrington and wanted to guide the visitors in the right direction.

The air smelled damp and the floor was slick underfoot as Hugh and Barrington headed deeper into the rock passageway. They were now regaining some control over their limbs and slowed the pace down to a manageable walk.

"That was too close," said Barrington, between heavy breaths.

"I know," said Hugh, clutching a stitch in his side. "I can't understand how he's managed it?"

"Who managed what?"

"Smithson, of course. He was the main suspect involved in the fire, and now he's turned the entire investigation on its back."

"I think Art is correct. Smithy has friends in high places. He must have called in a few favours to get this outcome. So, what are we going to do now? My shop's currently in the hands of someone incapable of running it."

"I say we focus on getting out of here first. We can worry about the shop once we are somewhere safe."

The tunnel was now heading upwards, and there were steps carved into the floor. There were a few places where they had to duck and squeeze through tighter gaps, sometimes having to remove their backpacks to get through.

Hugh's mind turned to the night Hamish McDougall, the old rune-master at the university, had to take this very route to escape the same powers who were after him. He could now sympathise with the emotions he must have gone through, having to flee one's home, not knowing when or if you would ever make it back.

A cool breeze that fell across his face brought Hugh back to his senses. The air had an edge to it, the smell of coal soot, and the walls of the tunnel had turned the colour of dark tar.

"I think we're nearing the end of the tunnel."

"I think you are right, old bean," said Barrington, still out of breath from behind him. "Tell me, what do you think we should do once we get out of here?"

"Well, Balinas said it would be obvious what to do once we are out here. It sounded like he was going to arrange something, but how he'll do that, I do not know … Ah, here we are."

The smaller passage that they were in opened up, and they found themselves in a large railway tunnel. It was wide enough for two sets of tracks, which glowed dimly from the daylight flooding in from the gaping hole. The breeze was greater here, and they followed their noses and the instructions from Balinas, aiming for the outside world. After what seemed like an age, the end of the tunnel was in sight, the breeze now seeming more like an icy gale hitting them in the face, the sound growing in intensity.

"Well, I'm pleased to be getting out of the tunnel," said Barrington.

"I'm just pleased that we didn't meet a train."

"*Shhh!*"

"What? Oh, come on, Hugh! I'm sure we are safe to say it's now ..."

But Barrington had now cottoned on to what Hugh was already far too aware of. The wind hitting their faces slowed, then changed direction. The tracks were pinging merrily away to themselves, in expectation of what was to come. The noise, however, had not stopped, and as Hugh looked behind, he saw the unmistakable lights of a train thundering down the track towards them.

Hugh grabbed Barrington by the arm.

"*Run!*" he shouted over the growing noise.

They scrambled to reach the mouth of the tunnel, the train now sounding its whistle in warning, the deep tone seeming to go straight through Hugh. He felt an energy surge into his legs, and he only hoped that his friend was also experiencing the same.

He could now feel the weight of the beast bearing down on the tracks behind them as they made it to where the end of the rock walls met the bright light of day. Temporarily dazzled, he veered left, falling down the steep embankment. He tumbled down the shingle and ballast slope, landing hard against a rock at the bottom, as the train thundered out behind him in a cloud of steam and smoke.

No sooner had he got his bearings than he panicked about Barrington, fearing that he didn't make it clear of the tunnel in time, before he looked up to see the outline of his friend heading straight for him. With no time to move, he braced for impact, as the full weight of his friend landing square onto of him, squeezing what air he had left in his lungs out, in a huff of pain.

Chapter 5

Smithson was in the first-class dining area of the *Silver Star Express* from Portis-Montis to Bansk. The way he had removed Geber and Delphin from the picture once and for all was simple in its planning. It now gave him the time to look for the book he so desperately wanted without impediment. By the time the train came out of the Corkies, he knew the deed would be done – Geber and Delphin in custody. It was perfect. He sat back with a smug smile on his face, rejoicing in the splendour of his plan.

The New World powers had sent him, with backup no less, to Portis-Montis on a specially chartered airship. Their mission was to sort out the mess that his servant, Collins, had left for him the last time he set foot in the city. He had marched into the main office of Art Gustoffman, the head of the city guard, taking his deputy by surprise.

He produced previously unseen and compelling evidence, proving he had no links to the stupid boy who had set fire to the alchemy laboratory. This was backed up by the powers of the New World. They didn't have a shred of evidence to pin on him, especially now that it was all carefully removed to the fireplace.

They had arrived with a team to relieve Art from his post and install a new chief, Mary Ablator-Sedes. She had made a name for herself by being a go-to person to sort out unwanted situations. She was a full supporter of the New World and would not be so lenient with those dabbling in the old ways. It was an easy affair to take control, given the man wasn't there. All they had to do was wait for him to turn up.

It gave Smithson great joy to see the old head thrown into the street, much to the outrage of his comrades; however, there were some who seemed to approve of the change. He would, of course, still have a job, but Smithson had arranged a much lower placement for the man. Much deserved in Smithson's eyes, after showing him up in the street three months earlier and accusing him of a crime he hadn't committed – that he was ultimately responsible for it was beside the point.

Now he could relax in style and enjoy the finest Ranthian cuisine money could buy. He was keen to see if his servant and his new apprentice had completed the one and only task he had set for them – though, given their track record, he didn't hold out much hope for the pair.

A waiter appeared next to him, holding a menu.

"Might I interest sir in a bottle of the house red?"

"You know, I think I'll give the house red a miss today, thank you."

"As you wish, sir. Is there anything else I can get you?"

"Bring me the finest bottle of red you have, no expense spared."

"Sir." The waiter nodded and headed off to get the order.

As the train thundered through the darkness of the surrounding tunnel, Smithson tucked into a fish course. The low pitch of the train's whistle sounded, to announce its exit from deep within the mountain. He sat back in his seat chewing in a mouthful of food, looking out of the window, watching the approaching light. The view that greeted him made him choke, and he sprayed half-chewed fish onto the window in front of him.

From the brief glimpse he got as the train went by, he saw Delphin windmilling his arms and what only could have been the mop-headed Geber rolling down the embankment. It appeared his plan hadn't worked. He'd recognise those two idiots anywhere. Delphin wore nothing other than his old navy uniform, and Geber's spindly frame was, he could only hope, being broken to bits whilst falling down the steep embankment.

"*Damn you, Geber!*" he yelled at the window along with a few other expletives, which caused yet more fish to hit the window.

This was met with much distaste from the other passengers travelling with him. It also earned him a curt reprimand from the train guard and a reminder of the rules of etiquette for passengers travelling in first class. Unable to face any more food and frustrated at being spoken to like a mere commoner – *telling me the rules of etiquette indeed* – he retired to his day cabin, where he could plan his next move.

If it was a war that Geber wanted, then it was a war that he would get.

Chapter 6

The last of the train carriages exited the tunnel, and the train trundled off down the track, leaving silence and cinders in its wake. Now moaning in a crumpled heap, Hugh attempted to push his friend off from on top of him. It was a huge task, as Barrington finally rolled over to the side and Hugh could take a breath, which hurt with the effort. He felt as though his entire ribcage had collapsed from the impact, and pain shot across his chest each time he breathed in. Barrington was coming round, shaking his head.

Both of them had lost their bags from Balinas in the fall, with items scattered all down the embankment. Hugh had a moment of panic, fearing his satchel with all of his father's notebook and letters were missing, but to his relief he saw the bag had landed at the bottom of the mound unopened. He pulled himself to his feet, and then with some difficulty, helped Barrington up, before attempting to clear the mess left in their wake.

"So, what do we do now?" asked Barrington, holding up the remains of his bag, the last few items dropping to the floor.

"Not sure," said Hugh, "but I think we can safely say that these are no use to us anymore." He held up his bag from Balinas that wasn't in any better state than Barrington's. "So, do you think this officially makes us wanted men?"

"I guess so, my friend. I don't know how we will get out of this one, especially now that most of the supplies Balinas gave us are in pieces across the bank. We'll need to get a move on if we are to make any form of civilisation before nightfall. We don't want to be out here for too long."

"Why not?"

"Hugh, just think back to our lessons on Ranthina, to the type of people that frequent this area. We are standing in the middle of bandit country, easy prey to those who make a living out of other's treasures."

"Well, if that's still the case, we'd better not hang around."

Hugh shouldered his satchel, then his hand went to his pocket. His leg was sore from where the compass his friend had given him had dug into his leg. He pulled it out, expecting to see it dented and beyond repair, but discovered it to be in perfect condition. He had thought it was made from brass, but whatever metal this was, it was certainly strong. He opened it up to see if he could get a bearing from it, but the needle spun round and round. The outer needle spun back and forth, unable to find a bearing to latch onto. Hugh shook his head.

"This is no good," he said, pocketing it once more. "It seems to have survived the fall on the outside, but the inner workings appear shot."

"I already told you back at the shop that it doesn't work. Please try to pay attention, dear Hugh, otherwise this will be an awfully long journey."

"*Alright*, no need to be cranky. I was only making an observation."

"Likewise."

"What's wrong?"

"*What's wrong?* Let me think. Maybe the fact that we're stuck out here in the open with no food and a lack of water might just have something to do with it. Oh, and let us not forget that we're wanted men once more."

"That's not my fault though, is it?"

"Depends how you look at it."

"And what's that supposed to mean?"

Barrington huffed impatiently.

"If you hadn't delayed going to see Balinas for all of that time, instead of keeping your nose in that damn book, then maybe we could have left earlier without having to abscond from the authorities. Instead, we now find ourselves as wanted men, with no food, no plan and nowhere to go. I dread to think what will happen to my shop."

"Is that all you care about, your bloody shop? I still can't see how it's my fault that we are in this situation. Besides, you're one to talk, burying your head in the sand and not facing up to your parents."

"Don't you *dare* bring them into this! We wouldn't be here if it wasn't for that damn book, and you know it."

"You *encouraged* me to go. I mean—"

Whatever Hugh was about to say disappeared from his train of thought as fast as Barrington pulled him to the ground. Hugh tried to fight him off, but his friend overpowered him again. "What are you doing now?"

"*Shhh ...*"

With no way of removing himself from his friend's hold upon him, Hugh gave in and attempted to see what the problem was. He heard it before he saw it. A steady, monotonous drone was coming from the mountains above.

A sense of dread came over him. Sure enough, a large, polished nose cone, followed by a gas sack, appeared from within the mountains.

"How? How have they found us?" asked Hugh.

"I don't know, but I don't intend to sit here and get caught! Come on!" Barrington was onto his feet again and running back up the slope.

"Where are you going now?"

"Back to the tunnel. I doubt they have seen us yet, and I intend for it to stay that way."

Hugh shouldered his bag once more and scrambled after Barrington, who was already a good way ahead of him. The beast of the airship slowly made its way out of the mountains, the light above him being blocked out, as Hugh eventually made it to the tracks and chased after

Barrington into the tunnel.

They hid behind the brick archway, out of sight from the eyes above, waiting with bated breath for the great ship to pass over.

The engines sounded as though they were being throttled back until it left them in an ominous silence.

They waited.

And waited.

"What's going on?" said Hugh in a low whisper.

"I don't know, but I don't like it."

A strange scraping noise came from somewhere above them, and shards of rock bounced off the embankment, narrowly missing the tracks. The engines briefly roared back into life before being backed off again.

"Wait a minute," said Barrington, coming to a realisation.

He was about to step out from the cover of the arch when it became eclipsed, as the airship headed towards the tracks nose first. It throttled up hard once more just in time to avoid smashing the gas sack into the ground, but not quick enough to avoid the gondola rubbing along the tracks, causing them to buckle, scraping and screeching as it went. The airship rose skyward, sending stones and debris toward Hugh and Barrington, who shielded their faces with their arms. The airship disappeared somewhere above them as Barrington turned to Hugh.

"Augustus!" Barrington yelled as they dared to step out from the protection of the tunnel.

Up above them the *Pearl of Ranthina* was levelling off, as the captain regained control once more of the lumbering beast. Hugh and Barrington looked skywards towards the gondola as Captain Augustus Volatus leaned out from a door. He was talking into a brass megaphone to be heard over the noise from the engines.

"What ho, chaps! Got a message to pick you up, wot wot! Mind out below, and I'll get the lads to drop a ladder down to you." Hugh and Barrington stood back as the call came out. "Heads up below!" A rope ladder landed at their feet and Hugh felt his stomach drop.

"He doesn't seriously expect us to climb that, does he?" A shiver of anxiety ran up the back of his neck.

"Calm down Hugh, it will be alright," said Barrington. "Look at me and listen to my instructions."

"Come on, you two! Stop dilly dallying and climb the damn ladder. I've a schedule to keep to."

Barrington looked up at Augustus, visibly holding back a curt response.

"As I was saying, I have guided many people up ladders like this numerous times in the past. It's a technique that we used in the navy, and we can use it now. It's very safe, and I will make sure you get to the top of the ladder."

Hugh nodded, saying nothing.

"What I need you to do is trust me. I'm sorry for the words we spoke before Augustus arrived, but I would like you to put that to one side for now. You need to concentrate on the job in hand, alright?"

Hugh nodded again.

"Right, I would like you to get onto the ladder, and begin climbing. Have you used a ladder like this before? No, of course you haven't, sorry. You need to keep yourself tucked in and pull up with your hands on the rear of the ladder."

Hugh gripped onto the ladder as instructed and climbed. He was gripping on so tightly for fear of letting go and falling to his death, and he dared not open his eyes, for he didn't want to see how high he was. He could not focus on the action of climbing as his head was spinning. After what seemed like an age, he called out to Barrington.

"How am I doing? Please tell me I'm somewhere near to the top?"

Barrington coughed awkwardly.

"Why are you so loud? Are you climbing up behind me?"

"Hugh, old chap. You've only made one rung so far."

Hugh opened his eyes and looked up at the airship, and his head fell forward to the ladder in disbelief.

"How am I to achieve climbing up there?"

"It's alright, you just need to climb two more rungs, then I will climb on behind you." Hugh followed Barrington's instructions before feeling his friend step on below him, his arms encompassing Hugh's body in a ring of safety. The ladder swung around, and Hugh whimpered with fear.

"It's alright Hugh, you are not going anywhere. I'm right behind you. Now all you need to do is slowly climb up. I'll be with you all the way."

"Oh, here we go. Bit of the old navy come out eh, wot wot! Save it for the cabin, lads!" Augustus bellowed out, and he guffawed loudly.

"*Bugger off!*" the pair called in unison.

"It's only a bloody joke. I don't know, make a comment and everyone takes offence these days ... what do you mean take the megaphone away from my mouth ... oh, blast!"

Hugh and Barrington looked up, shaking their heads.

"Right, Hugh. Are you ready?"

"Not really."

"It'll be fine. Just take one step at a time. Let's count. One ... Two ..."

It was slow going, and Hugh knew all the people on board were watching them. The airship that they were boarding appeared to be full of passengers. He dreaded to think what they must have looked like to the onlookers. He put it out of his mind as they continued to scale the ladder, and he felt reassured that his friend was right behind him. The scary part for Hugh was when they ran out of the ladder at the top.

"Well, come on lad, climb in!" Augustus barked at him over the noise of the engines.

"I can't let go of the ladder!"

The captain tutted to himself and instructed some of the crew to help. Hugh made the fatal error of looking down, and his world spun once more. He lost his grip on the ladder, but Barrington was ready. He pulled himself onto the ladder against Hugh to stop him from moving.

The crew sprang into action, and Hugh felt pairs of hands grabbing him under his arms and hauling him into the ship. They moved to help Barrington before retrieving the ladder and closing the door. The pair sat recovering as the captain throttled the engines into life.

Hugh looked to his friend.

"Well, I can safely say that I wish to never do that again."

"You're telling me? I thought I was going to lose you at one point. It took all my energy to stop you from falling."

"Thank you, I really appreciate your help back there. I couldn't have done that without you. Listen, about what I was saying on the ground, I didn't mean for it to come out like it did."

"It's alright. We've had a lot of stress these past few months, and I think it has taken its toll on us both. Let's put that behind us for now. We can discuss everything when we're both in a better frame of mind. Come on, let's find Augustus. I'm curious to know how he found us."

He helped Hugh up from the floor, and they made their way to a door marked 'BRIDGE'. It was being guarded by a crew member, who dutifully guided them through the door, down a small corridor, and onto the bridge. Augustus was just finishing an announcement.

"... so it will please you to know that the little diversion hasn't cost us too much time. I expect our arrival into Ranga to be later on this afternoon, and with any luck, I'll have us on the ground in time for dinner. This is Captain Augustus Volatus signing off, wot wot." He stepped away from the microphone, and his second in command quickly stepped in to switch it off. "Well, this is a lovely surprise! We seem to make a habit of catching up with each other like this, don't we, dear cousin?" He gave Barrington a friendly punch in the arm, and he frowned back at Augustus.

"Tell me, how is it you found us in the first place?" he asked, now rubbing his arm.

"I'll fill you in on that once we are in the privacy of my cabin," said Augustus, dropping his voice to a loud whisper still audible to all. "We don't want to be overheard." He winked at Barrington, whilst fumbling for a switch on the control board. He lifted a flap and was about to press the button when his second-in-command rushed over.

"*Not that one, sir!* That's the emergency gondola release button. We wouldn't want that, would we?" He carefully removed the captain's finger away from the danger of pressing the button, closing the flap.

"Well spotted, Enderby! You saw my test and passed it with flying colours, wot wot."

Enderby looked at Hugh and Barrington, blowing out his cheeks with a large sigh, as they stared back, open-mouthed and shaking their heads. George Enderby looked like a man who was under stress, as any Flag Captain would be in his situation. Though he kept his cool, a vein was throbbing near his right eye, causing it to twitch. He was dressed in the same white uniform as Augustus, with epaulets and tassels that hung over his shoulder. His jawline was stiff as he looked at Augustus, wide eyed.

"Well, it appears you have everything under control here, so I'll just leave you to it whilst I take my cousin and his friend here for a chat in my cabin. Come on, you two." And with that, he marched off with Hugh and Barrington in tow, leaving a bemused Enderby to take control.

To get to the captain's cabin, they had to pass through some of the public areas. This airship wasn't as big as the *Princess of the Skies*, but it was no less opulent. Everything was to a high standard, with plush carpet underfoot and the finest carpentry, as befitting a ship of this class. Hugh couldn't help but notice that everyone was sitting firmly in their seats and glared at the latest arrivals as they walked past. Given the ordeal that they had just been through, it didn't surprise him.

The captain came to a stop outside a pair of double doors, where another crew member was standing by to let them in. The crewman brought his feet together, nodded and opened the door for them before re-assuming his post outside the door.

"At ease, dear boy," said Augustus as they entered the room.

"This is all very formal, Augustus," said Barrington.

"One can't be too careful these days, what with the growing tensions in the world as they are."

"I take it you are referring to the uprising coming from the Old World?" said Hugh.

"Why, of course! These past few months have seen many changes in the world as we know it. The powers that be are getting jittery with the movements within the old kingdoms, and from what I can gather, they have every right to be worried."

"How so?"

"You get a feel for this sort of thing, especially when you run a company such as this."

"Sorry, did you say your company?" asked Barrington.

"Yes, dear cousin, all this is mine. Everyone thought I was mad, but I saw the future in air travel. Besides, nobody else would employ me. I don't know why."

Hugh glanced at Barrington with raised eyebrows.

"Why, I was the first to carry passengers," said Augustus, "instead of just using these beauties to ship cargo around the world. That's why I had the authority to pick you up."

"Yes, I was wondering about that. Hugh and I thought you were initially the authorities coming to take us back. How did you know we were here?"

"Well, it's simple, really. I had a message come through from Balinas just before take-off, saying that you were in a spot of bother. Naturally I said that I would do anything to help and, seeing as I was heading in this direction anyway, so I was more than happy to do my bit for the cause."

"For the cause? Are you telling us you are one of the family?" said Hugh.

"Shhh, keep your voices down, will you! Well … after you," said the captain, his brow furrowed. Hugh and Barrington rolled up their shirtsleeves to reveal their tattoos.

"Old school, eh?" The captain rolled up his left trouser leg, revealing a forest of hair. He reached into his sock and pulled out a card. "I knew I could trust you, as Balinas instructed me to find you, but it's important to keep up with tradition. I'm surprised to see the tattoos though, I heard they were phasing those out. You must be long-standing members." Hugh and Barrington exchanged a confused glance. "It was pretty simple to find you, really. I just had to follow your energy, Hugh. You really ought to get yourself trained up, you know?"

"Energy? Do you mean to say that you have gained use of the sight?"

"Of course," said Augustus, tapping to his monocle. "It was only a few months ago that I visited you whilst you were on your way to Skellig-Krieg. You didn't really think that I was there with you on the ship, did you?"

"Erm ... no, of course not," said Hugh unconvincingly.

"Anyway, you are here now, so how may I be of help? Balinas instructed me to take you to where you needed to go."

"We need to get to Bansk. I think we need to pay a visit to a friend out there. If you could drop us off en route, we would be very grateful."

Augustus started laughing.

"What are you laughing at? I don't recall Hugh saying anything funny?" said Barrington.

"Oh, my dear cousin, of course he did. I can't just alter my route that drastically.

I have a flight plan and a timetable to uphold. Small amendments are fine, but I need to be in Ranga by tonight, or I will face a penalty. Besides, are you sure that you want to go to the capital city? The authorities are after you."

Hugh looked to Barrington as the fear rose inside him.

"It was to be expected, Hugh. We ran from the law. I dare say that they are ransacking my shop as we speak, trying to find where we have gone."

"Ah, that reminds me," said Augustus. "Balinas also sent word about that. He said that he would make contact with Wanda, and he's also assigned a Collins to help look after the shop in your absence."

"That's very reassuring," said Barrington.

Hugh knew his friend was fearing his shop being left in the hands of Jenkins, who was nowhere near ready to take charge of the business. With a Collins there, Barrington could rest now the shop was in safe hands.

"So, how are we to get to Bansk, then?" said Hugh.

"Well, this old girl will need to be taken in for repair on the way there tonight, a bit of touching up to do no doubt."

Hugh looked at Barrington, who shook his head.

"I can get you into the city tonight," said Augustus, "but not earlier than midnight. Once I have dropped this one off, I can use my personal Air Steam Turbo ship to take you where you need to go. You will be fine whilst in my company, but if you try to enter through the normal channels, I fear the authorities will pick you up. I will have to drop you within the city limits."

Hugh's heart sank once more.

"Do you think it will be that bad?"

"I'm afraid so, but not to worry. I can drop you off wherever you need to go."

"We need to get to the marshes, to see an old friend."

"I take it you are referring to Hamish. Yes, I know of him,"

said Augustus, in reply to Hugh's reaction. "I used to take him and your father all over the place. Those were the days ..." He tailed off into some unseen distant memory.

"Yes, well, thank you. We really appreciate it," said Hugh. He looked at Barrington encouragingly, but his friend looked at something interesting on the carpet. "Barrington?"

He looked up. "Err, yes, we are very grateful for any help you can give us," he said awkwardly.

Hugh's mind returned to the last flight with Augustus, which resulted in an argument and Barrington storming from the room.

"Like I've said before, I am always here if you need help. You only have to ask, wot wot."

Hugh didn't want to admit it, but he was warming to the old aviator. Augustus said they were free to use the ship and his cabin as they needed; then he left them to it whilst he headed back to the bridge.

The pair explored the ship, which appeared to be a smaller version of the *Empress of the Skies*, though it was larger than the Air Steam Turbo ships, which were designed for high-speed flights around the world. They ended up at the bar, where Hugh opted to sit away from the window.

"So, how are we going to get around now there's a price on our heads?" said Barrington. "If what Augustus says is true, we won't find it easy to walk around Bansk. Then we have to figure out how to get to Skellig-Krieg, let alone pass through the border guards. We won't be able to explain that one easily, and I dare say that our faces will now be on some sort of list."

This made Hugh's stomach churn. Looking for one book was enough of a task, and that was without the pressure that Balinas had added on top by requesting them to find another hidden item.

"I'm really not enjoying this book-finding task," he said. "The whole thing just seems to be growing more difficult by the minute. I think we need to get to Hamish as he will have a better idea of how to evade the security measures. After all, he has been doing it for some time now."

"That's very true, my friend. I still say this would have been easier had you dealt with the task sooner, though. We wouldn't be under as much pressure as we are facing now."

"Look, I wasn't avoiding going to see Balinas, or avoiding looking at the letter from my father ..."

Barrington leaned back into his seat and looked at Hugh with a raised eyebrow.

"I wasn't ... I just ... well ... besides, you had your shop to think about."

"Don't pin this one on me."

"All I'm saying is that it's been a difficult time, especially since we lost Thomas."

Barrington looked out of the window, avoiding his friend's gaze.

"It's alright," Hugh said. "I know that you are still struggling with the loss."

It took a while for Barrington to find the right words, which he said whilst holding back the pain.

"It's just that I feel so responsible for what happened. I should've been more attentive to his needs, more caring, and I feel I let him down somewhat." He still couldn't meet Hugh's eye.

"I think he still would've left in the end. He had his own path to walk and his own destiny to fulfil. I understand it's hard for you, carrying on each day without him by your side. He was a big part of your life. You said yourself that he was like a son to you, so you're going to feel the loss. But we have to move on together.

"Maybe my focus was on the book, but I have a lot of pressure on me to get this right. Ever since Theo died, I've had to give up a lot. It wasn't just the loss of my brother, but also the loss of my freedom."

Barrington gave him a knowing look.

"What?"

"Are you sure that you are not still missing Adelia?"

"I've already explained that situation to you, and I don't want to do so again. What I'm trying to say is that I never expected to take on any of this. But now that you mention it, I have the added complication of Adelia and the children to consider."

Barrington looked back at him, confused.

"I thought you didn't know where they were, except for somewhere around Bansk. How can that be an issue?"

"I haven't told you this, but she has been in contact more regularly. She hasn't said where she is, but she is expressing some interest in coming back to Portis-Montis life. I've explained to her that the situation is difficult, but she still insists that she'll be coming back. I can't tell her they will all be in danger, without having to reveal everything that is going on."

"So, do you still have feelings for her, or not?" said Barrington, pushing the issue.

"What's that supposed to mean?"

"I mean, do you still like her in that way. I always saw you with her whilst Theo worked. You were more of a father to his kids than he ever was."

"What are you trying to say?"

Barrington raised his hands in defence. "I'm not saying anything, but if you were going to spend all of your time hanging around with your brother's wife and children, well ..."

"Well, what?"

"Well, people are going to talk, and talk they did. Besides, you don't get a crooked nose like that without there being some element of truth"

"You know it wasn't like that." Barrington looked back, nonplussed. "*It wasn't!*"

"Your crooked nose may have a different opinion on that."

"I've explained this to you before. Yes, things became ... complicated, but I would never do that to my brother."

"So, you admit you had feelings for each other?"

"Look, I think we are straying too far from the point. The fact of the matter is, I have been feeling the pressure of late, and some days it feels too much."

They sat in silence, and Hugh turned to look vacantly out of the window, avoiding looking down to the drop below. He hated being questioned on the subject, and he was now wishing he were somewhere else. His mind turned to Emily, the firestone glowed warmly upon his chest, and he knew that, somewhere far away, Emily's would do the same.

Chapter 7

It was coming on dusk as they arrived at the small trading outpost of Ranga, a large township an hour and a half flight west of Bansk. It had made its wealth mining gold, and its large houses which belonged to the mine owners dotted the hillside above the main town itself. To the east of the built-up area was the airdock, which appeared much smaller than those in Bansk and Portis-Montis.

As they dropped towards the landing gate, they passed a water tower, which was lit up like a beacon. It loomed in close next to the airship, and for a moment Hugh thought they were going to collide with the structure, but the airship swung outwards at the last moment, enough to avert the danger. Hugh and Barrington had barely spoken to each other for the rest of the journey, both lost in their own minds.

The passengers disembarked, and Augustus set a new course to take the airship in for repair. During the short flight, the crew worked around Hugh and Barrington, preparing to transfer to their next ship, which seemed to be a well-rehearsed move. Hugh listened to the conversations playing out as people walked by, oblivious to the two stowaways left on-board.

"I can't believe he's done it again," said one.

"Tell me about it. We spend more time transferring airships than we do in the air," said the other.

"How he funds this is beyond me?"

The second crew member dropped his voice.

"Well, from what I've heard, he's well rich. Got a huge family fortune from the old days, if you catch me drift."

Barrington, who was listening in on the conversation, cleared his throat. The pair stopped talking, looking over to where Hugh and Barrington were sitting, and took their gossip elsewhere.

It was fully dark by the time they arrived at the engineering dock. Hugh saw they were heading towards an immense set of hangars, one of which had INTERNATIONAL MORCARTHIAN AIRWAYS across the side, lit up for all to see. They flew over the top of it, nearly skimming the top of the buildings. Hugh could see that the IMA complex was quite impressive.

There were nine hangars, all facing a large landing pad, with a cross on it. He saw glimpses of the other airships, all mid service, having some sort of bodywork repairs being carried out. He watched as the ground crew attached a mooring line to the landing pad and felt the subtle jolt as the winch kicked into life.

Once they were safely down, Hugh saw they were on a turntable, which was being hand cranked around to line the airship up with an empty hangar. They attached the winch to a weighted train bogie on tracks, and the ground crew attached this to another line which disappeared off into the hangar. It went taught, and slowly they moved towards the cavernous space. The ground crew were already inspecting the latest damage, and Hugh could see them all shaking their heads. The P.A. clicked into life:

"Hello chaps. I don't have a clue where you are ... but meet me by the port-side door near the bridge. Wot wot [CLICK]*."*

"I suppose we'd best get a wriggle on then," said Hugh.

They made their way through the empty ship as the outside world disappeared behind the hangar wall. It felt eerie to be the only ones walking through the empty passenger areas. When they made it off the ship, they could view the damage more clearly. Hugh saw the front of the ship had scrapes and dents which carried on all the way underneath it to almost halfway along the gondola.

"Bugger!" said Augustus, to the chief engineer. "It must have been the train track we kissed outside the tunnel. Got right in the way it did."

The chief engineer let out a sigh, shaking his head. "And the tail? That's all bent as well."

"Ah, yes, well, that would explain the steering issues we had then." He looked at the engineer, who stood open-mouthed. "There was a small bit of rock in the way as we dropped to pick up my dear cousin and his friend, wot wot."

"That would be the mountain, would it, sir?" said Enderby.

"Rock, mountain, whatever you wish to call it. Still got in the way."

"We'll transfer everything over to the *Empress* and have her ready by the morning and— *Put that pipe away, now!*" Enderby barked at Barrington, his voice echoing around the hangar. "Is destroying airships a family thing?" He marched off at speed, talking irritably to himself, leaving Barrington red faced.

"I wasn't planning on lighting it," he said grumpily, stowing the pipe back inside his jacket.

Augustus guided them out of the main hangar to a smaller one at the side of the complex. He switched the lights on, and the lamps flickered into life.

"I love this new electricity thing," he said with a smile.

Hugh and Barrington stopped dead in their tracks. They were looking at a small AST ship, its body glistening under the light. These ships were built with a lightweight metal around the gas sack, which made it strong enough to fly at high speed, but prevented the gas sack collapsing, without making the overall weight too heavy.

Hugh took in its polished nose cone on the end of the stiffened gas sack, freshly replaced from its last outing, his warped reflection looking back at him. The slender shape reminded him of a large bullet. Automated bellows were gently priming the engine, ready for flight.

"*The Jewel of Ranthina.* Isn't she beautiful?" Augustus walked up to the side of the ship, giving it a pat. Some crew entered the hangar, and Augustus instructed them to open the main doors.

"We'll head on in; they can join us shortly." He marched up to the awaiting steps, ignoring the worried look on the crew's faces.

"You drew the short straw, eh?" said Barrington.

They nodded back, but said nothing, tending to their duties. Hugh followed Barrington into the airship. The smell of leather and beeswax greeted them. It was cool from lack of use, and everything gleamed in the lights shining in through the windows from the dock.

They made it to the bridge where Augustus was preparing the ship. Hugh could see that the captain was very proud of his baby. He didn't flick the switches and spin the dials but seemed to caress them carefully into life. A whirring noise began, the sound of something spinning extremely fast. The more things Augustus activated, the more the ship came to life, with lights and instruments flickering on.

"She's a gorgeous ship," said Augustus.

"I can see that," said Barrington, who looked on admiringly at his cousin's work.

It looked to Hugh like Augustus was an organist, but instead of the sound of music, came the dings, buzzing and lights, as the ship sang back to its master. A voice came through the P.A. behind them, making Hugh jump.

"*Ready to track out, sir.*"

"Right you are chaps, steady as she goes," said Augustus into a microphone on the console.

The ship bumped, and they began backing out from the hangar. The lights of the hangar disappeared from view, now replaced with the stark difference of the darkness from the outside world. They slowed to a stop, and Hugh heard the ground crew climbing aboard.

"This is ground control. You are clear to begin engine start-up."

"Right, chaps, if you would like to take a seat and strap in, we can get this show on the road."

Hugh and Barrington headed for two plush leather seats, more comfortable than the AST they last went on, and strapped themselves in. Augustus went over to a side window, opened it, shouted *"Clear engines,"* before closing it and taking a seat behind the centre of the console. Hugh was about to ask Augustus why he hadn't strapped himself in, but he thought better of it.

Augustus pressed a series of buttons, then reached overhead, and held one in for longer that the others. Hugh heard an engine whizzing into action, and then the captain's finger moved to the next button, depressing it in the same manner. Again, the sound of an engine springing to life came from somewhere behind Hugh. The ship was gently vibrating, as they were slowly rising into the night sky. It came to a stop with a gentle bump, and the ship began pulling against its mooring line.

"Clear to wind up engines."

Hugh watched as Augustus pushed up two levers to the halfway marker and felt the power of the engines keen to propel the craft forwards. Augustus operated the controller, and Hugh saw the world outside move sideways.

"Release in ten ... nine ..."

"Hold on to your hats chaps, wot wot!" He pushed forward on the levers, and Hugh began bobbing up and down in his seat.

"... four ... three ... two ... one ... RELEASE!"

Augustus slammed his hand down on a big red button, and Hugh sank into his seat, as the world around them disappeared in a blur. This was certainly faster than the last AST they travelled in. Augustus let out a whoop of joy.

"*Captain Volatus, this is ground control. How many times do we have to remind you not to leave on full power! Mr Criggens lost four sheep the last time you ...*"

The sound of ground control faded away as Augustus turned the speaker down.

"That's enough of that rubbish," he said.

As he moved his hand back to the control, he knocked a pad of paper and pen to the floor.

"Dang and blast ..."

He let go of the controls to pick them up, his knee leaning on the controls, and the ship lurched downwards. Hugh's fingernails dug into his chair.

"Augustus, hold on to the bloody controls!" said Barrington in alarm.

"What? Oh, yes, yes, whatever you say. No need to be a whinging ninny about it."

"There is when it's our lives on the line!"

"Stop moaning. It might distract me. Now let me think, button ... button ...which one was it ...?"

"I take it you are qualified to fly this thing?"

"...meenie ...miney ... What? Of course, I can fly this thing. Ah ha! MO!"

He hit a green button which illuminated, and the aircraft steadied off, leaving the bridge in an uneasy silence. Hugh sat wide-eyed, fingernails still firmly implanted into the seat, whimpering. Augustus jumped out of his seat and went to exit through the door.

"Now, where are you going?" exclaimed Barrington.

"To get a cup of tea and some food, *of course*."

"But who's flying the ship?"

"Oh, I leave that to the auto-thingamabob."

And with that, he exited the bridge.

It took Barrington some time to coax Hugh from his seat, leaving behind the indents where his fingers had been. He shakily followed Barrington through to the main area of the ship. Instead of there being rows of seats, Hugh saw they had kitted it out with a bar, some sofas, wing-backed chairs and a writing desk. Further on towards the back, he could see doors that presumably led to a bathroom and sleeping quarters. Augustus had already placed himself in one chair, and a crew member was handing him a cup of tea. Hugh watched as the sugar bowl arrived and the captain shovelled seven heaped teaspoons into his cup.

"Surely there's more sugar than tea in that thing?" said Hugh.

"Don't be silly. How on earth could I drink that? Now sit down, you're making the place look untidy."

He poured the tea into the saucer and continued to drink it from there, making large slurping noises each time the saucer met his lips. Tea dripped from the saucer, down the front of his white suit. Hugh sat agog.

"Cover your mouth up when you yawn, boy! I don't want to see your tonsils."

He slurped again, and the hairs on the back of Hugh's neck stood on end, and his eye twitched. Barrington was looking just as horrified. They both declined the offer of a drink of tea, opting for water, but were grateful when some food came out. Hugh's mouth watered as a trolly appeared next to him, smelling of a roast meal.

"I took the liberty of ordering ahead for you," said Augustus. "I hope that's alright?"

The serving staff showed Hugh and Barrington the hidden table on their armrests and they placed a tray in front of Hugh with a plate of roast beef and all the trimmings on it. They put an obligatory glass of wine on the side table next to him. As soon as Barrington received his tray, Hugh dug in.

Augustus didn't wait, as he dug into his plate, chewing with his mouth open, now adding gravy drips to the tea stains.

Hugh remembered the limited eating time from their previous mealtime experience with the captain and would not make the same mistake again. Sure enough, as Augustus finished his last mouthful, the staff took the plates away. Hugh was pleased as he ate some of the tasty delights before they disappeared.

He hadn't had the time to think before the deserts arrived in front of him — a chocolate steamed pudding and custard — which was hoovered up at great speed by Augustus. The crew attempted to wrestle the bowl from Barrington, who hadn't quite finished his, and he won the toss. The crew waited for him to finish, the captain's eyes drilling into him as he ate.

"It's normally considered polite on this airship to finish when the captain does.

"And greater society finds it polite to wait for the guests to finish before removing the meal. Now let's get down to business. What's the plan for our arrival in Bansk?"

Augustus scowled.

"Well, you can't just wander off here as if all is normal. We've to assume that the authorities will now know of your departure from Portis-Montis and will be on the lookout for you. I can get us to the marshes and land near Hamish's. Then we can all pay him a visit, see what he has to say about all of this."

"Sorry, did you say … *we?*" asked Hugh. "Are you coming too?"

"Yes! He's an old friend, and I wish to say hello, if that is alright with everyone?" He sat wide-eyed, eyebrows raised.

Barrington let out a sigh and shook his head.

"Alright, but please be on your best behaviour, no funny business. We need Hamish to be onside with us."

"Don't know what you mean, wot wot!"

"*I'm sure you don't!* Are you intending to join us for the whole caboodle?"

"Don't worry, I won't be hanging around for long, if that's what you're worried about. I have to get back for the morning flight to Skellig-Krieg. Besides, you wouldn't want me to cramp your style."

A pang of guilt dropped through Hugh.

"That's not what we mean."

"No, no, in all seriousness I have to be back, but it is nice to see that some people care." He glared at Barrington. "Now, we are about an hour away from our destination, so if you don't mind, I'm going to take forty winks."

"But what about the ship, who's going to fly it?" asked Hugh.

"Oh, Cocker here can monitor things on the bridge, and besides, the auto-whatsit is on, so I'm sure he'll be fine." The crew member to his left – who turned out to be Cocker – didn't seem too confident in the captain's decision.

"But I only joined the company last week, sir. I'm only here because they said it would be character building."

"And so it is, lad, so it is. Now's the perfect time to learn. There's a manual on the side; the basics are in there. That's how all the best learn."

Cocker stood, frozen to the spot.

"Well, run along lad. You're not on holiday. Come and fetch me in three quarters of an hour. That should be plenty of time to prepare for our arrival." With that, he stood up and left the room, leaving Cocker to run to the bridge and have his first flying lesson.

"Go on then, say it," said Barrington.

"Say what?"

"Well, this is the point where you normally tell me to go easy on him because *he only means well*, or something to that effect."

"I certainly do not! But, seeing as you've raised the issue, yes, you could try to be more polite to him. I know he can be a little obtuse, but I'm sure he is quite the educated man."

Barrington just stared at him.

"What now?"

"Are you actually standing up for the fellow? We are talking about the same captain, the one who let go of the control at full speed, has the table manners of an ape, and the observational skill of a dead mule, *that* captain?"

"They are all qualities in their own right ..."

He paused long enough for them to burst out into laughter.

"*Keep quiet out there! Wot wot!*" came the voice of the captain, trying to sleep.

Still suppressing small giggles like naughty schoolchildren, Hugh and Barrington agreed they ought to get some sleep before their next adventure at ground level. They settled down for a nap.

—

"*Excuse me, Mr Geber, Mr Delphin, the captain requested me to wake you up ...*"

"I asked you to wake them up, not whisper them a lullaby, Cocker. You two, *wake up!*"

Hugh woke suddenly, as Augustus kicked his foot, and then shook Barrington by the shoulder.

"Thomas, *no!*"

Barrington opened his eyes, looking around, stunned.

"Who the hell is Thomas?"

"What? Oh, none of your business." Barrington yawned and looked down at his feet.

"Right, well, come and take your seats up front with me. We're approaching Bansk."

They trudged their way through to the bridge, where they could see the bright lights of Bansk in the distance between the clouds.

They took their seats and, knowing the track record, strapped themselves in for good measure. No sooner had Hugh done up his seat belt than a message blurted out of the speaker which Augustus had just turned back up.

"... *I repeat, this is AST 196. You are on our flight path. You must yield immediately ... Over.*"

"What the devil?" said Augustus, as he leaned over to the microphone. "Now you listen here. I am Captain Augustus Volatus on a special mission. I will *not* yield. I have permission to be here from the highest authority."

"Do you have permission?" asked Barrington sotto voce.

"Nope, but they don't know that."

"Oh, it's you. Volatus, get your damn ship out of the way. We're coming through!"

Everything happened quickly. Augustus swore, and gunned his ship towards the ground, just in time to miss the AST which barrelled out of the clouds in front of them. But they still weren't out of the woods yet, for Hugh saw the open fields coming at them fast, the notepad and paper seeming to float in the air, until Augustus pulled back on the controls, causing the note pad to land on the captain's face.

With one hand on the control, barely keeping a grip, the other scrabbling at the paper on his face, Hugh screaming for his life and Barrington shouting at his cousin to get a grip, the airship shot back into a cloud.

Everything seemed to go quiet. Too quiet. The airship had stalled completely; the engines had flamed out, and they were now pivoting back towards the ground. An alarm bell rang with red lights flashing.

"What does that mean?" Shouted Barrington.

"It means there's something wrong!"

"No, shi—"

Barrington stopped mid-insult.

Augustus appeared to glow, cupping his hands over his mouth. Then released a ball of energy across the console in front of him. A wind appeared as if out of nowhere. The windows opened of their own accord, and the ball of energy went outside to envelop the ship, bringing it to a stop. It was as if they landed on a cushion of air. Hugh and Barrington looked on in amazement and the alarm bells stopped and the ship levelled off. Augustus was back on the controls, restarting the flamed-out engines. At the reassuring sound of the engines restarting, Hugh let out a muted sigh of relief.

"Erm, what …" was all that Barrington could muster.

Augustus turned to the pair behind him.

"You didn't see that, understand?" They both nodded in stunned silence.

"This is Bansk ground control. Is that you up there, Volatus? Do you need assistance?"

"Hello Bansk ground control, this is Volatus. We're all fine, thank you. Just a little engine flame out. I think we sucked in a bird or something."

"Do you require an emergency landing, or we could deploy the catch net? We can give assistance. Please update, over."

"No thank you, we will be fine. I am passing through and do *not* require assistance, over."

"Fine, all received. Please keep out of restricted airspace. Have a good night, over."

"Roger, will do, over and out, wot wot!"

"Augustus, not wanting to stick my nose in," said Hugh, "but didn't you ought to take their offer of help and get your engine fixed?"

"You know as well as I do that the engines are fine," he said, not even turning to face Hugh.

They sat in silence as Augustus flew them around the city, aiming to land in the marshes. They came to a stop above the green fog, the smell already seeping its way in through the open windows.

Augustus got up and closed them before returning to his seat.

"Ghastly smell."

"So, erm, how do we get down? There are no winches in the marshes," said Barrington.

Augustus turned around, winked, and hit a button to his right. A horn blared out into the dense night sky.

"Blasted contraption! Meant to do that, of course," he said, hitting the next button to the right. Hugh heard a whooshing sound, followed by a hollow thud. A flashing red light turned green, and the ship jolted before descending into the murky cloud.

"Ground anchor, my invention." He smiled at Barrington, who tutted to himself.

"That's reassuring," said Barrington. "And if it fails, then what?"

"I can always shout an order to the chaps below. They will take it from there."

"So, how do you know if we are in the right area?"

"My dearest cousin, I know these marshes like the back of my —"

Augustus grimaced as a loud crunch shook the ship.

"Bugger!"

"Actually, I think the word you were looking for was *hand*," said Barrington with a smug look on his face.

Barrington undid his lap belt and went to the window.

"It's not a bad attempt, if I say so myself. You only landed on the decking around the cottage, though I think Hamish might not be too pleased. Tell me, do you carry such things as masks and goggles on here?"

Augustus pressed a series of buttons, with numerous implements and gadgets appearing, then disappearing. It reminded Hugh of the photoplayer machine he had seen at the Portis-Montis music hall, with many bells and sounds, hissing and clicking, each time he pressed a button. Eventually, he found the one he was looking for.

"Ah ha, here it is!" A tray of breathing apparatus slid out from the wall. They donned the breathing aids and headed out into the gloomy fog to assess the latest damage to one of Augustus's ships.

Chapter 8

Smithson was sitting in his hotel room in Bansk, digesting the news that his servant, Collins, had just brought to him. He was very pleased that at least one of his plans had come to a successful conclusion, and he had now gained the package that he so desperately needed. He had just dispatched Collins to go with his new apprentice, to send a message back to his contact in Skellig-Krieg. It was important that he inform them about the latest events.

On his arrival into Bansk, he had headed straight for the Capitol building on Weaver Street to consult with the powers that be. He had informed them of his bad news about Geber and Delphin, and they had confirmed to him they were indeed on the run. With this latest intelligence report of their location, they would send a team out to locate the pair.

Oddly, they had received another message an hour earlier, saying the Silver Star Express to Portis-Montis had derailed at the mountain tunnel, in the exact spot where Geber and Delphin had last been spotted by Smithson. Early indications had assumed some sort of sabotage by the pair and so, egged on by Smithson, an international warrant for their arrest had been issued. How and why the pair had vandalised the tracks in that way was yet to be determined. Geber had slightly shocked even Smithson, as he had found it impossible to believe he could stoop to such a heinous crime.

One thing was certain. Innocent lives had been lost, lives that could have been saved had the pair just come in quietly. All this over a ridiculous laboratory fire. He had been sought for an interview from one of the papers, and he could give his version of events. This would be all over the morning's papers and would hopefully put an end to Geber and his antics once and for all.

The powers had thanked Smithson, paying him generously for his good work so far before asking him to carry out the other task they had then assigned to him. He was turning out to be a great help to the powers. Not only had he removed the last subject relating to the Old World from Portis-Montis, but he had also brought news of a book that would solve the New World's financial woes. He had promised them great riches, and although they were suspicious at first, he had reassured them that the book would be safer in their hands than those of the Elf King, who was currently threatening to get the book and overrun the New World.

Smithson had left with a spring in his step, knowing that Geber and Delphin wouldn't get far – indeed, perhaps they were already in custody. It had been disappointing to find out that his overnight flight to Skellig-Krieg had to be delayed because of an issue with a damaged airship. All he knew was that he would have to wait until morning to catch the flight.

In the hotel, he spent the evening looking through the old book that his father used to log his trips with Geber's father. He seethed at the thought of the pair always hanging out with each other, travelling together and dabbling in the old ways.

He had always hated the Old World. It had plagued his entire life, always getting in the way at the most inconvenient of times. He had grown up with his own father giving more attention to Geber than himself – as though Geber was his son. He sometimes wondered if his father had ever cared about him.

Things became worse when his mother ran off with an elf. He didn't know the creature personally, but he knew the elves had links with Portis-Montis and the university. His father had thrown himself into working with Frederick, never once giving any thought to how his son felt at being sent off to boarding school in Bansk.

There he'd immersed himself in the culture of Bansk and the New World. Now he was free from the shackles of the Old World, and he'd got to know some people in high places. When he'd received the news of his mother's murder, he shed no tears. He had wanted nothing to do with that woman or the Old World she had lain down for.

It was at the point, after graduating from university in Bansk, that someone from the Capitol building approached him, offering him a job. It wasn't great money, but he could work on that once he got there. He gleefully accepted the offer, finding that he was one of the few graduates from his year to gain employment. This bolstered his confidence, and he soon made his way through the ranks.

Then, one day, he received a message from his father. He was attempting to rebuild the bonds of father and son. Too little, too late, in Smithson's opinion. His father mentioned a trip to the Old World, something about a book that he shouldn't know about – a book Frederick seemed to be obsessed with. Why he didn't just grow a pair and throw the man from the university, Smithson couldn't understand. He even put this forward to his father but received the response that he couldn't fire a man who had recently lost one of his sons. A pathetic excuse. Smithson's father had also requested that he return to help run the university in his absence whilst he was away in the Old World.

This latest development of his father and Frederick's trip hadn't gone unnoticed. His superiors in the Capitol had pulled him aside, for they frowned upon such trips, and reminded him where his loyalties should lie. He was ashamed to have brought dishonour to the doors of the New World. Something had to be done. He devised a plan to change the ways of Portis-Montis and drag it into the New World once and for all.

Smithson returned to Portis-Montis in secret, gaining a new contact and ally within the city at the same time. Knowing that he would need help, he reluctantly reached out to the head of the Collins family, saying that he needed to go on a trip but felt helpless without a guide by his side.

It had worked, his family name was useful for something at least, and the man dutifully came to his aid. He appeared almost eager to get on with the task, and they left for the Old World straight away.

When they arrived back in Portis-Montis a week later, they were jubilant about the success of the trip. It had all gone sour though, when the true reasons surfaced for the man's keenness to help.

Ever since then, it had been a daily battle of wits between himself and Collins, yet neither's ambition would come to fruition without help from the other. But now he had a chance not only to clear his name within the Capitol but also to get one over on Collins at the same time. A horn sounding somewhere off towards the marshes brought him back to his senses. Probably some kids messing around.

"Hooligans," he muttered to himself.

Knowing he would have a long day ahead of him, he headed to bed. He had a lot of work coming his way if his plans were to succeed.

Chapter 9

The Eternal Marshlands of Bansk were a bleak if storied landscape. It was here the Battle of the Bog had been halted during the Great War, before being pushed back to Skellig-Krieg. They remained unconquered to this day. It was described by the locals as a desolate place where, if you listened carefully, you could hear the screaming souls of the dead. The area was subject to an unrelenting miasma in the form of a thick layer of green fog which blanketed the area day and night.

The putrid air coming off the Marshlands meant most people couldn't breathe without the aid of a mask to help filter out the stomach-churning smell. If you wanted to open your eyes without them being descaled, it was best you wore a pair of protective goggles for good measure.

However, all was not as it first appeared. Hugh and Barrington had uncovered the truth during their previous visit three months ago. It was here that they met Heather McDougall, daughter of Hamish McDougall. She ran the local tour company for those who dared venture closer to the Marshlands. It was also her job to mislead locals and tourists alike away from the truth.

Hamish had been on the run from the New World authorities for over twenty-seven years and was hiding in his cottage on the Marshlands. The 'screaming souls of the dead' were nothing more than Hamish playing his bladder pipes. Though he insisted the music was magical, to all other ears it sounded more akin to a dog whose tail had just been trapped in a closed door.

Hugh, Barrington and Augustus were assessing the damage to the decking and the ship outside Hamish and Heather's cottage. The airship had missed the little house by a matter of inches, the gas sack dangerously close to the stone clad roof. The one bonus of Augustus landing so close to the building was that they did not have far to go to reach Hamish. The lights from the airship were illuminating the surrounding fog, bathing them in an eerie green light.

"Well, at least you didn't hit the house," said Hugh, his voice muffled by the mask that he was wearing. "There's something bugging me though." His goggles had misted up, and he was having trouble distinguishing between the fog and the moisture building up on the glass in front of his eyes.

"Really, what's that then?" said Barrington.

"I can't put my finger on it. Maybe it's the lack of noise; there's no ear-splitting screech from those blasted bladder pipes."

"It's the middle of the night. I wouldn't expect there to be any."

"Yeah, that's the other issue. If you had an airship nearly smash into your house in the middle of the night, wouldn't you want to investigate it?"

"Well, that would depend on how regularly someone hit your house."

"I didn't nearly hit the house; I landed exactly where planned, wot wot! It's not my fault if he has built a deck since my last visit!" said Augustus. Barrington looked at him with what Hugh assumed to be raised eyebrows.

"I think, dear Hugh, you may be onto something. Why has nobody come out to greet us?"

They walked around the outside of the cottage and found a chilling discovery. The front door of the building was hanging off its hinges, revealing someone had forced the airlock open. There were no signs of life coming from within.

"Heather!" Barrington shouted as he pushed past Hugh to get

into the building.

It was dark and lifeless, the once homely feeling now replaced with the cold, thick air of the outside world. There were signs that someone had turned the room over, with the table on its side and items strewn everywhere.

"Heather, where are you? Are you alright?" Barrington was searching the room for her, visibly panicking as he expanded his search area into the kitchen.

"Hamish?" Hugh called out, an uneasy feeling in the pit of his stomach. "Hamish, are you here?"

"Hugh!"

"Barrington? What is it? What have you found?"

"Both of you, quick, I need your help …Heather …answer me … Heather!"

Hugh and Augustus ran through to the kitchen and found Barrington fussing over the motionless body of Hamish's daughter. He looked at the pair from behind his mask.

"Help her!"

Augustus clicked into action.

"Hugh, you go through and right the table in that room. Barrington, you help me carry her back in there."

Hugh stood for a moment, stunned, before coming round and carrying out his orders. He hotfooted it into the middle room and mustered the strength to lift the heavy table over onto its feet. Barrington and Augustus staggered through, carrying the limp body between them.

"Come on, onto the table … lift, Barrington, lift … Hugh, get me some water, either in a bucket or a bowl. The more, the better."

"Why?"

"Don't question me, just do it!" said Augustus. Though he had his mask on, Hugh could tell he was in no mood to suffer fools.

The Augustus that Hugh had seen up to this point seemed to dither and came across as pompous, but now the man had taken control of the situation. He ran through to the kitchen, searching the cupboards for anything useful. He opened up a door in the corner of the dim room and found a mop bucket. Next, he turned his attention to looking for a source of water, desperately searching for a tap. His initial thought of the sink turned out to be a dead end.

"Hurry! We have little time. I can sense her link diminishing!"

Hugh frantically searched the room for any sign of water. It was hard to see anything in the semidarkness. His goggles were steaming up, and it was impossible to see anything. He stubbed his toe on something hard and swore. He had found what he was looking for, a brass hand pump. He placed the bucket under it, then filled it up, before rushing back to the room next door, water sloshing over the sides.

"Ah, at last. Steady with the water, I need as much as possible."

Hugh passed Augustus the bucket. He placed it onto the floor and wedged his foot into it.

"What on earth are you doing?" asked Barrington.

"No time to explain. Just stand back over there in the corner."

Hugh and Barrington stood back and watched Augustus with renewed interest. He placed a hand on Heather's chest, and Barrington went to step forward before Hugh stopped him, shaking his head. His friend huffed and turned his attention back to the table.

Augustus had now cupped both hands over his mouth, and a small glow appeared within them. As it grew in brightness, the room became illuminated, strange shadows covering the wall in the glimmering light. He leaned over Heather and opened his cupped hands over her mouth. A thin line of light was flowing between the two of them.

Hugh noticed he and Barrington were unable to move, as if they were stuck to the floor by some invisible force. His body seemed to tingle all over as the energy filled the room. He could hear Augustus, though he seemed far away.

The captain was calling out to Heather from a distant place, and Hugh could hear someone crying somewhere in the distance. He closed his eyes and suddenly felt himself being pulled by his naval towards the direction of the noises. It was as if he were being pulled through a closing gap, then popping out again on the other side. All around him was semi-dark, except for two glowing dots in the distance which he aimed for.

'*Hugh? How did you get here? Are you aware of where you are*' asked the glow related to Augustus.

'*I don't know? I think I know where we might be, but I'm not sure.*'

'*We are in the sight. Remember when I visited you on the airship? Well, this is how I reached you. Have there been any times you've had a knock to the head?*'

'*Yes, in Portis-Montis. I fell into the street, into the path of the runners. I was out cold.*'

'*That was you, was it, eh? Well, that can trigger deep inherent abilities, locked inside oneself, and with your family history, I'm not surprised. It will only get stronger the more you re-enter the sight.*

'*Anyway, you didn't ought to be out here without a guide or protection for your life-link. I have enough strength to get us all back, but you will have to play your part.*'

His light encompassed Hugh's, and he felt warmth enter him, as though he and Augustus were one, and Hugh heard his voice inside his own energy.

'*There, I can protect you, but we will need to work together to help Heather.*'

'*Is that Heather?*' he asked, looking at the diminishing light between himself and Augustus.

'*Yes, but she is not aware of us. She is weak, and we need to get her back. Others are already wearing her life-link down.*'

'*Others? Life-links? Augustus, I don't understand what are you talking about? Please tell me what is going on.'*

'No time to explain. Seeing as you have made it this far, I want you to try something. Can you picture your light as if it were encompassing Heather? Then I will guide us all back.'

'I don't know. I can try. How do I do it?'

'We haven't time for idle chitchat. Trying isn't good enough. You must believe you can encompass her with your light, picture it in your mind's eye, tell the universe, and it will be!'

Hugh tried to picture his light expanding, but when he looked, he saw it had only expanded slightly.

'This is no good. I don't think I can do it.'

'It's important you listen to me, and you must do as I say. You have to believe you can encompass her. Believe you can do it with all of your soul. I wasn't planning on bringing two back with me, and without help, I can get either you or Heather back by myself. If we are all to leave together, then we need you to do this.'

Hugh summoned deep inside his own light, repeatedly telling himself that he could do what had been asked of him. An amazing feeling of peace washed over him, and he could feel himself expanding. He could sense Heather, and the urge to help and protect her. His light spread around the fading light to join with Augustus, and he sensed himself becoming a part of her. Augustus guided them back with the help of Hugh's energy, and they were now moving, though Hugh couldn't explain how. He saw the faint wisps of an outline, a pathway of sorts, heading out into the darkness. It was then that he heard him.

'Hugh ... Hugh? Is that you?'

'Father?'

He lost his concentration, sensing Heather slip away from him.

'Ignore him. You must stay focussed on your energy!' Augustus said, strain sounding in his voice.

'*But it's my father!*'

'*I don't bloody care who it is! It could be the queen of the Sylphs, and it wouldn't matter right now. Just concentrate on getting Heather back home.*'

It was difficult, as the urge to seek his father was strong, almost overwhelming, but he knew he had to stay in control for Heather's sake.

Everything went silent.

−POP−

He was back in the room, back in his body. He could sense the space forming around him. He opened his eyes and looked towards the table, seeing Augustus standing upright once more. His hands were hovering over Heather, still glowing. He saw Heather's entire body was surrounded by a warm haze which soaked into her body.

Then she flinched, gasping with a deep intake of breath.

Barrington ran over to her, the invisible bond that had stuck him to the floor giving way, and held her hand.

"Heather, are you alright?" His voice now wracked with concern and worry. She lay for a moment, not saying anything, before attempting to get up onto her elbows, with a little help from Barrington.

"Aye, I … I think so …" She looked to Augustus, then to Hugh. "Ye … both of yese … were there … ye saved me." She broke down into tears, Barrington doing his best to console her.

It took a while before she calmed down, and Hugh could speak.

"What happened? Where's Hamish gone?"

She began shivering, and Hugh realised that he too was freezing. He reached for the firestone around his neck and cleared his mind. It was only a matter of moments before they were bathed in warmth and light, and Hugh radiated from within.

"What is that?" asked Augustus.

"It's a firestone," said Hugh. "I will explain to you how it works when the time is appropriate. Tell us, Heather, who did this to you?"

"I ... I dinnae know. One moment dad was out on the deck, playing his bladder pipes, the next he was fighting with someone. I didnae have time to put me mask on. I just opened the airlock and ran outside. I barely had time to make it to the outer door, before someone pushed me back in."

"Who was it? If you can tell us who they were, we can find them, can't we, Hugh?" said Barrington.

"Hold fire, Barrington. Heather, where is Hamish, is he still here?"

She shook her head, but said nothing, and began coughing.

"Are you alright? What can we get you?" asked Augustus.

"Mask ..." was all that she could muster.

Hugh realised they were all standing around her, with masks and goggles on, but Heather was open to the elements. He scanned the room, looking for Heather's own mask and goggle set up, finally seeing the hat with the pump attached. He fetched it to her, and she placed it on her head. Her fingers appeared to glow, and the pump sparked into life. After a minute of gasping in the clean air, she could speak.

"Thas better," she said, muffled, but sounding relieved. "I could barely breathe. There were two people, wearing full face masks. I didnae see who they were ... they came in, and pushed me to the floor, hit me over the head with something hard. I saw stars, and dad was fighting them, but they were too strong, even for him. I think they knocked him out, but I was too far gone to see what happened."

"Did they say anything to you; did you recognise their voices?" asked Barrington.

Hugh could hear the anger in his friend's voice.

"Only one spoke, the other used some sort of hand gestures. I think they were both men, but I cannae be sure. The one who spoke kept saying 'leave her, we only need him' and I felt myself being dragged through to the kitchen, before it all went dark."

Hugh could see Heather's goggles misting up as she sobbed.

"It's alright, we will find him, I promise you," he said.

She looked at him, releasing small pools of water from her goggles.

"Ye were there. Ye helped bring me back."

"Yes, I was, but I couldn't have done it without Augustus here."

"Thank ye, Augustus. And thank ye, Hugh!" She let go of Barrington's hand and leaned forward to give Hugh a hug of gratitude so tight his goggles and mask nearly fell off. Hugh could feel the look Barrington was giving him as he glared through his goggles.

"It's not a problem at all, wot, wot! To be fair, I'm relieved Hugh was there to help. He enveloped you and protected you for the journey back here. I must say, I didn't realise that you were so well trained in the sight?"

Hugh looked across to Augustus, releasing himself from Heather's grip. "I'm not. I don't even know how I made it to you?"

"Well, it appears you have a knack for the sight, then. When time allows, you must build on the skills you have. I must admit, I've not seen anyone this gifted for a long time."

"Yes, well," said Hugh, feeling his cheeks flush. "The question now is, what are we going to do next?" he said, wanting to move the conversation forward.

"I'm afraid, chaps, that I have other duties to attend to elsewhere. I have a delayed flight to get to Skellig-Krieg, then I am overdue a much-needed break, wot, wot!"

"That's fine, Augustus," said Hugh, partially relieved that they would not have to endure another journey in the airship. "See to your duties. Will we be seeing you again soon?"

"Well, I can't guarantee my shift patterns, but I am always available through the sight, when you are trained up enough to go solo, of course. You can always rely on the great Captain Augustus to be at your side whenever you need help."

Hugh nodded, not sure what he meant.

"Right-o, if there is nothing else for me to do, then I shall be off. It's getting light out there already."

Hugh looked outside and could see the fog was changing to a dim green, brighter than the light from the airship. Augustus bid them all farewell and made his way back to the ship. They listened to the engines starting up, watching the lights rise away from the window. Minutes later, they heard something whipping onto the roof of the building, followed by the sound of a window upstairs breaking. Augustus had dropped the mooring line. He throttled the engines up, and the noise disappeared off into the distance.

"Well then," said Hugh, "let's see if we can't get this door back onto his hinges and close the airlock."

Barrington nodded. "Yes, and we need to fix that window if we are going to be airtight."

They kicked themselves into action, helping Heather down from the table and sitting her on a stool, before getting on with the jobs at hand. Heather directed them to a store shed outside, where they found an array of items and tools needed to keep the building going. Whilst they were working, Heather felt well enough to restore the fire to working order, light some lamps and get breakfast underway. Hugh admired her ability to carry on, given all that she had been through.

After a hearty breakfast, where they filled Heather in on their trip to reach her, they all went outside to inspect the damage left by Augustus. Barrington let out a large sigh, his mask complementing it with a raspberry.

"The man's a lunatic."

"Well, it could be worse, I suppose," said Heather.

"In what way?" asked Hugh, turning to look at her.

"He could've hit the house or, if Dad was out there, hit him."

"True. So, how are we going to find your father? I think we will need some help, but going back to Portis-Montis will be out of the question, as will wandering through Bansk. I feel uneasy enough standing out here in the fog, let alone out in the open where all and sundry can see us."

"Maybe we could go undercover, keep to the shadows and get a flight to Skellig-Krieg," said Barrington. "Then we can catch up with the rest of the team."

Hugh's heart sank at these words. He didn't fancy playing the undercover agent today, and the thought of stepping aboard an airship again filled him with dread.

"Maybe we could get a steamer ship?"

"I would rather not if it's all the same."

"Oh, come on, Barrington. If we're going to Skellig-Krieg, then we have to use some form of transport."

"Ahem! If yese two laddies have finished bickering, I may have a solution." They turned to Heather, who was standing with her hands on her hips.

"Sorry," said Hugh and Barrington, looking down at their feet.

"There's nae time to be embarrassed. If ye would like to follow me, I can show ye the solution to yer problems." Hugh and Barrington looked at each other, shrugged, then followed Heather around the outside of the cottage on the marsh.

She led them down another walkway, which was raised up the same as the decking around the cottage. They walked for five minutes, nobody talking, until a large building came into being from out of the green haze.

"Right then, gents. Before you I let yese both in here, ye must promise me that ye'll reveal nothing ye see inside this building ..."

Barrington raised a hand.

"Yes, Barrington?"

"How, exactly, were you able to build that out here?"

"Never ye mind, it's an old family secret. Now, do ye promise or not?" They both nodded, which seemed to be enough to please her.

Heather rolled up her right sleeve, revealing a bracelet with runes on. She turned to a door, seeming to slot one of them into an impression on the frame, and with the briefest of glows, the door opened. They walked in, finding themselves behind another airlock, as the door hissed closed behind them, plunging everything into a chilling darkness.

Chapter 10

They stood in silence, as the sound of a pump rattled into action, a ding, then the door in front of them hissed open. They were all able to remove their masks as Hugh and Barrington looked around in awe. They were in a cavernous room full of the smell of oil and grease and filled with many inventions and experimental vehicles. Hugh couldn't see the other end, as it appeared to disappear off into infinity. Heather turned to address the pair.

"Welcome to the rune workshop. Please touch nothing," said Heather (and Barrington stopped short of touching something on a workbench). "This is mine and dad's space, where we get to create all manner of items, which we then infuse with the power of runes."

"I'm amazed," said Hugh. "I didn't realise that all these ... things, could all relate to rune works."

"Technically they dinnae relate, but dad always encouraged me to invent new things. It was always a passion of his, and he passed his knowledge onto me. Anyway, I want yese two to come here and look at this."

She led them over to the middle of the space where a huge triangular metal object was sitting, polished to a high shine. All the edges were rounded off, and Hugh carefully approached the thing, in awe at its sleek beauty.

On closer inspection, he could see that someone had laced the entire structure with a covering of runes. They seemed to glimmer in the light, their power itching to get to work — *whatever* that work may be.

His hand tingled as he touched the edge of the surface, then the sensation ran up his arm, the hairs standing to attention. He followed to where the edge returned on itself, heading off to his right. It rose upwards into what Hugh thought was a tail, similar to those of the airships.

"Wow ... just ... wow!"

"Do ye like her?"

"Yes, she's beautiful. What is it?"

Heather moved to stand opposite him, with only the depth of the main triangle between them.

"It's a rune wing, mark one, or RW1 for short. She's the only one in the world, and this is what'll get us to Skellig-Krieg." She stood, looking into Hugh's eyes, running her hand through her hair.

"That is amazing. I've never seen anything so beautiful in all my life ..."

Barrington cleared his throat.

"*This* is very nice indeed," he said, drawing his friend's attention back to the rune flyer. There was a moment where he caught Hugh's eye before carrying on. "Tell me, where are we to sit on this, and how do we get about unseen?"

"Ah well, here's the beauty of it. We've created many runes to go with the inventions over the years, and these are our best yet. It can be in plain sight, yet still be unseen by those all around."

Hugh was now inspecting it from every angle.

"So, where does the coal go?"

"What do you mean?"

"Well, the coal, to power it ... where does it go?"

Barrington jumped in, ready to shine. "Please forgive my friend here. He spends too much of his time looking in alchemy books, rather than the coherent world around us," he smiled smugly at Hugh. "This runs off *runes*, Hugh." He went around to stand next to Heather. "It's really quite obvious to see."

Hugh stood chewing his cheeks, whilst glaring at Barrington with a furrowed brow.

"Oh, yer a proper joker, aren't ye?" said Heather, ducking under the wing to stand next to Hugh. "If ye feel the wing with me, I can show ye the power." She went to lift his hand, with Barrington looking on, peeved. At her touch, Hugh felt the strangest sensation, as if it compelled his body to move towards Heather's. She let go of his hand and looked him in the eye.

"What's happening?" she said in a soft voice, looking at Hugh.

"I don't know," said Hugh, swallowing hard. "I just … don't … know …"

"Well, isn't this a heart-warming situation?" Barrington spoke so sharply it cut the bond between Hugh and Heather. "Don't mind me, only I thought we had to be getting to Skellig-Krieg?" He stood tapping his foot, taking in a deep breath, then releasing it slowly.

"Look, Barrington, it's not like that. I think it's something that's happened since being in the sight together. It's … hard to explain."

"So you now think I can't understand the complexities of your private club?"

"But … I didn't mean it like that."

"Look, I may not have a clue about certain things, but give me some credit. I can see that I'm in the way here. I'm going back to the cottage."

He turned on his heel and marched off towards the airlock, snatching his mask and goggles off the hook. He turned and glared at Hugh, before putting on his mask and slamming his hand on the button to close the airlock.

"Barrington, wait …"

"Ye'd best go after him," said Heather.

As Hugh went to leave, she grabbed his hand. "You felt it too?"

Hugh nodded.

"Go easy on him, he disna understand." She let his hand go, and he looked at her before running after Barrington.

Hugh had feared that his friend had stormed all the way back into Bansk, so it was with relief that he found him sitting at the table back at the cottage on the marsh. The airlock hissed open, and Barrington sat scowling at Hugh.

"Come to gloat, have you?"

"Oh, come on, Barrington, it's not like that."

"Really? could have fooled me. Tell me, is it not bad enough that you are after our best friend and your brother's widow without going for Hamish's daughter as well? It's a tad greedy, don't you think?"

"Hey! That was below the belt."

"That's charming, coming from you! I just thought that Heather might have taken a liking to me, that's all. I really don't know how you do it."

"Let me get a few things straight. First, I have no clue where Adelia is, and as for everyone accusing her and I of having a thing for each other, well, it's just ridiculous. And as for Emily, well, who knows what's going on there. I think you have got things all out of perspective. This is Hamish's daughter we're talking about. It's her choice, and I'm sure she doesn't like me in that way. I'm unsure of what's going on, we seem to have an odd connection, but there's nothing behind it all."

"Could've fooled me! You looked like you were both getting on very well."

"Oh, I give in! We haven't got time to fight over this. We need to get to Skellig-Krieg, to Alfred and Emily. At least then we might come up with a plan to find Hamish and the books."

"Books?"

"Yes, *books*. We now have two to find if you've forgotten. Then there's the case of whatever is under the floorboard in Dallum. Heaven knows what delight we will find under there. So, if you could kindly remove the chip from your shoulder, then maybe we might have a chance of getting out of here today."

"Fine, but this conversation isn't over."

The airlock hissed open, and Heather walked in, the sound of the pump on her hat filling the awkward silence.

"Right, are yese two ready to leave? We have a flight ahead of us, and I want to get there before it gets dark." She looked at the pair and Barrington got to his feet. "I just need to get my bag ready. If ye need to use the room for convenience, may I suggest ye use it now."

It wasn't long before the trio were heading back out across the marsh, Heather stopping at the rear of the cottage to collect a dead deer, which she deftly flung over her shoulder with ease.

"Sorry, but what's that for? It looks a little uncooked for an in-flight snack," said Barrington.

"Don't be silly. It's nae for us, it's for Betsie."

"Betsie? Who and what is Betsie?"

"Why, it's the family pet, of course," she said, rolling her eyes.

"Of course, how silly of me."

"Well, I say pet, but she's more of a family protector."

She turned and marched off down the deck, leaving Barrington and Hugh in a confused and uneasy silence. They quickly went to catch up with her, scuffling over who would get in front, with both of them nearly ending up in the marsh.

They reached the warehouse and entered, making their way to the RW1. Heather placed the deer carcass on the floor, then rubbed her palm down the belly of the machine. A door opened, revealing a small set of steps on the inside just large enough to push the carcass through. Heather then squeezed herself in, beckoning Hugh and Barrington to do the same.

Barrington looked at the door, assessing it for size.

"How am I supposed to fit through there?"

"Ye'll manage, I can assure ye of that. Dad can get through it, so ye should have nae bother getting in."

"Mmm, I'm not so sure …"

"Ah, quit yer whining and get in, will ye. I wanna get going. Oh, Hugh, can ye pull that lever over there? Once you've done that, get aboard quick, otherwise ye'll be on the outside of the cylinder. Ta."

She disappeared into the RW1, leaving Barrington to figure out how to get aboard. Hugh walked over to the lever, checking which way he would have to pull it. He realised the craft sat on a large turntable of sorts, with the lever outside the ring. Thinking nothing of it, he went to pull the lever. Nothing happened. He tried again, and still nothing happened.

"Squeeze the smaller lever on the handle, then push," came a voice from inside the RW1. Hugh couldn't believe how gormless he was being. He squeezed the small lever to the handle, trapping the palm of his hand, letting out a yelp of pain. He released his grip immediately.

"Bugger!"

"What? Oh yeah, there's a pair of gloves on the table over there. Use those, and ye won't trap your hand."

"Yeah, thanks," said Hugh, shaking out his hand.

Now gloved up, he tried again, this time the lever moved with ease, and he heard something clunking below the floor, followed by a grinding noise. He saw two great counterweights slowly making their way down the wall next to him and could hear cogs turning. He admired his handiwork when he realised something was rising out of the ground, a cylindrical glass wall of sorts, which was picking up speed.

It was also now he realised he was on the wrong side if this glass wall and risked being locked out from the flight. He had to jump to reach the top of the wall, only clinging on by his fingertips, and he had to pull himself up and over. A burst of energy pumped through his body as he heaved himself on top of a thick glass ledge.

He was now considerably higher than he was comfortable with, but knew that if he didn't jump down soon, he would risk being squashed at the top. He closed his eyes and hoped for the best, waiting for the pain to come as he landed, yet it never came. Hugh opened his eyes to see that Barrington had caught him from underneath. He dropped him to the floor, and they ran to the rune wing.

As Barrington struggled to get through the door, Hugh wasn't watching where he was going, bumping into him, causing Barrington to burst into the craft. Above them, two semicircles of roof were opening up, the green tendrils of fog making their way in. The platform rose, corkscrewing out of the floor. Hugh rushed to get on-board, the door closing behind him with a whirring sound, followed by a hiss. He scrambled through the inside, which turned out to be spacious, finally reaching a door labelled COCKPIT. Hugh wondered at the strangeness of the word as he clambered into a spare seat.

"So, this is a cockpit then?" he asked, seating himself down.

"Well, I originally wanted to call it the pit, but dad said he'd nae even fit his—"

"Yes, alright, *that's* an image we don't need to see, thanks."

"Well, anyway, we put the two together, and it kind of stuck, so cockpit it is."

Heather began pressing many buttons featuring glowing runic designs as the outside world moved around them. The glass cylinder wall had reached the roof, and the craft was corkscrewing its way upwards into the dim light of day. Heather pulled her right sleeve up once more, pulling out a carved rune that would pass as a key. She inserted it into the panel in front of her as an array of lights lit up. Hugh heard a strange humming noise, and the hairs on the back of his neck stood on end.

"You say you built this yourself?" asked Barrington.

"Aye, well, it was a joint project between me and Dad. Yer not worried, are ye?"

"No, no. It's just we're not used to this form of travel. Just out of interest, how do the runes make it fly?"

"They tap into the power of the natural world. What else would it be?"

"Of course, how silly of me." He looked to Hugh, who just shrugged and gripped his seat tightly.

The spinning sensation had stopped, and Hugh saw the thick green fog surrounding them once more. Heather began pressing more runes on the panel, and Hugh sensed the RW1 rising upwards. He did not know how fast they were moving, only the sensation inside of being pulled down giving anything away. It wasn't long before they popped out of the fog bank and into the bright light of day. Hugh and Barrington shielded their eyes from the stark change of light whilst Heather pulled out a pair of tinted goggles to put on.

They hovered over the murky fog bank, and Heather placed her hands on two domes, one on each armrest of her seat. Hugh watched as she twisted the dials and saw the outside world move slowly around, coming to stop in line with a mountain in the distance.

Heather pushed forward on the controls, and the craft began moving. Hugh noticed his seat tilted backwards with the movement, making the flight feel very smooth. They were now travelling at a fair old rate, and he could see the if they didn't change their course they would hit the mountain.

"Erm, Heather? Didn't we ought to avoid the solid rock coming up?"

"Nae, we're going into it." And she increased the speed.

"What do you mean *we're going into it?* That's ludicrous! You're going to get us killed!"

She appeared to lift and pull the controls, and the RW1 altered its course, initially straight up, before beginning a large loop. Hugh felt his sides squeezed tightly by the seat as it appeared to adjust its grip on him, holding him tight. They were now upside down and heading towards the downward part of the loop. Hugh thought he was going to see his breakfast for a second time. Heather let out a whoop of enjoyment as they plunged into the fog once more.

"You're crazy!" exclaimed Barrington, whilst gripping on tightly to

his own seat, his face the colour of beetroot.

"Nearly there now. Hold on to yer pants boys." She pushed the controls forward, gunning the ship straight for the mountain, or where it would be if Hugh could see it. He closed his eyes and braced for impact ...

And waited ...

Everything went dark around him, but he could sense that he was still sitting in his seat and not being concertinaed into the side of the mountain. He dared to open his eyes, where he saw they were in a rock tunnel, with torches glowing in sequence to guide the way. They were slowing down. Both Hugh and Barrington were panting heavily.

"That was fun, wasn't it?" said Heather, turning around to look at the pair.

"*NO!*" Hugh and Barrington exclaimed in unison.

Hugh wiped his palms on his trousers as Heather guided the RW1 towards a landing pad glowing softly at the end of the tunnel. Hugh felt the craft slow to a pace not much faster than walking. The energy flowing through the wing was reverberating against the tunnel, which caused the inside of Hugh's ears to vibrate. Heather swung the ship around over the landing pad so that they were now facing the long tunnel they had travelled through, and Hugh saw the greenish light disappearing, as a set of doors covered the entrance.

"Right, we are here. Let's feed Betsie."

"Sorry, but your pet lives inside a mountain?" asked Barrington.

"Yes," said Heather, giving him a strange look. "Where else would we keep her? Don't tell me you believed the rumours of volcanic activity?"

"*What rumours?*" said Hugh, his mouth going dry. He didn't fancy stepping into an active volcano.

"Ah well, not to worry. Come on."

They heaved themselves out from the tight seats as Heather walked past them, humming a tune to herself as she made her way back towards the exit. Hugh looked to Barrington, who shrugged, and they followed.

She pressed a flashing rune, and the doorway slowly opened into the alien landscape. The RW1 was filled with a waft of warm air to the point where it stung Hugh's face. Barrington struggled in the doorway for a moment, before freeing himself.

"I think I'm getting the knack of this," he said. "Oh, wow!"

Hugh could see what his friend meant as he joined him outside the rune wing. The air in the tunnel was hotter and burned his nostrils, and the air smelled of charred sulphur. As they walked further into the tunnel, Hugh couldn't shake off the idea that something wasn't right. Why would you keep a family pet so far down here? As they walked between the stalactites and stalagmites, he could see the walls were blackened with some kind of soot, and he wondered if they were in some sort of train tunnel again.

He wiped a bead of sweat from his face but could do nothing about the sweat prickling down his back. He was definitely overdressed for the occasion. Up ahead, Heather's silhouette appeared in the strange golden light that was shimmering in the distance, the outline of the dead deer on her shoulders. It reminded Hugh of the light in the cavern behind the waterfall in Dallum, but that was blue. Maybe the sun was shining through, giving it the eerie appearance.

There was a low continuous rumble in the background, which pulsed up and down, unlike any body of water that he had heard before. He slipped on the uneven surface and stumbled. Barrington threw out a hand, grabbing Hugh at the last moment.

"Thanks."

"No problem. What is that noise?"

"I don't know, but my gut feeling says we're not going to like it."

Maybe it was the open sea beyond the mountain, and it was the waves he could hear. They rounded a corner, and the tunnel opened up into a great chamber. Hugh and Barrington stopped dead in their tracks, the breath being taken from both of them. They stood open-mouthed, slowly taking in the scene.

There, in front of them, was a pile of gold coins and precious jewels. Hugh thought for a moment they had stumbled upon the location of the book of alchemy until Barrington nudged him. Hugh followed his gaze further upwards.

He saw something coiled around the pile towards the top, a large tail, a slender body, legs and wings, and as Hugh's eyes continued their way up to the very top, he saw they belonged to a dragon. Its scaly skin seemed to ripple as they entered the room, as if it had sensed fresh prey had arrived. Its large head lifted from the pile it was protecting and looked Hugh in the eye with a piercing, reddish gaze.

Hugh felt the presence of the beast reach right inside of his head, reading his every thought, and knew his friend would be feeling the same sensation. Barrington had a hand on Hugh's shoulder, and he could feel him trembling. The room seemed to vibrate with each lumbering breath the beast took.

"Morning Betsie. I've brought ye some breakfast."

The beast took in two long breaths before it spoke.

'Mmm, they are usually dead before you bring them to me, mistress. Have you brought me a challenge?' Her gaze didn't leave the pair in the doorway. The words seemed to rattle Hugh's bones to the core.

Heather turned to look at Hugh and Barrington, then laughed out loud, slapping her thigh. They replied with a nervous chuckle. From where Hugh was standing, he couldn't see anything funny.

"Betsie, ye cheeky thing. Ye know we've spoken about this before. Humans are not for eating, well, the good ones at least. Nae, these are my good friends, Barrington and Hugh." They gave an awkward wave. "This deer is for ye, enjoy."

She threw the carcass to the floor, and it landed with a resounding thud.

'Humph. Well, that will have to do then, I suppose. But if you change your mind, I'll gladly assist you in their … capture.'

119

The dragon looked at the pair, as if it were deciding which would be the main course and which would be pudding. She opened her eyes wider, and they were filled with a malevolent look.

"*Ah, Betsie! Bad dragon.*"

Heather stood with a finger in the air, the other hand on her hip. Barrington stood with his mouth moving up and down, but no sound appeared.

"Are ye alright there? Ye've gone whiter than me dad's legs."

"*D-D-Dragon!*" was all he could muster.

"Aye, that's correct, have ye nae seen one before."

"Let's just say, they are not as common as you may think," said Hugh, filling in for the Barrington's lack of words.

"What are ye talkin' about? There're *loads of dragons* in Morcarthia. Just because ye haven't seen them, it doesn't mean they don't exist."

"Oh well, that's reassuring."

Heather turned away from the pair, shaking her head, as if it were totally normal to have a pet dragon. "We've to be away from here for a short trip. Do you think ye can hold tight until our return?"

'*I suppose I can. Where is the master? I sense he is in trouble.*'

"Well … he's in a wee spot of bother … we've to help if we can."

For the first time, Hugh could detect a hint of fear in her voice. Whether she was putting on a brave face for them, or Betsie, he couldn't be sure. He felt it unwise to show weakness in front of such a powerful beast.

"Anyway, as I say, we've to be off, so I'll see ye on our return."

The dragon let out another sigh. '

As you wish, mistress. If you require any help, I'm only a moment away, as always, and as is true to the bond between master and dragon.'

"Aye, thanks Betsie. Yer the best family protector we could have."

Betsie lowered herself down onto the pile of treasures, not taking her eyes off Hugh and Barrington. Heather turned to leave whilst the pair slowly backed out of the cavern, not wanting to lose sight of the beast. They didn't trust it, however much Heather did. Nobody said anything until they were safely back in the tunnel, heading towards the ship.

"But why a dragon?" asked Hugh.

"I dunno, she's always followed Dad wherever he lived in the past. I suppose Betsie chose him, so he had nae choice in the matter."

"I never saw him with Betsie in Portis-Montis," said Hugh.

"Well, of course ye didn't. She's nae the sort of beast ye jus' take for a wee walk down the street. People have them mistaken, they're lovely creatures when ye get to know them. They make great friends."

"Well, I, for one, had the impression that it saw us as more than just your friends. I think if you had left us there, we wouldn't have lasted ten seconds!" said Barrington. "Another thing, why Betsie for a name?"

"Because Betsietonusnormarandus is a bit of a mouthful. And for future reference, she's a she, not an *it*. Ye wouldn't want to offend her; she has a tendency to bite."

"Why on earth would you keep a thing like that?"

"Well, we give her a home, she protects the family fortunes, and she also comes to our aid if we ever need it. She used to protect the gates to the old family business, and she followed him when Dad moved here. Personally, I thought she should've stayed where she was, but Dad said Betsie insisted on being nearby. They've a close bond, one which has also passed onto me. Either way, I still have to look after her when Dad's not around."

"What was the job he had before? Was it the at the university?" asked Hugh.

"Nae, it was way before then. He was on duty in a prison of sorts, making sure that everyone was in the right place. I think the powers that be were annoyed that he left them in a bit of a mess, but ye know Dad.

Once he gets an idea to do something, there's not much stopping him."

"I thought you said it was the family business?"

"I did. Why do ye ask?"

"You said the powers that be weren't happy. Surely if it was the family business it would be up to him if he wanted to move on."

"Ah Hugh, I wish it were that simple. Everyone has to answer to someone. That's the way of things." She now spoke with a tear in her eye. "I just wish I knew where he was. I'm lost without him, and he disna even have his whisky." She finally broke down, and Barrington rushed in to support her.

"Hey, come on," he said, putting an arm around her. "We'll find Hamish, and then we can find those responsible and give them what for. Isn't that right, Hugh?"

"Erm, yes? Though I think you overestimate my abilities somewhat."

"Not with that attitude, you won't. We just need to focus on finding Hamish and keep positive. I'm certain we can catch the two vagabonds; they'll be no match for the great Barrington Delphin, I can assure you of that."

Barrington continued to comfort Heather as he turned and guided her back to the ship. They headed towards the glowing light in the distance, shining from the launchpad of the RW1. As they approached the wing, it appeared to glow, as if sensing its owners return. Barrington guided Heather up the steps, then followed her up, with a quick nudge from Hugh to get him back in through the door. The door closed behind Hugh as he stepped on-board and made his way to his seat. He sank into it, feeling its grip tightening as Heather powered up the RW1.

"Ready?" she said to the pair, who both nodded.

Heather turned to look forward and gunned the ship down the tunnel. Hugh couldn't help but notice that the end of the tunnel was still looking rather gloomy.

"Heather, shouldn't you slow down a bit?"

"Ah, it'll be fine," she said, pressing a button on the control panel.

Up ahead, a chink of light appeared and slowly began growing into a small opening. Hugh looked at Barrington, who wore the same worried look on his face which he felt inside. Hugh closed his eyes, not wanting to see their inevitable doom. He waited for the crunch to come but was greeted by another whoop of joy from Heather. They shot out into the fog once more, and she pointed the rune wing skywards. It wasn't long before they were out of the green fog and in the bright sunlight once again.

"Right-o, I think it's time we headed to Skellig-Krieg," she said, "unless anyone has any better ideas?"

"Fine by me," said Hugh, with palpable relief, "though where you are going to land this thing, I don't know. You can't just park it at the airdock."

"We'll cross that bridge when we come to it. For now, why don't yese two sit back and relax, ye look absolutely shattered."

"I could say the same for you. Are you sure we can't help?"

"Nae, I'll be fine. I can activate the auto-fly. It'll alert me to any issues, but most'll avoid us. The joy of using yer own runes. Anyway, I think Barrington wouldn't be much use right now."

Hugh looked across to his friend and saw that he was gently snoring away to himself. He chuckled to himself, as Heather pressed some controls on the panel, and a footrest came out of the front for her to rest her legs. She set the RW1 to auto-fly and tilted her seat back for the flight. Before he knew it, Hugh had passed out, shattered from the trip so far, and too tired to concern himself with the complexities of operating an RW1.

Chapter 11

Hugh awoke with a jump. The rune wing was banking round to the right, and Hugh could see the streets of Skellig-Krieg lit up beneath him. The sun had not long set, and the clouds were lit red from the remnants of its glow. Hugh's stomach was grumbling loudly to itself. He was about to see if the other two were awake, when a packet landed on his lap.

"Here ye are. I could hear yer stomach through there," said Heather, as she came through from the back of the craft.

"Is that Skellig-Krieg down there?" he asked.

"Aye, it is. I've been circling around, trying to find a place to land, but I've had nae luck as yet."

"Where's Barrington?"

"I'm here," he said, coming through from the back. "We were just discussing what to do. We cannot land this thing anywhere people can see it, or discover it by accident, but we cannot think of anywhere."

Hugh thought, then had an idea.

"Have you considered up in the mountains? There will be nobody travelling up there with the weather at this time of year."

"No good," said Barrington. "It will be too uneven to land up there."

Hugh shook his head.

"Not near the old Ranglestaff mine. There was that flat area next to it, and I'm sure it will be big enough to fit this in."

Barrington considered his friend's proposal, then began nodding.

"I think that will be as good a place as any. Only thing is, how do we get into the city? We can't just walk in and wave our papers. My guess is that the authorities will be on the lookout for us."

"I may have a solution for that," said Heather. "Dad told me once about an old tower that he used in the old days, when travel restrictions were still in place, somewhere near the greenhouses. There was a secret door that he accessed; it was his only way in and out."

"I think I know where you mean," said Hugh, turning to Barrington. "Do you think it's where the pub in the wall is?"

"You know, my friend, I think you may be onto something there. Let's call it a plan and get going. We can't keep flying round in circles all night."

They all agreed to the plan, and whilst Hugh ate his food, Barrington guided Heather to where he thought the landing spot was. They followed the river up to the gorge, then headed towards Riddors Pass. Heather turned on a spotlight which seemed to illuminate half the hillside, causing Hugh great alarm. She reassured him that nobody would see it, but it still made him feel uneasy.

It wasn't long before they found the spot and landed. It was a tight fit, but Heather was a skilled pilot of her craft, making the manoeuvre to get in look like child's play.

As they stepped out of the rune wing, a cold blast of air greeted them. Hugh moved quickly to activate the firestone around his neck, and soon they were glowing inside from the warmth it produced.

"How are we going to hide this thing, it's too big to cover," said Hugh.

Barrington immediately jumped into action. "I'll see if I can find any large material to cover it with," and before Heather could stop him, he strode off down the track.

She shook her head, then turned to the wing. She appeared to draw some symbols in the air and collect them in her hands. Hugh watched as they gently glowed as she worked, before cupping her hands together and blowing gently. The glow increased, and she directed it towards the craft. To Hugh's astonishment, it disappeared.

"Wow! That's amazing!"

"Ah, it's nothing, just a little trick Dad taught me ..." she seemed to drift off, the thought of her father bringing home the reality of why they were there. Barrington appeared, dragging a small tree that he had uprooted. Hugh could see from the glow of the firestone that he was out of breath.

"What ... where's the ... what have you done with it?" he dropped the tree and began walking quickly towards where the rune wing was.

"No, Barrington, it's still—"

A resounding 'DONG' cut Hugh off as Barrington walked headlong into it.

"Hey, careful!" said Heather, who came back to reality at the noise, running up to where the wing was and checking the invisible area with her hand. Barrington stood for a moment, then spun on the spot and dropped to the floor in a crumpled heap.

Hugh and Heather ran to Barrington's aid. After a few minutes he came round, disorientated, wincing at the pain in his head. He looked around as if searching for something.

"It's all right, Barrington. You're safe. You just knocked yourself out there for a moment, that's all," said Hugh reassuringly.

"But there were voices, I definitely heard voices, and it was dark and cold."

"It was probably us, just trying to revive you."

"No, it wasn't you. Believe me, Hugh, when I say, I heard people talking. It sounded like my old crew members, but it couldn't be, could it? Then I saw the triangle of the firestone, lit up like a beacon, and I headed for that, which is when I woke up."

Hugh looked at Heather, who seemed to have the same thoughts as he was. He looked back at Barrington with a smile.

"What, what is it? Tell me, is it serious?"

"Ah stop worrying, ye wee ninny," said Heather. "Yiv just dipped yer toe into the great expansive wonder of the sight, that's all."

"What do you mean?"

"I said that it was a hard one to explain," said Hugh. "Look, it's a strange feeling at first, but trust me, you will be alright. Let's get off this mountain to a place of safety, then we can explain a little more there. I don't have a huge grasp on how it works, but I can probably explain the basics."

Once Hugh and Heather had helped Barrington to his feet, they began the descent back down the mountain. The light from the firestone was enough to light the way, but not enough to reveal the large drop off the side of the path. Hugh took a deep breath in when they passed the gorge, trying to keep the memories of the past at bay.

It was a tough job to keep Barrington on the straight and narrow, as he kept wavering close to the edge, and it relieved Hugh to see the long track leading down to the main route into the city. They reached the fork in the track and had to wait for a caravan of horses, carts and people to walk past.

"Where do you suppose they are all going?" said Hugh.

"I don't know," said Barrington, "but I don't think I want to know the answer."

Hugh looked down the track in both directions and could see the torchlight procession making its way down the valley pass. From the sounds of the carts going past, there were all manner of things being transported out of the city, including livestock, their hooves banging on the wall of a cart as it passed. As the noisiest cart passed, his skin tingled all over, making him uneasy. People stared at them as they went past, and Hugh felt exposed.

"Can we get off this path? I don't like the way we are being watched," he said.

"I couldn't agree more," said Barrington, "but I can't remember seeing any other pathways heading off here on our last venture down this track. Perhaps we should head towards the city. We may see something heading in the right direction."

Aye, though I wonder if the old entrance is nae longer in use. Nature will have run its course and hidden the old path. It'll certainly make it harder to find," said Heather.

They began walking against the flow of people leaving Skellig-Krieg, having to yield to the larger carts as they passed. They were getting close to the gates and could see the guards thoroughly checking the documents of a group of people wishing to enter the city. They hung back to see what would happen.

As they watched, they saw the guards shake their heads to a group of travellers wishing to enter Skellig-Krieg, and some people had begun protesting and were trying to push past the security. The guards, now fed up with the troublemakers, pulled out their batons, and began hitting one of the group, driving him to the ground.

Some of the person's friends tried to jump on the guards to get them to stop, but the guards shook them off like rag dolls. A woman was standing with two children, with all of them sobbing and shouting at the guards to stop. Reinforcements arrived, and they neutralised all those involved with force and dragged them through the gates, presumably arrested and heading to a cell.

The trio of friends stood staring in shock, unable to take in what they had just witnessed.

"Well, that confirms our suspicions about using normal entry into the city," said Barrington, shaking his head. "I dread to think what is going to happen to those poor fellows, but I fear the outcome won't be a good one."

Hugh began scanning the opposite side of the track, towards the direction of the greenhouses and the hole in the wall. Something caught his eye. He would have missed it, if it were not for the slight path of trodden-down grass heading off into the undergrowth.

"There, look." He pointed it out to the others. They pushed their way across the line and onto the path which led to a thicket. Hugh began pushing his way through, following the line of broken branches and brambles flattened by whoever had passed through recently. If it were not for that, he wouldn't have been able to see the path at all. He pulled out the firestone and used it to illuminate the way.

Now and then they heard voices, coming from the high wall to their left, as the path brought them closer to the edge of the thicket. There appeared to have been an increase in the number of guards since their last visit.

"I think you ought to put the firestone out," said Barrington. "There's more than enough light coming down from the wall now, and we don't want to give our position away."

Hugh nodded, pulling the pin out and replacing it into its holder, his body going cool as he did so. They continued in silence until the path turned towards the wall. Up ahead, Hugh could see the old tower they were heading for.

In its past, it would have been out on its own, an outpost for Old Skellig, as the area used to be known. Once upon a time there was a chain of them, running across the valley leading to the mountains, guarding the once farmed plains from attack.

When they built the wall, they incorporated the towers into the construction, making a formidable barrier to keep any foe out. The wall was manned day and night to protect the New World from the Old.

As time passed, tensions decreased enough between the realms, and the need for defence became second place to the demands of progress. The maintenance of the walls became less important, and they had been left to the elements, causing them to partially collapse in places. This tower had all but crumbled into a hollow shell of its former self until an entrepreneur saw potential in the old building and turned it into a pub – and so the Pub in the Wall was born.

It didn't escape Hugh's attention that new repairs were being carried out along the old wall. Even at this late hour, he saw people beavering away to make restorations to the old defence. Any sections which had collapsed beyond repair had been completely rebuilt. It was obvious to all watching that they feared an attack from the Old World at any moment. They watched guards on duty marching across the ramparts.

"Do ye think the pub's still open?" asked Heather.

"Who knows?" said Barrington. "If they have any sense, they'll have kept it open. These guards will need food and water."

"We can only hope so," said Hugh.

He looked across to the old tower. He could see the base of the wall, but there was no easy entrance visible. The other problem was the twenty feet that lay between them and the wall, for it had been recently cleared of all foliage, no doubt to offer those on the wall a better view. "The question is, how do we get from here to the bottom of that wall?"

They all gazed across the expanse of no-man's land, to where the wall met the ground, unable to see where they would enter the tower. Hugh started thinking that the task looked impossible.

"How are we to get across to there?"

"I've got a few wee tricks up me sleeve."

"What's that?" asked Hugh, unsure if he wanted to know the answer.

"Well, Dad and I used to play around hiding each other all the time. They're the same runes that I hid the RW1 with, so you know they will work. What do ye think?" She stared back at them with raised eyebrows.

Hugh looked to Barrington, who gave no signal of what to do, and he looked back to Heather. "I suppose we could give it a go. Is it dangerous?"

"Nae, ye'll be fine. We've not lost each other … yet."

"Erm …"

Without waiting for an answer from Hugh, she began tracing out shapes in the air. Hugh worried that the light from the forming runes would give away their hiding spot, but the guards were too busy in conversation to notice. Heather cupped her hands, blew gently, and they glowed once more.

She guided them across to Hugh, who stood frozen to the spot, as the numerous symbols drifted over his body. They felt cool, giving him goosebumps from head to toe. He heard Barrington gasp, a sign that the method had worked.

"Well, I never," he said in amazement. "Are you still with us, old bean?"

He brought his hand across where Hugh's head was moments before, poking him in the eye.

"Ow! Yes, I'm still here, I'm only invisible." He brought a hand up to his sore eye, realising he could still see it. "Why can I still see myself?"

"That's totally natural, nothing to worry about. We cannae see ye, and that's the thing to remember. Right, Barrington, yer turn."

"Well, hang on a minute I uh—"

"Don't be such a ninny," she said, as she began repeating the process again, and letting the runes flow over his body.

Hugh watched as his friend seemed to melt away, leaving a space where he once stood. The only sign that he was there was the flattened undergrowth beneath his feet.

"And you are positive you cannot see me?" he said, sounding unsure.

"Aye, it's fine. I can't promise that there won't be any side effects, though. Ye may grow an extra head, or limb."

"What?" the pair exclaimed in unison.

"Shh, I'm joking, keep yer hair on."

She looked over her shoulder towards the wall. The guards had stopped talking and were looking in their direction. Heather moved deeper into the undergrowth, until the danger had passed, the onlookers deciding it was nothing to worry about. She drew up more of the same runes and covered herself, melting away like the other two.

"Alright, let's give this a go then, shall we? Let me go ahead of you two and see what I can find," she said.

Hugh heard her stepping out from the tree line and could see her feet depressing the freshly cut vegetation as she went. They watched as the depressions made their way to the base of the old tower. There was a metallic sound, like that of a crowbar being pulled out.

The sound of tapping from the workmen on the wall was joined by another noise, caused by Heather gently tapping the stones at the base of the old tower. Now and then it would sound slightly hollow, and to his amazement, he saw part of the wall detach as though it were on a hinge, revealing what looked like a tight gap, but an entrance, nevertheless.

He set off into no-man's land, trying to be as quiet as possible, but then he heard footsteps coming up behind him. It was Barrington who was walking at a faster pace and misjudged where Hugh was. He caught the back of Hugh's heel and tripped, taking them both to the ground. There was no hiding the noise this time, as they both landed heavily with an "*oof*" that echoed off the wall.

Neither of them dared to move.

"Halt! Who goes there?" said one guard.

"Yeah. We know you are there," said the other guard, though he didn't sound too sure. "Come out, reveal yourselves!"

Hugh and Barrington lay as still as possible, trying not to breathe. They could hear Heather, quietly making her way through the narrow hole which she had opened up.

"This is your last warning. Come out now or face the consequences!"

Still, they did not move. Hugh could see the small patch of the wall moving in the dim light, signalling that Heather had made it.

"Sound the alarm!" came the call from above them. "Get some men down there, search the area!"

The next moments passed Hugh by in a blur of activity. He looked up at the wall and saw someone cranking a large handle. A long warbling sound followed this, which rose and fell. The pair struggled to get to their feet. They were making so much noise now, but that didn't matter, for the sound of the alarm drowned out all the snap of breaking branches and undergrowth. However, they were still out in the open.

Hugh saw many members of the city guard, pouring out of the gate and running towards them at speed, as he and Barrington ran for the gap in the wall. Heather was awaiting their arrival, and an arm came out, beckoning them in.

To his horror, Hugh looked down and saw the faint outline of Barrington just appearing as he ran past him. He watched him dive for the gap, seeing him get momentarily wedged before Heather began pulling from the inside. Hugh ran headlong into him, which was enough to get him through. He didn't waste any time in doing the same, but misjudged, scraping his back on the sharp stone before Heather quickly closed the hidden door behind them.

They sat in the darkness, nobody daring to move, as the warbling alarm ceased. They were now listening to the muffled conversation on the other side of the door.

"*I'm tellin' ya, I saw something move over here.*"

"*And as I've said to you before, Reg, you ain't seeing things right, as usual. There are weird things on this side of the wall.*"

A muffled voice called out from above, but Hugh couldn't make out any words.

"*I'm telling you, Sarge, there ain't nothing here … but … fine. Come on, let's search the area. They can't have gone far.*"

Hugh listened as the sound of people hacking through the undergrowth disappeared off into the distance.

"That was too close for comfort," said Barrington, still getting his breath back, rubbing his back. "Hugh, can you give us some light?"

Hugh found and illuminated the firestone, the now familiar warmth filling his body. There was something dripping from his hand, and he realised he must have cut it when he jumped through the door. He rummaged in his bag, pulling out a piece of material, which he wrapped around the wound. Heather helped him tie it off, before they discussed what to do next.

"Well, I say that we find our way out of here, and get to the Rangles Inn," said Hugh, "wherever the exit may be."

They all looked around for an exit to the dark hole there were in. Hugh could hear people moving around in the bar above him, with bits of dust falling through the cracks and into his hair. The space initially seemed only tall enough to crouch, but eventually opened up to a larger disused cellar, high enough to stand up in. It smelled musty, and as they walked through the space, the hanging cobwebs tangled across their faces. It wasn't long before they found a set of stone stairs leading up to a door.

"Do ye think it's safe to venture out there?" asked Heather.

"Well, there's only one way to find out the answer to that," said Barrington.

He carefully lifted the latch on the door and opened it into the world beyond the cellar.

Chapter 12

If there was one thing that Smithson despised more than anything else, even more than the Old World he was currently clattering his way through, it was travelling by horse and cart. The fact that he had to use anything relating to the Old World made him feel degraded and downright dirty. He was sitting in the back of the canvassed transport which Collins had arranged for them.

It was lucky for them the city governors had passed a new law, ordering all people with links to the Old World to leave the city. It gave them the perfect cover to leave with the package without being discovered, even if it was making an awful racket.

The sirens that had echoed their way down the valley shortly after their exit from the city were a cause for concern. He'd heard of the new warning systems in place on the wall, but to hear them in action sent chills down his spine. The rear flap of the cart opened, and Collins jumped in with his new apprentice.

"Collins, are you sure you can't get the cargo to be a little quieter? The noise is driving me *mad*."

"I assure you, it is most annoying to myself as well, sir."

"Can't you use more sedative?"

"We've been down this road before. If we use any more than we already have done, we risk losing the package all together. I'm surprised at the current resistance to the sedative already used; it's enough to drop a bull. Short of killing the poor thing, I don't think there is anything we can do."

Smithson looked at his servant, holding back the comment he wished to make.

"Tell me, has your little apprentice come up with any *better* ideas than you? I see he has decided to model his hair style on yours. Very … *fetching*."

"He is yet to come up with anything suitable, indeed, anything at all, come to think of it. I believe he may be in shock after all he has been through. His previous employers were keeping him in less than standard conditions for someone of his heritage. If I hadn't come across him when I did, I dread to think what state he would be in now. He will be of great use to us. I can assure you of that."

"Hmm, well, make sure he is. I'm not in the mood for any hangers-on." They looked across at the apprentice, who appeared to be vacantly staring out the back of the wagon, a tear falling down his face.

"What's wrong with him this time?"

"I'm not sure, but he's been acting strangely since we left the city. I think the alarm going off spooked him. I guess it probably got triggered by the amazing duo on the track back there."

Smithson whipped his head round to look Collins in the eye.

"What do you mean?"

"Well, you know … Hugh and Barrington … the ones you *sorted out*. They also appeared to have picked up their own added extra, but I didn't have time to see who it was, other than it was a woman. That's the reason we came to see you."

"*Emily* … Damn it. Damn, damn, *damn!*" Smithson pounded at the canvas, putting a hole through it with his fist.

"OY, watch it! You'll have to pay for that, you will!" called a voice from the front.

"Shut up, driver. You'll get your money, now keep quiet!"

"There's no need for you to spit your dummy out, sir." Collins sat back with a wry smile on his face.

"You know, Collins, I could really learn to despise you."

"So, what are you going to do about them?"

"Me? I'm going to do nothing."

"What, you're going to let them get away?"

"No. I said *I'm* going to do nothing. You, on the other hand, will have to take your apprentice and head back to Skellig-Krieg."

"But we're nearly three miles down the track!"

"Good. It will give you the chance to remember the position which you hold, won't it?"

"When we get there, what would *sir* require of us? A bit of spying perhaps, or maybe just a visit to the retail district for a souvenir? Maybe a little model of the airdock for you to make on your journey to Kings Seat?"

"*That's enough!*" snapped Smithson. He pulled out a piece of parchment and a pen from his bag, then began writing a note. "I can always have you replaced, you know."

"I think you'll find you can't. It goes against the rules of the university."

"I can change rules. It's *my* university after all."

"But you are in *my world* now, one which you need me to guide you around."

Smithson ignored the comment.

"Here, take this. It will get you back into the city. Head for the main office of the city guard and give the note to them. They will understand it. Tell them the Rangles Inn would be a good place to start."

Collins snatched the note from Smithson's hand. He read it, screwed up his face, shook his head and made to leave.

"You may think you can manage without me, but you need me.

I know the truth about what you are doing. Wouldn't it be terrible if the authorities were to … oh, I don't know … find out about this little adventure. I'll leave you here to think about the position in which you find yourself in. Come, boy!"

Collins and his apprentice jumped down from the cart before Smithson could retort, leaving him to seethe in silence.

Chapter 13

The only noise from the street outside came from the Pub in the Wall, which appeared heaving with off-duty guards, now returned to their merriment after the ceasing of the alarm. Beyond that, the world fell silent. With the alarm silenced, the residents of Skellig-Krieg were prepared for an attack that would never come.

The sound of a creaking door cut through the silence, its rusted iron hinges reluctantly giving way to Barrington's strength. It seemed to fill the empty void, echoing off the surrounding buildings.

From the street, the door was concealed by a bush, which moved slowly outwards as the door opened. Moments later, a mirror on a stick cautiously appeared out from the edge of the vegetation. It tentatively scanned the area for any signs of danger, before disappearing back in. Hugh, Barrington and Heather cautiously stepped out from the doorway. Heather was busy folding the mirror and collapsing the extendable sneak stick – one of her many creations – and she placed them into her coat pocket. They looked carefully around the street, still checking for signs of danger.

"It seems safe enough," said Hugh, looking around. "I think we ought to get to the Rangles as soon as possible. I don't want to get caught out here."

"I think that's a good idea, my friend," said Barrington.

They lifted the hoods on their cloaks, whilst Heather pulled out something flat from her pocket. It was a flat circle which she depressed with her thumbs. It expanded with a soft pop to form a bowler hat, similar to the one she wore in Bansk, just without the air filtration system and mask. The sound of footsteps now bounced off the buildings, and the trio quickly headed toward the Rangles Inn.

They moved swiftly and quietly through the city streets, their breath forming a mist as they breathed out. Hugh was glad when they turned down Billy Lane, and the Rangles came into view. They approached the back door, Hugh rapping hard, which stung his cold knuckles. They heard the thudding sound of footsteps tentatively approach the door, followed by silence. It seemed an age for Trevor the innkeeper to reach the hatch and slide it open.

"Who is it?" he said in a harsh whisper.

"Trevor, it's us, Hugh, Barrington and an extra guest. Can you let us in?"

The sound of locks being opened came from inside, then the door swung open. "Mr Hugh, sir! And Mr Delphin too! What a lovely surprise."

"Shh, Trevor! Not here! Mind out the way."

Worried that the innkeeper may have blown their cover, Hugh pushed past Trevor with Barrington and Heather in tow.

"Well, I must say, this is most out of the ordinary, Mr Hugh sir."

"Trevor, please, close the door. We can talk when we are in the room, if it is free, of course." This appeared to spark the inn keeper into action. He closed and locked the door, then turned back to the group.

"Right you are, ladies and gents, if you would be so kind as to follow me, please."

He walked them halfway down the corridor, stopped to clear his throat, and a doorway appeared.

"Through here, if you please."

They followed Trevor's direction, entering the hidden room off

· the corridor.

"So, tell me Mr Hugh," said Trevor, closing the door to the room, "what brings you to my inn on such a cold winter's eve, and who is this fine young lady you have brought with you?"

"It's a long story Trevor, but may I introduce Heather McDougall, daughter of Hamish."

Trevor looked in awe at Heather.

"Tis an honour to meet you, my dear. Your father is a welcomed guest at this inn, and so are you. Will he be joining us tonight?"

Heather looked stunned at the mention of her father's name.

Trevor looked mortified with himself, as she burst into tears and threw herself into Hugh's shoulder.

"Oh dear, is it something I said?"

"I'll explain all in a while Trevor, but for now, please could you fetch us all some food and drinks. It's been a long day." Trevor nodded and excused himself, whilst Heather continued to sob uncontrollably, still using Hugh as a human tissue. Barrington watched them, tight-lipped.

Hugh couldn't explain how, or why, he could feel Heather's pain, but he just could. He felt the firestone glow on his chest, and he sensed it would also take some of the sting out of Heather's sadness.

The door opened once more, revealing Trevor with a tray of drinks. "Here we go everyone, these are on the house. You wouldn't believe who else has just turned up?"

Hugh looked towards the door as Emily walked in with the day's copy of the *SK Daily News* tucked under her arm. She looked Heather's frame up and down, tilted her head, and raised an eyebrow, then looked to her firestone, which was also glowing upon her chest. Hugh didn't think her lips could get any tighter.

"Emily! What a lovey surprise it is to see you here," Hugh said cheerfully.

Heather lifted her head from Hugh's shoulder, her eyes red and puffy.

"Emily? Dad told me all about ye." She left Hugh's drenched shoulder and turned to Emily, her eyes red and puffy. "To be honest, I didn't think I would ever get to meet ye."

Hugh and Barrington looked on confused as Heather flung her arms around Emily, who looked taken aback.

"Yes. Well, I was only made aware of you recently," she said, stepping away from Heather, who looked embarrassed and hurt.

"Sorry," said Hugh, "but is there something that we're missing?"

"Nothing for you to worry about. Just something between me and her." She stood in silence, looking unimpressed at both Hugh and Barrington.

"Well?"

"What?"

"I see you two have been up to your usual tricks." She chucked the paper onto the table, and it landed front page up. Barrington recoiled in horror, and as he moved out of the way, Hugh saw why. His innards dropped to his boots, and the colour drained from his face. There, on the front of the paper, were two pictures. One of himself and one of Barrington. Above them, the headline read:

WANTED: THE PORTIS-MONTIS TERRORISTS

Under the pictures, the article read:

> *Wanted for the reckless act of terror caused to the Silver Star Express from Bansk to Portis-Montis. The current toll is 28 dead and 47 injured. The pair believed to be behind these atrocities are Hugh Geber (left), and Barrington Delphin (right). According to our sources, the pair were already on the run from the authorities in Portis-Montis. It is believed that they will stop at nothing in their attempt to evade the authorities... (Story continued on page 2)*

Barrington hastily turned the page over.

> *...(continued from page 1) The pair were witnessed at the scene by Robert*

Smithson, Chancellor at the university in Portis-Montis. He had this to say
to our Ranthinian SKDN reporter.

"I can reveal that I did indeed see the pair at the scene. I was on the train
heading in the opposite direction and saw the pair with my very eyes, skulking
around the area in question. I have known the pair for many years, and it
saddens me to think that they could stoop so low. I must admit, their behaviour
looked suspicious, and I reported it to the authorities at the earliest possible
moment, but alas, by that time I was already too late. My condolences go out
to the families of all those involved in this harrowing incident. One can only
hope that the pair either turn themselves in or are caught at the soonest possible
moment before they cause more carnage."

We can report that the pair fled from the scene by airship, as they were
witnessed boarding the daily flight to Ranga by many of the passengers travelling
on the flight. It is being said that the airship made an unscheduled pickup outside
the train tunnel, hitting the train tracks before the pair climbed on-board. The
investigating authorities wish to speak to Captain Augustus Volatus about
his actions and to find out why he offered the pair a lift. Perhaps he himself is
also in league with Geber and Delphin, but that will only come to light once
Volatus has been brought in for questioning.

The Portis-Montis terrorists are also wanted for questioning in relation
to a previous incident at the University of Science and Progression. Fresh
evidence has emerged, which implicates the pair with the blaze in the Alchemy
Laboratories. As previously reported, Geber had a falling out with Chancellor
Robert Smithson not long before the fire broke out.

It is believed that Delphin agreed to cover for Geber, alleging that the latter
was with him at the time of the fire. When the new evidence was uncovered,
the authorities wasted no time in heading to Delphin's shop, only to find the

pair had already gone.

Using intelligence information, the authorities tracked the pair to the infamous Great Library, but were thwarted in their attempts to reach them by the library staff. Though we cannot be sure what happened, we know the pair evaded capture before moving to the area of sabotage outside the train tunnel.

The newly appointed head of the city guard, Mary Ablator-Sedes, had this to say.

"Although it saddens me to hear of the help the pair received from those in the library, we also have suspicions they had help from within my team. I shall investigate this in due course, and I would like to reassure the public that we're doing all we can to bring the pair to justice. I have not long received an international warrant for the pair's arrest, so I am sure we will have them in custody soon enough."

Geber and Delphin are still at large at the time of printing and are believed to be dangerous. It is imperative that any sightings of the pair are reported to the local authorities, and members of the public are warned not to approach the wanted men. There are some reports that they may head to the Skellig-Krieg area, and citizens have been advised to be on the lookout for the wanted criminals.

The SK Daily News will keep you up to date on the unfolding events, as and when they happen. Jump to page 6 for more on the Elf King: What we know so far, and how to prepare your household for an attack.

Hugh and Barrington looked up from the paper, with stunned looks on their faces.

"Emily, we didn't know the situation was this bad," said Hugh.

"Well, that's an understatement. I take it the alarm was your arrival?" she asked.

Hugh nodded awkwardly.

"A subtle entrance, as always," she said. "Why not raise a banner, heck, throw some trumpets in to announce your arrival!"

"Emily, are you alright?" asked Hugh.

"Let me think. We last saw each other outside the city. Since then, you have disappeared from existence. A simple letter would have done, or a reply to one of my many attempts to get hold of you. I even contacted Balinas to see if everything was alright, and he informed me you were ignoring him as well!"

"It's not that I didn't want to talk to either of you," said Hugh, "we've just had a lot on. And then other distractions got in the way; you know how it is."

"Don't give me excuses, Hugh Geber. This isn't some sort of game you can drop in and out of. I don't think either of you are quite aware of how serious the situation is right now." She looked at them, shaking her head. "It's bad enough that you are on the run from the authorities in Portis-Montis, *but this*?" She was now looking at Hugh as if he were a stranger and someone to be feared.

"Emily, you must believe me when I say, we were not behind this. We would never want to kill or harm innocent people, or anyone else for that matter."

"So how is it you were witnessed at the scene, by Smithson no less, two hours before the accident? Not only that, you had the audacity to drag Augustus into this as well?"

"Please, you have to believe that none of this was our fault. Augustus knocked some debris down towards the track. Maybe that caused the accident? Besides, it was Balinas who asked Augustus to find us. You have to believe us."

"I don't know what to believe right now."

There was a long, uneasy pause whilst she stared at Hugh and Barrington. Hugh went to reach out to Emily, who batted him away.

"Don't touch me!"

"Emily? I don't understand what I've done wrong?"

Emily wasn't listening, however; she turned left the room, slamming the door behind her, Trevor wincing at the force used. Dust filled the void left by Emily, as the rest of them remained silent.

"I think I'd better rustle up some food for you," said Trevor, looking glad for any excuse to leave the room.

Hugh, Barrington and Heather walked across to the table and sat down, drinking in shocked silence. Trevor eventually returned with a plate of sandwiches, apologising for the lack of warm food. They sat eyeballing eachother, with only the polite noises of eating for company.

A knock at the door broke the stalemate. Trevor jumped to his feet and opened it, revealing Emily and Alfred. He bustled off out of the door once more, to sort out more drinks for the new arrivals. Hugh got up to greet his uncle with a massive hug. Never was he so grateful to see a friendly face.

"Alfred!"

"Hugh, goodness me," said Alfred, pulling himself free from Hugh's grip. "Let me look at you. Are you well?"

"Yes, I'm fine, thank you. What about you? Has Emily filled you in?"

"Erm, yes," He shot a glance at Emily, who stood uncharacteristically quiet, before turning back to Hugh.

"I'm fine, but you really should plan your arrivals better. I received a message from our contact in Portis-Montis that the tracks were blown up outside the tunnel. The papers are yet to find out that nugget of information, and when they do, it'll only make things worse for you." Everyone in the room turned to look at Alfred. "What? I received the message not long before Emily came to fetch me. I must admit the papers are all over the story, calling you terrorists, but that's the rag getting the wrong end of the stick as usual."

"Sorry, but did you say blown up?" said Emily.

"Yes, why? Surely you didn't believe what was written in the papers?

Anyway, I was informed to be expecting your arrival imminently. They said that Augustus had been dispatched to pick you up. You should have let him drop you at the airdock. Bernie was expecting you, but you weren't on the airship," he said, looking at Hugh with raised eyebrows.

"We had to make alternative plans after Augustus bashed his airship on the rocks and tracks. He also said we wouldn't be able to get past the security in Bansk, so he dropped us off at the cottage on the marsh."

"Well, that was good thinking from him."

"Exactly," said Hugh, "so we caught a lift here from Heather, and we had to land outside the city boundary."

Alfred looked at Heather, whose eyes were still showing signs of being upset.

"Ah, hello my dear. Is everything alright?"

Hugh set to in filling in Emily and Alfred on their trip to reach Skellig-Krieg, whilst Heather sobbed quietly to herself.

"… and that's why we had to find an alternative route into the city. We feared people would be on the lookout for us here, given what we left behind in Portis-Montis."

"So, let me get this right," said Alfred, trying to get things clear in his head. "You entered the sight unaided, found Augustus, then helped him to get Heather back by surrounding her with your energy?"

Hugh nodded, and Emily let out a sigh.

"You really ought to be trained up before you go on any more forays into the sight," said Alfred. "Your involvement in the rescue of Heather, and the manner in which it was carried out, means you are now linked to each other. Have you noticed any strange bond between yourselves since the incident?"

Hugh and Heather nodded.

"So why did you decide to enter the sight on your own in the first place?"

"I didn't knowingly enter it," said Hugh. "I just sort of fell in by accident. Balinas suggested I should ask you to be my mentor," he said, looking at Emily.

"Oh, did he now? Well, I'm sure I have a spare five minutes lying around here *somewhere!*"

Alfred let out a sigh. "*Emily*, don't shoot the messenger. Hugh's only relaying what he was told."

"Hmm, sorry," she said. "I suppose we can cross that bridge later. Just try to keep yourself out of mischief and the sight until I have time to explain it in better detail. As for you," she said, turning to Heather, "how do we know we can trust you?"

Heather looked Emily back in the eye and cocked her head.

"After ye," she said. Emily stood tight-lipped, still chewing the inside of her mouth. "Well, if ye want me to show mine, yiv to show me yers first."

Emily Huffed and pulled out her card with the EGF crest embossed on it. Heather sniggered.

"I'm sorry, but what is so funny?" said Emily.

"Well, it still makes me laugh when I see those, that's all."

Emily took a few steps back.

"Wait, you *don't* have one of these?" Her eyes widened, and Hugh could see the tell-tale signs she was gearing up for something big.

"Heather, just show her yours, *please!*" said Hugh.

"Oh alright, if ye insist," she replied and rolled up her right sleeve. Emily and Alfred gasped.

"Erm, what's wrong?" asked Hugh, gulping.

"Why on earth do you have the symbol tattooed on your bloody arm?" said Emily.

"Well, dad says the card is for wimps who dinnae like needles."

"I beg your pardon?"

"Emily, please go easy on her."

"Stay out of this Hugh! If your *dad* had bothered to stay around long enough, he would have found out that we moved on from that system years ago, and for good reason!"

"How dare ye insult Dad like that! They've kidnapped him, Emily. Does that mean nothing to ye? All ye care about is some petty card."

"A petty card it may be, but have you thought of what would happen if they caught you? How would you hide the evidence of being a part of the EGF, especially when it's permanently attached to you? We can easily dispose of the card if needed, unlike the permanent tattoo. Only a fool would have one of those now," she scoffed. Both Hugh and Barrington looked sheepish, subconsciously rubbing their right wrists.

Emily stood agog.

"Oh, do not tell me you two ... show me your arms ... *NOW!*"

They couldn't resist even if they wanted to. As Hugh and Barrington raised their right sleeves, revealing their fresh marks, Emily let out a high scream of rage, and Hugh had a blow to the chest so hard from the firestone it knocked him to the floor.

As Heather ran to his aid, the surrounding room shook. The sound of bottles falling from the bar came from the other side of the wall, and they heard Trevor cursing, whilst attempting to save his stock.

"*EMILY! Calm yourself, regain control!*" said Alfred, placing himself between Hugh and Emily. The shaking subsided, and Emily slumped into a chair. The sound of heavy breathing and the smell of disturbed dust filled the air.

"What the hell was *that*?" said Barrington.

"It's something I've not seen for a long time," said Alfred. "When Emily was younger and had less control over her powers, she would lose her focus and draw energy towards her. There are channels of magical energy which flow deep underground through this area. They can surface closer to particular individuals, like a conductor, if you will, especially if the person in question is experiencing emotions outside of their control. Anything from intense pain to anger can trigger it. If they lose focus, even for a moment, the power surges upwards to the surface towards them. We don't know why it happens, but if not kept in check, it could cause untold damage to the people involved.

"Emily, understand that I'm not blaming you for what just happened. I'm sensing that the powers are flowing close to the surface at this point in time. I know this is difficult, especially when you have heightened feelings, but please do as your mother taught you, go to your calm place. We cannot afford for you to lose control now. We need you."

She sat with her eyes closed, taking deep breaths. After one last exhale, she opened her eyes.

"I'm sorry. You should not have had to witness that just then. Heather, please accept my apology. It is not your fault that you and Hugh have become connected to each other. I'm just angry with Augustus for not explaining things clearly to Hugh *before* he did what he had to do."

"I don't understand," said Hugh. "What was it that happened when we rescued Heather, and why are we linked?"

"It's to do with the fact that you shared your energy with Heather. You will have inherited some of each other's power. It will need an in-depth discussion, and one which we don't have the time for today. We must talk about Hamish and the urgent need to rescue him."

"So, first ye mock Dad and then me for using outdated ways, then ye want to rescue him. I'll accept yer apology for being overprotective of Hugh, but insulting me and Dad, that was completely over the line."

"I'm sorry, I can't say it enough. But I want to find him too. He was a big part of my life too."

"So much a part of it that ye never bothered to look for him?"

"That's unfair. He was the one who walked out on us! He left me and my mother to fend for ourselves."

"Ye still could have tried to find him. He was always there. *We* were always there."

"He was *not* always there. He used to run off every summer on little expeditions to god knows where, leaving us behind. Then one day he left for good. He gave us no option to go with him, left no forwarding address and no money. It was difficult for my mother to make ends meet."

"We were living alone in the middle of a marsh. We saw nobody, not one person. Do ye have any idea how lonely that was?"

"Not as lonely as fleeing in the middle of the night, leaving everything that you have ever known. We had no home to go to and ended up sleeping rough in caves for six years!"

"Yeah, cos Dad never had to run, did he? At least you had fresh air. Marsh air is something you can never get used to. We were lucky Dad invented the air filtration system."

"Fresh air's great, apart from when it's *freezing!*"

"Will you two just shut up!" said Hugh, tired of the one-upmanship currently happening in the room. "Your behaviour is more like squabbling siblings ..."

Emily and Heather turned to Hugh, both with eyebrows raised.

"Oh ... right."

Chapter 14

They all sat in silence, the sound of Trevor sweeping up broken glass, the only noise filling the room. Hugh didn't know why he hadn't spotted it before now. Apart from the obvious difference in hair colour, Hugh could see some similarity between them in their eyes and their noses.

"It's not so obvious unless you are looking," said Emily, seeing to answer Hugh's unspoken question. He hated it when she looked inside his head.

"Sorry," she said out loud.

"So, you never knew about each other?"

Emily shook her head.

"I found out the night you were last in this room, and it came as quite a shock. I didn't have time to speak to Hamish before he left."

"But you never refer to him as your father, only by his name. In all the time we spent in Portis-Montis growing up, you never mentioned it."

"Well, I barely saw him. He was always away, so he never seemed like a father to me. We had our alternative ways of talking to each other, but that died off a long time ago. Anyway, that's enough chit chat for now. I'm not here for a family reunion; I want to figure out how we are going to rescue Hamish. Do you have a plan?"

Hugh looked at her and shook his head.

"We haven't had the time to plan as yet. The only thing remotely relating to a plan are the instructions we need to follow on this letter."

He dug around in his bag and pulled out the letter from his father instructing him to go to Dallum. Emily scanned it through, then looked up at Hugh.

"When did you receive this?"

"If you remember, Hamish gave it to me before we separated outside the city gates. We now have to get to the room in Dallum."

"Why didn't you read this when we were still together? It would have saved a lot of hassle. You must stop procrastinating on these things, Hugh."

"Alright, I get the picture. It was Hamish who stopped me from reading it when he passed it to me, as he was keen to get moving. On our return home, I didn't feel up to reading more cryptic messages, which may have taken us on another trip away. Then we were caught up with the hearing at Runners House, and that took up a lot of time.

"I now realise it was an error to avoid opening the letter and that I should've moved quicker on this. But if we can get back to the room at the Hotel Alpine, I think it will give me some idea of where the book we were looking for may be located."

"Let's not forget the *other* book that we have to find," said Barrington, "not to add to the workload, but Balinas said we had to find it."

Emily let out an exasperated sigh.

"What book are you talking about now?"

"It's the book relating to the element of earth and the lore of magic." Emily's face lit up.

"Did he at least give you any idea of where to look to find this other book?"

"No," said Hugh, "only that the *Book of Prophecy* said we needed to retrieve that one as well. Sorry, there's nothing else to go on."

"It's barely a clue! I mean …"

Emily stopped talking. A red light began flashing on the wall behind her, then stayed on constant.

"What's that mean?" asked Heather.

"*Shhh*," said Emily. "It's a warning that there is something wrong in the bar!" she said in a hushed voice.

They sat and listened, trying to pick up any discernible words from the conversation through the wall. They could just about make out someone barking orders at Trevor, followed by the sound of the innkeeper's steadfast response.

"*Sit down, you lot. We'll question you in a moment. Now then, Innkeeper, tell me where they are.*"

"*I really don't know what you are talking about, sir,*" said Trevor, his voice unwavering.

"*Don't play the fool with me, innkeeper. We've had a tip off from an informant that they would be here. Now tell us where Geber, Delphin and Miss Le Fey are, and we will cause you no harm.*"

Emily looked across at Hugh in alarm, and he shrugged his shoulders in response, just as confused as she was.

"*I really don't know what you are talking about. Search in the back for all I care.*"

"*That we shall do. Buckmore, Featherwell, set to your duties. Leave nothing unturned. We will find them, innkeeper, and when we do, we will have this place shut down for good. We have it on good authority that you harbor people of an unwanted nature here. Now you wait nicely whilst the rest of my men question your punters.*"

They heard footsteps walking around the bar, followed by the door to the corridor slamming against the wall. Hugh counted the footsteps stomping up the stairs, then heard the furniture being moved around somewhere above their heads. They sat with bated breath, hoping the hidden room which they were in remained so.

The noise upstairs seemed to go on for an eternity, the people searching, showing no regard for anything. They heard furniture breaking and the sound of glass smashing upon the floor. With each bang and crash, the occupants of the hidden room jumped, and dust dropped onto their heads. Eventually, the sound of footsteps came back downstairs, and the room let out a collective sigh of relief, thinking they were safe.

"Nothing to report, sir. They must have got away. Maybe someone tipped them off?"

"Thank you, Buckmore. Where is Featherwell?"

"He said he was going to search the perimeter. They can't have run far."

"Good, good, now you listen here innkeeper ..."

Hugh sat wide-eyed, for they had not heard the locks being undone on the back door, nor the unmistakable sound of the back door opening or closing. Someone was pacing the corridor outside the room. The sound of something rubbing along the wall, a hand maybe, or an ear? Hugh mouthed "what do we do?" to Barrington, who shrugged, panic-stricken, then looked at the door.

Everyone sat in silence, as the sound made its way along the outside of the room, stopped, then returned on itself, as if the person outside knew there was something wrong. It stopped outside the door, and everyone held their breath.

A bead of sweat made its way down Hugh's face as the unmistakable sound of the door latch clicking open filled the room.

Chapter 15

The Elf King was sitting in his room above the Horn of the Unicorn. He was awaiting news about the current happenings in Skellig-Krieg and had dispatched his newly appointed servant to assess the situation for him. The final warning went out to all peoples not of New World origin to leave the city with immediate effect. Many people opted to leave when the order first came out. Now only the stubborn remained.

He now pondered the task laid out in front of him. The time he needed to locate the books of lore was diminishing, especially since that bumbling fool from the university in Portis-Montis had joined the trail to find the book, and he desired to impress those in control of the New World. He needed to get back to his people, if he were to stand any chance of getting to the prize first. There was a knock at the door, and his servant entered.

"Well, what news? Have all the carts left?" The servant handed his master a note, then bowed in respect. The Elf King read the piece of paper, before screwing it up and tossing it into the fireplace. "It would seem that our stay here will be short-lived then. Well done, we must move quickly if we are to get onto the last transport out of here."

"Sire." His servant nodded and left the room.

There was nothing for it. They had to leave now, or risk being left behind and out of the race. Word was that people were convening at a new camp set up for the displaced in Dallum, but those more loyal to him had begun moving onto Kings Seat, to await his expected arrival. It was to these loyal followers he knew he must return, for with their help, he would track down not only the lore book for alchemy but also the other three books of lore. Once he was in possession of them, he would be all-powerful, and nobody could stop him. He grinned to himself as he grabbed his cloak and headed for the door, his gold ring catching the light of the fireplace as he left.

Chapter 16

Hugh sat watching the door for movement. He could tell the person on the other side was preparing for their next move. There was no way they could escape this time, with no easy way out apart from the way they came in. He looked at the others, seeing that they were also coming to the same realisation. They sat and waited, unable to move, as the once hidden entrance to the room slowly creaked open.

A hand now gripped the outer edge, as if to steady the speed of the moving door. The person was backing into the room, and Hugh prepared himself for a battle, maybe a scuffle to overpower the new aggressor, to get out of the room. There was only one person, so it wouldn't be hard for the group to overpower the newcomer.

"Bernie?" said Barrington, his voice loud in the quiet room, making everyone jump.

"*Shhh!*" Bernie checked over his shoulder cautiously. "Listen, we ain't got much time. I can buy you five, maybe ten minutes, but that's all." He spoke in a harsh whisper.

"What do you mean?" asked Barrington in a more cautious tone.

"I don't have time to explain, so you are going to have to trust me. There's a new gaffer in charge of security, sent over from Bansk. He's in the bar with Trevor now, and he's got a real issue with you two, gawd knows why?" He looked to Barrington and Hugh. "I don't know what you've been up to, but there's talk of you being linked to the Elf King, aiding him somehow. They think you're behind the train crash as well."

"Bernie, you know we are not working with the Elf King. You must believe me. And we're not behind the train crash."

"We all believe you are not with him, well, me and the lads, and we know you didn't cause the crash, but the gaffer ain't so sure. He got this message from two chaps earlier, seemed to rile him up. One of them was that chap who's always with Smithson. He had a friend with him, quiet fella, just followed the other one around."

Hugh looked at Bernie. "Collins was here? That means Smithson's not far away."

"We ain't got time to discuss this now. You lot need to get moving and …" He paused, clocking Heather for the first time. "Who's this?"

"This is Heather McDougall, Hamish's daughter. It's a long story, one which we don't have time for now," said Emily.

"Nice to meet you." He briefly nodded to her. "Right, well, I need to get back through to the bar before they come looking for me. Alfred, you'd best go back to your shop. I'll swing by there later. I'll sort the back door, and Emily, you know what to do. Steer clear of all checkpoints, and don't use the old routes. They're being watched."

"These three found that one out already," she said.

"Yeah, so we heard!" He looked across at all three of them, who avoided his look of disapproval.

"I'll take them out and go with them," said Emily. "Alfred, you'll have to cover for me."

"Right you are," he said. "Hugh, please stay safe, keep in touch and watch out for the crows. They're everywhere."

"Yes, I know, I know," said Hugh, rolling his eyes.

"Hugh, this is serious. We are in enough trouble as it is. Promise me you will be careful."

"Alright, sorry, I promise. Now what do we have to do to

get out of here?"

"Leave that to us. We have things ready for this sort of situation. Emily, take the new route. Stay safe."

With that, Bernie left the room, leaving a nervous tension in his wake. They listened to him walking down the corridor, then heard the back door being subtly unlocked. It creaked open, then closed with a slam. Bernie headed back towards the bar, and they listened to him giving an account to his superior.

"So how do we know what the signal will be?" asked Hugh.

Emily looked at Hugh, deciding honesty was best in this situation.

"We have a well-rehearsed plan. Bernie will divert the guards out of the bar, and Trevor is going to get himself arrested."

"*What?*" said Hugh.

"*Shh!*" Emily clamped a hand over his mouth. Hugh went tingly inside. Her hand smelled like soil and vegetation.

"Hugh, pay attention. It's the only way that we'll get out of here alive. We agreed to this plan long before you turned up on the scene. It's one of our fail safes. There's no need to worry about Trevor. Bernie will see that he's alright."

Just then, a noise from the other side of the wall distracted her. The sound of a scuffle came through, along with the sound of orders being hastily given, and more glass smashing onto the floor. Emily jumped into action.

"Let's move!"

She guided them quickly and quietly from the room, with Alfred following on behind. Hugh heard the ominous sound of Trevor being restrained with the use of a fist, knowing there was nothing he could do. Bernie was instructing other guards to give chase, saying he had seen the wanted men running in the opposite direction towards Old Skellig.

They found the back door had been left unlocked, and made their way out into the cold night air. Alfred bid them farewell, and melted into the darkness, leaving Emily to get them out of the city. They half walked, half ran down the empty street. Now and then, Hugh would see a person peeking from a window, watching their every movement.

"Emily, we're still too exposed."

"I know, get a move on, will you, and keep your voice down."

They turned away from the street they were on, towards the direction of the greenhouses. Hugh remembered walking down here in the warm sunshine not three months before, on his way for lunch at the Pub in the Wall. It was more relaxed compared to this situation.

"Hugh, stop dawdling and keep up!" Emily hissed.

He caught up with the rest of the group, as they entered the courtyard to the Great Greenhouses, the metal gates squeaking loud into the silent night. She led the group through the first doorway she came to, ushering them in quickly. They were all out of breath and already plenty warm enough.

The wall of humid air came as a shock compared to that outside, and Hugh found it hard to breathe. His skin itched all over as they ran down a path, Emily not hesitating to stop for junctions and pathways. She knew the greenhouses inside and out, calling out trip hazards and turns as she went. The others dutifully followed, whilst attempting to avoid the foliage whipping back in Emily's wake. They came to a clearing, and Hugh realised where they were.

It was here where he had met Emily for the first time since her departure from Portis-Montis all those years ago. He had just cycled through the deadly vipera fronde, and would have become another victim to the plant, if it weren't for Emily and her student's quick work.

Hugh had ploughed into them, and the team worked together to save his life. He had no intention of going back into the death trap down the path, as he watched Emily run to a pile of protective suits.

"Here, put these on, quick!" she said, passing them all a set to put on, before getting one for herself.

"You're not telling me we're going in there?" said Hugh.

"Yes, we are, so I suggest you get suited up, quickly," said Emily. "The vipera fronde is where it's hidden."

"Where what's hidden?"

"The entrance to the new way out of here, so put this on. We have little time."

Barrington stared at her in alarm. "Sorry? Are you saying that we have to walk *into* the vipera fronde?"

"What's that?" said Heather.

"Only the most poisonous plant known to man. It nearly finished our dear friend here."

"What?"

"Barrington, stop filling her mind with stories," said Emily. "These suits will protect us. Now hurry and put them on."

They rushed to get covered up, arms and legs getting tangled up in the unyielding garments. At one point Hugh had one hand in the foot hole and a foot in the armhole, earning him another chastisement from Emily. After much fuss, they were ready to enter the hazardous nest of plants.

The suit restricted Hugh in all the senses. He waddled in the clumpy suit and struggled to hear Emily's instructions, her voice sounding muffled. It was hot and claustrophobic, but he knew it was better than the alternative. Shivers went down his spine as he remembered his last encounter with his plant.

Emily, realising she was getting nowhere fast, spoke to them inside their heads, a useful skill that paid off in situations such as this.

She led them into the evil plants. Even through the thick suit, he could feel the fronds wrapping themselves around his arms and legs, this time without the bonus of being poisoned. He snapped them clean off at the head and saw Emily turn into the mass of vegetation, swiping it away with a machete like a true explorer, whilst being dimly lit by the lamplight from above. It was hard going, as the plants had overgrown the path.

Hugh couldn't understand the point of heading deeper into this deadly nest of plants. He was wondering if they were to hide in here for the rest of the night when everything opened up around him. Emily had stopped in a clearing in the centre of the mass of vegetation, pointing to the floor with the blade in her hand. Hugh looked down and saw a trapdoor revealing itself as Emily cleared off the topsoil. She opened it up and gestured for them to climb in, which was easier said than done.

Hugh watched first Barrington, then Heather squeeze into the tight hole. Now it was his turn. He looked down into the dark abyss, seeing a ladder going into a deep shaft. His head spun as he took in the drop, and Emily had to catch him before he stumbled over.

'*It's alright, Hugh,*' she said in his head once more, whilst batting off vines. '*You can do this. One step at a time.*'

Hugh whimpered as he lined himself up with the hole. His stomach churned as he went down onto hands and knees and placed a foot onto the top rung of the ladder. He went to move his hand closer to the hole, when he realised he couldn't move it. He had stood still for too long, and a vine had wrapped itself around his wrist. In the effort to remove it, the plant took his glove.

Fear rose within him as the plants sensed a fresh victim for the taking. He then realised the plants had a hold of his other arm and watched in horror as they made a move for his ungloved hand. He could feel the plants attempting to pull him back, as if they could sense the bare flesh, wanting to devour it.

Before he could think of what to do, the machete swung down through the air, freeing his trapped arm. It came down again, swiping at the mass of plants coming towards his hand. The surrounding vines cowered back, the ones around his body falling to the floor. In one move, Emily removed the danger, turned, shoved him into the hole and booted him down the ladder with her foot.

Hugh scrabbled to get a grip of the rungs as he bounced his way down the shaft.

If he were not wearing the thick suit, he would have broken bones for sure. He was halfway down when he grabbed a hold of a rung, nearly wrenching his arm out of its socket. He looked up, seeing Emily had closed the trapdoor and had descended into the shaft. He tried to hurry to get a hold with his other hand, but Emily was on top of him before he knew it, her foot landing hard on his hand.

Hugh let out a muffled yell of pain before continuing his bumpy descent, landing in a pile by Barrington's feet.

"Very elegant," he said in a muffled voice.

Hugh was rolling around on the floor, battered and bruised from the fall. He looked up just in time to see Emily jump the last four rungs to land on top of him. She stood up quickly and removed her mask.

"What are you doing, laying underneath the ladder like that? Come on, we have to keep moving. You can remove the suits now, there are no plants down here."

Hugh scowled as he stood up and removed his safety gear, rubbing himself from being bumped and jumped on.

The tunnel smelled earthy, and it was warm and damp. The air tingled with the raw power that he now knew ran below their feet. The tunnellers who dug the underground path used wood and metal to hold the walls and roof up. The roots from above pushed ominously through the cracks.

After what felt like an age, the ground beneath their feet started to slope upwards. Hugh felt fresh air on a breeze fall across his face. They heard running water and came to a stop next to a rock face with hand and foot holes cut into it. Emily scaled up as nimble as a mountain goat, followed by Barrington, who puffed his way up the damp stone face. Heather seemed as nimble as Emily, taking to it with ease. Hugh, still sore from his previous ladder acrobatics, wasn't looking forward to the task ahead.

He took in a deep breath, then began scaling the rock wall. It was cold.

The edges of the rock dug into his hands, and the higher he climbed, the more dread clawed at his insides. His breathing became shallow, and he was finding it hard to avoid looking down. He was nearly at the top when his overwhelming urge to look won the battle. As he did so, the world spun below him, a whirl of torchlight and shiny rock face, illuminated by the bright moon above. He felt his hands losing their grip. He scrabbled for a hold, his fingernails painfully scraping the rock surface.

On the cusp of falling, hands reached down, grabbing his own, and dragged him upwards. His belly grazed on the rock face, as he emerged into a leafy undergrowth next to a fast-flowing river below. Behind them, the dense woodland rose upwards back towards Skellig-Krieg into the darkness.

It appeared the tunnel designers had cunningly concealed the entrance to the tunnel within a hollow tree trunk, which, for all intents and purposes, looked dead. Sore and tired, Hugh lay on his back, regaining control of his senses. He was looking up into a silhouetted canopy of branches.

"Thank you," he said, sitting up. "I thought I was a goner there ... now what are you listening to?"

He looked at Emily, who flapped her arms, signalling for him to be quiet. He turned his ear, to hear what the rest of the group had already tuned into. He could hear voices coming in their direction, and the sound of undergrowth being hacked away. The sound of tracker dogs barking sent fear coursing through his veins.

"What are we going to do?" said Hugh in a whisper.

Emily was busy sealing the exit point with protective runes and covering their tracks with soil and leaves.

"We need to get moving, we'll have to stick to the river," she said, before making her way down the bank.

The sound of the search party and dogs was getting closer. Hugh's nerves were almost shot from the panic. They reached the edge of the river, its gradual slope shallow enough to walk in.

"We can't go in there. They're bound to follow us," said Barrington.

"If you have a better idea, then please share it with the group."

Barrington remained silent.

"No? Then let's get moving. The sound of the river will cover our movements, but don't step too far out, or the current will grab you Come on."

Hugh shuddered at the thought of falling in as Emily set off into the river. The cold water was like a thousand knives digging into his legs. They were not in that deep, but it was enough for Hugh. Emily paused and suggested they used the firestones to keep warm. Without hesitating, Hugh pulled his stone out and placed the pin into a hole. The riverbank illuminated instantly, and he whipped the pin out, nearly dropping it into the river.

"What the *hell* are you doing?" said Emily.

"*Sorry!* I can't see a thing, it's too dark, and my hands are numb."

He could already feel the heat radiating from Emily's stone. She had used the first hole for heat, and not the second for heat and light.

Emily took the pin from his hand and placed it into the correct hole. "Well, at least try to be a little careful." She huffed and turned to walk away, with Hugh scowling at the back of her head. "Don't scowl at me."

Hugh turned to see Barrington struggling to balance in the fast flowing river.

"Barrington, will you get a move on," said Hugh, urging his friend on.

"I can't. It's slippery, and these are new boots I'll have you know."

"Well, you're going to have to get a move on, unless you wish to get caught by that lot out there. And keep your voice down, will you?"

"Well, you're the one who's shouting right now. This is really difficult."

"You think it's an easy experience for us?" said Hugh.

"What are you two bickering about?" said Emily. She had stopped and turned to see what the problem was. "I can hear *both* of you, and so will they. Get a grip on yourselves, this is no time to have a spat."

Hugh went to answer back, but Emily cut him off.

"Don't you dare, Hugh Geber! I've walked away from my job, *again*, to get you out of a sticky situation. The least you can do is try to keep up. Heather, would you mind taking Barrington's hand? You'll be able to support each other."

Heather went to Barrington's aid, and they continued on slowly through the river. They waded in silence, keeping themselves low. Hugh was finding it difficult, as they could not see the roots from the many trees that lined the bank of the river. He kept stumbling and heard more splashing from the pair behind them, suggesting they too were finding the going just as tough.

More than once, they had to duck down into a thicket to hide from searchlights scanning the river. Hugh noticed the sound of the dogs had disappeared. He guessed someone had probably called them off, or they had picked up the scent from the road. Either way, the sounds coming from the search party spoke of frustration.

Eventually, after a long game of hide and seek, the searchers gave in. Hugh heard them discussing the change in shift, and how they could pick up the search when the light was better. Together with Emily, after one last check that they really were on their own, they used hole two on their firestones.

The light made all the difference. They stepped out onto the bank, shielding the stones with their tops, to prevent the light giving their position away. Their bodies were steaming from the warmth flowing through them, with gentle wisps of mist fading into the night air.

"Right, so what's the plan to get to Dallum?" asked Emily.

"Well, we don't actually have one," Hugh said sheepishly.

"What? Then why are you here? Did you think it would all just sort itself out when you arrived?"

"Emily, please listen. We were going to talk it through with you when the guards arrived. We know that we have to get to Dallum, and we have to rescue Hamish, wherever he may be. Beyond that we don't know."

Emily appeared to be assessing this in her head, and Hugh worried she was heading off into another rant.

"Alright, so what do you want to do first?" she asked.

Hugh was taken aback. "Erm, yes ... well, I suppose we need to get to the Hotel Alpine, so probably head to the road first?"

"Then what? We can't just walk down the open road like all is fine. There will be people looking for us."

"Please give us a break. It's difficult for us, being on the run too."

"And you think it's easy for me to be dragged away in a rush, with no time to plan?"

"And what do you think we had to do?"

Emily took in the soggy group, realising all the eyes were on her.

"Sorry, I'm struggling to get to grips with everything today. I'm being rude and insensitive. I knew deep down that this day would come, just not as soon as this. Does anyone have an idea that might work? We need to be out of sight before daybreak."

"Maybe we could hitch a ride with one of those carts we saw earlier?"

Everyone turned around to look at Heather.

"What? It was just a suggestion."

"That's a brilliant idea," said Barrington.

Emily jumped into action.

"Right, we need to move fast. The last of the carts were due to leave by this evening. We don't want to miss them." She jumped to her feet, signalling that she was ready to leave. Everyone else stood, more disjointed than Emily, stiff from the effort of walking through the river.

"So why are all the carts leaving?" asked Hugh.

"There's been a big clamp down with all things regarding the Old World, something that you would have known about, if you had bothered to write once in a while."

Hugh looked down, choosing not to reply.

"It's been getting harder to live in Skellig-Krieg, since the start of the uprising."

"Uprising? Balinas mentioned that and said it was all to do with the king returning to power in Kings Seat." said Barrington.

"Yes, he is correct. The Elf King has many followers still, who were all waiting for the signal to come and take arms once more. That makes anyone living in Skellig-Krieg with links to the Old World a possible threat, meaning they're no longer welcome.

"Not only that, there's talk of the old resistance movement starting up again. They were never happy with the wall and the nation being split into two. We have faced numerous inspections these past few weeks, making work nearly impossible. It's been in all the papers here, so I would be surprised if it hasn't made the news in Portis-Montis. But then I suppose you *are* the news in Portis-Montis."

"That's not fair. We had the update from Balinas," said Hugh.

"She has a point though, dear Hugh. You tell me all the time how much we've been in the papers recently. All the accusations about the fire seem to me like a good cover up for what is happening in the outside world. Then there was the case of poor old Art, of course."

"What about Art?" asked Emily.

"You know him?" asked Hugh.

"Of course, I do. He's one of our main contacts over there. What's happened to him now?"

"They have removed him from his position as Head of the City Guard." Emily stopped walking, and Hugh walked into her.

"Careful," she snapped at him. "I was already aware of that news. I thought you were about to reveal something bad."

"And Art being removed from his position isn't bad news?"

"No, it's bad alright, but at least he's still alive. Things are heading downhill fast. The word on this side of the wall is the Elf King is building an army, or so they say. That's what those in charge of the New World are getting worried about. With Skellig-Krieg bordering the Old World, it's feared that it will be the first to be attacked." She took in a deep breath and let out a sigh. "Let's get to the track and find these carts."

They continued on in silence, as the situation they were finding themselves in dawned on them all. The track was quiet when they reached it, no sign of the wagons, nor any of the guards that were after them. They kept to the edge, ready to dive into the woods at a moment's notice. It wasn't long before they caught up with the tail end of the procession.

"Here's what we're going to do," said Emily, as they stalked the end of the line as if it were their prey. "We'll, need to jump into the back of that trailer without being seen. They won't take kindly to extra passengers."

"What if we end up getting caught? Won't they notice us getting on?" asked Hugh.

"There is a possibility they could catch us getting on-board, but it's a risk we need to take."

Hugh looked at her in alarm.

"There's no other choice. We need to get off this road," she said.

"We just have to hope the driver isn't keen on stopping. He will want to keep up with the rest of the party. If we are lucky, we might make it most of the way to Dallum."

The trailer in question appeared to be extremely sturdy and well built. It was carrying bales of cotton, probably the life's work of a trader, who couldn't prove their New World status. Hugh saw the heavy load was no match for the massive steam tractor that was pulling the wagon, its nameplate THE GOLDEN WEAVER shining by the light coming from the oil lamp above it.

He saw people walking alongside the trailer, and they looked to be armed. A man sat on top, who appeared to be giving instructions via a talking pipe to those operating the tractor. There was also one going to the side of the trailer so he could communicate with the guards.

"Are you sure we couldn't just take our chances and walk to

Dallum?" he asked.

"Hugh, you know as well as I do that by first light, this road will be swarming with guards looking for us. We can hide well in there, and hopefully, if the fates are on our side, we'll not get caught. Come on, let's move, they're nearly out of the trees."

Before Hugh could raise another objection, she darted off towards the rear of the trailer. They all watched as she deftly leapt into the cart in one swift move, not making any sound. She hung onto the outside of a bale, then scrambled upwards, disappearing between the load and the roof of the trailer.

Hugh looked at Barrington and Heather, who just shrugged. He went for it. He ran out from the protection of the ditch they were walking in, heading for the rear of the trailer. What seemed like an easy task moments earlier, now looked like an insurmountable job.

Close up, the cart appeared a lot higher and turned out to be moving at a considerable pace. On his first attempt, Hugh misjudged the speed, missing the back of the moving object, looking like he was doing a bizarre dance ritual.

Emily's head popped out from above the bales.

"What are you doing? Stop larking around and get in, before you get us caught!"

"What do you think I'm trying to do?"

He tried again, this time doing the splits between the rear of the trailer and the ground. He stifled a yelp of pain.

"*Shhh!*" said Emily.

She had now leaned down, and attempted to grab at his foot, but she could not reach it. His right knee was hooked over the rear of the moving trailer, whilst his left foot dragged along the ground. Now half upside down, and in incredible pain, Hugh found he couldn't move, unable to get himself into an upright position.

As his head bobbed in time with the rhythm of the trailer's movement, he saw Heather and Barrington coming to his rescue. To his relief, they lifted him onto the bales of cotton. He scrambled up to the top to join Emily. Next up was Heather who did a hop, skip and a jump onto the bales, clinging to them with ease. She scampered upwards towards the gap.

Barrington strayed behind the trailer, before attempting the same manoeuvre as Heather. He looked at Hugh, giving him a cocky wink before hopping, skipping, jumping. He deftly leapt through the air, as a deer would jump over a high hedge.

The look of smugness soon changed to one of realisation that he had misjudged the distance and speed by a large margin. He landed flat on his face with an audible *'oomf,'* causing the others in the cart to wince with pain. He scrambled to his feet, alarm on his face, and Hugh knew why.

From the front, Hugh heard the muffled conversation of the driver asking the guards to check out the back of his trailer. Barrington half hobbled, half ran towards the cart, this time leapt harder, wincing as he did so. Hugh, Emily and Heather grabbed him by the arms, leaving his legs to flail around wildly behind him. The other three dragged him upwards with a surge of adrenaline, hiding themselves on top of the bales just in time, before the guards appeared at the back of the cart. Hugh watched from above from the shadows, saw the pair give a brief check, shrug, then disappear back to resume their positions.

Hugh let out a sigh of relief. He found the trailer had been partitioned according to its load. Planks were attached to the tops of the partitions, so the packers could still move about whilst loading the trailer. They had been rubbed smooth over the decades by those who shimmied across to the different areas below.

Hugh carefully pulled himself along the top, squeezing between the gap. It was a struggle, as every bump in the road jostled the trailer, nearly causing him to fall off more than once. Beyond the bales, there were areas for linen already woven, which showed signs of being hastily packed.

Ladders were built into the walls, making it easier to climb up and down. He picked a compartment with dark cloth in and carefully made his way down from the narrow board he was on. It was comfy enough for a short ride. Emily appeared next to him, climbing down from the bales.

"Are you alright?" she asked.

"Yes, thank you, just in a bit of pain, that's all."

"Not as much as Barrington."

"No, that looked painful! Where are the other two?"

"They have themselves settled in a compartment further forward. By the looks of things, this was one of the last trailers to leave. The order was for everyone to be out by sundown today, and it looks as though some compartments further forward have been packed hastily. They are in the section for the offcuts and oddments. I left Heather tending to Barrington's wounds."

"Mmm, lucky Barrington!"

"Oi!" Hugh turned to Emily, grinning. "Git!"

"You know, I still don't understand why, but since we rescued her, I've felt this strange connection between us. It's as though I'm attracted to her, but not in a wanting to be with her kind of way, and I can't explain it? I know you said it was something to do with when I surrounded her energy in the sight, but why would that make me be attracted to her, but not, if you know what I mean?"

"Inter-connectional link," said Emily.

"I beg your pardon?"

"It's what happens if you have to shield someone whilst using the sight. It's what Augustus should have explained before you undertook the procedure. It's not only part of your power that is now connected with each other. Part of your soul will link with the one you were shielding. In essence, you're linked together internally; a part you resides in her and vice versa."

"So that is why we are drawn to each other?"

"Yes. It will feel like love, but it's much deeper than that. The parts

173

of your souls you both inherited will reach out to each other. They will always live in both of you and inside Augustus too."

"A bit like when you rescued me, then? Is that why we are..." he tailed off.

"That's different. I liked you before that." She settled herself further into him.

"Oh," said Hugh, his throat going dry. "I ... erm ..." All he could think was *not now, not here!* He tried to adjust his position to make it less obvious.

"What do you mean?" she whispered into his ear, before pulling back with a wry smile on her face. "Look, I'm sorry for being a grouch earlier. I was just so worried, and I can't stand the idea of losing you."

Hugh swallowed.

"Nor I, you."

She was looking into his eyes.

"Now why don't you let me tend to those wounds?"

It was a long journey on the track that night. In more ways than one.

Chapter 17

Hugh awoke with a thin shaft of daylight streaming across his face. The trailer was still moving, swaying gently from side to side. Emily was asleep next to him, with Hugh's arm around her, softly snoring to herself. A muffled giggle told him that Barrington and Heather were also awake. All should have been good and fine with the world, yet there was something niggling at him in the pit of his stomach. He couldn't put his finger on it.

Emily had stopped snoring and was watching him with interest.

"Morning, you. What's wrong?" She kissed him lightly on the cheek, and he pulled her in closer.

"Morning. It's nothing really, just a feeling I can't shake off."

"Everything will be alright. You're just overthinking things as usual." She yawned and stretched.

"You say that, but there is definitely something there."

"Hugh, you just need to relax."

"No, *listen* ..."

Emily stopped talking and focussed onto what Hugh was hearing. It was so faint that it almost blended in with the background noise of the steam tractor, but the longer that they listened, the louder it became. It was a low drone, one only associated with that of an airship.

"There aren't any scheduled flights that come this way, are there?" asked Hugh.

"Not that I'm aware of, and I don't like the sound of those engines, they're far too close for comfort." They looked at each other, then made moves to clamber across to the compartment where Barrington and Heather were.

"Good morning, my fine friends," said Barrington.
He had a graze on his chin from his previous night's engagement with the ground. "What's wrong? You look worried about something."

"We are," said Hugh. "Be quiet and listen for a moment."

Though they were closer to the mechanism of the steam tractor, the sound of the airship passing overhead drowned out all other noise as it vibrated the surrounding partitions. The trailer slowed, eventually coming to a stop.

"What is it?" asked Heather, in a shaken voice.

"I don't know," said Hugh, "but I think the search area has been expanded."

They listened as the sound of the airship engines slowly came to a halt. They sat in fear, nobody wanting to speak, so they could hear what was happening in the outside world. They heard confused conversations between the driver and his guards.

"I don't care what they want, they ain't gettin' me cotton! They've taken me business, me home and me family from me. They can bugger off if they think they are gettin' all that I have left!"

"But, sir, what if they wish to search the trailer? We won't be able to stop 'em," said a guard.

"You ruddy well will! And that's an order!"

"Yessir!"

It turned out that the trailer they were in belonged to Stanley Weaver, one of Skellig-Krieg's largest cotton importers from the Old World. He'd had to leave his family behind, as it was only his heritage that was under suspicion.

The Weaver family were well known for their skills with cottons, and if myth were to be believed, the weaving of time itself. An amplified voice called out across the morning air.

"This is Major Rufus Volatus of the New World Air Corps. I am halting this convoy for an official search for traitors to the New World. Anyone refusing to cooperate will be viewed as conspiring with the enemy and, as such, will be treated as traitors of the New World."

"You ain't got no jurisdiction this side of the wall, *Volatus*," Stanley called out from his cart.

"Who said that? Make yourself known … Right, that's it!"

Hugh, Emily and Heather looked at Barrington.

"I didn't know," he said, looking as surprised as the rest of them. "I haven't seen that side of the family for years." Barrington stopped talking, as someone appeared above them like a head in the clouds, startling them all. It was Stanley.

"Will you lot keep quiet?"

"What? You knew we were here?" said Hugh.

"Of course, I knew you were here. I'm a weaver, we know everything. Besides, your attempt to get into the trailer last night was less than subtle, let alone what happened after that." He looked at them with raised eyebrows. "Now keep quiet and let me deal with this fella."

He disappeared back towards the front of the trailer. They all sat in silence as they listened to the unfolding scene outside.

People were sounding disgruntled with the progress of their journey being interrupted. There were protests from some, who called the actions unjust and a downright crime against the Old World. There were scuffles, and it sounded as though Stanley was standing up for people up the line. The sound of men approached the cart they were in.

"State your name and business."

"Stanley Weaver. I deal with cotton imports and weaving. I am heading to Dallum after being forcefully evicted by *your lot*!"

"Now, now, Mr Weaver. There's no need for that sort of tone. We are aware of your links to the Old World, but we've been lenient on you. We wouldn't want that to change now, *would we?*"

"You effin' bastards! You don't have the right to do this. I give you no right to search me trailer."

"We'll be the ones deciding that. Men, go about your business."

Hugh felt the trailer being rustled, as though someone had been pinned against it, then the sound of more scuffling. Stanley's guards were setting to their job.

"Call your men off *this instant!*" said Volatus.

"Never! I invoke the rule of the weft!"

The scuffling ceased at once. The sound of heavy breathing filled the silence.

"Men, arrest this man, that is an order."

Nothing happened.

"I said, arrest this man!"

"We can't, sir. He invoked the rule of the weft," said one of the New World guards warily.

"I don't care what bloody rule he invoked," said Rufus. "I want this man in custody. *Now!*"

Still, nobody moved.

"You see," said Stanley, "what you appear to be forgetting is that you have no jurisdiction here, and even if you did, the rule of the weft would still overrule your lacklustre powers! I invoke the rule of the weft for myself and the rest of my people in this convoy. Now would you respectfully let me go, and you can *bugger off!*" He spat the last words out.

The sound of cheering made its way down the line, as news of the latest turn of events moved through the people like a wave.

"You haven't heard the last of this, *Weaver!* We may not have control yet, but mark my words, the days of this fanciful world are ending. Men, back to the ship!"

The sound of the retreating men, was followed by the jeering crowd, throwing insults as they passed by. The sound of an airship starting up, followed by a low and threatening pass came through into the trailer. Hugh listened to the sound as the engines disappeared off into the distance. Stanley's head popped out above them once more.

"Well, are you coming out or not?"

They all headed up through the partitions towards the front of the trailer.

The whistle on the steam tractor blew, and the convoy restarted its journey, as Hugh and the other three sat on the bench seat next to Stanley.

He was a broad man, with a round face. He wore a suit and a long oilskin coat, and on his feet were wooden clogs. Hugh studied them with interest.

"You think it odd that I wear the shoes of me trade?" said Stanley.

"Erm... no, just curious, that all," said Hugh, embarrassed at being caught out.

"There's nothing to be ashamed of in a little curiosity. We don't wear the hobnailers like everyone else. The risk of sparks is too great near a weaving machine... KABOOM!" he shouted into Hugh's face, causing him to startle backwards and nearly fall off the trailer. "Sorry, my little joke." Hugh didn't find it funny, as Stanley laughed and slapped his thigh.

Positioned atop of his trailer on his high-backed padded seat, Stanley commanded a view across the entire line, and looked like the king of his own mini empire.

"There's food and water in the sack," he said, nodding to the hessian bag swinging behind his head. "I packed enough for all of us."

"Thank you," said Hugh, grateful for the help their protector was giving to them.

"It's alright. You ought to be more careful, there are lots of people looking for you, even this side of the wall. There's a price on all of your heads."

Hugh looked alarmed.

"It's alright, you can trust all these folk here. But just sayin' be careful, tha's all."

"Thanks, we will, and thank you for the heads up. How did you know we were in the back again?" asked Hugh, as he ripped off a hunk of bread and began eating it.

"Well, I'm a Weaver to start off with, and we Weavers have an attuned sense for that sort of thing. There was also the unsubtle way you tried to get onto me cart," he said, shaking his head. "I asked my men to check none of you were left behind, so I knew you were all in."

"Well, I don't really understand how you knew to expect us," said Hugh, "but we cannot thank you enough."

"No worries. I take it you are heading to Dallum? You're more than welcome to travel with me for the rest of the way."

"We are, and thank you, that would be most appreciated. What about your family, do you have any? Are they in danger now?"

"No, they're fine. I sent 'em ahead to me wife's parents. They should be safe and warm by now, well, as safe as they can be with everything that's going on. What you need to be doin' now is gettin' some rest. Oh, and take some of that food to your companions in the back. You have a long journey ahead of you, Hugh Geber."

Stanley gave him a wink.

Confused and tired, he climbed back to the others, who had made nests within the different compartments. The idea that he had caused unrest and put others in danger didn't sit very well with him.

He had a thousand questions running through his head, but the most important was how on earth did Stanley know his name. He confided his worries with Emily.

"There's a lot of things you will need to learn, Hugh, one of which is that we can trust the Weavers. We have a long-standing agreement with them, one which spans the centuries. It is said that they are the ones who not only weave the fine cloth, such as is found in this wagon, but it's also believed they weave the weft of the cloth of life itself.

"The law that he invoked back there wasn't born out of fantasy, it is a rule as old as the world itself. The Weavers have many powers, one of which is immunity in certain situations. Naturally, they have to abide by the laws of the land, but they can use the rule of the weft if they believe their world is being intruded on.

"The disrespect he was shown was enough to invoke the rule, especially as we are this side of the wall. Anyone can see that he is a man of high standing, just by the fact he has men and a steam tractor, not the standard horse and cart setup.

"We are in the Old World now, so Volatus has little power here. He doesn't have the power to search the wagons now he is away from Skellig-Krieg, though I fear the New World powers are going to push it as far as they can."

"But what happens if the rule of the weft is broken?" asked Hugh.

"Well, you heard how fearful the guards were of the rule? They were correct to be so. The Weavers have certain powers, which, once invoked, can alter certain people's journeys through life. That's not to say that they can alter the fabric of time or the end destination, but they can tweak certain elements. Life can become very hard for those who get on the wrong side of the Weavers."

"That sounds impossible."

Emily nodded.

"Yes, it does, but would you want to risk it? Most people are superstitious, including a lot of those in the New World. Old wives' tales which have been passed down through the generations still stand strong today."

"But I thought the New World shunned all things to do with the Old."

"Some do, but where do you think the old wives' tales come from? All the family lines can be traced back to the Old World, as that is where we are all from. Behind closed doors, the old tales are being spoken of once more, kept alive by those who feel trapped in a world of futurists, who just want power and domination."

"So why don't they stand up and fight?"

"Because the fear that's instilled within them is holding them back. Most people want to get on with life and live in peace. Standing up against the machine would mean war, and that doesn't sit well with the majority. That is what the New World powers rely on to keep hold of the reins of control. Of course, the Elf King would love nothing more than to see the New World destroy itself from within. It won't take much to ignite the powder keg, and that day is fast approaching."

"Things are moving at quite a pace."

"Yes, which is why we have to find the books of power before the Elf King or Smithson. If either side get hold of them, it would spell disaster. Listen, we need to rest, we have a long journey ahead of us, and last night was energetic for all of us." Emily yawned and looked over to Barrington and Heather, who were already fast asleep.

"I see what you mean," said Hugh, but when he turned to Emily, he saw that she, too, had drifted off. With nothing left to do, Hugh entered an uneasy dream world filled with airships, search parties, and then, unexpectedly, his father.

—

The Elf King hid in a cart full of lumber with his servant. It wasn't the most pleasant of journeys, but at least they were heading in the right direction. He had panicked when the cart slowed to a stop, and an inspection was ordered. Luckily, their driver stowed them away in a hidden compartment, and they could remain undiscovered.

By the end of the next day, they would be back in Dallum and reunited with his loyal supporters. It was there he would make his plans.

It was there he would begin his come back to regain the power he so rightfully deserved.

Chapter 18

It had been a long night's travelling from Skellig-Krieg, and Smithson was tired and fed up. Their procession through the Old World was moving at too slow a pace for his liking, so when the offer came up for a faster ride, he jumped at the chance.

The owner of the cart he was in had a cousin who was transporting horses to Dallum, and he needed some help in keeping them under control. Smithson quickly offered his services, the cart owner glad to be rid of his grumpy cargo.

Smithson knew he could get himself booked in at the local hotel before heading to view his package when it arrived. It was early morning when they set off, and by lunch they were safely at their destination.

It was a crisp day, with the fresh snow on the ground crunching under Smithson's feet as he walked up to the entrance of the Alpine Hotel. Few people had trodden the path to this door. A fire was roaring away in the open fireplace, filling the air in the lobby with the heavy scent of woodsmoke.

Smithson marched up to the counter and, seeing that there was nobody there, rang the service bell. He waited, then rang the bell again. Still no answer came, so he impatiently rang the bell continually, until eventually someone came to serve him.

"Alright, alright, *alright!* You'll wear me bell out doing that," said Eric, the owner of the Alpine Hotel, as he slid the bell from Smithson's reach.

"About time," Smithson said under his breath.

"Less of that attitude, sir, or you will be forced to find accommodation elsewhere, and I assure you there's very little, given the current situation."

"I would like a room."

Eric stood looking at him, waiting for a further response.

"*Please.*"

"That's better. No excuse for bad manners, sir. Now, it's nine hundred dragoons for a room with facilities."

"*900 dragoons!* That's outrageous. I shall not be paying that, *hotelier.*"

"Then you shall have to find accommodation elsewhere, *sir.*"

Smithson chewed the inside of his cheeks, attempting to give Eric a good hard stare, but it turned out the Eric was a practiced foe in the art.

"*Fine*, I'll take a room ... *Please.*"

Eric smiled smugly in return.

"Now then, if we could start with your name."

"The name's Smithson, Robert J Smithson."

"Now there's a name I haven't heard in a while. Any relation to the Smithson family from Ranthina? Portis-Montis way, I believe?"

"What *are* you twittering about now? How are you aware of my family name?"

"We had a Mr Smithson stay with us a few years ago. Came to do some sightseeing at the falls I seem to recall. Don't worry, the bill's been cleared now, so there's no need to panic."

"That's alright. I wasn't," said Smithson, looking down his nose at Eric. "So, this is where my father stayed, was it?"

"Why yes, I was one of the last to see him alive. It was tragic to see a man cut down in his prime. If only I had known what was going to happen, then perhaps I could have prevented him from going out that day."

"Well, he's gone now, there's no need to trouble yourself over it."

"Show some respect for the poor man; he was your father after all.

Do you not feel any loss for him?"

"Let's just say that we had our differences, but they are settled now."

"Hmm," he frowned. "Well anyway, let me see which rooms are available."

Eric turned around to the full keyboard behind him, studying it carefully, whilst Smithson raised an eyebrow and tapped his foot impatiently.

"I hardly think that is necessary," he said, gesturing to the empty lobby.

"I tell you what, sir, why don't you let me do my job, and you can do yours!" Eric turned back to the keyboard, picked out a set, then returned to Smithson. "Here we go, room nine. Should be suitable. After all, it's where all you Portis-Montis folks like to stay."

"Who said I was from Portis-Montis?"

"You did, didn't you?"

"No, I believe it was you who mentioned the place."

"Are you not then?" Eric offered a sour smile.

Smithson glared at him.

"What do you mean Portis-Montis people like to stay there."

"Just that," said Eric, truculent now. "I get requests, that's all."

"Why?"

"I don't know. Maybe they're superstitious. Anyway, breakfast is served at seven, there's no dinner service on, so it'll have to be one of the fine establishments in town. May I recommend Mather's Wine House, a truly fine establishment if I say so myself."

"Suggest all the names you want," Smithson said. "I shall not be frequenting those sorts of ... *establishments*." Sneering, he walked off.

Eric watched as Smithson tutted at the out-of-order lift, then climbed the stairs to his floor.

"Hmph, suit yourself."

Chapter 19

The last of the carts rattled into Dallum late in the evening. The amount of traffic attempting to pass through the small town had caused a bottleneck, the result being a two-mile queue heading out of the town, along the river road from the low pass to Skellig-Krieg. A small tent city was taking shape on the plains along the Kings Road, which was already twice the size of the small town and still growing. Even though the hour was late, it was alive with music and people milling about, all looking for food and somewhere to lay their head for the night.

Stanley dropped Hugh, Barrington, Emily and Heather off at the edge of the encampment, saying that he had some urgent business to tend to, and he would no doubt see them along the road in the future, leaving the quartet to explore the new settlement.

"This is crazy," said Hugh, as they walked through the maze of tents. Food stalls and street entertainers had already set up shop, spotting the business potential of lots of people in one small area.

"They have been pouring out of Skellig-Krieg to here for the last month," said Emily. "Many people left before they were forcibly evicted. Each tent here represents at least one household that has left Skellig-Krieg. The old Skellig area has been decimated by the loss, and it's so quiet nowadays. I've not seen Ranny for weeks, and there are still some who will refuse to move, no doubt. Goodness only knows what fate awaits them ..." She tailed off, the sadness showing in her voice.

"Come on," said Barrington. "Let's see if we can find a bed for the night."

Having arrived on the last trailer in meant that all the good tents were taken, leaving only the ones on the outer edges, their outer skins flapping in the evening breeze, all rammed with the latecomers. Snow was falling heavily, so Hugh and Emily lit their firestones to keep them all warm.

"This is ridiculous," said Barrington. "We won't find anything out here. Let's head to the hotel. Maybe we can try our luck there. We can follow up on your father's letter whilst we're there, Hugh."

"But surely that'll be full too," said Heather.

"Never fear, my dear. I have a way with words. Besides, I don't think most people can afford the prices being charged there."

——

"... and I'm telling you that if you wish to book a room, you needed to be here earlier." Eric had come to the desk wearing a nightshirt, nightcap and slippers. He was not in the mood for latecomers.

"But we were delayed out on the track. Surely you have heard about the congestion trying to get in here?" said Hugh.

"Of course, I've heard about the hordes of unwanted visitors making a home on our beautiful plains. I've seen them with me own eyes. They've destroyed all the local habitat."

"Surely there is something you can do?" asked Barrington, who was getting desperate.

"No, nope, not at all."

"But—"

"*Right!* I've had enough of refugees trying to get a room for next to nothing, or for free. I have a business to run here, and I ain't gettin' much of that either, not with all you travellers scaring off the tourists.

You have pulled me out of my warm bed, ignored the sign on the door about booking times and have obviously struggled to find a bed for the night. This has happened every night for two weeks now, and I'm fed up with it. I'm going to have words with the nightwatchman about this."

"Eric, my dear fellow. We don't expect a room for free. We are loyal customers, willing to pay cold hard cash." Barrington pulled out a wad of krune notes, enough to match Eric's annual income and then some. The man's eyes lit up.

"Well, why didn't you say? That makes all the difference; however, there is a small fee of eighteen percent, plus admin fees, for exchanging krunes to dragoons."

"*Eighteen percent!* That's steep. I'll pay five percent and nothing more. Oh, and you can forget about the admin fee."

"It's eighteen percent, with fees, or *no room!*"

"Five, with no fees, or we walk."

Eric remained silent, staring at Barrington.

Barrington took in a deep breath and sighed.

"Right! Come on everyone, those tents are looking quite appealing to me now." He pocketed his money and walked away.

Hugh tried to plead to his friend's better nature.

"But Barrington, the room, the cold tents, the snow?"

"I refuse to do business with a crook!"

"Oi! I ain't no crook."

"At those prices, my friend, you most definitely are. Come on, we're taking our money elsewhere."

"There's nowhere else ..." Eric began but stopped when Barrington opened the door and began ushering the group out of the door.

"Wait!"

Eric ran out from behind the counter, running up to Hugh and dragging him back through the door by his arm.

"I've reconsidered the deal, and I think there may be enough movement to within the price to accept your offer."

"Well, if you unhand my friend here, then we'll consider it a done deal," said Barrington.

"Right you are," said Eric, finally conceding, holding out a hand to shake on the deal. Barrington grasped it, clamping his other hand over the top.

They all headed back to the desk, so Eric could check them in.

"So, are you paying for the account Mr ..."

"Delphin, Barrington Delphin."

"Ah, that's right. Are you planning on passing out today?" said Eric.

Barrington shot him a look, and he glanced down to the bookings list.

"Let me see what we have ... bit of a rush on at the moment ... lots of people waiting ..."

They all looked around the empty lobby, listening to Eric's voice echo off the wall, then turned back to the desk. Hugh rummaged in his bag and pulled out his father's letter and nudged Barrington.

"Ah, yes, you don't have the same room we had last time, do you? We like the view from there. Room nine if memory has it."

Eric looked down at the room lists.

"That rings a bell ... here we go, room nine. Ah yes bit of a name from the past, that one."

"What do you mean?"

"I have Robert Smithson staying there."

"Sorry? Robert E Smithson, who was here with my father?"

"Eh? No, not him. He's dead, *remember!* Cor, you ain't half forgetful. Nah, this is a Robert J Smithson. His son, apparently. Seems a bit of a prat if you ask me, but you get all kinds. You know him?"

"We do, and I don't want you talking to him about us," said Emily, stepping towards the desk.

Eric had a fearful look in his eye, and took a step back, remembering his last run in with her.

"No, no, of course. I wouldn't dream of doing such a thing, madam.

It's just that I assumed you may be acquainted somehow."

"Don't assume. Now please kindly sort the room out. We are tired and wish to go to bed."

Eric gulped and quickly scanned the list.

"I can get you two rooms next to each other, one floor up. One zero nine is the room above number nine, same view ..."he chuckled nervously.

"Well, that will have to do," said Barrington.

"Good, good," said Eric, turning to the board. "There's no rush to check out, but how long do you think you will be here for?"

"Unsure as yet, we have a few jobs to sort out before we leave town."

"Alright, well, just keep me posted. Here are your keys. You can settle the bill when you vacate the rooms."

Barrington tipped his head to Eric, and the four of them started their trek up the staircase. They reached their floor and walked the short distance to their rooms. On opening the doors, they discovered they were both doubles.

"I could go down and asked Eric for two singles," said Barrington. "Or you two can share one, and myself and Hugh the other?"

"No, I don't think we want to encounter him again," said Emily. "Hugh and I will take this room. You and Heather can have the other."

Hugh and Barrington stood open-mouthed.

"Oh, come on, get over it. You're both grown men, I'm sure you can manage without each other for a night or two." She grabbed Hugh by the hand, and Heather gave him a wink as she took Barrington off to the adjoining room. As soon as the door was closed, Emily rounded on Hugh.

"Right, to the bed, now."

Hugh couldn't believe his luck. Emily tutted.

"No, not for that. We have some learning that we must do."

"But I thought you said you were tired?"

"I only said that to get us moving from the lobby. We don't want to get caught by Smithson. I'm not tired, and I'm guessing you aren't either."

Hugh had to admit, his adrenalin was pumping.

"Alright, so what are we going to learn?"

"The sight, of course. You need bringing up to speed if you are to gain control over it."

She went to the bathroom and returned with two glasses of water.

"What are they for?"

"Lesson one. You need to be close to, or better, have contact with, water to enter the sight. I take it Augustus had something similar for you to use?"

"Well, *he* did, certainly."

"What do you mean, *he* did? You can't enter the sight without the use of water, well, not humans anyway."

"Well, that's just it. He put a foot into a bucket of water, and I just sort of fell in."

"Fell into the bucket?"

"No, fell into the sight."

"But that's ridiculous, you can't just fall in like that?"

"That's how it happened, but I don't know why? Augustus seems to think it has something to do with when I fell in Portis-Montis?"

"Well, I have heard of people's abilities being unlocked after a knock to the head. Your family history would point to you being able to access the sight. Alfred certainly helped me with my training. Tell me, when you were unconscious, did you hear or see anything?"

"It was dark and cold, and I kept hearing my father, but I couldn't see him. Then there was the time I saw Augustus on the airship. He was talking to me from within the sight, but I could see him on the airship."

"Wait, you actually saw him? An exo-transitional apparition? That takes many months of training to see one."

"A what?"

"An exo-transitional apparition, ETA for short. It's where you can deliver a message, via the sight, to someone who is skilled enough to see you. Was he in full form, or just a hazy outline?"

"He looked solid, if that's what you mean."

"Hmm, you are a curious one."

"How come?"

"I, for one, have never heard of anyone progressing so fast, so early on, without training. I suppose you were up in the clouds, therefore near a lot of water, but that doesn't explain how you entered with Augustus at the marsh?"

"Maybe the water content in the air? The cottage is in the middle of a marsh after all."

"Possibly, but to just *fall in?* It makes little sense."

"Why don't you try it now?"

Emily mulled the idea over in her head, before heading over to the bed. "Fine, sit opposite me, cross-legged. I'm going to enter, and we can see what happens."

She seemed very sceptical about the idea as she and Hugh set up on the bed. She placed a glass between them, then dipped her finger in. She emitted a glow, that seemed to light up the room. Hugh felt himself being drawn to it and then ...

–POP–

'Emily?' he said into the emptiness.

It seemed partially brighter than the last time he was here.

'I'm here,' said a shocked voice from behind him.

He mentally turned himself around, expecting to see a white light as before, yet this time, he could make out the outline of Emily, the firestone glowing on her chest.

'I can't believe you are, too. And look at our firestones.' Hugh looked down to see his own firestone was also lit up. *'Are you sure that you haven't been shown how to do this? Your finger is not in the water?'*

'Nope, I just kind of followed you in here.'

'*And you didn't take time to clear your head beforehand?*'

'*Nope, I just fell in.*'

'*Wow! And your form, it's, well, it's coming on. I can see your outline.*'

'*Yes, and I can see yours. Is that normal?*'

'*Yes, it's normal to see outlines, but that's level two stuff. Mine would be stronger if I had more training. I can't believe you can do all of this without any practice.*'

'*Why is it so cold here?*'

'*That's a worrying sign, one you should take heed of. Your life-link is unprotected, meaning any wandering spirit can take over your body. Hang on …*'

Hugh watched as Emily's outline drew symbols in the air which floated off towards a white line connected to him. As they made contact, Hugh felt himself warm up.

'*That's amazing. How do I do that?*'

'*It'll take time to learn how to protect your life-link, but I can show you as my mother taught me. May I?*'

'*By all means.*'

She reached out to him, and Hugh felt a tingle in the centre of where his body should be. Images began flashing in his vision, and he could see many runes floating around, some of which he didn't recognise. Emily's knowledge was flowing into Hugh at an incredible rate.

'*You must learn the runes, learn them until you know them off by heart. This is what you should have learned before you stepped in here for the first time*'

'*I didn't have any control over that I'm afraid, given that it first happened when I banged my head in Portis-Montis. I guess I fell in then too. Then it happened again when we were at the waterfall.*'

'*Interesting. You must learn how to gain control over it, at least until you have mastered the runes,*' said Emily.

It sounded as though she was inside of him.

'*That's because I am inside of you. I can see where you helped Heather, and we can use this to our advantage. You both now share a part of each other, which cannot be undone. I can also see a bit of Augustus in you and that you've been here more than once with him.*'

'*Yes, but I didn't know the first time, did I? He came to visit me in the airship. I was still present there when he just turned up.*'

'*You say you saw him in full form?*'

'*Yes, why?*'

'*Was there anything to say that he wasn't there in person?*'

Hugh cast his mind back to the night in question, sensing that Emily was watching. He was there on the airship, about to have a drink, when Augustus seemed to just appear beside him, before taking a seat. He remembered looking out of the window at the moonlit clouds and the reflection of the empty chairs.

'*That's it,*' said Emily.

'*What?*'

'*Look carefully, and you'll see that the chairs are empty in the reflection, yet when you look at Augustus, he is clearly sitting down.*'

'*Wow, I never realised that.*'

'*Oh, well, it just makes your case more curious by the second. You shouldn't be able to see full forms for some time yet.*'

'*But I can see your outline.*'

'*Yes, you said. Right, that should do it.*'

Emily finished casting her runes, and Hugh sensed her leaving his energy. He looked back, seeing that his life-link shimmered and swirled with golden runes.

'Alright, I need you to focus on the part that Heather left behind, and what I have just passed onto you. See the runes and learn them. You will have access to them, both in the sight and in the world plane.'

Hugh searched inside himself, trying to find the part of Heather that had latched onto his soul. As he searched, he sensed parts of Emily there, too.

'Yes, I'm there, and always will be. In fact, I have been with you since I rescued you after your run in with the Elf King.'

Hugh could have sworn that he felt Emily's embarrassment. He looked deeper into himself and found what he was looking for. Numerous runes were now filling his vision, and he realised he could follow them, read them and understand them.

He had learnt the basic runes and their uses from his father and from his extra lessons with Hamish when he was younger. He had wanted to question his father about them in further detail before he left on the trip with Smithson's father. There were also some runes there which he didn't recognise.

'She is a great master of the runes, that's for sure,' said Emily. *'Hamish has taught her well. I think it's time we left this place and headed home. It's doesn't do well to hang around here. There are too many malevolent spirits lurking in the shadows.'*

It was then that Hugh heard it once more. His father's voice calling to him across the darkness of the plane.

Hugh, Hugh, is that you?

'Father?'

'Hugh, we have to go, now!'

He saw that Emily now had the outline of a great unicorn stood next to her.

'Erm, Emily, what's that?'

'Not now, Hugh!'

He sensed her pulling him back to his body, away from his father.

–POP–

Hugh opened his eyes, he was back on the bed facing Emily, who was strangely out of breath.

"What happened? Why did you pull me out of there, and why was there a unicorn standing next to you?" There were so many questions now filling Hugh's head that he didn't know where to begin.

"First, I'm amazed at what you have been able to achieve, especially without any training. Second, we had to get out of there before we lost the connection with our life-links. It takes a lot of control to not lose your way in the sight."

"But what about the runes protecting them?"

"They require constant maintenance, Hugh. It's not something that sustains itself, which is why it's imperative that you learn the runes that you see inside your soul. I don't have the power yet to cover the both of us. I am amazed at how much information you have retained from linking with Augustus and Heather. If you learn to harness the power of them, along with my own which also resides within you, then you will have no trouble stepping in and out of the sight."

"But what about my father, did you not hear him?"

"Yes, I did, but then Aeolus showed up."

"The unicorn?"

"Yes, he is my spirit guide, and protector. He normally turns up in my time of need in this plane and in the sight."

"Do I get one of those?"

"In time, you will, but you are new to this. It takes time for you to find your spirit guide. There will be a time when you come together, but when that time will come, we cannot predict. Only you will know when it has happened, for it's a very personal thing."

There was a loud bang from the room below. Hugh assumed Smithson had returned in one of his foul moods. He put this to one side, as he wanted to know why the unicorn had appeared next to Emily.

"So why did your guide turn up, then? I really don't understand why I couldn't look for my father?"

"There was something about your father's voice, Hugh, something that even spooked Aeolus," said Emily, her gaze coming back from the floor below. "I urge you not to seek whatever that is. I believe it could something trying to mislead you. Aeolus would only come to me like that if the situation was dangerous."

Hugh sat in silence. He didn't want to believe that the sound of his father was actually something more sinister.

"Hugh, please, give me your word."

He looked up, to meet Emily's eyes.

"I promise, never to go looking for the source of my father's voice."

Inside, he sought the part of Emily, called all of his will to block her out briefly, before promising to himself that he would never give in, no matter what anyone else thought.

Chapter 20

Smithson was lying in bed. The sound of footsteps and muffled voices of the people talking in the room above had woken him up. The breeze flowing in from the ornate air vent in the ceiling had left the room extremely chilly, and he had gone to bed fully dressed, pulling the covers tight up to his chin.

Daring to bring an arm out into the cold, Smithson checked his Ever-Right pocket watch, which told him the hour was just past two AM. Just as he was considering making a complaint or heading upstairs to give the offending parties a piece of his mind, they had quietened down. He huffed irritably, as he thought over the day's events in his mind.

After waiting all day, checking the many carts that came trundling into town, he had no luck in re-locating Collins and his apprentice, and half wondered if the two of them had deserted their posts. The pair should have returned after delivering his message, so naturally, Smithson had expected them to arrive with the evening's carriages.

As he lay there with his thoughts, a note was posted under his door. He quickly jumped out of his bed, the chill of the room hitting him full on as he headed for the door but tripped on his way over. He landed head first into the frame, nearly concussing himself in the process, before landing heavily on the floor, cursing the loose board. Picking up the note and standing once more, Smithson made his way back to the bed to read the mystery message, when something caught his eye.

The loose floorboard had remained dislodged, and something glinted in the light. He lifted the board, then pulled out what appeared to be a box covered in runes. His eyes must have been deceiving him, as he could have sworn they shimmered and moved of their own accord. He realised it had something to do with the Old World. Smithson knew his knowledge on the subject was limited, but he could recognise runes when he saw them.

He took the box and the note over to the bed, feeling dirty being in proximity to some dusty box from the Old World. Even so, there was something drawing him in, begging him to open it. He looked closely at the runes, running his fingers around them.

A closer inspection of the underneath revealed a symbol that was strangely familiar to him, but he was unsure what this was. It took him back to his school days and the extra lessons he had had on runes. His father had insisted that he take the subject, saying that it may come in useful down the line. Smithson detested the subject, always falling out with the teacher.

"Ye have to remember the runes and symbols, laddie," the old lecturer would tell him.

"But I can't."

"Can't means won't, and I *won't* have this in my class. Is there anyone else who can help young Mr Smithson out here? Aye, Hugh."

"It's the old symbol for fire, sir."

"That's correct, laddie. Well done. Ye want to learn from Hugh, young Robert. These symbols are important."

Smithson had looked at the desk, which stood in front of a blackboard full of symbols from the Old World. He despised them. None of the symbols were in use except the one with a question mark next to it –

the *missing element*.

That was the only one which appeared on the centre of the compass in the atrium at the university, and that was only there at the insistence of the then head librarian, when the university was built. The teacher had told the class that the other 'New World' symbols between the cardinal points were another nail in the coffin of the old ways.

"Are ye even listening to me, laddie?"

He had drifted off into another daydream.

"*Yes*, I'm listening, *sir*. I hate those symbols, and I hate this class."

"I beg yer pardon, laddie?"

"I'm sorry, are you deaf?" There was an audible gasp from the rest of the students.

"Out, *now!*"

"Gladly!"

Hugh had leaned back in his chair, and Smithson had seethed at the way he had shown him up. He had slammed his book to the floor, grabbed his bag and stormed out of the room.

He was back in the room in Dallum, sitting on the bed, the hatred for Hugh still fresh in his mind. He had dropped the box on the floor, which had left a sizable dent in the board where it had landed, but the box was remarkably strong and still in one piece. Smithson picked it up and studied it once more. There was no obvious way to get into the box, and it seemed locked shut. Putting it to one side, he read the note.

Hmm ...

Then he remembered something and picked up the box again, casting his mind back to the classroom, back to the teacher's desk.

"That's it!"

Smithson placed the box the bed and made himself presentable. Then he grabbed the note and the box and headed out into the corridor, slamming the door behind him. He was about to go when he realised he had left the key on his nightstand. Cursing himself, he left a note at

reception, before heading out into the cold night air. The key would
have to wait for his return.

Chapter 21

It was long after breakfast and Hugh, Barrington, Emily and Heather were currently in room one zero nine of the Alpine Hotel. They were attempting to figure out how to gain access to the room below and were planning their next move.

"It's obvious that we need to get into that room," said Barrington. "The question is how."

"We can go through the door," said Hugh. "We just need someone to look out whilst we are in there."

"And the lock? How were you planning to get past that? Or were you thinking the heavy-handed approach, and then we make a run for it?" said Barrington, cracking his knuckles.

Emily shook her head.

"I don't think there will be a need for that approach. We don't wish to get caught in the act."

"I can pick locks," said Heather, pulling out a set of picks from her pocket. Everyone turned to look at her.

"What? I had a lot of free time as a kid, so I put it to good use. Unless yese have a better idea?"

"Where are you keeping all these items?" said Barrington, who took a step back to look at her.

Hugh had to agree that he too couldn't fathom how she fitted the picks into such a small pocket.

"I have bottomless pockets," she said, shaking her long coat. They heard clunking and rattling, followed by a large clatter. She looked into the pocket. "Damn it, that was the socket set. So, do ye want to try picking the lock, or not?"

"It's certainly worth a shot," said Hugh.

"Failing that, I can always use wee Jimmy."

"Who's Jimmy?" asked Heather.

"Not who, but what ..."

She dug deep, ferreting around for something, then pulled out a jimmy bar.

"That would do it," said Barrington, rubbing his hands together.

Emily huffed, but with no other objections, they headed out of the door. Five minutes later, with Emily and Barrington and Hugh on lookout, Heather set to work on the door. She knocked, calling out, "Room service ..."

With no answer from the room, Hugh came to stand behind her, and they presumed it safe to crack on. Heather pulled out her tools for the job but seemed to get nowhere fast.

"How are you getting on?" he asked in a harsh whisper, clearly nervous.

"Not bad, but I'm a wee bit rusty, and it appears there is more to these locks than just ... the ... key ... mechanism," Heather replied in a low whisper.

Barrington came to see what was taking so long.

"Come on, we don't have all day."

"It's nae use, I cannae do it."

"Pass me that jimmy bar," said Barrington, now sizing up the door.

Heather passed it to him, and he attempted to pry at the edge of the door, which creaked under the pressure.

"Good morning, having a party, are we? I didn't expect to find you on this floor today." said Eric, making them all jump. "If you are looking for Mr Smithson, I believe he's gone out for the day. He was out before breakfast. He left a note saying that he would be back later on and something about leaving his key in the room. Anyway, it's best not to loiter in the corridors. It makes the other guests suspicious, thinking you are up to no good."

"The key's in the room, is it?" said Barrington.

"Yes, but nothing for you to worry about."

"Oh no, of course not." He was now edging away from the door with his hands behind his back.

"What are you hiding?"

"Erm ... nothing?"

"Yes, you are, and you were just fiddling with that door. Show me your hands, where I can see them." Barrington swallowed hard and moved uneasily on the spot.

He slowly raised his hands, revealing them to be empty. He smiled and shrugged. "You two, hands up."

Hugh and Heather raised their hands, revealing nothing.

"Well, if you would excuse me, I've just remembered, got to get something from my room," said Barrington, dashing off. If Hugh wasn't mistaken, his friend appeared to have grown a metal tail, which bounced as he walked. Heather had also spotted this and distracted Eric.

"Oh, would ye believe it, I appear to have also left me ... overcoat in me room ..."

"And what's wrong with the one you are wearing?" said Eric with raised eyebrows.

"Erm ... disna go with me shoes, silly!" and she shuffled sideways, smiling, before darting back down the corridor and up the stairs, leaving Hugh to deal with Eric. He let out a nervous chuckle.

"And you, Mr Geber?"

"Would you believe it? I think I left my bag on the bed."

"Hmm, a likely story,"

Eric ushered him back to the stairwell.

"Oh, and what luck. Here's your last friend, conveniently arriving at the right time. You'd best give Mr Geber a hand. He appears to have left his bag in his room. It might be wise for you all to go for a walk; you wouldn't want to miss the day."

"What a lovely idea. Come on Emily, *let's get my bag*."

They walked calmly up the stairs, Hugh waiting until they were out of earshot of the hotelier, before turning to Emily.

"You were supposed to be keeping watch!"

"I was, but Eric must have been using a service corridor or something because he didn't pass me. Come on, let's get back to the room."

Back in room one zero nine, Hugh sat and flopped back onto the bed, deflated.

"Well, that's it then. We will not get into that room, and we can't carry out my father's wishes."

"Now come on," said Barrington, "let's not get so down in the dumps about all of this. We just need to find another way to get in there and be out quickly without being caught."

"But there is no other way."

"Once again, you are wrong, my friend." He pulled out the jimmy bar and dropped to the floor, prying the boards up.

"What are you doing now?" said Emily.

"Well, if I'm not mistaken, the rooms here are laid out in a similar fashion," he said, pointing up to the air grill in the ceiling. "The grills line up with the gaps in the floor, which lead to air bricks, I think." He lifted the plank he was working on, then smiled with glee. Hugh saw an opening into the room below.

The patterned grill was caked with years of dust, but as Barrington cleared it off, he saw it was only held in with catches. Barrington poked his fingers through the tight holes, released them and gave the vent a wiggle. Nothing happened. He tried again, and this time, the grill came off, sending dust upwards into his face, with the rest falling into the room. He carefully turned and lifted the grill up through the hole.

"Ta-da!" Everyone looked at him, with blank faces. "Well, don't all thank me at once."

"For what?" said Emily. "You've destroyed a hotel floor and left a mess in the room below."

"Now, now Emily, no need to join Hugh on the bench of negativity." Hugh sat up and scowled at him. "No, the important bit is what's down there in the room."

They all gathered around the hole, joining Barrington. Hugh peered down into the room, the smell of eau de Smithson wafting on the air. He scanned the room, trying to see what his friend was so excited about.

Then he saw it.

"The key!"

"Correct, my dear friend. The question is, how do we get it?"

The keyring with the room number on it was resting tantalisingly on the nightstand and attached to it was the room key, which dangled off the edge.

"I may have something," said Heather, reaching once again into her pocket. She pulled out a ball of string and a magnet, which she tied to the loose end of the string. She then lowered it into the room and began swinging it. With each pass, she let out a little more string, until it came within reach of the nightstand.

"Just a wee bit more…"

She let out a little more string, and the magnet brushed the keyring. It momentarily grabbed a hold of the keyring, pulled it off the nightstand, and the key dropped to the floor with a '*THUNK*'. Heather slapped a hand to her forehead.

"I can do this," she said, letting out more string.

Hugh noticed the end was coming up fast, but before he could say anything, it passed through Heathers fingers.

"No!"

Emily muttered something, and everything seemed to slow down apart from Emily's hand, which seemed to move ever so slightly faster. They all watched as she snatched the end of the string in time. Time resumed its normal pace, with everyone letting out a communal sigh. The magnet lay still on the floor, but as Emily pulled it up to swing, it was clear to all there was just not enough to reach the key, with the arc of the swing coming up too short. Emily relaxed her arm back down through the hole, and the magnet dropped to the floor. She seemed to stare vacantly at it.

"What's wrong? Are you not going to pull it back up?"

"No, I have a better idea."

She flicked the string, which made the magnet jump across the floor. The others realised what she was doing and began encouraging her. With each flick, she moved closer to the key, but she was now working blind, as she needed as much arm length as the tight hole would offer. After each attempt, she carefully pulled back the magnet back up, seeing if she was anywhere near the mark.

Ten minutes later, Emily was ready to give up, but with one last flick of the string, a metallic clink was heard. Tentatively, she pulled up from the hole and they all peered through the hole. There on the magnet, was the key, stuck firm. Emily pulled it up and sat back, leaning on the bed, rubbing her arm.

"That's amazing!" said Heather, removing the key and dropping the magnet with string still attached into her bottomless pocket.

"Thanks, I didn't think I was going to do it."

Barrington was busy replacing the grate so he could re-lay the floorboard. "I say we get in there right away."

"Hang on there, Barrington," said Emily. "We need to plan this better. I say Heather and I stay on lookout. I can watch from up here in case Smithson comes back, and Heather can wait on the stairs, looking out for Eric. We can whistle to warn you, agreed?"

They all nodded.

"Good, we can leave the floorboard up for now, so you can hear my whistle."

Moments later, Hugh and Barrington were back in the corridor, one floor down. Hugh was tingling with nervous tension. With his hand slightly shaking, he slotted the key into the lock, and twisted. They opened the door and crept into the room. It felt odd to be in the lion's den, and they didn't want to hang around. They started tapping the floor with the feet to find the loose floorboard. Hugh found it and dropped to his knees, with Barrington beside him.

"Ready?"

"After you, my friend." Hugh lifted the floorboard with the anticipation rising within him. He sat staring blankly into the empty void. "Well? Where is it?"

"I don't know. The letter definitely said to look under the floorboard, and this must be it."

Hugh reached right into the hole, attempting to see if he could feel anything further in. Still nothing. A whistle sounded from the corridor.

"Quick, that was Heather, Eric is on the way."

"But it has to be here."

"I know Hugh, but alas, it appears not. *Come on*, we need to hurry or risk getting caught."

"You go ahead," said Hugh, "I'll be right behind you."

"I really think you should come now."

"*No*, I just want to check something else first."

Heather whistled again.

"Fine, just don't get caught."

Barrington stood up, and, with a quick glance back at Hugh, ran out of the room. Hugh started frantically searching the room, lifting the mattresses on the beds, looking behind the curtains, under the duvets, but it was no use. He heard another whistle, then heard footsteps in the room above.

"*What are you doing? Get out of there now!*" hissed Emily, but it was too late.

He could hear Eric walking down the corridor, talking to Heather and Barrington, who failed to put the man off the scent. Hugh panicked, unable to find a decent hiding place. He dived behind one of the floor-to-ceiling curtains at the last moment, and held his breath as Eric entered the room, who saw the open floorboard, then the still moving curtain.

"I've gotcha now ..." said Eric, marching up to the curtain. Hugh panicked. He was done for. He had to get of the situation, fast.

−POP−

"What the ...? Where are you then?" said Eric, and flapped the curtains around, making sure Hugh wasn't hiding on either side of the window. A cough from behind Eric made him jump out of his skin.

"May I enquire as to why you are here in Mr Smithson's room?"

Collins had entered through the open door behind the hotelier, blocking his exit.

"I was, well, just, housekeeping." He plastered an over-egged smile across his face.

"What, by lifting the floorboards and flapping the curtains around? You're doing a poor job." He gestured to the dust on the bed and floor, which had fallen from the vent. "Anyway, if you are housekeeping, where is your cleaning apparatus? You should at least be wearing a tabard and holding a duster. You know what I think? I think you were searching for something."

"Erm ..."

"I'm sure Mr Smithson would be very interested to hear that you were snooping around his room."

Collins turned on his heel and headed back down the corridor, with Eric following quickly after him, begging the man to reconsider his decision.

–POP–

Hugh was back in the room, unsure of what had just happened, the sound of Eric's pleading fading off into the background. Refusing to give up hope, Hugh carried on his search.

"*Psst ...*"

Hugh looked up. Emily was looking down at him from above.

"Heather's watching Eric, he's outside. Hurry up!"

"It's not here? I just can't find it."

"What do you mean, it's not there?"

"I mean, whatever I'm looking for has gone. The hole is empty!"

"Well, have you tried looking harder? Get a move on ..." she tailed off. "He's coming back, *run!*"

Hugh dropped the floorboard back into place, and bolted down the carpeted hallway. As he made it to the stairs, he heard Eric making his way across the lobby, out of breath and chuntering to himself. Hugh ran up the stairs, three at a time, tripping at the top. He heard Eric tail off and figured he must have headed back to the room. Hugh made it back to the open doorway where hands reached out and dragged him in, the door slamming shut behind them.

"Eric's downstairs, he's livid. He's searching all over the place for you now," said Emily. She and Heather were looking down through the grate.

"He's left the room," said Heather, looking up from the hole in the floor.

"Quick, open the curtains, put that floorboard back. You, in there, get into the shower," said Barrington, shoving Hugh into the bathroom.

Hugh, unsure of why Barrington wanted him to wash, rushed to get undressed, getting tangled in his sleeves and trouser legs, before stumbling into the shower. He turned it on, letting out a yelp and a howl as the shower went from ice cold, to piping hot, before levelling out.

The door opened. "Will you keep the noise down in there," said Barrington, then slammed it shut again.

Hugh calmed himself down before hearing someone knock on the door to their room. There came the sound of muffled voices, as Hugh tried to wash himself down. He was glad for the chance to get clean, given that he'd not washed since arriving in Dallum.

The water stung, as it ran over the many cuts and grazes he had gained over the past few days. He stepped out of the shower, wiped the mirror down and gasped. He was clean, which was good, but looked as though he had been in a fight with a bull – and lost. He wrapped himself in a towel and went to face the aggressor in the room.

"… and I'm telling you, I know that there is something underhand going on around here. I don't believe your cock and bull story … ah, here he is. The man of the moment. Would you mind telling me what sort of racket you and your friends are trying to pull here?"

Hugh looked at him nonchalantly.

"I don't know what you're talking about."

"Don't play that game with me, *sonny,*" he said, pointing a bony finger into Hugh's damp chest. "You and your gang here are up to something. I know you were in that room. How did you get out, where did you hide?"

"Hiding from whom? I don't have the faintest idea what you're talking about, as I've just returned from being outside."

"Oh, have you now? Well, if that's the case, you won't mind confirming for me what your friends say you were doing?"

Barrington stood behind Eric, mouthing run, and tried to imitate someone running. He ceased immediately, when the hotelier spun around to glare at him. He ran his hand through his hair and smiled at Eric, who returned his piercing gaze to Hugh. Barrington mouthed, *run* repeatedly behind Eric.

"I was partaking in some, *exercise* …?"

Barrington willed his friend on. He was now jogging on the spot, until Eric spun round, and he attempted to lean nonchalantly on the wall behind him and stretch out.

Eric rounded back onto Hugh, and Barrington resumed his

running motions.

"What are you up to?"

"Nothing, honestly. I have just returned from a … from a …" His forehead furrowed, as he attempted to decipher what his friend was doing. "Oh … a run! That's what I was doing. I went out for a … *run?* Of course, silly me."

"A run, *A RUN?* What the bloody hell is a run?"

"You know, quicker than walking, slower than sprinting?"

"I know what running is. Why were you running, who was chasing you?" He looked at Hugh as though he had him cornered.

"I was doing it for, erm, fun, you know, exercise. It's all the rage in the New World, don't you know?" He waggled his finger in an authoritative I-know-better-than-you kind of manner.

"*Running? For fun?* You're weird, all of you. Where did you get these injuries?" he said, taking in Hugh's battered body. "Sure you haven't been *running* headlong into any doors?"

"I got these from the journey getting here. I took a fall, climbing up onto a wagon."

"And a ladder, don't forget that," said Heather, stifling a snigger. Eric turned to her.

"You think this is funny, missy?"

"Excuse me, you leave her alone." Barrington stepped in between Eric and Heather. The hotelier's eyes followed all the way up his great frame, to the point he had to crane his neck to meet Barrington's gaze. He spun back to Hugh.

"I will find out what you are up to, and when I do, I'll be the one with a smile on my face, just you mark my words!"

DING … DING … dingdingdingdingdingding.

"*Where are you Hotelier? I want a word with you. HOTELIER!*" said the booming voice of an irate Smithson.

213

Eric rolled his eyes. "Oh, for the love of all things spritely! That bloody man!" he said as he turned and left the room.

Hugh went to shut the door, but Barrington stopped him, holding up a finger. They all listened keenly, to the stammering Eric, trying to explain why he was in Smithson's room.

"*... And I'm telling you, that bell will wear out if you keep doing that. I've had enough trouble from your friends.*"

"*What friends? I didn't come with any friends?*"

"*Well, no, but Mr Geber—*"

"*Geber! You told them I was here, didn't you?*"

"*No, well yes, but not like that.*"

"*Where are they?*"

"*Well, Mr Geber was out for a run—*"

"*A run? What the hell is that?*"

"*Well, you should know. It's all the rage in the New World. Anyway, I caught them by your door earlier.*"

"*I will not stand for this breach in security. How dare you let them into my room!*"

"*I did no such thing! In fact, I nearly caught him on several occasions, but—*"

"*And you failed to tell me? Collins, come with me. You stay here. We're leaving, immediately. I don't want to hear another word from you until I have vacated my room, which I shall not be paying for!*"

Barrington shut the door, leaving Eric to his pleading, then turned to look at Hugh.

"So ..."

"So, what?" said Hugh.

"Well, the last time I knew, you couldn't do magic."

"And that is still the case."

"Then may I enquire where you disappeared to, when you were in the room below?"

"I was there. I mean, I slipped into the sight by accident, but my body was there still, wasn't it?"

"My dear friend, you were not in that room. We all saw it with our own eyes."

"Hugh, if what you are saying is true, then you achieved something quite miraculous," said Emily. "Not only that, it was a dangerous move to pull."

"I don't know what you mean. I was hiding behind the curtain, that's why you didn't see me."

"I'm saying that you not only entered the sight, but you also took your entire body in with you. Eric looked behind the curtain, and you were neither there nor anywhere within the room. You should not be entering the sight unaided and certainly not attempting a full-body cross over alone. You never mentioned entering full body to me."

"But I didn't enter the sight on purpose, it just happened. And I certainly didn't intend for my whole body to come with me."

"You must learn to control this, otherwise—"

Emily was cut off by the sound of the door in the room below. Smithson was back.

"Quick, to the floorboard. Emily, close *the curtains again*. We don't want any light to show through the hole." Emily did as Barrington asked, making it back to the hole in the floor just in time to see Smithson return to his room with Collins.

"Useless oaf of a man. Letting Geber get so close to my things … what on earth is all this dust doing here on the floor?"

"Like I said before, sir, I caught the hotelier in the room with the floorboard up. I can't be certain, but it looked like he was looking for something. Then he started blithering on about Geber and his cronies."

"I want to know how on earth they are here in Dallum, and why they were permitted to enter the hotel. It should be guests only. This is all your fault, Collins."

"And how did sir come to that conclusion?"

"You let them escape, again."

"I delivered the message. I had no control over any events that occurred after that point. We had to get back onto the road to catch up with you."

"Where is your shadow, anyway?"

"I gave him the afternoon off to explore the tents. He's quite fascinated with all the different people milling around."

"Well, I would prefer to be out there, than be stuck in this ... hovel any longer. That hotelier is sniffing around, and he will ruin my plans if we are not careful."

"I totally agree with you on that point. If you were to ask me, sir, I would say that he was definitely up to no good and just using Geber as a ruse. He was most flustered when I discovered him, and there was no way that Geber could have escaped past me."

"Hmm, that's a very interesting take on things. Well, I have a feeling that he may have been looking for *this*. You may look at it, but remember who it belongs to. I tried to open it, but it's locked shut."

"May I ask where you found this?" Collins asked.

"Under that floorboard."

"Exactly where I found that hotelier sniffing around. So this is what he was after, was it?" Collins looked in awe at the box. "This is exquisite work, sir, carved by the finest hands. I would dare to go as far to say, it's a relic from the Old World, maybe the work of elves."

Smithson shuddered at the use of the words.

"I'd remind you not to use those filthy words in front of me!"

"Yes, *sir!*" Collins sneered back. He went back to the box, studying it closely.

"I dare say the hotelier uses these rooms to hide many things and ... What are you looking at now, man?"

"Oh, nothing, just some of these carvings seem familiar to me, that's all." He was studying one on the underside.

"Well, of course, that one is from the centre of the compass at the university. I don't know about the one on top."

Collins rubbed his fingers over the box, his eyes taking it in avidly. Smithson looked at his servant as though he didn't trust the man with the item in his hands. "Right, that's enough looking at that for now," he said, snatching the box from Collins. "You and your squire, wherever you left him, can pack my cart. Don't forget the package."

Collins went to take the box.

"*No*, not this one, you fool, the other package. Meet me north of the camp in half an hour. We must get to Kings Seat before nightfall. I have some unfinished business with the idiot downstairs."

Collins lingered for a moment to look at the relic in Smithson's hand.

"Well? Run along man, we haven't got all day."

Collins went to speak again, but Smithson cut him short.

"I'm more than capable of managing with my one bag and this. Now, get a move on!"

"As you wish, *sir*."

There was something in the quiet way Collins spoke and quietly left the room, that unnerved Hugh.

As they continued to watch Smithson, a drop of water rolled off Hugh's nose, managing not to hit the grate on the way down. It landed square on Smithson's thinning hair. He stopped, wiped it off his head, then looked directly up at the grate. Hugh was sure that he could see them and would surely connect the dots and realise what was going on. The time he spent looking at the grate seemed an age. All four of them had stopped breathing.

To everyone's utmost relief, Smithson shook his head, muttered something about '*shoddy rooms*' then went about, collecting the small amount of belongings he had, placing the box on the bed. All four of those viewing had to hold back their gasps.

There, embossed into the top of the box for all to see, was the EGF crest, gleaming in the afternoon light.

Chapter 22

Hugh stood up slowly from the hole in the floor, unsure of what to do next. He walked in circles before deciding that he had to go after the box and headed over to the door. Emily and Heather carefully replaced the floorboard, whilst Barrington went to stop Hugh.

"Where are you going?" he asked in a low voice.

Hugh already had his hand on the handle and had half opened the door.

"To get my box back. He can't take it; that box belongs to me."

Barrington closed the door gently and stood in front of it, preventing Hugh's exit from the room.

"Barrington, I'm warning you. Get out of my way!"

"Or what? Hugh, look at you. You're still in a towel and need to get dressed. Just stop and think about the situation for a moment, will you."

Hugh stood, breathing deeply, staring Barrington in the eye, eventually backing down.

"Fine, but I want that box back. It belongs to me."

"Alright. Well, we'll add it to the growing list of items we need to get."

"Growing list of items?"

"Yes, or have you forgotten about the original plan? This is not all about you, Hugh. Other people are involved."

Hugh looked to the floor but said nothing.

"There's Hamish, who's caught up in all of this, plus we have to get the book of alchemy, and this other book Balinas has asked us to find. Then there's the other notebook from Smithson's father. We need to sit down and plan our next move, instead of running from one crisis to the next."

They heard a door closing in the room below them, signalling that the chance to confront Smithson was ebbing away, which only made Hugh more frustrated.

"But he's here now, and if we let him go, then we won't get another chance again."

"That's not true. We know he's making his way to Kings Seat, so we can follow him there. Right now, you need to stop being so selfish and think of the others. Heather put off finding her father so we could divert here. Emily's left her post at the university, and I my shop. We are all in this together, so why don't you start acting like one of the team!"

There was an uneasy silence in the room. Nobody came in to join Barrington, but nobody stood up for Hugh, either. He ached inside, whilst his brain concluded that his friend was right. He flushed, realising the error of his ways. He felt a fool, standing there in a half damp towel, undressed and no steam left in him to fight.

He went to sit on the bed, looking down at his feet.

"I'm sorry. I have been very selfish. It's not that I meant for any of this to happen. I just became transfixed with finding what my father had left for me. I'm such a fool."

Emily came and sat next to him, the bedsprings creaking as she put an arm around him. He felt the firestone glow warm upon his chest and a tingle of excitement as Emily touched his bare skin.

"My dearest Hugh. Nobody blames you for focusing on what was important to you," she shot a glance at Barrington. "I suppose we are all to blame for some of this."

Barrington went to speak, but Emily raised her hand to stop him.

"We could have easily stopped you if we'd wanted to, and for that, we are sorry. We all have our reasons for being here and our own worries too, but unless we work together as a team, we will never achieve our end goals." She was now speaking to the room at large.

"We all want what's best for ourselves, but we must keep in mind the bigger picture. Yes, there are items to find, jobs forgotten and people taken from us we dearly love. But there's more at stake here. If we get this wrong, the world at large is in great danger. Now is not the time for petty arguments amongst ourselves but a time to come together as the Book of Prophecy has foretold. Now, why don't you get dressed, and we can then think about planning the next stage."

Hugh nodded slowly and rose from the bed. He was sore, numb and exhausted. All his energy had been spent trying to get to this point. He plodded to the bathroom to get dressed. The only clothes he had were the dirty ones he was wearing before. He pulled them on and returned to the room as they prepared for their next move.

They all agreed that they would have to scope out the situation in the camp. There could be someone there who might shed some light on the situation with Hamish, and most people could be persuaded if the price was right.

Barrington and Emily both needed to get messages back to Portis-Montis and Skellig-Krieg. Then they would make ready to head to Kings Seat. They still needed to get the items from Smithson, but that would have to wait. With the plan in place, they collected the few items they had before heading out into the cold light of day.

They reached the lobby where Eric was waiting behind his desk, hopeful for any customers.

"Ah, Mr Geber, I would like a word with you."

"What now?"

"Oh, nothing, nothing. In fact, I wanted to apologise for any upset that I may have caused earlier. I really don't know what came over me."

"Erm, alright ..." Hugh was uneasy in the change of tone from the man.

"I realise that I may have been coming across a little harsh, and I would like to offer you my sincere apologies. May I also offer you all a complimentary meal on the house?"

"I'm afraid we have urgent business to tend to elsewhere, my good man," said Barrington. "We would like to settle our bill, if we may."

"Really? So soon? Are you sure that I couldn't convince you to stay a night longer? You must be exhausted from your journey."

"No, really, we have to be away today," said Hugh. "What we have to do cannot wait any longer."

"Very well then, let's see if we can't soften the blow a little." Eric began working out figures on a pad. "Are we heading anywhere nice? Off back to see my cousin Trevor, no doubt. You must say hello from me."

"No, we are headed in the opposite direction, for Kings Seat if you must know."

"Really? Then, maybe I can be of help to you after all. Let me pass you a name of a contact that I have there. After all, you can't be too careful these days."

"In what way?" asked Hugh.

"Well, the word is that the Elf King has returned to Morcarthia, and he and his people are on the move to Kings Seat once more."

At that, Hugh shot Emily a worried look.

"You must be careful who you trust," said Eric. "The world is becoming a dangerous place. There are many people that would try to stop you if they could."

"Eric, are you trying to tell us something?"

"Erm, no, why would you think that?" he moved uneasily on the spot.

"You don't seem too sure about that," said Barrington.

"Really? Sorry, I'm a bit rattled by a conversation with another guest, that's all. Right, here we are, your bill." He said, moving the conversation with the skill of one who is used to doing so regularly. He passed the bill over to Barrington as he spoke, who looked it over.

"I see you haven't added the exchange rate on. Is this correct?"

"Oh yes, call it an apology for my behaviour."

Barrington raised his eyebrows. "Well, if you're sure, then I won't fight," he said, pulling out the krunes to cover the bill.

He handed them over. In exchange, Eric went to hand him the name of his contact in Kings Seat.

"Barrington, a quick word, if I may?" said Hugh, preventing his friend from taking the note. He dragged him to one side, and they spoke in hushed whispers.

"What?"

"Are you totally sure this is a good idea?"

"When have I ever steered us wrongly? Listen, we need all the help we can get right now. Let me deal with this. We're more than capable of looking after ourselves."

"Is everything alright, gentleman?" asked Eric.

"Yes, yes, all fine here. Now you were saying about a contact in Kings Seat?"

"Why, yes, it's here," he said, waving the bit of paper in the air.

"Thank you," said Barrington, taking the paper without reading it.

"No problem whatsoever. I will message ahead on your behalf, to let him know you are coming."

They all bid Eric farewell and headed out of the front door. It was a crisp day. The sky was cloudless, and the sunlight reflected off the freshly fallen snow. As they headed towards the tent city to find out what was going on, the snow turned to a muddy slush. As they walked past the station, a voice called out to them.

"I say, Emily, is that you?" A lean man with dark hair and blue eyes stepped out from the veranda at the front of the station. He was wearing a navy-blue suit with a waistcoat, stationmaster's hat and black shoes polished to a shine.

Hugh looked at Emily, worried that they were getting unwanted attention, but she signalled that all was alright.

"Hello, Alden, how are you doing?" she said in a lower voice.

"Fine, thank you. I wondered if we might see you at some point. I've seen a lot of old faces around town recently, not that I'm surprised, given the state of things."

"Yes, we're back, and trying to keep a low profile." She tipped her head and gave him a look of annoyance.

"Oops, sorry. Tell me, is this who I think it is?" he said, turning to Hugh.

"Hugh, this is Alden Paxton," she said, and Alden held out his hand in awe.

"Mr Geber, I am very honoured to meet you." He was speaking in a quieter tone, and Hugh took a step back wearily. "It's alright, you can trust me."

"How do I know that?" said Hugh.

"After you."

Alden kept his eyes on Hugh, who looked around cautiously. There were many groups milling around, not paying attention to anyone, and he deemed it safe to continue. Hugh raised his sleeve, and Alden returned the gesture. This also prompted Heather and Barrington to roll their sleeves up.

"Careful, don't all of you do it out in the open. The crows are all around us. I already knew Emily was a safe contact, and I can surmise that you are also part of the extended family, but Hugh was still correct to ask me. Now I have proved my allegiance, that should clear up any suspicions anyone may have."

"I'm Barrington Delphin, lifelong friend of these two," he said, holding out a hand.

Alden smiled and shook his hand.

"And this," said Emily, "is Heather McDougall, Hamish's daughter."

At the mention of her father's name, Heather's eyes welled up, but she managed to hold it together.

"It's alright, I've heard the news. I spoke to Alfred just last night. Trust me when I say, we are all working towards locating your father." He gave her a gentle hug.

"We?" asked Hugh.

"Yes, we, Hugh. There are many of us out here, and Alfred has been working hard to rally the troops. Tell me, have you any leads to go on?"

"No, not as yet. We're currently following someone else, who looks to be headed towards Kings Seat."

"Smithson, I take it?" Barrington frowned and stared agog at Alden. "There's no need to look surprised. We're well aware of his movements, and those of his little helpers too."

"Sorry," said Barrington, "did you say helpers?"

"Why, of course, and keep your voice down will you? His servant and that new minion of his that he's picked up since they were last in town. You really ought to keep up with what's happening. We've been tracking Smithson and his entourage since they arrived in town. They've been walking to and from the hotel all day. It seems he has a large party with him, and as far as we can tell, they are making plans to head out of town shortly. He passed here not too long ago in quite a rage."

Hugh let out an awkward cough.

"We may have had something to do with that. Do you have any idea what he may be up to?"

"I'm afraid not, but I must warn you to be wary of him. He is definitely up to no good. Look, I won't keep you, but please promise me you will all try to keep out of trouble? We need you for the cause, and if the rumours are true, for what is coming."

"What rumours?"

"I cannot speak of them here." Alden looked around uneasily.

225

He nodded to an alleyway cast in shadow. "You see over there?"

Hugh looked and saw the edge of a cloak disappear.

"The crows are everywhere. I must warn you to be careful who you talk to, and plan carefully. They will be waiting for you to do something unexpected. Tell me, have you somewhere to stay in Kings Seat?"

"We have been given a contact," said Barrington, holding out the piece of paper for Alden to look at.

"Don't waft it around out here, man," he said, snatching the paper from Barrington. He studied it, then looked up. "Gambi, eh? Yes, you can trust this man. I know him well. I will send word to our people in Kings Seat to let them know you are coming."

"How many people are there in the EGF?" asked Hugh with concern.

"It's alright, Hugh. We have a network of resistance fighters on this side of the wall, all wishing to see the worlds re-united as one. Only the top-ranking people are a part of the family." He looked around once more, before leaning in closer. "All you need ask is 'are the owls out tonight'. Normal folk will look confused, but those in the resistance will reply with 'eagle, hawk or owl'. You must reply with the word 'eagle' to signal your rank."

"Why?"

"Those three birds are the enemies of crows and the three ranks of the resistance on our side. Eagle is top and are only those within the EGF. Hawks and owls are the lower ranks. That way, we need not mention the family unless talking to another eagle." He handed the paper back to Barrington. "And where, may I ask, did you get this contact?"

"From Eric, the hotelier at the Hotel Alpine."

"Hmm, he's a bit of a weasel, always sticking his nose into places it didn't ought to be. It makes sense that he'd know Gambi; after all, they are in the same business. Anyway, like I say, you can trust ol' Gambi."

"Well, that's good to know," said Barrington, who glanced at Hugh.

"Right, well, I'm afraid this is where I leave you. I have work to be getting on with. Please be careful and trust the resistance network. Without it, we are lost."

With that, Alden left them to it, busying himself at the entrance to the station. They walked off towards the camp on the edge of town. As they reached the top entrance to the field of tents, they could see carts heading off down the Kings Road. There seemed to be an exodus.

On enquiring with the first food tent they reached, it turned out that an order to move on had been given to the camp. Most of the locals were fed up with having the rabble on their doorstep.

They ordered some lunch to eat along the way and took a walk through the encampment. The ground underfoot was thick mud, churned up by the hundreds of feet stomping over the area, which sucked at people's feet as they walked. Here and there, Hugh could see the odd abandoned shoe or boot sticking out.

With the noise, people and animals, the area had a feel of home to it. They asked around about the whereabouts of Smithson and if anyone had heard anything about the disappearance of Hamish.

The first question was easy to answer. Smithson had come through in a rage, not caring who was listening to his rant. He was apparently furious with his service from the hotel and made sure that everyone was aware of the situation. It was reported that he had left for Kings Seat, and on the whole, most of the people were glad.

The issue of Hamish was more difficult. There were no sightings, nor whisperings, of where he might be. At a loss as to what to do, they left the tent city to head for the nearest messenger office. Both Barrington and Emily needed to send messages back to their respective homes to update the relevant people on their progress.

Though there were no cables this side of the wall, messages could be sent via a runner for a small fee or by a carrier bird for an express service. When it arrived at Skellig-Krieg, the message was delivered to the nearest telegraph office. Hugh was unsure if either of them ought to send messages, given they might be intercepted en route, but Barrington insisted it be done.

"I really must see if Wanda has any news on the shop. I can fill her in on what's going on."

Hugh huffed and frowned at him.

"I'm sure Balinas will have it all covered. Don't you trust him?"

"When it comes to the shop, dear boy, I would rather a trained professional monitor my establishment. I will only be a minute, and if it makes you happy, I won't use our names. Wanda will understand."

Without giving Hugh a chance to respond, he and Emily stepped into the messenger office. His mind swung round to the situation in Skellig-Krieg, and Trevor. He wondered what the outcome of the search in his bar had resulted in, and hoped they hadn't caused too much trouble for Trevor. Whilst he and Heather were waiting outside, a familiar voice spoke to them from behind, bringing Hugh's attention back to the real world.

"Hugh, is that you? So it is, what brings you back to this side of the wall?"

Hugh turned and was glad to see a familiar face, though it was not as familiar as it might have been.

"Jeb? My goodness ..." Hogwinkle was virtually unrecognisable from the last time they met.

He was clean and clothed and had grown a short beard. He wore round goggles to protect his eyes from the glare of the sun.

"Not so loud, Hugh. So, who's this fine young lady you are with? Are the others not about."

"Oh, they're in there, sending a message. Heather this is Jebediah Hogwinkle, an old friend of ours. Jeb, this is Heather McDougall."

Heather tilted her head, looking at Jeb with curiosity.

"What?" said Jeb curtly.

"Oh ... nothing, it's just yer name's familiar to me."

"I'm not surprised you've heard of me. Me name's known far and wide in these parts, though it's not helping me right now."

"Aye, I've heard of ye, Jeb Hogwinkle, from me dad."

"Hang on, your father, he wouldn't happen to be ..."

"Hamish McDougall," said Heather, her eyes welling up.

"My poor girl, whatever is the matter?"

Hugh stepped in to bring Jeb up to speed with the events that had transpired over the past few days, and Jeb went white with horror. He turned to Heather.

"Oh, you poor thing. I'm saddened to hear this news. I am sorry to say that I've heard nothing about your father, and trust me, I would tell you if I had heard anything."

"But how do I know if I can I trust ye?" she said, wiping her eyes.

"After you my dear."

Heather looked around, then carefully peeled up her sleeve to reveal her mark. Jeb leaned on Hugh, whilst struggling to take his boot off.

"What are you doing now?" he asked.

"What I'm supposed to do in these situations." Jeb pulled off his right boot, reached in, and pulled out a slightly damp card. "So, as you can see, I'm trustworthy. Your father gave this to me the last time we were together, Hugh." He replaced the card and put on his boot again.

"So, what are you doing here?"

"Ah, well I'm in a spot of bother."

Hugh saw that the man had gone red in the face.

"Really, why?"

"Well, if you cast your mind back to the last time we met, it was at the Banishment Day festival, where I was supposed to rid the town of evil spirits."

"Am I correct in thinking it didn't work?"

"Well, not according to the elder council. Apparently, all these people arriving are my fault, and then there's the return of the Elf King and talk of the old resistance starting up again."

"But that's nothing to do with you?"

"Try telling them that. Anyway, I think there's more going on here than meets the eye. I think there's someone pulling some strings higher up."

"What makes you say that?"

"I was hauled up in front of the town elder council today, and they appeared to have updated their wardrobes. Apparently, they went on a little shopping trip, before asking me to leave. If you ask me, I'd say someone bunged them some cash in return for a few favours. That was just before all of this trouble started, and all these people began turning up here."

"But why would someone do that?"

"Think, Hugh. People are picking sides, hoping to hedge their bets who they believe will be the winners of all this mess. Anyway, I've decided to get out of here, before I'm physically removed. I'm going to lie low with an old friend of mine in Kings Seat."

"That's where we are headed, once Barrington and Emily are done sending their messages."

"I doubt they'll get through."

"Really, how come?"

"Most lines of communication are blocked at the moment. All to do with this Elf King business. Unless it reaches someone who favours the Old World, I doubt they'll get far."

Hugh's insides churned.

The door behind them opened, revealing Barrington and Emily, who scanned around the area cautiously. Barrington's eyes lit up when he saw who they were now joined by.

"Jeb? My dear fellow, what a lovely surprise."

Jeb flapped his arms, pulling Barrington and Emily from the doorway. He began marching the group down the street at speed, filling the pair in on his situation.

"That's preposterous," said Barrington.

"Be that as it may," said Jeb, "the case still stands that my face is not currently a welcome one around here. So that is why I am heading out of town, the sooner the better. I hear you are going to Kings Seat. Tell me, have you arranged somewhere to stay?"

Barrington nodded and pulled out the piece of paper that Eric had given to him. Jeb looked at it, then stared open-mouthed at Barrington.

"What's wrong?"

"Oh, nothing, nothing at all. Ol' Ned Gambi is an old friend of mine. Well, as I'm also headed there, we can all travel together. It will be nice to have the company."

"Why is it everyone around here seems to know of Ol' Ned Gambi?" said Emily.

"Ah, well, the Gambi family were once well known on both sides of the wall; they still are in these parts. It's an old family name, that goes back generations."

"So, we can definitely trust him then?" said Hugh.

"Why, of course. Right, if we are all present and correct, we ought to get a move on. It will be nightfall by the time we get there."

They headed out along the Kings Road, though to call it a road was generous. It was barely wide enough for two carts to pass each other and woefully incapable of coping with the amount of traffic currently using it. There were furrows filled with mud, carved out by the many wheels heading out of town and puddles so deep, you could almost lose a person in them. Some carts became bogged down, much to the frustration of the drivers whilst other carts passed them, jostling for room in the tight space left over.

Hugh found himself, along with the other pedestrians, having to step aside each time a cart approached, as everyone fought for space on the narrow track. By mid-afternoon, they stopped for a break, if only to empty their boots of muddy water. Barrington huffed, looking at the state of his once new boots and shaking his head.

There was a large, disconsolate crew, whose job it was to mend and maintain the track, but they had given up all hope of trying to make any repairs for the day. They sat with their protective hats on their laps and could only look on in dismay as each cart that passed only added to the damage. Hugh saw they were carrying all manner of household items, with those that couldn't be packed within strapped to the outside. They clinked and clacked with each dip in the road.

"How far do you think it is to go?" asked Hugh, who was caked from the waist down in mud.

"A few hours, yet I'm afraid," said Jeb, as another noisy covered cart, with what were presumed to be cattle thumping on the side walls, rattled past. "Everyone really did just up and leave, didn't they?"

"Yes," said Emily, "some people were on their way to the cattle market in Skellig-Krieg, only to be turned away on arrival. The annual cattle fair draws in people from all across Morcarthia, and it's normally the boost the farmers need to get them through the winter. There will be many people affected by the ruling of the New World powers, and I fear this is only the start."

They all sat in silence, taking in what Emily had said. Hugh wondered if this was this the start of something bigger, and he was drawn to a memory from the day before, to what Major Volatus had said.

"… the days of this fanciful world are ending!"

Those words, coupled with the scenes they were watching, now gave Hugh an uneasy feeling in the pit of his stomach.

Chapter 23

Smithson was sitting in the back of a cart again being buffeted by the ride. He had to complain to the driver more than once that the ride was most unpleasant. They had stopped regularly to give way to larger carts, and he was eager to get to Kings Seat. He was tired, sore and wished to be at his destination as soon as possible. Collins and his apprentice had just joined him, both caked in mud, which dirtied the floor.

"Do at least try not to drop mud in here. It's bad enough that I'm having to endure this uncomfortable ride without the smell and muck of the outside world joining me as well. How on earth do these heathens live like this?" He wrinkled his nose and cast a hand around to the world beyond the canvas.

"It must be such a hardship for you, sir, to be cooped up in this all day long, not even able to get your feet dirty. I don't know *how* you cope," said Collins.

The apprentice silently chuckled next to him.

"Less of that tone, Collins. I don't have to let you ride up here with me. You can pack it in too."

The apprentice stopped his chuckling at once and looked wide eyed at Smithson, going red in the face.

"And you can cut that tone with him," said Collins. "He is not yours to chastise, and any issues you have with *him* will have to come via me.

Do I make myself clear? He's a Collins now and therefore under my jurisdiction."

Smithson scowled at Collins but said nothing.

The Collins family rules were in place for a reason. Even Smithson knew he had to follow them, though he pushed against the rules regularly. The head Collins served the chancellor and had to answer to him up to a point. But it was deemed better for all that the running of the family, and indeed and any reprimanding thereof, fell to the head of the Collins family. This left the chancellor free to take care of the more important duties of university life.

"Maybe we don't have the privilege to ride up here with you, but then you wouldn't have the ride if it were not for our swift dealings with the driver. Now, would you like to get the news you so desperately want to hear or not?"

"Oh, do enlighten me with more of your words of wisdom then."

"Certainly, but we ask a little more respect from you first."

"*We?* Do you mean to tell me that the boy has spoken at last?"

"We converse with each other on a different level. I know his every thought, and we would like some more respect, *sir!*"

"Alright, alright. Please, can you tell me the message you have come to give to me, *oh exultant ones.*"

"Now, now. There's no need to go over the top. Just a simple please and thank you would suffice."

"Fine, just get on with it will you."

Collins raised an unimpressed eyebrow.

"*Please,*" said Smithson.

"That's better. It would appear that Geber is, indeed, still on our tail."

Smithson hit the side of the cart, gaining him a reprimand from the driver.

"We had to scrabble back through the mud to find this news out for you. Please don't let it go to waste this time."

"Never you worry, Collins, I already have plans in place. I intend to make sure he doesn't get away this time – nor the other two, for that matter."

"Three."

"I beg your pardon?"

"There are three of them with him now. He appears to be gathering himself a bit of a following. You ought to be careful; he may be more popular than *you* soon."

Smithson scowled.

"How many more does he intend to drag down with him? I don't suppose you found out the identity of this mystery person."

"One of them is Emily le Fay, she unto whom you seemed to place all of your trust."

Smithson hated it when Collins reminded him of his failings, but his servant hadn't finished yet.

"There was another woman who I was surprised to see again, but I don't know her name, but she had ginger hair. I thought we had removed her from the picture." Collins looked at his apprentice, who shied away.

"Ah, so it's not only me that makes mistakes then. Not so perfect after all, eh? Who was the fourth person?"

"Funnily enough, we both know him very well. I must say, I was under the impression that *you'd* dealt with the problem, sir, but apparently not," said Collins, outmanoeuvring Smithson. "It's none other than the old shamanism tutor from the university."

"*What?* How? I thought I had removed him from the picture. I spoke to the town elders on my arrival into Dallum. They promised me they would deal with it."

"It would seem your influence is not as strong this side of the wall."

"Just you wait, Collins. If my plan works, I will hold more cards than anyone either side of the wall, then nobody will have the power to stop me."

"Hmm, I'll believe it when I see it. Anyway, talking of cards, you'll have to excuse us. We have some unfinished business two carts back. I have a game with my name on it. Come, boy."

Collins and his apprentice jumped from the cart, leaving Smithson lost for words. Somewhere deep within the inner workings of his mind, a small but significant realisation was bubbling its way to the forefront, above all the other chatter.

He was losing control over his servant.

Chapter 24

It was getting dark and, were it not for the lights of the carts travelling along the route, they would be walking by the dappled moonlight alone. They were walking alongside a great lake that seemed to go on forever. The breeze coming off the lake was cold, and they were all tired. Conversation had long died and only the sound of the water lapping on the lake's edge kept them company.

They came across the Lakeside Coaching Inn, which was revelling in the travel boom currently taking place. There was no debate over whether they should stop, for they were pulled in by the promise of warm surroundings, a hot meal and some well-earned ale.

It was crowded inside; the bar was doing a roaring trade. The air was thick with pipe smoke, and Barrington's eyes lit up. He rooted deep in his pocket and pulled out his prized possession and began loading it with tobacco as a serving wench came to seat them. The room was so crammed with people that Hugh didn't think they would get a seat anywhere. Barrington was busy tamping the tobacco into his pipe, enjoying the experience.

"You wouldn't have such a thing as a quiet table anywhere, would you?" Hugh said over the noise.

"Not out here," said the wench, barely audible over the hubbub in the bar. "But we 'ave out the back. Follow me. He'll have to put that away though."

She pointed to Barrington, who had just lit his match, but had stopped, hovering mid-pipe ignition, as if unable to grasp the words reaching his ears over the noise, the pipe now hanging limp from his mouth.

"Come on, put that away. We have a table, and no, you can't stay out here. We have things to discuss," said Hugh, already reading the next question on his friend's face.

Barrington grumpily shook the match out and put his pipe away. In the act of putting out the match, he caught the back of someone's head, but was already on the move through the bar. Behind him, the scene was unfolding rapidly, unnoticed by the group.

The large man Barrington caught on the head, turned to square up to his innocent neighbour, unaware of what was about to come his way. The party of five made it through to a saloon bar just as the fight in the main bar was getting into full swing.

With the door shut behind them, the room was a lot quieter. A fire crackled away in the hearth, with the room smelling of wood-smoke. The furniture looked more comfy with its upholstered seating, and to Hugh, it was almost homely. He momentarily wondered if they could stay here for the night.

"Now then, what can I getcha?" asked the wench.

"Ales all round and a look at tonight's meal, please," said Hugh.

"Right you are my luv." She winked at Hugh then exited through a door to the kitchen.

A barstool smashed through the window of the door that they had just walked through, making them all jump.

"It sounds raucous through there," said Hugh.

A man's head appeared briefly through the newly created hole. He was the colour of freshly picked beetroot and had another person's hands around his neck. No sooner had he appeared than he disappeared to re-join the fray once more.

"Goodness only knows what set them off," said Barrington.

It wasn't long before they had food on the table and drinks in their hands.

The meal on the menu was stew – though what was in said stew was anyone's guess. At one point, Hugh chased an unknown item around the wide bowl with his spoon – chased because it had refused to die through the cooking process – and eventually gave it up as a bad job. The fight in the bar had been cleared, and the people moved on. It wasn't long before it filled up once more.

"So, Jeb, this Gambi fellow," said Barrington, attempting to chew something gristly. "Are you sure he is the kind of man we can trust?"

"What, ol' Ned? Of course he is," said Jeb. "Known him for years. I'd trust him with me life, I would."

"Well, that's reassuring to know. So, once we arrive in Kings Seat, we can get settled in then try to find ... what are you laughing at?"

Barrington looked across at Jeb, who was wiping the tears away from his eyes.

"Oh, excuse me, but that is *hilarious!*"

He laughed harder and began slapping his leg, part of the food he was about to chew crawling from his mouth to escape death once more.

"I don't see what the joke is?" said Hugh, and gauging by the looks of everyone else, neither did they. Jeb stopped laughing long enough to speak.

"I think you missed the part about the Elf King coming to retake his throne. The hordes returning to carry out their duty in his name? My dear friends, the atmosphere is just a powder keg ready to blow. That fight in there is just a taste of what is coming. You won't be able to stroll into Kings Seat like it's a sightseeing trip, especially not at night. You missed the boat to buy a souvenir, I'm afraid."

"What are you talking about? We're not going for a sightseeing trip," said Hugh, feeling unsure that he would not like the answer.

"Well, the numbers of guards have swelled in recent months with those loyal to him, what with all this talk of the Elf King returning to power once more. They still hold true to him in these parts. We ain't getting within a mile of that place on this road; well, you ain't, anyway."

Everyone stopped eating, staring open-mouthed at him.

"What?"

"Wouldn't that information have been more useful *before* we set off?" asked Heather.

"I thought you all knew?"

"Erm, *no!*" said Emily. "So, we've walked all afternoon to find out that we won't be able to get in?"

"I didn't say that. I just said it's heavily guarded. You forget, I'm a shaman of the city. We have certain rights, shall we say. I can get me in, no worries there, and I'm sure that I can blag the rest of you as well. You just leave it to me."

———

Three miles down the road, some of the carts were peeling off from the Kings Road into a field. They were joining the new camp growing outside the city of Kings Seat beyond the castle walls, not being granted access to the city itself. Those who didn't wish to join the growing camp carried their journey onwards, heading along a track to the right, which guided them around the outside of the curtain wall into the heartlands of Morcarthia.

However, some carts were not diverting from the track, which had now changed from rough terrain to a smooth ride. The track had become an avenue, recently decorated with the king's colours. There was some excitement in the air as the carts travelled towards the city gates.

In one of those carts was Smithson, who was enjoying the smoother ride, but unaware of the path he was on. From out of the semi-darkness, trumpets sounded — trumpets that hadn't sounded for over three hundred years — and Smithson jumped at the immense sound.

"Driver! What the devil's going on out there?"

"Announcing his arrival, of course," said the driver.

"Whose arrival?"

"King Riddor! Yer part of his arrival party. Yer lucky yer servant got you a space in me cart, otherwise you wouldn't be gettin' in."

"What do you mean?" said Smithson, poking his head out through the canvas to talk to the driver directly.

He didn't need an answer.

Wide-eyed, Smithson took in the surrounding view. He looked back to see most of the carts behind them rolling into the new tent city, one which was decorated with banners and flags flying above it. He turned back to see the large imposing curtain wall. They were currently travelling towards a drawbridge, in its final stages of being lowered, covering a large moat below.

Up above the gate, a flag was being raised, unfurling in the night breeze, heralding the return home of the long-lost leader. Smithson saw the blue and yellow flag with its gold cross border separating the four squares, and within each was a beast. A phoenix, a manticore, a sea-dog and a dragon. Behind that, rising into the night sky, was the mound of Kings Seat, comprising spiralling streets lined with houses and many alleyways.

At the very top, like a bird sitting upon a large nest, was a castle in the shape an enormous throne for which the city was named. Underneath this was carved Numquam Victa, Semper Timui – a message to the New World – Never Conquered, Always Feared. A great cheer went up from the camp outside the gate, as the onlookers watched the parade go by.

"Do you mean to say the Elf King is *real*?" said Smithson, suddenly overcome with nerves, unable to process the surrounding scene.

"True is true."

"What about my servant, will he make it in?"

The driver chuckled. "Oh, don't you worry. He'll makes it in a'right. He's in the ale wagon."

"Of course he is."

"All you needs do now is sit back and relax. We'll be at our stoppin' point soon."

Smithson went back under the cover of the cart. He could hear guards being called to attention. He would have to have words with Collins about this one. In the ale wagon, indeed. Though it was a surprise to enter the city in this manner, he thought that it would have been a harder job.

He had heard the stories in Dallum of the Elf King, of the city going into lockdown and its new motto carved into the wall. Smithson's secret orders were to make contact with the king himself – though he had always thought the man to be nothing but stories and hadn't thought for one moment that he would locate him.

Of course, he had his own itinerary to think about. How was he going to find the book he needed if he was stuck in an armed city? Well, plans would have to be amended. He would have to get Collins to sort out an audience with the king as soon as possible and then see where that got him. Maybe the king could supply him with extra men to help find the book.

Then there was the gravitas that this would gain him back home. His mind was now whirring with ideas. He could get the king onside, and if he failed to listen, remind him of the power that the New World held. No motto would scare the New World into submission; after all, they were only words. He would convince the man to bow down to the immense force and give the New World the foothold it so desperately needed within the Old World.

—

Further back down the road, word was spreading of the return of the Elf King, who had come to reclaim his throne. Could it be true? In the distance, Hugh could see the avenue leading to the walls of the once great city, its massive stone seat dominating the skyline. Even from here, Hugh could see that it was an imposing structure, commanding power over all who set eyes upon it.

It seemed to take an age before they made it to the tent city. They had to pass through newly erected check points, but these were all passed with ease, thanks to Jeb's status. The newly appointed guards were overwhelmed with the number of people passing through the area, and meeting a party with a vaguely important person, let them pass without too many questions.

They reached the gate of the field where most of the carts were now heading. The banners and flags were flapping in the wind, and it was a hive of noise and activity, briefly reminding Hugh of home. The smell of smoke and sound of metal being worked brought him back to the situation in hand. He was reminded of how tense everything was, and that, from the looks of it, people were preparing for war.

Behind him, above the curtain wall, he saw what he took to be the royal flag, flying from a huge flagpole. The seat itself was lit with large torches, giving it an ominous presence. A large beacon was being lit, and as Hugh watched it flare into life, he looked out to the hills in the distance. One by one, he watched the beacons light across the land, signalling to the Kingdom of Morcarthia that the King was back in power.

A shiver went down his spine.

"Are you sure you know what you're doing?" Hugh asked Jeb, as he walked up to the edge of the moat to where the drawbridge should be. He was beginning the feel like a tiny player in a very large game.

"Yes, yes, it's fine," he said, waving Hugh away with his hand, "though I've never seen the drawbridge up before now." He cupped his hands over his mouth. "Hello ... can you hear me?"

His voice bounced back at them from the wall.

"What do you want?" came a gruff voice called from the battlements.

"I'm the city shaman. Missed the carts to get in. Would you mind lowerin' the drawbridge so we can enter."

"*Bugger off!*"

An arrow thudded into the ground at Jeb's feet. It appeared to glimmer in the light and gently hummed to itself.

"Now look here, there's no need for that sort of business!"

A second arrow landed in his boot, narrowly missing his big toe.

"Jeb, I think we need to move from here," said Hugh, looking back towards the chuckling guards on the wall.

"I suppose you're right," said Jeb, downhearted.

As he went to move, Jeb found himself unable to move his foot, the arrow still stuck in his boot and pinning it to the floor. He pulled it out, scowling up at the guards on the wall.

"These were only cleaned this morning," he shouted back at the un-yielding wall.

"Jeb, let's just get out of here." Hugh pulled him away, so he did not fall prey to a third shot.

"That went *really* well," said Barrington. "What next? Do we have to beg on hands and knees? Or shall we dress as royal jesters? Maybe that will see us across the ditch."

Hugh shot him a look of disapproval.

"Not helpful," said Emily.

The camp outside the wall had the energy of a crowd coming together before something big. Hugh could see that most carts were stopping, but some moved on, leaving the rabble to their business. As they made their way through the milling crowds, Hugh could hear the odd mention of the King's arrival, and people wondering if this was going to be it – whatever *it* was.

"Let's find somewhere to sit down. We need to discuss what we are going to do next," said Emily.

They found a tent which wasn't too crowded, but noisy enough to cover any conversation.

"I dinnae like the feeling of this," said Heather as they took their seats. "It feels kinda wrong, do ye know what I mean?"

Hugh nodded.

"There's something going on alright, and I don't think we should spend too long in this camp. I feel like everyone is watching us."

"You always feel like everyone is watching you," said Barrington.

Hugh scowled at him.

"On a normal day, I would agree with you, Barrington," said Emily (Hugh looking at her in shock), "but on this occasion, I would have to agree with Hugh." She looked warily around the tent at the numerous pairs of eyes now watching their every move.

Hugh noticed that she and Heather were the only women in the tent.

"Thank you, Emily," he said, feeling partially vindicated. "Jeb, there must be another way to get in?" They all looked to the shaman, who hadn't said a word since his run-in with the guards, and sat sour-faced, looking at his ale.

"Now, come on Jeb, that drink won't drink itself," said Barrington, giving him a nudge. "Don't let those guards put you off. I'm sure there's another way, it's only a wall … and a moat … and armed guards …"

"Let's not get bogged down with the problems," said Emily. "We have to find an alternative way to get into the main city. Does anyone have any ideas?"

They all stayed in silence for a few minutes, racking their brains for any ideas.

"Could we scale the wall, ye know, take them by surprise?" said Heather.

"And the moat? The guards? I'm pretty sure we won't be able to get in un-challenged," said Barrington.

"I don't see you coming up with any ideas, Barrington," said Emily, looking him directly in the eye. An unspoken conversation was taking place, but Barrington seemed thoroughly chastised. "Jeb, is there a back door, or a secret passage of sorts that we could use?" asked Emily Jeb mumbled something incoherent.

"Now you'll have to speak up so that we can all hear you."

"I said, you could always try using the tradesmen's entrance," he said, practically shouting at her, causing more attention to be drawn their way, the talking lowering.

They all looked at him once more, open-mouthed, with Emily choking on her drink.

"*What?*"

"Again, Jeb, a little more information at the right time wouldn't go a miss," said Hugh.

"Sorry, it's just that I never use that entrance, it's … you know?"

They all looked at him, nonplussed.

"It's degrading, alright! It's where the trades go!" He wrinkled his nose and sneered at the thought.

The surrounding noise ceased, and the barman stood agog, mid-polishing a tankard.

"But yer a trade, are ye not?" said Heather.

Jeb puffed his chest out indignantly. "*How very dare you!* Shamanism is a respected skill, not some plebby trade."

The barman dropped the tankard onto the bar – it bounced around, the sound filling the quiet space over the noise of flapping fabric, as the barman slowly shrunk under the bar.

"I think it's time we left," said Hugh, already grabbing his things and making a swift move towards the exit.

A small party of five people, soaked in ale, ran out of the guild of trades tent with stools, tables and tankards being thrown after them. They ran from the camp, and back down the road, until they thought they were far enough for any pursuers to stop chasing them.

"Good move, *Jeb! Real smart!*" said Barrington.

"What the hell were you thinking?" said Emily, rounding on the shaman. Hugh could see what was coming and did his best to calm her down. "Emily …"

"I, uh, well, err …" Jeb stammered in Emily's looming presence.

Hugh realised he would have to dig deep, finding the part of Emily that resided in himself, to prevent her going headlong into a full-blown explosion of fury.

'*Emily! Now is not the time. Keep yourself under control.*'

She jumped as he had spoken inside her head. She looked around, coming back to the real world once more, everyone surprised at the sudden comedown, none more so than Jeb. Emily blinked.

'*Hugh, how did you ...?*'

Hugh smiled.

'*I looked inside myself,*' he said once more into Emily's head.

'*Oh ...*'

Barrington cleared his throat, bringing them back to their senses.

"Right, yes," said Emily. "So then, Jeb, would you be so kind as to tell us where this other entrance is then?"

"Well, it's around the back, *of course.*"

It didn't take them long to reach the rear of the curtain wall. It only surrounded the newer part of the city, enclosing the upper part of the hill in a great circle, leaving the old village it grew from open to the elements.

The smell of the sea filled the air, as they wound their way through the maze of the old streets, finally reaching a large embankment holding in the moat. Hugh saw a set of steep steps which led up the side, and Jeb climbed them, with the others following close behind.

At the top was a small jetty, leading a short way into the moat, and a set of bells. Hugh looked down into the dark waters, not sure that he liked the idea of falling in.

"So, now what do we do? I can't see a way in over this water, and I, for one, don't fancy a swim," said Barrington.

"Aha, watch and learn my friend, watch and learn," said Jeb.

He pulled a lever below a flaming torch. This was connected to a pulley system, leading to a weight which dropped. More cogs and mechanisms wound into action. A fly wheel began spinning, and a set of bells rang out in a particular order, making it sound like the run up to a clock about to ring the hour in.

"Seriously?" said Barrington in disbelief.

Jeb held up a finger, and they all waited.

A call came from out of the darkness.

"*HEADS UP!*"

This was followed by an ominous creaking.

"You'll like this," said Jeb.

The sound of creaking and metal chains running at speed increased, then Hugh sensed something moving fast through the air towards them. With a loud thud and dust blown into their faces, a narrow drawbridge landed at Jeb's feet. The cloud of dust caused everyone to cough and blink.

"*Amazing*," said Barrington, flicking dust off his front. "What next? A spray of water for good measure?"

Jeb ignored him and marched across the narrow drawbridge.

"Make way for the city sha— *oomf!*"

He was stopped by two burly guards he'd walked headlong into in the semi-darkness. Barrington stood, shaking his head. The smell coming off the guards was a mixture of onion and mouldy cheese. The rest of the group retreated backwards to where the air was fresh.

"What is that smell?" said Barrington.

"That'll be these two. Troll guards, not known for their cleanliness," said Jeb.

"Clearly," said Barrington.

"Oi, we can 'ear you. State *yer* business," said one guard with a gruff voice. Jeb quickly composed himself, straightening himself out, and puffed out his chest.

"I am the city shaman, and I require access to the city."

The two guards burst out into laughter.

"Ooo! *City shaman requiring access* ... did you hear that?" said the second guard, between breaths.

Jeb stood looking unamused and folded his arms. Hugh wondered if he could purse his lips any tighter. The man could give Emily a run for her money. Eventually, the guards pulled themselves together enough to address the situation, realising the group were still there.

"'Ere ... I think he's bein' serious!" said the second guard.

The first cleared his throat, wiping the tears away.

"Right, err, Mr Shaman, sir," he said, stifling yet more sniggers, "let's see yer papers, then."

"The name's Jebediah Hogwinkle." He found his documents and thrust them into the first guard's hand, who looked to the papers, then back at Jeb.

"And what about this lot?"

"They're with me. They are, uh, apprentices. Yes, that's it, they're me apprentices."

"Apprentices? I didn't realise you could 'ave apprentice shaman?"

"Well, every day's a school day, ain't that right, you lot?" They all nodded in earnest. "So, if you'll just stand aside and let me go about me business, then all shall be good."

He went to snatch the papers from the guard's hand but was prevented by way of a large fist. Jeb stumbled backwards, holding his chest.

"I say, there's no need for that sort of business," said Barrington, stepping forward, sniffing, then retreating once more.

"There is when you try to pass us without permission. You lot wait 'ere with Effluentus, whilst I get the sergeant," said the first guard.

They stood in the temporary face off; the guard standing his ground, the rest of the party attempting to not breathe in the foul stench of the troll. Moments later, the first guard returned, with his human counterpart.

"'Ere they are sir. We stopped 'em just in time. They was about to storm us, so I punched 'im in the chest."

"We weren't storming anyone!" said Jeb, rubbing his chest. "These two … guards took me papers, and I want them back."

The sergeant looked at the band of travellers, then took the papers from the guard. With a deep sigh, he looked up.

"How many times do I have to go through this with you two? This is the fifth time tonight. My office, now."

"But …"

"*Now!*"

The two trolls stomped off into the sergeant's office, taking their protests with them.

"Honestly, you ask for guards, and you get trolls. Just because it's not the main entrance, I end up getting the new recruits. Now then, let me see. Ah yes, Mr Hogwinkle. We haven't had a visit from you in a while. It seems the king's return attracts people from all walks of life." Then the sergeant noticed the others. "Who are these people?"

"As I said to the pair of oafs just now, these fine fellows are me apprentices. I am allowed up to five, according to the Shamanism Act, paragraph fifty-four, section C. Go look if you don't believe me."

The man looked the four up and down, who were now smiling and nodding vigorously. He didn't seem too sure of Jeb's reason and was now paying attention to the hangers on.

"I say, old chap," said Barrington. "Are the owls out tonight?"

The sergeant stopped what he was doing and stared at Barrington.

"What did you say?"

"I said … erm … are the owls out tonight? You know … twit-twoo…" He flapped his arms for a moment, before Hugh nudged him. The guard walked passed Jeb and up to Barrington, who gulped. Hugh was sure the man was about to call for backup as he squared up to Barrington, who leaned backwards from his ankles.

"Eagle, Hawk or Owl?" he said so quietly, Hugh could only just make it out.

"Eag…" the word caught in Barrington's throat, and he cleared it before making a second attempt. "Eagle, all of us."

The guard stepped back, to give Barrington some space. His whole demeanour changed in an instant.

"So it is you, then. I must say, I didn't expect you to turn up at my gate. I can only apologise for the behaviour of those two oafs; they're not up to speed with all the rules and regulations as yet regarding the trades. Trust me when I say, I'll be having words with them about this. Do you have lodgings sorted?"

"Yes, ol' Gambi himself is expecting us, sir," said Jeb.

"Right, you may enter. I may remind you that the new curfew begins in one hour, so make sure you are indoors before then. The city's streets are no longer safe after dark, especially to those such as yourselves."

He stood to one side, letting them in – paying close attention to Hugh and Barrington. They went through a small stone passageway cut into the wall itself, only wide and tall enough to allow them all to walk single file. It brought them out onto a cobbled street which headed off in each direction, following the shape of the curved wall.

"Right, follow me," said Jeb, walking off with confidence.

He led them into a passage as a bell sounded somewhere far off, signalling that it was nine o'clock.

"Jeb, would it not be easier to follow the road?" said Hugh.

"Nah, it's incredibly long. It'll take us ages to get to the top. I know me way around these streets like me own backyard."

"But, for the sake of ease and time, couldn't we take the road?"

Jeb rounded on Hugh.

"When was the last time you was here?"

Hugh said nothing, this being his first time in the city, with Jeb fully aware of the fact.

"Exactly. Now we can take the long spiral road, which takes more than an hour, trust me, or we can take my shortcut and be in well before curfew, enjoying a nice jar of ale."

Not wanting to be out in the open longer than was necessary, Hugh kept quiet, which was enough of an answer for Jeb. After walking around in circles, with many changes of streets and hearing the quarter to peel ring out, they rounded a corner.

"It should be right around ... uh, here," said Jeb with confidence. "Ah, hmm. Well, this is most unexpected."

They were back where they started.

"I thought you knew this city like the back of your hand?" said Hugh, eyebrows raised.

"It all looks different in the dark. Plus, I normally use the main entrance, as befits me status."

"Well, we're here now," said Emily, "and only have fifteen minutes in which to find this Ol' Gambi."

"We could look on that board over there, I s'pose?" said Heather, pointing over to the wall in front of them.

In the years after the Great War, Kings Seat had become somewhat of a tourist attraction for the Old World. People were keen to learn more about the Elf King who lost not only the war but also his throne of power. As is universally expected of all tourist areas, many of its streets were now adapted to aid lost visitors.

One such group of disorientated travellers was currently studying one of the many tourist information boards in desperation, trying to get their bearings before the nightly curfew kicked in.

"Right, so where are we?" asked Barrington.

"Here," said Jeb, tapping the map with a grubby finger.

"And we should trust you *because* ..."

"*The map says so* ..."

They all turned to the map, seeing an arrow with 'YOU ARE HERE' hovering next to it. Hugh noticed it was literally floating on the map, illuminated in the dark.

"I wonder …"

"Wonder what?" said Emily, peering over his shoulder.

"Where is Ol' Gambi's Inn?"

"Well, that's the big question, isn't it? I mean …"

Emily stopped talking. Luminous dots were appearing on the map, showing the way to a flashing dot close to the centre of the map. It was right next to the massive picture of a stone seat.

Jeb slapped a hand to his forehead.

"Oh, I remember now. It's next to the King's Seat, the Palace of the Elf King."

Once again, everyone stopped to stare at him, shook their heads, then turned back to the map.

"Where's it gone?" said Hugh. The dots guiding the quickest way to the Ol' Gambi Inn had disappeared.

"Show us the way to Ol' Gambi's," said Barrington (nothing, he tapped on the map, then banged his fist on the side). "Show us the way to Ol' Gambi's now … ruddy things stopped working! For sprites sake … show us the way to Ol' Gambi's Inn, damn you!"

"Hang on a minute! I only got one pair of bloomin' hands!" came a gruff voice from the side of the map. "Bloomin' tourists waking me up at all hours, *'where's me hotel … which way to fair maidens' lane'*. I tell ya, I don't get paid enough for this job."

Hugh looked to Barrington, who shrugged. There followed the sound of pen on parchment, something humming to itself – like all good artists did when they worked – followed by "I'm finished, please insert me payment!"

Hugh looked to the side of the board and saw a slot to insert coins with D1 marked next to it. He looked to Barrington, who shrugged and shook his head, then to Jeb, who let out a sigh, before pulling out a one dragoon coin. He inserted it into the hole. They heard it rattle its way down, before ending in a hollow *'thud'*.

"Agh! Warn me, won'tcha! Bloomin' tourists. 'Ere!" A small, bony, taloned hand popped out from the side, holding a rolled-up parchment. "Ave a good day, and we hope you enjoy your visit to Kings Seat. If you have enjoyed this service, please recommend it to a friend, why don'tcha? Who needs sleep anyway?"

Hugh took the parchment. The hand disappeared, with the sound of indistinct grumblings coming through.

"Right, shall we?" he said, backing away from the map, taking charge of guiding the party to their final destination.

Even with the help of the map, it was still difficult to find their way through the maze of streets and alleyways. The main street spiralled up to the Kings Seat, but to travel along that alone would take too much time. To aid locals in their day-to-day movements, the street was dotted with hidden cut throughs to get them up to the next level.

Naturally, these had to be hard to find, as they would be a weak point in any invasion. This wasn't on the mind of the map designer, as the map pointed them out, and they soon got used to the different ways in which they were hidden. Some were behind bushes whilst others disguised themselves as ordinary passages like the ones leading to the rear yards of the residents of the city. The bell was tolling the hour by the time they reached the top of the mount.

"Now what are we supposed to do?" asked Emily.

"Avoid the guards," said Jeb.

They hung back in the alley that they were in. All seemed quiet.

"I think we're in luck," said Barrington hopefully. They crept out onto the street, moving out of the shadows.

"Halt, in the name of the king!" The soldiers seemed to appear out of nowhere.

They all stopped in their tracks, not wanting to get on the wrong side of the king's guards. The lead soldier walked up to them.

"Well, well, well, what do we have here then? Thought you could stay out past curfew, eh?"

"No, it's not like that," said Hugh, trying to keep his voice steady. "We're new in town and haven't had time to get our bearings yet." He waved the newly purchased tourist map in the air.

"I see, so you chose to ignore the new rules at the main gate then?"

"What new rules?"

"*No tourists.* Things are tightening up around here now that the king has returned. We don't want any unwelcome visitors."

"Ah, maybe I can help," said Jeb, standing forward from the group."

"And who are you?"

"Jebediah Hogwinkle, at your service."

"That name rings a bell."

"Why, of course it will, my dear man. I'm the City Shaman, and these are me new apprentices."

The soldier looked Jeb up and down, then looked back to his second in command, who was holding a scroll. He clicked his fingers, and his deputy passed it to him. He unfurled it, and his eyes darted back and forth, as he read what was written upon it.

"Hmm, Jebediah Hogwinkle, here we are."

"See, I told you I was important around here," said Jeb, to the rest of the group.

"So that must make you lot Hugh Geber, Barrington Delphin, Emily Le Fey and *unknown ginger female*," said the soldier, looking to the rest of the group.

"My, that's a very accurate list you have there," said Jeb, rocking back on his heels uneasily.

"That's because it's the list of the most wanted. Came in with the latest arrivals."

There was a moment, where everyone stood, staring at each other.

"*Run!*" said Hugh, darting for the nearest alley.

He could hear the rest of them following and the sound of whistles behind that. He went up the steps, two at a time. The soldiers were close behind as they burst out of one street and ran up the hill, before soldiers appeared in front of them. They appeared trapped with no exit. The soldiers had stopped running now and were approaching at a slower, more measured pace.

"What now?" said Emily.

"I don't know," said Hugh, looking up and down the street at the two groups of aggressors.

"Where are we?" asked Jeb, clutching at his chest. Hugh studied the map, but it was pointless. He needed a landmark to base their position. He looked up, seeing the great armrest of the King's Seat.

"We're about one level away from the top, I reckon," he said, pointing up at the imposing structure.

"So, which way do we go now?" asked Emily.

"*This way, quick!*" came a voice from their right. There, waiting for them in a concealed passage, was an old man, and they ran towards the place of safety. It was a hidden alleyway, not on the map. They followed the old man, who appeared sprightly for his age.

They came out next to the King's Seat and followed the man to an open doorway.

"Quick, gets yourselves in now!"

Hugh noticed the sign above it which read Ole Gambi's Inn.

As they scurried inside, Gambi shut the door firmly behind them and extinguished his lamp. He ushered them into a side room.

"Stay in 'ere and don't go makin' any noises."

Someone banged hard upon the door, making them all jump.

"Just a minute," said Gambi, as he re-lit the lamp.

He signalled for the newcomers to be quiet and keep down, closing the door to the room, leaving them in darkness. They listened intently.

"Who is it?"

"*It's us, old man. Let us in!*" The sound of a door being unbolted followed, then the sound of it being forcefully opened and slamming against the wall.

"I'm just a poor old inn keeper, trying to make me way in the world," said the innkeeper in a now feeble voice, "with no business in making trouble with the guards."

"Don't pull that trick with us, Gambi! Where are they?"

"I wouldn't know who you mean."

There came the distinct sound of a gun being cocked.

"Ah, I see what you mean now."

Hugh sat paralysed with fear. Something was wrong.

They had guns. Why did they have guns?

The door to the room flung open, revealing silhouettes.

There was a scuffle.

The sound of hand-to-hand fighting, punctuated by the blast a gun going off.

"*NO!* We are instructed to bring them in alive."

Hugh's eyes widened in the dim light being cast in from the doorway as he attempted to crawl away.

"*There!* Grab him."

Hugh felt hands land on his back as he was hoisted to his feet.

"Well done, *Ned*. You have helped us capture the fugitives."

"But I didn't..."

Hugh was dragged out past Ned Gambi, who was holding a bag of coins, open mouthed. Hugh momentarily looked into his eyes, before a blow to the back of the head made his world go black.

Chapter 25

Smithson was sitting by his window, watching events unfold before him. He had just witnessed Geber and his band of outlaws being apprehended from his room across the street. The plan had worked well – extremely well, in fact, as they also had the shaman. His tip off from the contact in Dallum came up good. When he handed the list over on his arrival, he didn't know if the soldiers would take the bait. It seemed that money really could buy you what you wanted.

This would go down well with the powers that be. Gambi was a useful pawn, but he had seen too much. He would have to be removed from the picture to stop him from blabbing about the night's events. His train of thought was disturbed by a knock at the door.

"Enter. Ah, Collins, oh and you still have him with you too. How sweet. Have you arranged an audience with the king like I requested?"

"That I have, but you don't have long. The Elf King is a very important man. I don't wish to trouble him for longer than is needed."

Smithson looked up at his servant.

"What?"

"You're afraid of him," said Smithson.

"No, not at all. I just like to show respect to those who deserve it. Why would I need to be afraid of the king?"

"I don't know, maybe because he is *the Elf King,* the most powerful elf there ever was."

Collins swayed uneasily on the spot.

"How much of the ale did you help yourself to during our trip from Dallum?"

"I wouldn't know what you are talking about."

"Gauging by the fact you smell like a brew-house, and your apprentice looks like he could heave at any moment, I would say you do. Light snack?" he said, waving a plate of uneaten sandwiches under the boy's nose (who then ran from the room).

"So, we've finally found someone to whom you will show some respect," he said, walking towards Collins. "You know, until a few hours ago, I would have said that the stories of the Elf King were all make believe. I know I've been tasked to contact him, but I only took the job on to get me a free pass into the Old World." At this, he shuddered. "But now I have a better plan, one which may gain me the book I want and more power than I could ever dream of. I wonder, Collins, if I were to gain his trust, where would that put me in the pecking order?"

"*Not as high as you would like,*" Collins muttered.

"I beg your pardon?"

"Oh, nothing, *sir!*"

"It appears the drink has made you overconfident. I've had enough of this conversation. Now, take me to your king."

—

Ten minutes later, Smithson was standing alone in the antechamber to the main throne room. Collins could not get this far, being only a servant. He had been dismissed by the guards, leaving Smithson to his thoughts.

He had been standing alone for some time, staring at the coat of arms on the door, which incorporated the flag and motto on a shield. The lack of a chair wasn't going unnoticed. Unusually, his nerves were running away with him, something he was not accustomed to. He was about to meet one of the oldest members of the world that he detested. Why was he worried?

Even in his wildest dreams, Smithson couldn't have imagined a situation like this. He was the envoy for the New World, and he felt the weight of the situation on his shoulders. He had to get this right. This was the last piece in a larger puzzle, one that – if he were successful – would see the end of the old ways forever, making way for a new, all-powerful world. One that he intended to be a part of.

Or maybe the head of.

The doors in front of him opened; a golden glow cast across his face. The smell of woodsmoke swept over him, and he saw the flickering of the flames in the fireplace.

"You may enter."

Chapter 26

Hugh opened his eyes and found himself in a dimly lit space. The smell of damp was everywhere, and there was something dripping over to his right. The back of his head was sore from where it had been struck, and he had a thumping headache. As his eyes adjusted to the light, he could make out the others, all slumped in various positions around the room. Something was moving around his outstretched legs, and he realised it was a rat. He yelped in fear, and flailed his legs about, scaring the small creature away.

"You're awake then?" said Barrington from across the room.

"Yes, how are you? Where are we, and what happened?"

"We appear to be in a cell. I'm fine, just sore and damp from being sat here for too long. It would appear that our new friend was easily bought. His offer of help was actually a trap, ready for the guards to collect us."

"So, it was a setup, then? I thought they held him at gunpoint."

"What we heard and what we saw were two different things. It's easy to feign fear at the sound of a gun, there were no witnesses other than those taking part in the capture. Going by the large bag of coins he was clutching, I would say he received a nice payment to retire on.

"Naturally, I tried to fight the soldiers off, but there were too many of them. They knocked me out briefly, but I came round as they dragged me across the street. I pretended to be unconscious, so I could pay attention to where they were taking us. We are in, or under, the Kings Seat."

"What about the others, are they awake?"

"I don't think so."

"No, I'm awake," said Jeb from the corner, sounding groggy. "I know one thing. I want to kill Gambi the next time I see him, the double-crossing bastard."

"He's over there, so why don't you tell him to his face? No? Thought as much, all talk and no show," said Barrington. "Anyway, it looks like his gamble didn't pay off if he's in here with us. Either that, or he was betrayed by those who paid him."

Emily was coming round. She was next to Hugh, and he could just about pick up her sweet smell over the musty air in the cell.

"Wha ... what's going on?"

Hugh shuffled over to her, putting an arm around her shoulder, and she leaned into him.

"It turns out we put our trust into the wrong people," said Hugh. "I saw Gambi with a bag of coins in his hands before I was knocked out. Though he didn't look overly pleased to be holding it."

"But, again my dear friend, who's to say he wasn't faking that too?" said Barrington.

"That confirms it then," said Jeb, "and I for one will not sit waiting for him to come round."

Hugh could just make out the outline of somebody standing up. He closed his eyes to will the pain away from his head.

"Take this, you old codger," said Jeb, followed by the sound of a dull thud.

"Ow! Do you mind?" said Barrington.

"Sorry, I thought you were Gambi."

"Well, as you can tell, *it wasn't!*"

"It's not my fault, I can't see a bleeding thing in ... woah." Jeb lost his balance and tripped over Hugh's legs.

"Dammit, Jeb, just sit down against the wall," said Hugh.

"What time is it?" asked Emily.

"I don't know, I figured we've been here for at least three hours, so possibly past midnight, though it's hard to tell," said Barrington.

"Has Heather come round yet?"

"No, not yet," said Barrington. "She's laying against me, I can feel her breathing."

"So, I guess we just sit here and wait it out then?" said Hugh.

"Well, unless you have any ideas of how we can get out of a locked cell, we have little choice, old bean."

Hugh let out a sigh, and they returned to sitting in silence. His head was really throbbing now.

Emily reached into a pocket and placed something in his hand.

"Here, take this. Chew it and swallow."

Hugh felt her hand put something into his. Her touch was so gentle, and he felt a tingle inside his chest. He placed the panacea in his mouth and followed her instructions. It was some leaves, and they tasted bitter in his mouth. The situation was really hopeless. Hugh felt a warm sensation flowing through his body, the pain easing as he did so. His eyes closed, and he nodded back off into an unsettled sleep.

He was there at the waterfall again, and could see it all replaying, as if he were above it, like a fly on the wall. Thomas was heading backwards. He had the gun pointed at Barrington, who went to stop the boy from falling backwards, but it was too late.

Hugh watched again in slow motion as the gun was knocked through the fall, followed by Thomas tripping backwards into the torrent of water cascading over the entrance. There was the sound of the gun going off somewhere beyond the water.

He saw himself running to stop Barrington from succumbing to the same fate as Thomas, having to use all of his strength to pull his friend backwards. "*No ...*" Barrington shouted, yet it seemed closer now, more real.

"No, Thomas ... Why, boy, why ...?"

Hugh slid his arm out from under Emily and made his way over to Barrington in the darkness.

"Barrington, wake up, it's only a dream, *Barrington!*"

"Wha ... Thomas? Is that you, boy?"

"No, Barrington, it's me, Hugh. You're alright ... well, as can be."

"But Thomas, I was there, and I didn't stop him, Hugh! I *should* have stopped him. I had to ..."

He broke down onto Hugh's shoulder, sobbing for all he was worth.

"It's alright, it's alright," said Hugh, rubbing Barrington's back. "Hush now. We're in the cell, remember? We'll find a way out of here soon enough. It's all going to be fine."

"You really think so?"

"I know so. We have to be strong, for everyone's sake." He sensed the others were awake and listening, but politely kept quiet. "Do you think you can do that?"

Barrington nodded into the darkness.

"I just keep having these same damn dreams, repeatedly."

"I know."

"You do?"

Hugh fumbled around his neck, finding the Firestone. The cell lit up, as he pulled the pin out, and inserted it into the hole to light it up. It was so intense that it hurt his eyes. He controlled it in his mind's eye, seeing it dim down to a more comfortable level. Emily was now sitting up and looking across at them, rubbing her eyes.

"Barrington, I've spent three months under your roof, listened to you on many a night, wishing there was something I could do. Most nights I just come and settle you down again, though I've never had to wake you up before."

"Oh, Hugh. You must think me such a fool."

"No, Barrington, I don't think you are a fool," said Hugh, shaking his head. "I remember you are human, and that even the strongest of people have times when they too need support."

Barrington lifted his head, wiping his face on his sleeve.

"You've known all this time, even helped me nightly, yet you've never said anything?"

"Yes, because I knew it would only trouble you further. Besides, you had more than enough going on with the shop."

"But I don't want to burden you with my troubles."

"Barrington, I've never seen it as a burden. I am doing the same for you as you would do, and have done, for me."

They sat in silence, whilst Barrington regained some composure.

"Thank you, my friend," he said, patting Hugh's thigh. "I fear I may have been awfully dreadful to you these past few months. I don't mean to be grumpy, it's just all the stress."

"No need to apologise. I know I haven't been the easiest houseguest to live with either. Can we just agree to talk more openly from now on and not hold things inside?"

"Yes. That sounds like a splendid idea." Barrington took in a deep breath and let it out slowly. They sat in silence, pondering their own minds for a while, before Hugh broke the silence, causing them all to jump.

"I don't understand it?"

"What?"

"Everything that's happened since the fire."

"Which part? There's so much to choose from."

"Good point. What I'm currently trying to figure out is why nobody told me about the sight before all of this happened?"

"Hmm, good question. Then there's Augustus. How come he has access to it, and not I?"

Emily let out a sigh.

"I think I know the answer to this one, but you both have to hear me out."

Hugh and Barrington sat themselves up, eager to hear what Emily had to say.

"Let's start with the sight itself. It's not that you didn't have access to it before this point, more that you had to open yourself up to it. Going back into history, all the races had the ability to step in and out of it. Naturally, you had to be trained up, as you do today, but it was a safer place back then. There weren't as many wandering spirits in those days."

"Wandering spirits?" said Hugh.

"Yes. It is said that there was once a guardian, whose job it was to guide those who passed over onto the next world. It's believed that the sight is where our energy goes when we die before we are guided on. Over time, the guardian grew interested as to where all these spirits came from. It is said that the guardian crossed over to the plain of the living one day and never returned, leaving those who passed over to wander the eternity of the sight for evermore.

"Now if you remember, I said that originally everyone had access to the sight. Well, over the years, some forgot, and others chose to forget, especially after the Great War. Those who sided with the Elf King were put into exile, into what's now called the New World. This comprised mainly the race of man, with some of those who chose the wrong side. There were some from the Old World, who attempted to keep the old traditions alive, and some who were placed there to keep things in order."

"So, what's that got to do with the sight?"

"I'm getting to that bit. Over the years, people forgot the old ways, and the powers that came with them. They shunned those who showed any loyalty to the Old World, and in recent years, it's become more extreme. Meanwhile, in the sight, the spirits were building up. Some even passed back over to this plane, but anyone in the New World dismissed this as ghosts or guardian angels. Have you have ever felt like someone is watching you even though there's no-one there? That's the sight at play."

"Right, so what's that got to do with us?"

"It's important to understand that all bloodlines run back to the Old World somewhere, and although a majority of those intermingled along the way, some of those lines are stronger than others. The Geber and Delphin lines are two such, along with Le Fay. Each family will have different ways in which the next generation is taught. A majority of the time it's passed down the generations via stories, which you have to learn, so you can pass the knowledge onto the future generations. I had to leave Portis-Montis when I came of age, and that's when my mother taught me about the old ways and opened my mind to the sight. Sadly, she passed before I could complete my training, but Alfred kindly stepped in and continued where my mother left off.

"Your father, Hugh, would have been training up your elder brother, as tradition dictates, the eldest child learns first, then the younger generations follow. The Geber family has had its losses over the years, so he invested a lot of time into Theo whilst trying to research the family history. He was keen to find out why the family had so much bad luck, or if there were any more Gebers out there other than Alfred. We think this is how he uncovered the mystery of the books."

Emily now looked at Hugh with sadness in her eyes.

"Alas, when Theo passed, he was already wrapped up in the emotion of losing a second son, and looking for the books, that your training was woefully inadequate. You must not blame him for this, of course, for as far as he knew, he had many years ahead of him."

"I fear some of that lays with me," said Hugh. "He was always on at me to keep up with the basics, but I always assumed Theo would be there, and his line would carry on the family work. I was learning some of it, but I had other things to distract me. The pressure when Theo died took its toll on my father. He was almost desperate in searching for something, which now I see was the lore book of alchemy. If only I had stopped him from going on the trip, maybe he and Robert would be here now."

"Hugh, you mustn't blame yourself. Your father had his path to walk, as you have yours, and I mine," said Barrington.

"He's right," said Emily. "We cannot choose our destination, only how we get there. Now, with your unlocking of the sight, I think you mentioned Augustus telling you about a knock to the head being able to trigger things. This is correct, as you can testify. When we are rendered unconscious, our minds relax and open up, unlocking certain powers deep within us.

"It turns out that your line is so strong, your abilities are far beyond what I could teach you. But it is this that you must learn to control. You have entered at such a high level that you will struggle to control your powers for some time. I can guide you through the process of how to enter and exit safely, but I think self-control is the key to you choosing when and where you enter and exit the sight."

"That's easier said than done," said Hugh.

"I know, but you must put more effort in, and please don't fight me on this one. It's important you do this."

"So where do I fit into everything that's going on?" asked Barrington.

"Well, you also have a strong line, as you very well know. If you hadn't fallen out with your father, then maybe you would have found out sooner. Because of that, you missed a great deal of training, especially being an only child.

"Your father sought you out on so many occasions, and I even discussed trying to plan a trip to Portis-Montis to talk to you. As luck would have it, you came to us. But you had so much other news to catch up on, you didn't get around to the subject of the sight before Hugh and I had to come and get you."

"So why did I enter the sight?"

"Because you banged your head on the rune wing, remember?" said Hugh.

"Yes, well, that would do it," said Emily, "and I think, if you look back over the years, there will definitely be times where you have entered unknowingly into the sight and chosen to ignore it. That's your

New World brain at work. You will have, of course, learnt some of the Old World knowledge, being in the navy. Until recently, the training arched back to its roots, in helping to keep the peace and order between the old and new."

"Yes, that is true. I was one of the last cohort to learn such ways, before the powers that be stepped in, decreeing that the training of the old ways had to stop. Of course, we tried to pass on the knowledge in secret, but it became harder as time moved on. I wish I'd spoken more to my father about it, then maybe I would be up to speed like Augustus."

"Well, he has many more years of training than you. He was taught from birth, for his line is directly linked to the Old World. In his lifetime, he has seen the old ways become shunned, and his family elders had to go undercover, portraying themselves as aviators, to fit into the new way of things. As far as the powers that be are concerned, he is a bumbling pilot, but this is only a ruse. He is very skilled in his arts and a force to be reckoned with."

"So why did they give all that grief to my mother?"

"In their eyes, she had gone across to something that supported the New World. You must remember that with the family lineage as strong as that, defecting to someone not chosen for her would have caused great offence, especially as it was not linked to the sylphs."

"The sylphs?"

"Spirits of the air," said Heather, making them all look in her direction. "Sorry, I hope ye didnae mind me listening in. All these names are like listening to dad remembering the old days."

"That's alright. I didn't realise you were awake. It's not as if you can ignore what we are saying anyway," said Barrington. "I really didn't know about any of that."

"This is where you missed out on your rite of passage," said Emily, "as did Smithson."

"What do you mean?" asked Hugh.

"Had things progressed as they have always done, he would've been inducted into the sight like every chancellor before him. In some ways, we're lucky that he doesn't know, otherwise he could cause untold damage. Anyway, everything passed over out of order, and his reluctance to learn anything of the old ways is his loss and our gain. We cannot undo what has already been done, but we can try to plan for the future."

She let out a long yawn.

"I think we ought to get some more sleep," said Hugh. "We will need all our energy if we are to come up with a plan to escape from this place."

"Escape?" said Barrington.

"You seriously think we are going to sit here for the next month, letting Smithson get away with murder?" said Hugh, who caught the yawn off Emily.

"No, Hugh, I don't think we will. Then sleep time it is, until morning, whenever that is."

He patted Hugh again before Hugh went back to Emily. He carefully put his arm around her, and she nestled back into his shoulder. Hugh reset his firestone, and with one long blink, he was joining the rest of the group, adding to the cacophony of snoring.

———

They awoke to the sound of the cell door being opened. The light flooding from the torch on the wall cast a painful ray across the floor and caused Hugh to shield his eyes. The smell of the troll hit him before he could make out its bulky silhouette filling the open doorway, choking off any chance of escape.

"*Breakfast,*" it said in a gruff voice. Six bowls on a tray were shoved in roughly, the door slamming behind it, plunging the room back into an inky black void.

Once he was sure they were clear, Hugh lit his firestone, then crawled over to the tray, picking up a bowl, and dipped his finger into it. It was slimy and lukewarm, smelling of plain porridge. He handed the bowls around the cell. Gambi had finally risen from his silent state.

"This is disgusting," he said.

"It's your own fault," said Jeb. "I thought you were a friend?"

"I am a friend," he said, between forced mouthfuls. "They forced their way in, then shoved the bag of money in me hand before they left. I noticed they didn't knock Hugh out until he had a good eye of the bag."

"Then how did they know where to find us then?"

"How do I know? Maybe you were followed, or they were tipped off, or someone else set you up? But you have to believe me when I say, I am your friend."

He whipped up his right sleeve. Hugh saw in the firestone's light, that it revealed an EGF tattoo. Gambi looked him in the eye.

"I would never betray a member of the family."

"So, if it wasn't you, then who was it?" asked Jeb. "Who else knew we were coming here?"

Hugh's heart sank.

"Eric."

"Sorry?"

"It was Eric. He was the one who gave us Gambi's details."

"But why would he do a thing like that?"

"Who knows? Smithson said that he had some unfinished business with him. I bet you anything that has something to do with all of this."

"How can you be sure it's Eric?" said Jeb. "I know him. He's a bit of an odd fellow, yes, but how do you know it was him?"

"I don't know, but I just think it's him. Who else knows where we are going?"

"There was that Alden Paxton fella," said Heather. "Ye cannae forget about him. Do ye think he was behind this? He knew all our plans."

Hugh thought for a moment.

"That's true, but he was angry with Barrington, remember, for flashing the paper around?"

"Aye, okay, so we think he's safe. What about those people he pointed out watching us in Dallum."

"Again, I think they were too far away to hear anything. I didn't see anyone else around acting suspiciously, and I don't recall speaking to anybody about coming here, apart from those in the room now, or the previous names mentioned. Alden Paxton is a member of the family and was extremely cautious. That only leads us to one person who knew where we were going. It has to be Eric."

Barrington let out a sigh.

"I fear you are correct, my friend, but what does that mean for us?"

"It means we can no longer trust Eric, at least, not until we have time to question him."

"I agree," said Emily, "though I don't think that he is a malicious character, just a bit naive."

They all sat in silence, the sound of bowls being scraped clean, and the last forced mouthfuls being swallowed.

"So, what now?" asked Barrington.

Emily sat more upright. "Seeing as we cannot go anywhere, I think we should work on your sight practice."

"Really?" said Hugh, not in the mood for anything involving effort.

"Yes, really. Unless anyone knows how to overpower a troll guard and get us out of here?"

Everyone remained silent.

"No? Right, sight practice it is. We need to get you ready, especially if you end up slipping in and out as easily as you have been doing."

"Do I get to practice this sight thing?" asked Barrington.

"I can't mentor several people all at once," said Emily. "I'm skilled enough for one person at a time, and that's all."

"I could do it," said Heather. "Dad taught me how, and I'm more than able to do so."

Barrington nodded. "Suits me, as long as it's all, you know, alright?"

Emily considered this, then nodded her head slowly. "Alright. We'll meet you on the other side then. Jeb, Gambi, you can keep a lookout for us, and Jeb, can you warn us if needed?"

"I can do that," he said.

"Right then, all we need now is some water." She began searching around for the source of the dripping. "Over here, look," she beckoned the others over to a small pool of water. Emily, Barrington and Heather sat themselves around it, leaving no space for Hugh, who sat back-to-back with Emily.

"Don't we need to make room for Hugh?" asked Heather.

"No," said Emily, "he can jump in without the need of water."

"Wow, that's ... unique. Doesn't that mean?"

"Possibly."

Hugh was getting confused. "What?"

"Not here, not now," said Emily.

"But—"

"Not now. Right, Barrington, hold hands with Heather and put your other one in the water. Hugh, you do what you normally do."

Hugh didn't pursue the conversation any further. He was aware of a glow emanating from the group behind him, then felt the unstoppable urge to step over the border between the planes.

He was back in the sight once more, floating next to the faint outline of Emily, looking back at his life-link. They were joined by Heather and Barrington, the latter sounding amazed by his surroundings. Hugh saw Heather busily weaving runes in the air and watched them fall along her own life-link, before moving onto Barrington's. They drifted off, further into the darkness. Emily had already started hers and turned to Hugh.

'Well? Are you not going to at least attempt to protect your life-link?'

'But how?'

Emily huffed. 'Search inside yourself, and the answers will be revealed. I shouldn't have to remind you.'

She sounded annoyed, and not wanting to anger her further, he reached inside himself. He could see the runes. They were there, but always just out of reach, slipping through his fingers.

'Hurry up, Hugh.'

'I'm trying, but I can't get them to stay still.'

'What? Oh, for goodness sakes!'

He felt himself warming up and realised Emily had stepped in to help protect his life-link.

'I tried,' he said pathetically.

'Yes, well, you need to try harder. Practice calling up a rune now. Show me how you are going about it.'

'Well, I look inside … I try to reach the runes, but, well, they keep moving away, see! This is ridiculous. I'm never going to get the hang of this.'

'Not with that attitude you won't. You have to see yourself getting the runes. Visualise it in your head and don't let it go. You must master this, Hugh. I won't always be here to help.'

'I know, but…'

'Hugh … Hugh, is that you?'

'Father? Father, where are you?'

'You made a promise to me, Hugh Geber! A promise to never follow him. Don't you dare break it.'

'But he's just there … just out of reach …'

He could feel himself drifting towards the voice before something jolted him, moving him away from where he thought his father may be. It was as though he were being pulled backwards through a plughole. It was whilst he was distracted by this new feeling, that he felt the presence of another energy. It was familiar to him, and he was drawn to it, but then pulled away again, Emily's control far greater than his own.

–POP–

He was back in the cell's dimness, and turned to look at Emily, who was drying her hand on her top.

"What did you do that for?"

"I told you not to follow that voice, and you promised not to go there, but you just had to look, didn't you?"

"But it's him, I know it is."

"You cannot trust it. It may be a malevolent being, and you don't want to face being attacked whilst in the sight. You'll risk not getting back home again, and we don't want that to happen."

Underneath the tone of annoyance, Hugh could sense care and worry seeping through. He had no time to dwell on it, as there was something else nagging in his mind.

"Did you feel it, Emily?" he said, looking into her eyes. "You did, didn't you?"

He looked at her, and she looked across at him, saying nothing. Hugh heard Heather and Barrington coming back into themselves, and he turned to look at them.

"Absolutely amazing," said Barrington. "In all my years, I never thought I would experience such a place."

"Ah, yiv been there once already. Get over it. Why did ye come back out, Emily?" said Heather, with some urgency.

"Just fantastic, I mean, I've seen some things in my time, but wow!"

"Enough, Barrington!" she snapped at him. "Tell me, Emily, why did ye come back out so quickly?"

"Hugh was heading for the voice of his father again. I had to pull him clear and stop him from drifting off."

Hugh looked at her.

"You must have heard it, or at least sensed it, surely?"

"Your father's voice? Yes, I heard it."

"Not that. There was something else there, and I'm not talking about *my* father." Hugh turned to Heather. "What about you?"

"Aye, I sensed something, or someone. Ye sensed it too?"

Hugh nodded, and she turned to Emily. "Ye did too, I know ye did."

"Yes," said Emily, nodding her head slowly.

"If we all sensed it, then that means ..."

She looked at Hugh, who took the word from her mouth.

"Hamish."

Chapter 27

They all looked at each other, their minds now in overdrive. If they could all sense Hamish was there, then that could only mean one thing. He was nearby, and possibly not conscious.

"I'm sorry," said Jeb, trying to get a grasp on the situation. "Are you saying that Hamish was there in the sight with you?"

"Yes, but not with us exactly," said Emily. "We all sensed him there with us."

"But that doesn't mean that he is close to us here. He could be anywhere in the world."

"No," said Hugh. "I definitely sensed he was close."

"I'm sorry, but I can't take the word of a mere *trainee*."

"Oh, you can take the word of *this* one," said Emily. "He's no ordinary trainee. He's already done a full step in."

"What, with a mentor?"

"No, on his own."

"And he made it out alive?" he looked at Hugh partly in awe, and partly with suspicion. "Who taught you to do that? I can only just do that, with many, *many* years of experience behind me. This speaks of dark training if you ask me."

"I didn't do it on purpose, and I've had little training so far," said Hugh. "Anyway, we're straying from the point. We all sensed the same thing. Hamish is nearby. It was the same feeling when we rescued Heather ..."

He tailed off and looked Heather in the eye. He felt a connection spark up inside him, and she must have done too.

"Hugh, concentrate!" said Emily, clicking her fingers in front of his face, snapping him out of the trance, and he looked down at the floor. "You have to at least attempt to control this. It's vital that you get a grip on things."

"Sorry," he said, "but it's difficult. I'm having to pick up so much in such a short amount of time."

"You seem to drop in and out easily enough." Hugh sensed her anger. He stayed silent, and Emily regained her composure.

"Sorry," she said. "I know this is hard for you, but a little more effort is required on your part. Anyway, we need to figure out what we are going to do about Hamish?"

"What about him?" asked Jeb.

"Well, there's the fact that we can sense that he's here. That alone is a reason to get out of here and try to rescue him ... what now?"

Jeb was laughing to himself.

"I don't know if you've noticed, but we're in a cell with only one way in and out. The cells in the Kings Seat are renowned for being impenetrable. Oh, and let me think? Ah yes, they are buried deep underground. I knew there was something I was forgetting. There's no other way in and no way out, except for the way we entered, or..."

"Or what?"

"Well, the only other way out is to be added to the library of lost souls."

"The what?"

"The library of lost souls," said Gambi, causing all in the cell to look at him. "It's where the Elf King kept what he took from those who didn't make it out of here. You could call them 'trophies' I s'pose."

"Why trophies? Isn't that a bit morbid?" asked Hugh.

"Of course it is. But you has to remember, this is the Elf King we is talkin' about. He used to rule with fear tactics. He kept the belongings of those he disposed of and then opened up the room for enforced tours regularly, like, to remind his *loyal subjects* what would 'appen if they stepped out of line." He shuddered at the memory.

"But why keep the belongings of the dead after the king was caught?"

"It's believed the spirits of those taken haunt the rooms. There were fears that disturbing the last known artefacts of the dead would anger the spirits, bring 'em bad luck, so they left 'em where they were."

"That sounds awful," said Barrington.

"It really does," said Emily, "and that is not how I wish to leave here."

"Well, unless you are planning on overpowering our troll captors, which would be an impossible task I might add, then we are stuck."

Emily shot him a look so deadly that Hugh was surprised to still see Jeb breathing.

"There has to be a way to rescue him," said Heather. "He's nae had any whisky for a few days, he'll need a wee dram as soon as possible."

"Is that all you can think about?" said Jeb. "We need to rescue him, me dear, not feed his alcoholic dependency."

"Don't ye dare go down that road, Jebediah Hogwinkle. He needs the whisky to keep him going. Without it, he'll be lost *forever*. Ye mortals would never understand."

"I understand," said Hugh, uncertain about what she was talking about, but wanting to support Heather (Emily turned to look at him). "We'll rescue him, regardless of what some people think."

He now shot a look across at Jeb.

"Hear, hear," said Barrington, not wanting to be left out of the party.

"There is a way," said a voice from the corner.

Everyone turned around to look at Gambi.

"I know of a way that we can save him, if you believe he is here, but we will only have one chance. I can sense his presence if that's of any use to you all, and I agree that he's close, but he's a fadin'. I think we can do it, though it will leave us with one less way to escape. It will require using some old magic."

"What do you mean?" asked Hugh.

"We can club together and get our power together as one force. Then we can use it to find Hamish, before pulling him back with us, if you gets what I mean?"

"Sorry," said Emily, "but are you talking about a full body extraction via the sight?"

"Of a sort, yeah."

"Are you also saying we can also use this to escape from here?" said Barrington.

"Yeah, but it's one or the other. Then we'll have to wait to recharge."

Barrington looked at Gambi, confused.

"Recharge? What are you talking about?"

"The more energy you use in the sight, the longer you needs to recover."

"And how long does it take to *recharge?*"

"A couple of days, unless you are special," he said, looking across at Hugh.

"But that means Smithson could be long gone and possibly reach of one of the books of lore before we do," said Hugh.

"I'm fully aware of the task you have been given. I've been in regular contact with Alden and the others. Like I say, the choice is yours to make. You just have to decide what is more important to you right now."

Hugh stood, feeling the awkwardness of everyone looking at him.

"So what you are saying is, we either save Hamish or escape from here?"

"Pretty much."

The room was left in silence whilst the various minds mulled the idea over.

"We have to save Dad!" said Heather. "That has to be the only choice!"

"I think we should escape," said Jeb.

Heather shot him a look of anger, and he replied with a shrug.

"I think we'd be better off out of here," he said. "Then we can figure out a rescue plan. Our escape doesn't preclude a conventional rescue. Besides, not being funny, but your dad gives me the creeps. He always insists on playing that screech bag of his."

"They're called bladder pipes, just for reference, and ye know the reason ye don't like his music, it's magic, and ye cannae resist the call if it's yer time."

"Can we just stop the bickering for one moment and get back on topic? I think Jeb may be right," said Barrington, earning him a scoff from Heather and a scowl from Emily. "What? I was only saying ..."

Heather looked away from him.

"I'm keeping out of this one," said Gambi. "I've already made a mess of things, and this is not for me to call."

They all turned to Hugh, who felt put on the spot again.

He was sensing, and even hearing, the inner workings of Emily and Heather, neither of which would be repeatable outside his head. He knew they must try to escape from this room, but if they didn't rescue Hamish, the old rune master might not see the day out. He looked at them all in the dim light.

"Whatever I decide to do, know that I am doing it for the right reasons, and that whatever I decide, we must all agree it is the plan." He looked around at them all in the dim light. Nobody moved. "I need your word on this, or I too will abstain, leaving us in stalemate." Reluctantly, they all nodded.

"Right, then my decision is that we rescue Hamish." Barrington went to speak, but Hugh cut him off. "No, my word is final in this, and you all agreed to go with it."

Barrington sat tight-lipped.

It took some organising to get the plan underway. They had to wait for the next lot of lukewarm mush to be shoved through the open door, to be sure they wouldn't be disturbed. Once their eyes had adjusted back to the light of the re-lit firestones and they had eaten their food – Gambi insisted they did this to keep their strength up – they made their way to the damp corner once more.

Gambi, like Hugh, was one of life's rarities and didn't need to be near the water to enter the sight. He sat back-to-back with Jeb, who squeezed in with Emily, Heather and Barrington around the small pool of water. Hugh resumed his place behind Emily, and he saw the glow, then sensed himself being pulled once more into the sight.

He was there in the darkness, and he turned to see the outline of everyone, with the more experienced already weaving runes together to protect their life-links. Hugh dug deep, this time finding some of the runes required to protect himself. It was a struggle to keep them in place, and soon enough Emily came to join him.

He soon had a long golden line heading off into the distance and sensed himself warming up once more. Heather had already finished weaving Barrington's protection for him by the time they joined the group. Hugh could see the outline of Gambi, as he brought them all together.

'*Right, gather round you lot, here's what we are going to do. First, we needs to concentrate on thoughts of Hamish. We ain't going nowhere until we know where he is. Picture him in your mind's eye – and makes it strong. If you sense him, call it out.*'

Hugh searched inside his mind for a firm picture of the man. He pictured woven wool, scratchy upon his face and the smell of heather, fragrant ... Heather ...

'*Concentrate Hugh,*' came the voice of Gambi.

Hugh jumped, before realising what had happened.

He sensed Emily's anger. He attempted to picture Hamish once more. He had images of walking with him, being inside the cottage on the marsh, the deep lines on the old man's face which had been weathered with time, then he was there. He had him.

'*I know where he is,*' he said aloud, whilst trying not to lose the sensation.

'*Alright, Hugh, you must be the one to guide us,*' said Gambi.

'*But I haven't a clue how.*'

'*You can do this. Jeb, you come join me in the centre, thas it. Emily, Heather and Barrington, you encircle us. Thas the one. Now Hugh, you need to encompass us all.*'

'*But wouldn't that mean I gain small parts of you all?*' asked Hugh.

'*Yes, but we'll have to deal with that. Now quick, form the bond, link us together,*' said Gambi.

Hugh did as he was instructed to do. He sensed himself flowing around the group, filling all the nooks and crannies of space not taken up. His mind was flooded with everyone else's, and he nearly lost the concentration to keep them all together.

'*Come on, Hugh, push yourself!*' Gambi urged him on.

He concentrated harder, his energy joining around the group, binding them together.

'*Right, everyone else picture Hamish, you too Hugh.*'

He felt the combined power of Gambi and the others flow into him. He felt strong. He had purpose. He liked it. '*Go with it, Hugh.*'

They were off, racing through the immense semi-darkness. Hugh chanced a look behind him, seeing a bright golden trail in their wake. He turned back, seeing other things floating around him, as if they wanted to be a part of the ride, but he had no time to focus on them.

They appeared to bounce off the group, as if it were an immense shield. He could see a ghostly outline ahead and headed straight for it. He knew it was him. It had to be. He saw a whip of a line heading off from the figure, which was curled up in the foetal position. Ahead him was a chink of light, not too dissimilar to a tear, and he raced forward to it, knowing it would lead him to the withering man.

    —POP—

Hugh was in the cell with Hamish. He looked rough, curled up into the corner. He couldn't see the others but could sense them inside. He seemed to glow, enough to illuminate the cell.

'*Hurry Hugh, we cannot hold like this for long!*' came the distant voice of Gambi.

'*Hamish, are you awake?*' said Hugh.

His voice sounded strange to him, as if there were hints of everyone else's voices within it. He chanced a touch on the old man's shoulder and saw his hand was glowing. It almost made him jump and lose his concentration. He regained his focus, and his hand grew bright as he nudged Hamish once more.

"Mnmph, Hugh?" said the pile of tartan. "Is that ye, laddie?"

'*It is.*'

"What? How? Is this a hallucination? Are ye really here?"

'*It's not a hallucination,*' said Hugh. '*It's a rescue party.*'

He held out a hand for the old man to hold on to. Hamish went to grasp it, but it passed straight through.

'*Concentrate Hugh!*'

"What the … who was that? It sounded like …" Hamish backed away from Hugh.

'*It's alright,*' said Hugh, concentrating harder. It was making him ache. '*Try again, we really are here to help.*'

He raised his right sleeve, and the EGF tattoo on his wrist illuminated the room. Hamish shielded his eyes from the light, and Hugh covered it up quickly. Hugh's eyes adjusted once more, and he could see the old man was on his feet. He was wavering slightly.

Without any warning, Hamish lunged at him. It was the strangest experience. Hugh, expecting to fall to the floor, braced himself for the pain which never came. They were back in the sight, this time with Hamish caught inside the group. Hugh could feel some of his power entering the old man.

'Hugh, you need to move now. Everyone else, focus on your life-links, make them strong. Now, Hugh, GO!' There was an urgency in Gambi's voice.

They were moving at speed, and the images floating past Hugh's eyes were all a blur. It was then that he heard it.

'Hugh, Hugh? Is that you?'

Before he had time to answer, several things happened.

First, Emily shouted. *'No!'*

Hamish turned. *'Fredrick ...?'* His eyes aglow, he was pulling against the will of the group.

'Hamish, no!' said Gambi.

Hugh watched as he and Jeb fought to keep him in the group.

'Let me do me job!' said Hamish, now physically fighting to break free.

'Yer not strong enough, Dad; besides, yer job is in the plane of the living,' said Heather.

Hamish stopped fighting, distracted by the sound of his daughter.

'Heather? Em? What are ye doing here? It's too dangerous, we're all in danger here!'

Then, from out of the semi-darkness, a large, slender dragon appeared in a flash of brilliant light. Its long slender body and tail curled under the group. Hugh recognised Betsie, who had come to the words of her master. Hugh sensed a feeling of protection, as the beast's mighty wings encircled and shielded the group from what was beyond the vision in the group.

'I protect my master, as I am duty bound, and I will give you time, to return to ground.'

'Betsie?'

Gambi surged forward, making use of Hamish's distraction, dragging the rest of the group with him. Hugh had the usual sensation of being pulled from the navel backwards.

–POP–

Then they were back in the cell, laying on the damp floor, all out of breath.

Nobody spoke. Hugh was dizzy from the effort he had put in, keeping the group together. He could see remnants of runes flashing in his eyes.

"Would someone like to tell me what the hell's going on? I finally had him!" said Hamish, a glow still in his eyes.

"Dad, take this, will ye?" said Heather, pulling out a hip flask from her bottomless pocket. He took it and necked a large mouthful, the glow in his eyes ebbing away.

"Thanks, I needed that," he said, looking gratefully at Heather. "Now what's going on?"

It took a joint effort from Hugh, Emily and Heather to explain all the events since he had been kidnapped from the marsh. He listened in shock to the news that the Elf King had returned and was more dismayed to hear they were being held prisoner beneath the King's Seat.

"In all my years, I widna think I'd be in this situation. Then, to see Betsie come, we must've been in a perilous position. Am I really a prisoner in the King's Seat, with the Elf King free to roam the lands?" He put his head in his hands.

"Don't worry, Dad. We'll get him," said Heather.

"Aye, I'm sure we will, but it shouldna come to this. I'm sorry, sorry to be dragging ye all into this with me."

"It's not your fault, Hamish," said Hugh. "You've been through a lot."

"Nae, laddie, ye just don't get it. It's my job to stop the king, and now he's out."

"Hamish? What are you talking about?"

"I'm supposed to monitor the Elf King. I'm supposed to find him and take him back to where he belongs. This whole job has just become a lot harder."

"I don't understand?" said Emily. "I thought your job was working with the runes?"

"Aye, 'tis, but I also hold the role of chief finder, amongst many others. I'm supposed to catch the Elf King and reign him in. I lost track of him before I went into hiding, and then I cuidna leave Heather behind on her own. Now he's out in the world again, and we'll be at war once more."

Emily looked at him, sorrow in her eyes.

"Is that where you went each summer, to look for him?"

Hamish nodded.

"Aye, I never told ye and yer ma because she'd only have wanted to follow. I'm so sorry Em."

She embraced the man with a hug, and they were quickly joined by Heather, who was in tears.

Hugh looked at Barrington, who was looking just as awkward as he was. They moved to join Gambi and Jeb, unsure of where to place themselves. Eventually, the three parted, wiping the tears away from their eyes. Even the eldest of the trio had found it hard to hold back the tears.It was some time before they stopped, giving Hugh the chance to ask the questions, begging to be answered.

"I'm sorry to drag you through this again, but do you have any idea who it was that kidnapped you and how you ended up here?"

"Well, there's a tale. I was out on the deck, playing me bladder pipes as usual, when I was attacked. They came at me from out of the fog, taking me unawares. Before I knew what was going on, they dropped a rune net over me, rendering me all but useless. I didnae have me aegis on, otherwise I would have stood a fighting chance."

"Did you see who it was?"

"I'm sorry Hugh, but the net made me weak. There were runes the likes of which even I had never seen before. I watched them break the airlock in, and I heard them take out Heather. I think they meant to kill her, but she's made of strong stuff. Isn't that right lassie?" He looked on with pride at Heather. "They took me back to the edge of the marsh and put me into a cart. They removed the rune net and shut the door. I had some strength left, but nae whisky to keep me going, so I had to reserve me strength.

"I was aware of the cart going up a long ramp and being loaded into a cargo airship. I had food and water thrown at me through a hatch in the roof. I banged my feet on the side of the cart, but it was nae use, the wood was strong, enchanted, I think. They tried to stop me making so much noise, but they cuidna do it. We were days on the move, and we then stopped overnight somewhere before the last leg to here. There were lots of people milling around, and it was cold, so, so cold."

"Did ye even know where ye were?" said Heather.

"I heard people speaking; Dallum was mentioned, so I figured we were in the Old World. I spoke to one of me captors. He sounded young, and all he said was they needed me for me skills as a guide. Anyway, when the airship landed they unloaded the cart and we hit the road again, and I resumed me banging, until I couldn't continue anymore. At one point I heard trumpets way off in the distance, so I figure I must've passed out. I came round enough to see a big building but cuidna make out what it was, before being dragged into the cells.

"The next thing I remember is seeing this laddie here. I don't know how ye found me, but boy, am I glad ye did. I was close to crossing over, and without Betsie, too. I was so glad to see her. When she turned up, I knew we were gonna be alright, though I dread to think what would've happened if you hadn't have reached me in time."

They stood in silence whilst Hamish's tale sank in. Hugh still looked confused. "So who was it you saw on the way back here?"

"What do ye mean?"

"You said, you finally had him. Who was he?"

"Ah, you'll have to forgive me, Hugh. Me memory's hazy; I was close to the edge." He shuffled on the spot as though he was holding back. Hugh tried to enter his head, but Hamish blocked him out.

"Right then," he said, clearing his throat, wanting to change the situation. "What's yer plan to get us out?"

He looked at all of them, hopeful that they would have found a way out of the cell. This was met with blank looks in return.

"Alright, so it looks as though it's down to me to get us out of here, then. Anyone up for giving me a wee hand?" Hamish stared at them all. "Well, dinnae all volunteer at once. I widnae want to interrupt any of yer busy schedules." Reluctantly, they all stood forward. "Thank you. What we're looking for is air."

"Air? I'm sorry, old bean, but I don't think you're quite with it yet. The air is all around us." Barrington went mute, as his comments were met with a hard stare.

"A breeze then, if yer going to be picky about it."

"Right, yes," said Barrington, looking down at his feet.

They began shuffling around the cell with their hands in the air, attempting to detect any signs of air seeping into the small room. Emily illuminated her firestone to add to the light from Hugh's, and moments later Heather called everyone over.

"Look, I think I've found it!"

"Let's take a wee look, lassie. Ah, yer ye daddy's gal, eh? Thas an air vent, that is."

"I hate to put a spoiler on things," said Jeb, "but it's six feet out of reach and the size of a brick. We'll need a miracle to get through there."

"Negative tones … a little whiney … why it can only be …" Hamish spun around on his heels, his kilt flapping outwards. "Aye, it's Winky!

How ye doing?" He ruffled Jeb's hair.

"Fine, thanks, Hamish," he said, batting him off.

"Ye don't change, do ye? Still got the voice of a pleading dog."

"Hey! I don't whine, thank you. I just think it's better to voice me concerns, that's all, Hamish."

The conversation was cut short by the sound of the door being unlocked. Hugh froze. If Hamish was caught in here with them, it would cause massive problems.

"We need to hide you, *quick!*" he said, springing into action. He and Emily extinguished their firestones, and Hamish was shoved into the corner. They all took their jackets off to hide him, just as the door opened. Hugh stood, leaning on the wall, with a hand behind his head.

"What'cha all up to in 'ere?" said the troll guard, their noses recoiling at the smell.

"Nothing," they all chimed at the same time.

"Hmm." His noise turned into a cough, and he hawked up a lump of troll gunk, which he spat to the floor.

The guard stepped inside the cell, and Hugh tried to steady his breathing as the troll walked up to him. He attempted to not breathe his odour in, as his eyes watered from the stench. This one was a mixture of sweat, onion and rotting cabbage, and he struggled to steady his nerves as the overwhelming aroma infiltrated his nostrils. It was all he could do to keep his food down.

The guard continued looking around the cell, moving towards Emily, who was standing on the other side of the pile of jackets on the floor, before he paused. Hugh's brow was soaked. The guard was about to inspect the pile when another guard appeared at the door.

"Oi, what'cha in 'ere for? His lordship said not to venture in here with them, and you went and left the door open, you plonker. Out. *Now!*"

The first guard held short of lifting a jacket. He stood up and looked around the room, looking at the smiling people, who had stopped breathing.

"They's up to summit," he said to the guard at the door.

"Yeah, well, they can stay up to summit behind lock and key. *Out!*"

The first guard looked them up and down, before plodding out of the cell in a huff, the door slamming shut behind him.

They all let out a collective sigh of relief and began breathing once more, then regretted the decision immediately. The stench still hung in the air. The troll guards of the King's Seat were known for their ability to knock a man off his feet at twenty paces by smell alone. If that didn't work, then a single punch to the stomach would normally be enough to finish them off.

The current occupants of cell six nine three, were scrabbling for the air vent, fighting to get some fresh air. As they clambered upwards, grabbing hold of the slimy grill, it decided it had had enough of prison life, and crumbled in their hands. They all landed in a pile on the floor in a comic chorus of groans and yelps.

"Shhhh ..."

They held their collective breath and listened to make sure the curious guard was out of earshot.

"Well, that was unexpected," said Barrington from within the pile of people, looking up at the hole where the grate once was.

On closer inspection, they saw some bricks had dislodged, showing a larger hole than before. They pulled at the bricks, finding that water had seeped in over the years, causing the mortar to degrade.

As they were pulling the wall apart, they saw a cavity behind the cell, designed to help airflow within the cells, and it was big enough for a person to fit through. Hugh noticed a flickering light reflecting off the rock wall from somewhere further along. They were about to see who could fit in when there came a lot of commotion from the corridor outside.

There was no need to find out what the fuss was about, as the answer was standing in the cell with them. They rushed to get through the newly created hole and began squeezing into the gap. Hugh was the last man through, as he heard the cell door being unlocked. He didn't wait to see who it was that was coming in. The smell alone was enough to give him an idea.

As he pushed his way between the walls, he heard the calls being shouted at the realisation of their disappearance. He knew the trolls wouldn't be able to fit into the gap and saw a gnarled and podgy hand fill the gap between the wall and rock. He hoped it would take time to get human guards down to the cells.

They scurried along the gap, which was slimy and pungent with the smell of mould. The narrow gap finally gave way to an access ladder heading upwards. The ladder, too, was slippery, and Hugh lost his footing more than once. Each time he nearly fell, he gripped the ladder tightly, for fear of falling to the bottom. He refused to look down, knowing that to do so would spell disaster.

He could still hear the commotion echoing off the walls below, and it sounded like the guards were getting themselves into order. The sound of people making their way down into the gap soon followed, and he knew it wouldn't be long before they reached the bottom of the ladder.

He was paying so much attention to the noise that he didn't realise that the party above had stopped. The sight that greeted him was most unpleasant, with something hitting him in the face. Letting out a cry of shock, he retreated down a few rungs, glad to be out of Hamish's kilt, wiping his face on his grubby sleeve.

"Whoa there laddie, that's a bit too close, even for me."

Hugh was busy spitting back down the ladder with his eyes closed. "Too much! Too much!" he said repeatedly.

"Will you keep the noise down!" said Emily.

The sound of a metal clang above told Hugh a hatch of sorts had opened. Light poured down the dimly lit shaft, causing Hugh's eyes to sting. They all clambered out into the fresh air, shielding their eyes from the intense light. It was a clear afternoon; the sunlight punching its rays into the alley they found themselves in.

"Shut the hatch, quickly," said Barrington.

Heather slammed it shut, then found a metal bar on the floor next to her and wedged it into the handle to prevent it from being opened. The sound of voices under the hatch told them how close a call it had been.

They needed to put space between themselves and the guards, who would now be making their way to street level. They crept along many alleyways and crossed the spiral road. When the coast was clear, they would move quickly to another dark alley.

A deep horn sounded from on top of the King's Seat. The drone seemed to reach the innermost core of Hugh's body, vibrating him from the inside out. It changed to an intermittent drone, and the streets emptied. Gambi informed them this was the signal for the streets to be cleared when the city was under attack. The sound sent shivers down Hugh's back.

"What do we do now?" said Jeb, looking distressed.

"We need to get off this street and out of this city," said Hamish.

It was then Hugh remembered something.

"We need our bags, Barrington."

"This is hardly the time for mementoes," said Jeb.

"These aren't mementoes. The notebook is in there. It has everything we need to progress. Without it, we're lost."

"Where is it?" asked Emily.

"The last time I remember seeing it was on the floor when we were dragged from the Ole Gambi Inn. They wouldn't have left without searching the place. That means ..."

They all looked up to the towering King's Seat.

"You have to be kidding me?" said Jeb. "We've only just escaped from there, and now we are going to break back in? Nope, not me!"

"We can leave you out here to fend for yerself, Wee Winky, if that's what ye'd prefer?" said Hamish.

Jeb glared at him, but it was no use.

"Fine. But I don't see how we are going to get back in there. We don't know where we are going?"

Gambi let out one of his now famous throat clearings, and they all turned to look at him.

"I has a good idea of how we can make it in."

Chapter 28

Ol' Ned Gambi was one of life's little wonders and full of stories from his past – of which there were many – as well as useful surprises. One such surprise was that this wasn't his first foray into the cells under the King's Seat. It turned out he had been quite the rebel over the years and had spent many nights in the cells under the seat. He reassured the group that the guards hadn't changed their routines in all the times he had visited the underground rooms.

He led them through the now empty streets, keeping to the long shadows, with the warning horn still blaring out. It was enough to put most people off heading outside, leaving only the guards and their prey to endure the appalling noise.

"So, you think that if we break in through that door there, we will be in the library of lost souls?" said Barrington, over the noise.

"I don't thinks, I knows for sure. I've passed through the guards office many times, and that's the room where I gots all me belongings back."

"How do you…" the horns stopped. "That's better. How do you know our belongings will be there?" he said in a low voice.

"Because that's where they keeps all the belongings of those who entered the cells over the years. It's in the library we was speakin' about earlier. It's situated behind the guards office. I walked passed the doorway on me way out of there each time, gave me right chills down me spine, it did. I doubt they'll have changed the habit of a lifetime."

"So why are your belongings not in there?"

"I was a guest after the Elf King was caught. They were less keen on removing people after he was put away. The only ones kept since then are the ones of those who died whilst in their 'care'. I had mine returned when they released me."

"Alright, so how do we get in then?" said Emily. "And more importantly, how do we know that this isn't another trap."

"First, I can open any door — just leave it to me. Second, you has to believe me, I didn't set you up. I was as much a victim in this as you, and right now you has little choice." He looked her in the eye, and there seemed to be some unspoken conversation going on between them.

"Chaps and lasses," said Barrington, "I don't wish to intrude, but can we chivvy things along a bit. We're still in great danger here."

This sparked Gambi into action, and they all watched with intrigue. He shimmied up a drainpipe, stopping next to a small window which was propped open. It looked impossible for anyone to squeeze through, especially one as old as Gambi. They looked on as the man reached out and pulled himself into the open window. With a wiggling motion, he slowly made his way through the hole with ease.

As Hugh observed Gambi's motions, he was reminded of a mole he once saw digging back into its hill. Gambi disappeared from sight, leaving the group to wonder whether he had made it. Moments later, the door that looked impassable from the outside, began rattling, before it popped open, revealing a smiling Gambi. With one last look over their shoulders, the group snuck in.

"How did you do that?" asked Hugh.

Gambi said nothing, choosing to tap the side of his nose instead. They found themselves in a room with hundreds of shelves full of belongings.

They clung to the shadows, as a guard walked past the open door.

"Well, this job looks like it will be *easy*," said Jeb in a low voice.

Hamish turned to look at him. Jeb flushed and looked at his feet, muttering something incomprehensible.

"Alright, what are we looking for, Hugh?"

"Well, it's a leather shoulder bag, and it's embossed with the family crest."

Emily looked at him. "Really? Was the tattoo not good enough? You had to go the whole hog."

"For your information, the bag was a gift from my father, and he had it done for me."

"Will yese two pack it in?" said Heather. "Have some respect for the dead, and don't give Hugh a hard time about his tattoo; it's better than the card system."

"Oh, really?" said Emily. "What happens if you're caught, and they check your arm. You'll be stuck then, won't you?"

"And if ye lose yer card or worse, have it taken from ye?

"Girls, will ye pack it in, and stop squabbling," said Hamish in a low voice. He looked at Hugh, tutted, and shook his head. "If ye keep clucking like this, that guard'll hear ye."

They began the search of the shelves. It was dawning on Hugh how large this room was. It seemed to go on for shelf after shelf, without an end in sight. They spread out across the room and began searching the musty aisles. The room revealed a more sinister side of the King's Seat.

There were rows upon rows of belongings and shoes, from the tiny to the large, all split and dried out. It sent a chill down Hugh's spine, as he pondered the fate of all these people. Gambi was lucky to escape with his life the number of times he did. He continued his search, taking care not to disturb the items on the shelf out of respect.

"Hugh, *over here!*" Emily hissed.

"Where are you?" he said.

"Three rows from the far wall. Where are you?"

"Somewhere in the middle, I can't see over the shelves."

"Head back to the end of your aisle, and I'll go to the end of mine."

He turned back on himself; the dust swirling in his wake. He made it to the end, looking left towards the far wall, and Emily popped out, beckoning him to come to her. He reached where she was standing, and saw the room had affected her too. Her cheeks glistened in the light.

"What is it? Have you found it?"

She shook her head but said nothing. She blinked large, fat tears, which rolled down her face.

"Emily, what is it?"

Lost for words, she led him by the hand, her grip shaking uncontrollably. They stopped by a shelf with some random items. Hugh looked at them, and his entire world spun. There on the shelf was his father's bag, spectacles and shoes. He looked at Emily then back at the shelf. A sense of finality hit him hard in the pit of his stomach.

He found himself out of breath and unable to get the words to form in his mouth. Tears now made their way down his face, creating their own tracks in the build-up of dirt. He fell onto Emily's shoulder. The pain in his chest was immense. He had always held onto a glimmer of hope, a possibility against all odds, that his father may still be out there somewhere. To see his father's belongings here and know that they were never collected, could mean only one thing.

Barrington appeared next to them, his face covered with concern, before he, too, turned to the shelf in question. He raised a dirty hand to his mouth and swallowed hard.

"Oh, Hugh. I am so sorry, old bean. I… I don't know what to say."

"What's this? A wee mother's meeting?" asked Hamish, who arrived with Heather and Gambi. He looked at the three friends, then to the shelf, and finally back to Hugh. "Ah laddie," he said, letting out a heavy sigh and resting a large hand on Hugh's bony shoulder, giving it a comforting squeeze. "It's not all as it seems in this place. Though I suspect he may well have passed over."

This made Hugh worse, and Emily shot Hamish a glance. He shrugged back, then turned to the shelf and gently pulled the bag off it, carefully clearing the dust off. He forced the lock until it clicked open. It revealed more paper notes with codes and notes all over them.

"If ye ask me, I think they didnae realise the importance of this bag. Oh, we also found this," said Hamish, holding up Hugh's bag.

Hugh wiped the tears from his face, striking muck across his cheeks. "Thank you. Where did you find it?"

"Near to where we came in. There looks to have been more shelves added to the room recently. I fear we may've been next on the list to be joining those others who weren't so lucky, especially given that the Elf King is back. Oh, and I also found this next to it." he said, handing a pipe to Barrington.

"Marvellous! Good find, old chap."

Hamish was putting the items from Frederick's bag into Hugh's when a flustered Jeb came running down the aisle. He was followed by heavy footsteps and familiar smell of two troll guards skidding to a halt at the end of the aisle, bumping into a shelf, which rocked ominously.

"Guards!" said Jeb, out of breath.

"Oh, aye, thanks fir that, Winkie."

The trolls turned and began thudding their way down the aisle.

"*RUN!*" said Hugh, grabbing Emily's hand and they took off in the opposite direction, the rest following close behind. He reached the end of the path to find out to be a dead end, the others crashing into him painfully. They looked around for a means of escape. The two troll guards who were in pursuit realised there was now no getting away, so slowed to a casual stroll, trying to get their breath back.

"Heh, they ain't got nowhere to go," said one of them. They began moving menacingly closer. Hugh tingled all over, then popped out of existence, then back again a few seconds later.

"Will you pack that in?" said Emily.

"I can't help it. It just happens."

"Then get some control over it!"

They looked back to the trolls who had stopped, looking at the group with confusion on their faces. Hugh took the chance to make a move and began climbing the shelves like a ladder. He reached the top and felt it wobbling as the others climbed up to join him.

"Oi! That's disrespectful, that is!" said one troll, who had come out of his confused trance, realising their chance to catch them was slipping away.

Hugh leapt across to the next shelf, landing awkward upon the pile of belongings. The others joined in, and they began leaping across the room, causing the shelves to sway. The trolls were attempting to climb up, but their sheer weight added to the rocking motion caused by the others jumping from the top.

Hugh watched in horror as the entire case of shelves slowly lurched forwards, hearing the contents sliding to the floor with a crash. It fell into the next case, then the next, causing a veritable wave of dust and noise to head in their direction. He turned and started leaping for his life. The sheer shock was causing him to enter and exit the sight repeatedly.

"Whoa!" –POP– "ahhh" –POP–"hang on" –POP– "yikes" –POP–

Meanwhile, he could hear Emily chastising him.

"Will" –POP– "you" –POP– "stop" –POP– "doing" – POP–"that!" –POP–

He wished he could.

"I" –POP– "can't" –POP– "bloody"–POP– "help" –POP– "it!"

This continued all the way to the end, where they gained the safety of the floor.

"Move, now!" said Hamish, and they ran for the open door, leaping out of it, followed by a plume of dust and noise. They landed hard on the cobbled street in a chaotic mass of arms and legs.

"There they are! Get them!" called a guard from down the street.

"Really?" said Hugh, getting to his feet, and helping the others.

They made for the nearest alleyway, the sound of whistles and footsteps following closely behind. They changed tack regularly, occasionally slipping down some stairs, then faced aching legs as they climbed up others, in an attempt to shake the pursuers off.

The guards, whose legs were more attuned to the city streets, didn't give them an inch. They ran past Ole Gambi's Inn, and Hugh saw something shoot out of the old man's hand, followed by a small explosion a moment later, as the building burst into flames.

They ducked and weaved through the debris that flew through the surrounding air before running down another passage. Hugh could feel the sea breeze hitting his face and knew this had to be the way to freedom. The sun was setting, and he hoped the tradesman's entrance was still open.

They picked up pace, this time heading in a vague downhill direction. Eventually the group burst out into the street by the curtain wall, seeing the tourist map they used to get to Gambi's place. Hugh thought on his feet and ran to the machine.

"Hugh, this way. We don't have time for a sightseers map."

Hugh didn't listen and ran up to the information board.

"Hugh?"

"Welcome to Kings Seat, the heart of Mor ... Oi! Gerroff me!"

Hugh had pushed his hand through the flap in the machine, grabbed the beast within and pulled it out hanging onto its wrist, pulling the door off in the process. He swapped the creature to his other hand and shook the door to the floor.

"What'cha think yer playin at? Put me down, right now. That's criminal damage, that is!"

"Sod that," said Hugh. "You show us the way out of here, and I'll set you free."

The beast looked at him. His taloned claws stopped attacking

Hugh's own hand.

"Deal."

Hugh nodded and ran back to the rest of the group, just as the guards arrived. They ran for the hole in the wall leading to the tradesman's entrance, ducking to get through the tight passage, which worked to their advantage. To Hugh's dismay, he saw the drawbridge was already raised and panicked as they still ran through the passage.

The guard at the end was taken by surprise by the newcomers, as Hamish shoulder barged him out of the way. He slammed a lever in the wall and kept running to the uncontrolled, opening drawbridge. Light flooded into the darkened gateway, as Hamish ran at the bridge that was already halfway down. He began running up the decreasing slope, his weight only speeding it up. He stood on the end, letting out a war cry, kilt flapping in the wind, as the drawbridge slammed to the ground so hard it splintered in the middle.

As the rest of the group followed Hamish, heading over the draw-bridge, Hugh thought it was going to split. They made it over, with their pursuers close behind, but as the guards chasing them headed over the weak spot, the bridge gave way, sending the lot into the moat.

The group momentarily stopped, being caught by the unfolding scene. The guards writhed in the grimy waters, looking like bog monsters from the deep. Hugh noticed something moving towards the mass of arms and legs, and one by one, the guards disappeared under the water.

The group returned to their senses and carried on going, heading for the tight streets of the old fishing village. They weren't alone for long, as Hugh heard more cries of anger coming from further up the street. The Portward Gate had been opened, and fresh guards were flooding into the street behind them. They darted into the nearest gap between the houses. The area was made up of narrow lanes and alleys, tighter than those in Portis-Montis.

"What is that thing you are holding?" shouted Barrington, as they took a sharp turn right.

"It's a Partem Goblin. Excellent at finding the way when lost," said Hugh.

"Good thinking, laddie," said Hamish, patting Hugh in the back. "Now, I'd be most happy if ye could ask it the way out of this mess."

Hugh held the goblin as steady as he could, so it could shout out the directions.

"We need to get out of here, fast."

"Right. Thank you for choosing the Partem service. Please tell me your destination."

"We don't know."

"I don't know, ain't no good. I need a destination."

"Out of this place."

"Right, calculating your route out of this place ... I'm sorry, I ain't got that in my range. Anywhere else you would like to go?"

"For goodness sakes! I don't know ... the port? Or anywhere away from that lot chasing us!"

"Oh, I know that one, easy. Take the next left." They turned left. "No, not that left."

"But you said left?"

"Yeah, well, I meant the other left, didn't I ..."

It tailed off, grumbling to itself, whilst the group doubled back on themselves.

They followed the directions, coming across the guards more than once and altering their route quickly.

"You appear to have made a wrong turn. Please carry out a switchback at your nearest convenience."

"What? That takes us back to the guards. Find us a different way," said Hugh.

"Cor, I dunno. The rudeness of some people! Recalculating route ... again. Take a right ... no, left ... or was it right?"

"Which bloody one?"

"Hang on, hang on, just getting' me bearings. Right …"

"Right, it is then."

"No, not *right*, I was sayin' right. You wanna go straight on."

The sound of footsteps was getting louder behind them.

"Alright, please can you get us off this path and away from the people behind us?"

For once the Partem Goblin listened without a fuss, and took them down a series of streets, leaving their chasers somewhere lost within the maze of buildings. The air was cool, as they ran between the tightly packed buildings, the smell of fish hanging strong in the air.

Where there were pavements, they were high, and Hugh nearly dropped off the edge more than once. Where they had no choice but to run on the streets, they found the cobbles were slippery underfoot, and Hugh was finding it hard going. He was constantly looking down, making sure he didn't lose his footing.

After what seemed like an age, the goblin said, "You have reached your destination."

Hugh looked up, ready to see the open sea in front of him, only to have his hopes dashed.

"This isn't the port?"

"You said the port, I took you to the port."

"This is the Portward Gate! We wanted the port, the harbour area, the place where the boats leave from."

"Then you should've been more specific from the start. I ain't no mind reader, you know. Bloomin' tourists."

"Fat lot of use you are," said Barrington.

"I don't have to sit here takin this sort of abuse, ya know. I've had enough, I'm off."

Hugh watched, mouth open, as the goblin opened up a pair of wings and took flight.

"No, please don't leave us!"

"Too late. If you want a hint, head that way," said the goblin, pointing away from the city.

"*Thanks.*"

"Another idea might be to run. See ya later."

Hugh watched as it flew off, then saw another lot of guards coming around the curtain wall.

"I think now's a great time to make a move," said Hamish.

They all agreed and set off back into the maze of streets. Without the aid of the goblin, it was nigh on impossible to find their way around. The only bonus was the guards were having the same luck as them. Eventually, after many dead ends and learning to hide in the growing shadows, the buildings turned more industrial, with yards full of nets and coils of rope.

The smell of seaweed was strong on the wind, and they turned the last corner into the harbour area. They ran towards a pontoon, finding the tide nice and high. The area was deserted. The only sound came from their own feet, reflecting off the warehouse walls. Numerous guards were now filtering their way through the maze of buildings, and they appeared to flow from the many alleys and streets facing the harbour area.

"Erm, guys, not to worry you, but we have company," said Jeb.

They all looked around and saw the swelling numbers of guards pouring onto the quayside. Hamish ran to the end of the pontoon, signalling for them all to follow. When they caught up with him, they saw he was untying the mooring lines to a small boat called *Ship Happens*.
Hugh hoped it wasn't a sign of what was to come.

"Who here knows how to operate one of these?"

Everyone stared at Barrington. He stood, shaking his head.

"I've sailed lifeboats bigger than this."

"Barrington, you're the only one who knows how to sail a ship," said Hugh. The others were busy boarding the vessel.

"That may be true, but if we attempt to outrun those men in this, they'll have us in no time. It'll be the end of us for sure. Why can't we use that boat?" he said, pointing to a larger boat on the next pontoon along.

"All ye days will be over entirely if ye dinnae get on this boat, laddie! It's this boat, or no boat."

He nodded to movement happening behind them. The guards were getting into formation up on the quayside, ready to flood onto the pontoon, cutting off any other means of escape.

"Barrington, *please*," said Hugh. "We need a captain, one who is seaworthy, who is marked with honour, and you're the man for the job." Barrington glanced a look at Hugh. "Please Barrington?"

A bolt flew over Barrington's head.

"Righto, make way, captain coming aboard." He took a deep breath, puffed out his chest, then boarded the small vessel. He made his way to the small wheelhouse.

"Barrington, do you need any help?"

"My dearest Hugh, you can take the man out of the navy, but you can't take the navy out of the man. I've had plenty of experience with this type of vessel. We used them for training back in the day. Now if you will excuse me, this old sea dog needs to set sail once more." He turned and walked into the wheelhouse.

"Is he gonna be alright?" asked Heather.

"He'll be fine, just you see. We'll be casting off any minute now … any minute …"

They stood looking back from where they had come, watching the guards making their way down the pontoon.

"Any minute now … Erm, Barrington, now might be a good time to start the engine … Barrington?"

Lanterns flickered into life, then extinguished themselves.

Winches wound forwards, then reversed back again, followed by a fishing net landing heavily on the deck. Gambi stuck his head into the wheelhouse, then turned back to Hugh.

"He might need a hand in there," he said, nodding his head back to the wheelhouse. Hugh, Heather and Emily ran into the small space to find Barrington muttering at the controls, hitting random buttons at will.

"Bloody thing, all symbols and runes."

"Barrington? Not to worry you, but half the guard of Kings Seat are currently making their way towards us. Ought we not be getting a move on?"

"What mad lunatic designed this? This is like no ship I've sailed before."

Hugh peered over his shoulder, seeing a control panel full of oddly shaped runes. Emily and Heather pushed him to one side, and started working together, pushing buttons and mastering the panel like pros. It lit up and beeped into life.

"Cast off," said Emily.

"Er, yes. Cast off," said Barrington through the open door.

The hairs on Hugh's neck stood upon end, as the boat rumbled to life, and he saw the harbour wall begin to move out of the window. They had done it.

They were finally on the move. With Emily and Heather mastering the controls, and Barrington still muttering to himself about the layout, Hugh made his way out on deck.

The front of the pack had made it to the end of the pontoon too late. Golden bolts were now flying overhead, hissing as they hit the sea, but the boat picked up speed and cleared the harbour wall. The sea became choppy, and Hugh had to steady himself on the rail as he had began to feel unwell.

"I'm glad we cleared that lot," he said to Hamish, attempting to take his mind off the rocking motion.

"I widnae be too sure of that, laddie," he said, pointing back to the harbour. A fleet of small boats was taking up the chase.

"Barrington, we've got company!"

Barrington put his head out of the door, seeing the mass of moving lights heading towards them. "Damn, kill the lights … Ladies?"

"Hang on a minute!" snapped Emily.

"That's, hang on, *captain* to you."

The choice words that Emily and Heather shouted back at him, told Hugh who was really in charge at the helm. All the different lights around the vessel began flashing on and off, as they struggled to find the right control.

At one point a flare went off, which turned out to be Barrington losing his footing and slipping onto the wrong control. This had the effect of illuminating the entire bay area, the complete opposite of what they were trying to achieve. After another berating from those in charge, Barrington made himself scarce.

"Err … I'll just tend to things out here, ladies," he said, walking out onto the deck.

Hugh saw their pursuers, illuminated nice and clearly by the flare, noticing they had fallen back somewhat. They appeared to be turning, following a line of buoys which marked out a shipping lane.

"Is there a reason that we are not taking the same route as those ships?" he asked.

"Ah, well, they are larger ships, whereas we're on a smaller boat. That allows us to go straight past the small island over there," said Barrington, knowledgeably, pointing to something beyond the bow.

The trailing ships now sent their own flares into the sky, illuminating the bay further.

"And you are sure we won't bottom out?" said Jeb, looking concerned.

"Jeb, my dear fellow. I am an experienced seafarer with years of experience under my belt. I think I may know a little more about boats than you."

"Aye, well if that's true, then can ye explain why we've stopped moving forwards?" said Hamish, gripping the rail.

"It may appear that we have stopped, but that's because we are at sea without reference points. We're still moving. I can sense it in my bones. Old naval habit." He gave them a wink and a smile, rocking side to side with the motion of the little boat.

"Well, I use me eyes, and ye can stick yer wee naval habit up yer arse. Boats tend to move forward in my world, not upwards."

Everyone looked around and saw that Hamish was indeed correct. They were slowly rising out of the water.

"*Barrington!* A little assistance if you will, please," said Emily from the wheelhouse. Barrington backed his way to Emily and Heather, a forced smile on his face.

Everyone held their breath as snippets of words from Barrington came out.

"What? ... that's not right? These must be old charts ... but it's impossible ... just a myth ..." He made his way back out on deck, still smiling.

"Is there an issue?" said Hugh, his stomach flipping over, ready to spit its contents across the deck.

"Erm, well, uh ..." said Barrington, raising a shaking hand and pointing towards the island.

Hugh's eyes opened wide as he turned to see what his friend was pointing at. The small island had risen out of the sea, revealing two large, menacing eyes.

Behind him, Jeb let out a yelp. Hugh turned back to face the harbour, which had now been blocked from view. He craned his neck as he took in the scene in its place.

A large, suckered tentacle was slowly rising out of the sea behind them, glistening in the light given off by the flares. Hugh turned back to Barrington for an answer. He stood wide eyed, still smiling and pointing, his jowl quivering. Only one word could pass his lips.

"Kraken."

Chapter 29

The door to his temporary office burst open, making Smithson jump.

"What the devil's this all about? You don't just barge in here unannounced. Explain yourself this instant!"

"Lord Smithson, sir. They've escaped ... again," said the guard.

Smithson sat there in stony-faced silence. He took a deep breath in, then released it slowly through his nose.

"You assured me they could not escape from the harbour. Did you station your men down there as I requested?"

"Erm ..."

"No, of course you didn't. Why does nothing work around here? I'm going to have to make some changes if things are to be working better in the future."

The guard looked at him, a look of confusion on his face.

"It's not that we meant for them to escape, your lordship. It's just we don't know the harbour area. We is just city guards, we never venture near the fisherman. We have a long-standing dispute with 'em."

"I don't care for your excuses. I'll deal with you all later. Now get out of my sight."

"Sir." The guard brought his feet together with a stomp, turned and left the room, bumping into Collins and his apprentice on the way out.

"What do you want?"

"I see you've just received the bad news then?" said Collins.

"Yes, would you believe it, but I think we have finally found some people more incompetent than you two."

Collins stood with raised eyebrows. The apprentice stood mute.

"You know, I don't have to serve you."

Smithson turned on his heels and rounded his desk.

"What did you just say? I think you ought to remember who you are now talking to."

"Oh yes, how easily I forget, your new title. How you humans love your fake levels of authority."

"And what, exactly, is that supposed to mean?"

"Nothing," said Collins with a pleasant smile on his face.

"You ought to take a leaf out of your apprentice's book and keep your gob shut once in a while."

"But then, how would I torment you?"

Smithson scowled at his servant.

There was a long pause whilst they stared each other out before Smithson finally broke the tension.

"Well? What have you come here to say, or is it just to gloat?"

"So, I may talk then?"

Smithson shot him a look.

"Ah, good. Well, I'm here to report that though your current bumbling garrison have let Geber and his friends escape, they have currently strayed out of the safety of shallow waters, and over the depths of Kraken Bay." He stood with a smile on his face.

"What on earth are you on about?"

Collins and his apprentice walked up to the window.

"Come and see what I'm talking about."

Smithson came over to the window and saw the current action taking place out in the bay.

"What the devil is that?"

"It's the Kraken's nest. The buoys mark out the shallower waters, deep enough for shipping, but too shallow for the Kraken. It lives in the collapsed volcano which once was in the bay."

They watched the mass of tentacles rising out from the depths, looming over the small boat. A smile as large as a side plate grew across Smithson's face.

"Collins, we need to take a trip."

"Where to now?"

"To the powers that be in Bansk, to report the untimely demise of Geber and his posse of followers."

Chapter 30

Hugh stood on the deck of *Ship Happens*, watching the mass of tentacles rise out of the surrounding water. Nobody was speaking. All were transfixed by the situation unfolding around them. The small island had risen right out of the water now. The Kraken loomed over the boat, assessing the best way to devour its prey.

"What do we do now?" said Hugh. He was whispering, but he didn't know why.

"My coat ... I don't have my coat," said Barrington.

"What? I think that's the last thing you need right now."

"That's where you're wrong, my dear friend."

Before Hugh could ask his friend what he was talking about, Emily and Heather staggered out from the wheelhouse. The boat was now out of the water enough that it teetered upon the tentacle it had balanced on. A suckered end crept out of the water and slowly wrapped itself around the vessel. It creaked under the strain, as the beast squeezed the hull.

"Barrington, you will be alright," said Emily, seeming to know what he was talking about.

"But what do we do now?" asked Jeb.

"I s'pose we needs to abandon ship, but it's the captain's call," said Gambi.

Everyone looked to Barrington – now affirmed in the role of captain

– who looked back to Emily and Heather.

"Well, you said you were the captain," said Emily.

"Erm … yes I did, didn't I? Well, I don't suppose we have any choice, really?"

"What? Yuu have to be kidding? Take a swim … with that thing?" said Jeb, eyes opened wide.

"It's that or be squished. Unless you has a better idea?" said Gambi.

"Aye, we hivna got a choice in the matter. But the decision really falls to the captain," said Hamish, wiping drips of water off his face from another tentacle rising above the boat. "I'd make it quick, though. I dinnae think she's going to wait."

"Well … I …" he began, but whatever he said was drowned out by the large tentacle slamming onto the deck of the small boat, right over Hugh.

"Hugh!" Emily cried out as it crashed down through the space where he was standing.

Everything else was drowned out by the sound of splintering wood.

'Bugger,' said Hugh into the darkness.

He was aware of the large tentacle coming down towards him. A fear rose inside of him, then he was sucked into the abyss of the sight once more. He patted himself down, realising he had brought his body with him.

'Well, that was lucky I guess.'

He began trying to find the runes needed to protect himself. He struggled to get a grasp on them, but the light feeling of warmth within told him that something had worked.

He looked around in the semidarkness, expecting to be sucked back into the real world, but it never came. Something nudged him from behind, and he turned to see Aeolus.

'Hello, boy. It's good to see a friendly face.'

'Hugh … Hugh … Is that you?'

Hugh knew he shouldn't, but he wanted to follow the distant voice;

but he knew also that his friends were in great danger and needed his help. He was torn about what to do. He didn't even know how fast or slowly time passed when he was in the sight.

'*What would you do?*' he said to the unicorn, not expecting to get a response (so he was surprised when it answered).

'*Hmm, I would leave the voice for now. Go get help and save Mistress Emily.*'

'*Ah, yes, Emily,*' said Hugh, as calm as if he were having a pleasant conversation on a dry summer's day.

All the stress in the world appeared to disappear in this place. His mind was full of clarity. '*But I have no way of getting out of this place. To be fair, I don't know how I got in.*'

'*Fear and emotion brings you to a place of safety,*' said Aeolus. '*That is why you are here in the sight.*'

'*Oh,*' said Hugh, nonplussed. '*So, we need help. Augustus maybe?*'

The unicorn nodded.

'*Can you take me there?*'

'*Climb on, I can cross you over to the living plane.*'

Hugh climbed onto the great beast, thinking that he ought to hold on tight, but as they moved – or what Hugh presumed to be moving, given the lack of wind and reference points – Hugh realised he needn't worry about falling off. The ride was serene, most unlike that of riding a horse in the real world. A point of light shone ahead and grew as they moved towards it.

'*Get ready,*' said Aeolus.

'*What for?*'

The unicorn leaned forward, kicking its hind legs high above its head, sending Hugh flying through the nothingness of everything that was. He felt the sensation behind his navel as he was sucked back into reality.

–POP–

Augustus was busy enjoying a night flight above the clouds, watching a peculiar thunderstorm from above, when Hugh popped out of thin air, onto his lap.

He screamed.

Hugh screamed and, leaning back into the controls, sent the airship into a nosedive. Augustus fought to get Hugh off from his lap whilst the airship pointed down through the clouds. They cleared the base, to see the sea coming towards them at speed. Augustus hit out at all manner of buttons whilst attempting to reach the controls, as Hugh dropped to the floor headfirst.

Augustus heaved back in the controls, and the airship levelled off, before rising back towards the direction it had come from. They popped up above the clouds and levelled off once more. He grabbed the mic on the console in front of him.

"Apologies there, chaps. Had an unexpected visitor. All's level and safe." He clicked the mic off and rounded on Hugh. "What the bloody hell do you think you are playing at, man? Wot wot! You don't just pop out into thin air onto someone's lap. Where is your mentor?" He looked around, to see if there was anyone else stood behind him.

"I don't have one. Well, I don't think I do anymore," said Hugh, the realisation hitting him in the chest.

"You don't have one? What were you doing in the sight, full body, with no guidance? Are you mad? How did you get back out?"

"It's hard to explain. Aeolus threw me back out."

Augustus was piecing the puzzle together quicker than Hugh could explain it.

"Wait a moment, did you say Aeolus? Who's that? Hang on, where are Barrington and Emily now?"

Hugh explained the most urgent of the news, as quick as he could.

"… and now they're in the sea!"

"That explains the flashes of light that I saw then."

"Hang on, you saw the flares going off?"

"You're lucky that I was flying the *Jewel* here so close to the area you were in. I thought it was a thunderstorm happening down there, but no time to talk now. Sit down, we're going in!"

Chapter 31

It was safe to say that, up until now, guard duty in the city of Kings Seat had been a pretty dull job. Every day always followed the same pattern of eat, guard, eat, sleep. Sometimes, if you were lucky, the sleep part would replace the guard part. However, since the Elf King had returned, things had picked up pace. Lessons learned many years ago were being dug out from deep within the memory, dusted off and readied to be put into use once more. Where the current scenario fitted in with basic training, nobody could be sure.

After watching the great beast called the Kraken being awoken by the foolhardy group of convicts – such a brazen move had to be commended, even if they were enemies of the king – they were treated to a spectacular scene of carnage and excitement.

They were distracted, however, from the foaming sea, by the sight of an AST ship of all things, bombing out from the clouds. Its outside lights flashed on and off before it levelled and went shooting upwards once more. For the first time in their working career, the guards had no regrets about signing up.

—

Up above the clouds, Augustus was heading back towards the sea, readying himself and his new passenger for a bumpy ride. He hit a button on the control panel and a spare seat popped up next to him.

"Come next to me. I need your eyes." Hugh did as instructed and sat himself next to the captain. "This is going to be one hell of a ride, and I need you to warn me about any obstacles that arise."

"Obstacles?"

"Yes, tentacles and whatnot, wot wot?" He was saying all this, looking at Hugh whilst heading towards the chaos below.

"Erm ...?"

"What is it now? You need to be clear when talking to me, otherwise we—"

"*Look out!*" screamed Hugh, hiding behind his hands. Augustus looked out the window, pulling back, then turning the control to avoid a large tentacle. Hugh sat whimpering in the seat next to him.

"That's it, nice and clear. Right, let's get to work."

"How are we going to — arrghhh, tentacle! And boat ... I think."

Hugh clung onto the seat as they dodged another tentacle, currently waving the remnants of the prow of the boat, as if it were a baby's rattle.

"How are we going to rescue them?"

"This old girl has a few tricks left in her yet. Hang on." He pressed a button on the control panel, then disappeared with a ...

–POP–

leaving Hugh spluttering random words of fear. The ship avoided a large tentacle with luck more than accuracy.

With another ...

–POP–

Augustus reappeared next to Hugh, drenched, with a bit of seaweed in place of his hat.

"Erm?"

"What? wot wot!"

"Nothing."

"Right, well, you will be pleased to hear I've found them. Right, let me see, aha!" Augustus hit a button, and Hugh heard cogs and machinery rattling into life. The ship headed for the sea once again.

Hugh screamed, "Tentacle, tentacle, tentacle…" like a deranged person, unsure if the captain was listening.

"We need to perform a rescue, chaps. Are you ready down there to collect some packages?" said Augustus into a mic, not looking out the window, but still missing the tentacle.

"*Aye, Captain.*" This the response from a crew member stationed below.

"Right, here we go."

He dipped the nose of the ship down, nearly getting it caught up in the chaos.

"*Three on-board, Captain. Two to get.*"

Augustus went up in a large arc, before heading back for a second attempt.

"*Missed.*"

"Dang and blast!" he said, hitting the control column.

"*Tentacle!*"

"What? Oh yes," said Augusts, looking up briefly, swerving out the way of a large sucker.

With one hand on the controls, the other rooted around for something in a cubbyhole. He pulled out a half-eaten, fluff-covered sandwich and glanced over at Hugh.

"What? I always get hungry at moments like these." He bit into the sandwich then waved it in front of Hugh's nose.

"Do you want some?" he said, spraying bits of food which landed on his lap. Hugh looked back, gob-smacked. "No? Suit yourself." He looked forward just in time to avoid a fishing net flying through the air.

Hugh didn't know how much more his heart could take. As the ship rose once more, readying for another dive, Augustus pressed another button. Hugh heard gurgling and hissing, somewhere to his left, followed by the ding of a bell, and a small flap opened.

Swallowing the half-eaten mouthful, Augustus looked at Hugh.

"Well? what are you waiting for? Pass it here, I'm thirsty."

Not believing he was following the orders, Hugh reached into the hole, and pulled out a steaming cup of tea. He passed it to the captain, spilling some on his hand, scalding himself. He let out a yelp.

"Careful with that, it's hot. I don't want to get burnt."

Hugh passed the cup of tea to the open hand next to him, shaking his head.

"That's better," Augustus said after a long slurp. He now balanced the cup on his lap.

"Are you sure that's a wise thing to do?"

"What? Yes, of course. I do it all the time." Augustus grabbed the mic once more, with Hugh now watching the tea and the Kraken. "We have to get them on this run, do or die," he said into the mic.

"*Right you are, sir.*"

Hugh looked wide eyed at Augustus.

"Erm, do I get a say in the dying part?"

"Nope."

And with that, they went in for a last attempt. Hugh saw the foaming water from the writhing mass of destruction coming towards them, feeling for sure that they were done for.

At that moment, the captain took in a deep breath and sneezed. The tea went everywhere, across the console, the captain's lap and – to Hugh's horror – his eyes as well.

"Argh! Dang, blasted thing. I can't bloody see! Grab the controls."

"What?"

"I said, grab the blasted controls!"

"But we're coming in hot!" he said, grabbing the controls, pulling back on them, sending the ship skywards again.

"Not as hot as my lap and face! And where are you going? They are in the sea, not the sky."

Augustus was busy blindly pushing buttons, blinking the tea out of his eyes, with many items popping up and disappearing again. Eventually, a box of tissues jumped out at Hugh. He passed them over to Augustus, who wiped his eyes and re-took the controls, pointing the ship downwards once more.

"There they are." He mopped himself down whilst looking at Hugh. "Why didn't you take the cup of tea off my lap? You could see I was going to sneeze."

Hugh stared on in amazement, before looking forwards, seeing the sea coming towards them at an alarming rate, and he let out a yelp.

"What's wrong with you now?" said Augustus, turning his attention to the mass of writhing tentacles coming their way, and he grabbed the controls. "Come on, old girl, you can do it," he said, fighting with the mass of levers in front of him.

Hugh saw a vein on the side of the man's head, bulging with the effort he was putting into keeping the airship from being pulled under the waves. A large sucker attached itself to the front window, making Hugh jump. He watched it pulsate, as it increased its hold. Another smaller tentacle rapped on the side window.

"Oh, no you don't, you little blighter!" Augustus punched another button on the console. A flash of light filled the bridge, followed by a loud squeal, as the beast released its grip on the ship.

"Are they in?"

"*Yessir!*"

"Right, hold on to your pants, lads!"

Augustus pulled back on the control, forced the throttled forwards and closed his eyes, emitting a white glow. Every nerve ending in Hugh's body fired up, as he felt as light as a feather. The AST ship shot out of the sea and out above the clouds in a matter of seconds.

Everything was serene. The noise from the chaos below had ceased to be, and above the clouds, the moon was shining. It was disturbed by the sound of voices, high on adrenaline, all trying to talk over each other.

Someone was crying, and Hugh heard his name mentioned.

"But he's gone, Hugh's gone!" said Emily, still in shock and upset at the thought of Hugh being wiped out by the Kraken.

"Ye dinnae know if that's true Em." said Hamish.

"You all saw it. He was crushed … crushed! There's no way he survived that, and we left him behind … Oh Hugh, what have I done?"

"Don't blame yourself, Emily," said Barrington. "It's all my fault. Another innocent life taken by my poor leadership! I will never forget this for the rest of my life." He sounded dreadful.

"No Barrington, ye mustn't blame yerself," said Heather.

"I can't believe he's gone …" said Emily.

"Me neither," said Jeb.

Gambi cleared his throat, and everyone looked at him. He nodded over to the doorway to the bridge.

"Nor me."

"What? Hugh!" said Emily. She ran across the room, appearing to fly the last few feet, and threw her arms around him, sobbing into his shoulder. "How, what, but how?"

Barrington and Heather made their way over and joined the embrace. Barrington broke off, to speak to Augustus.

"Here, you dropped this," he said, handing over the captain's hat.

There was a pause, whilst the captain slapped the wet hat onto his head. He splatted the seaweed into Barrington's hand before bear-hugging his cousin with joy. Barrington, being overwhelmed by the situation, embraced his cousin back.

The seaweed swung around Augustus's back and slapped the pair in the face. Once everyone had calmed down, Hugh could recount the story of his miraculous escape.

"You saw Aeolus?" said Emily.

"Yes, and he delivered me here to Augustus." The rest of them looked on in confusion.

"You told me you didn't have your mentor with you," said Augustus.

"I didn't. I said she was in the water, but I met Aeolus in the sight."

"Then who is Aeolus? Wot, wot?"

"He's Emily's uni—OW!"

Hugh yelped as Emily cracked him in the shin.

"Spirit guide," she said. "Aeolus is my spirit guide whilst in the sight."

"Ah, I see. That makes more sense now. Well, if it's alright with everyone, I'm going to get myself dry. I've an Aqua Dry 900 in the back, if any of you wish to use it? We're currently on auto pilot, held in a circular pattern, so nothing to worry about there."

"An Aqua Dry 900? I've heard of those," said Barrington. "Dry you out fully clothed if I'm not mistaken? I bet the person who invented that made a bob or two."

"Aye she did, and I'm proud of her for it." said Hamish, giving Heather a squeeze, wringing more water out of her.

"You mean to say that's *your* invention?"

"Aye, I am an inventor after all, and we have to make ends meet like any other family. I hope ye like the ship, that's a family invention too. I found the missing link to get the AST engines working safely." Barrington stood open-mouthed. "There's nae need to look shocked," said Heather.

She turned and walked off, offended. Hamish tutted, shaking his head, looking at Barrington.

"Heather, I didn't mean it like that ... Heather."

Barrington went over to talk his way out of the hole he had dug for himself.

Hugh began looking through his bag, checking that all was in order.

"So your bag survived, then?" said Emily, leaning her head on his shoulder.

"It looks to be all there. They didn't have the sense to search it in Kings Seat at least."

"Well, they're mainly trolls who share a single brain cell between them.

What's that?" She pointed at the broken compass.

"Ah, it's just some trinket that Barrington picked up. I think at one point it was a compass, but it no longer points in any direction."

He opened it up, and Emily looked in awe at the intricacy of the item.

"That's beautiful. What does the second needle around the outer edge do?"

"I wouldn't have a clue. It moves around as randomly as the main compass needle."

He passed it to Emily to have a look at. The needle went crazy, spinning this way and that. She closed it up and turned it over, looking at the symbol and writing on the back. She rubbed her fingers over a circle with two curved horizontal lines passing through it, one top, one bottom. There was one more across the centre.

"There are runes here too," she said.

"What ye got there, lassie?" said Hamish.

He, Jeb and Gambi came over.

"Hamish, would you gets a look at that," said Gambi. "Is that, I mean, can it be …"

"Look at what?" said Hugh, looking up at him.

"That's rare," said Hamish. "It's one of the missing relics, and I didnae think I'd see it this side of half a century."

"What are you talking about?" said Hugh, looking from Gambi to Hamish.

"Don't be panicked, laddie. What you have there is a thing called the Orbis."

Hugh stared back at him, open-mouthed, then across to Barrington, whose ears pricked up at the mention of the name.

"Did he just say what I think he did?" he said, walking back over to Hugh with Heather.

"Yes, he did."

"So yer aware of the Orbis, then?" said Hamish.

"Aware of it and searching for it, but I didn't know we had it until now. How does it work?"

"Ah, 'tis a beautiful thing to see it back in action. It's the book finder. I take it you tried it as a compass and thought it broken? That's the idea. It hides the true identity of the device. Though I think its third needle might be hiding. May I?"

Hugh nodded. He passed it over to Hamish, and it glowed in his hands, the light reflecting in the old man's eyes. Everyone seemed to fall silent, as the power of the object drew them in. As they watched, a third needle slid out from under the main compass needle.

"So, as ye can see," said Hamish, sounding reverent, "there's three needles and two faces, the outer and the inner. The one looking like the compass is the book locater dial. Ignore the compass markings and focus on the symbols. Outside, is the marker to show how much control you have over the Orbis. It works with the sight, using the power of the plane to help locate the books."

"How?" asked Hugh.

"Well, the four books of lore link into the sight. All power, be it magic, runes, natural or otherworldly, needs the sight as an energy source. That's why whoever gets the books will have all the power of the world."

These words sunk in, making Hugh feel uneasy.

"So if we get the books, then we have the power?" said Barrington. Hamish looked up at him cautiously.

"Yer nae getting it, laddie. No-one can hold that much power, except for the one who will find the missing element."

"So there definitely is a missing element," said Hugh.

"Oh, aye. Ye remember the extra rune lessons ye had at the university? Well, they link into this mystery. It's widely known that there's a missing element, but nobody knows where or what it is. The Elf King is desperate to find it, of course, but without knowing the location or what the item might look like, he's as stuck as the rest of us."

"I'm glad we have the Orbis, then. He won't be able to find the books without it."

"I widnae jump the gun there, laddie. There are replicas out there. Granted, they are not as strong as this one, but someone like the Elf King could make it yield to his power. It wouldn't get him exactly there, but it would get him close."

"So he may already have one of these book finders and be ahead of us?"

"Again, this is all speculation. I cannae say for sure that he has one yet, and even then, it wouldn't be able to locate the missing element."

"So that's what my father was after?"

"Yes, and no. Everyone's keen to find it, but it has to be found by the correct person. The prophecy spoke of someone who can combine the elements, work them in such a way that they become one. Only then will the fifth element reveal itself. I'm sorry Hugh, but yer father wasn't the one, and until we can find out who it is, we're stuck."

"But we can operate the elements between us, surely?"

"No, again yer not listening. The prophecy speaks of one who will come along, who will know all the powers. There's only three of yese younglings to start off with, four if ye include Heather here. I believe you all have a role in this, most probably to find and track down the one, before the Elf King does."

"So, that could mean I could be the one? And they have found me," said Jeb.

Everyone looked at him, paused, then laughed in hysterics. Jeb stood up, his face going red.

"Ye?" said Hamish, "Wee Winkie … the one! Thas a corker, that is! Ye cuidna find it even if it was in a box labelled *missing element* hidden in a room called the *missing element room!*" He wiped the tears away from his eyes. "Ye can always rely on Wee Winkie to come out with the jokes."

"Oh dear, it hurts so much," said Gambi, clutching at his side.

"So, how does the Orbis work?" said Hugh, bringing the conversation back to reality.

"Oh aye, sorry. So, ye have the outer dial here. Yiv to control that before you control the inner dial, and only then can ye look for the book. Ye must choose the element, by lining up the outer needle with the relevant symbol, then lock it in, by controlling the third needle to line up with the outer one. That leaves the compass needle, which will guide you to the book. Quite clever really."

"That seems like it will be quite difficult."

"Nonsense, ye just have to clear yer head and look at it with the right frame of mind, thas all."

He passed the Orbis back to Hugh, who held it in his palm. It tingled for a moment, as though it were vibrating, before stopping and losing its lustre.

"Why's it gone out? Where's the third needle gone?"

"Because yer wee head's fulla bunkum."

"My head is not full of bunkum."

"Some would disagree with that, anyway, give over fighting with me and get on with the job in hand. Ye have to clear the mind. Only then will the power flow through ye."

Hugh scowled at him, then looked down at the Orbis, squinting.

'Concentrate, laddie.'

'Like I showed you with the firestone.'

'What they said.'

Hugh looked at Hamish, Emily and Gambi, speaking aloud to their silent probing.

"Would you all mind naffing off out of my head. How can I clear my mind if you are all in there?"

"Well, if ye dinnae want the help?"

"It's not that. I just need space, and you are all putting me off."

Hamish held his hands up in front of him.

"Alright, no need to be a whinging ninny about it."

Hugh closed his eyes and cleared his mind. Something began glowing, and as he chanced a look, he saw the Orbis glowing bright.

"Is that any good?"

"Aye, perhaps a little too much power there, laddie," said Hamish, shielding his eyes. "Ye have to learn how to control the power of the sight."

The Orbis went dim once more.

"You sound just like Emily."

"Well, maybe you should listen then," said Emily with a raised eyebrow.

He looked to Hamish, who was pulling the same expression, then back to Emily and smiled.

"What?"

"Oh, nothing."

He turned back to the Orbis, and this time he was able to get it to glow with less intensity. He watched the outer needle slow down and come to a rest in line with the top above the north on the face. The third needle revealed itself once more.

"Very good. Right, now ye need to think of the book ye want to find."

Hugh concentrated on the book of alchemy, and both inner needles began spinning so fast, they turned into a blur.

"What in all things spritely are ye doing? Ye must remain calm and clear, slow the mind down."

"I am."

"Not gauging by the Orbis, you're not. Which book are ye trying to picture?"

"The book of alchemy."

"Ah, well there ye go then. Too much emotion attached to that one. Pick a different book."

Hugh looked up at Emily and decided that the lore book for magic would be a good place to start. He watched the Orbis glow gently. The outer arrow swung round to the symbol for earth.

"Very good. Right, you see the inner needle, the one that appeared?"

Hugh nodded. "Alright, try and turn it around to line it up with the outer needle to lock it in."

Hugh did this, and watched the third needle line up with the outer one.

"Thas good, but ye need to concentrate to get the compass needle to fix on the location of the book."

Hugh tried harder, but no matter how hard he focussed, he could not get the last needle to fix to one steady position. It slowly moved around.

'Concentrate, laddie!'

'I am!'

"Hamish," said Emily, putting an arm out to prevent him from retaliating.

"He is concentrating. Look, the outer and inner needles are still."

They gazed down at the Orbis and saw that Emily was correct. Even with Hugh stood in one place, he could still see the compass point slowly turning.

"Oh aye, so it is. Apologies, young Hugh. I wonder what's causing that?"

"Didn't Augustus leave us in a circular pattern, I think he called it? Could that be the issue?" said Barrington.

"That'll be it," said Heather, nodding.

"Then I think we had better leave this for now. It will be impossible to get a good fix on anything whilst we are moving," said Emily.

"Aye, ye'll get the hang of it laddie," said Hamish, patting Hugh on the shoulder.

With everyone else in agreement, the group separated once more, and Hugh stowed the Orbis safely away.

Augustus appeared through a door, looking remarkably dry and clean. All those who had been into the water took it in turns to get dry before they sat down to plan the next step. They agreed they needed to get back to Skellig-Krieg, and Augustus said he would drop them up near the Ranglestaff Mine – though it would be best to wait for first light so they could see the landing site.

From there, they could head down the track into the city. With a plan in hand, they settled themselves down for the short trip over the mountains. It wasn't long before they all nodded off, all exhausted from the day's adventures.

Chapter 32

Smithson was standing at the desk of the library of lost souls and had found another bell to ring – repeatedly. An annoyed guard came around and moved the bell out of reach. He was covered from head to toe in dust.

"That's enough of that. What do you want?"

"A little more respect, if you don't mind," said Smithson. "Does anyone do any work around here?"

The guard looked up, then realised who he was talking to.

"Apologies, I didn't realise it was you, *your lordship!*" said the smirking guard, showing no respect.

"What's your name? I'll be making a note of it for future reference."

"I don't answer to you. Now what do you want?"

"But I'm a lord, and I demand respect."

"And I'm in the King's Guard. We're all lords and ladies around here, requirement of the job, and we only answer to the king, so I suggest you drop your attitude. Besides, it's only a title."

Smithson stood looking agog at the guard.

"But—"

"But what? Now, if you're finished flaunting around, you can tell me what you want, or I'll have you removed."

Smithson let out a large sigh.

"I'm looking for a bag."

"You're in the wrong place. You want to go out the side door here, down the street to the Bag Emporium. Massive range, should suit the title of *lord*." He went to turn, but Smithson stopped him.

"No, wait."

"What? I got a load of angry spirits to deal with, and you're gettin' in the way."

"I need a bag that's in storage. The prisoner's name was Frederick Geber. I believe his bag is in here."

The guard looked at Smithson.

"Well, there's a name that's plagued us more than once."

"What do you mean?"

"Frederick Geber was a prisoner here, but he escaped. We had another member of the family in here too until he escaped."

"Dear me, what a sad state of affairs. Two escapees right under the noses of the king's own guard, and from the same family, no less. What would the Elf King say?"

The guard stared back, unimpressed.

"What we can't figure out is why they broke back in."

"They broke back in?"

"Yeah, two of our security trolls caught them in here. Caused great carnage they did, smashed the whole room up. Now everyone's panicking that they angered the spirits of the dead, but I keep telling 'em that it's Geber who'll get it. Anyway, from what I heard they got what was comin' to 'em. They ended up as supper for the Kraken. Just goes to show, don't anger the spirits."

"What were they looking for?"

"I dunno, do I? They looked lost, by all accounts. Listen, if you want a bag, fill out a form. It's going to take us ages to clear the mess up in there, and I bet the spirits are proper angry now, and we got to get it back to how it was. If we find anything, we'll let you know."

He passed a form, quill and ink pot to Smithson, who looked from the guard to the archaic equipment in front of him. He was about to make a comment but thought twice about it after looking at the guard. He pushed the quill to one side, pulled out his own pen and filled it in.

"I'll leave a forwarding address in Bansk. I have to be away today."

The guard looked at him suspiciously.

"What'cha going there for?" he said, reaching for his whistle.

"There'll be no need for that. I'm on a mission, ordered by the king himself."

He pulled out a letter sealed with the king's mark. The guard went to take the letter, but Smithson pulled it back. "I don't think so. This was a job for me, not you."

"Right. Well, you'll have to leave this with me, and I will be in touch."

"Oh, one more thing, don't talk about this with anyone." He passed the form over with three gold pieces.

"Oh yes, right you are. Your secret's safe with me, Lord Smithson."

Smithson turned and left the room. He had another uncomfortable ride to look forward to, but it would be worth it in the end, and now, with Geber finally gone, he could launch his plan knowing that nothing could stop him. He left the King's Seat with a smile on his face, and he heard an airship fly by somewhere above the clouds. Oh, what he would do to be on one of those right now.

Chapter 33

Hugh awoke to the sound of the ship's engines humming away. The others were still fast asleep, so he wandered through, bleary-eyed, to see Augustus. It was getting light outside as Hugh sat himself in the seat next to the captain.

"Ah, good morning, did you have a good sleep?"

Hugh noticed the large bags under the captain's eyes.

"Yes, thank you. Do you ever stop to sleep?"

"Me, no, never, not whilst I'm on duty at least. I catch up when I can, but I find I can run on very little."

Hugh chanced a look out of the window and saw they were still above the clouds.

"I thought we would've been there by now?"

"Well, I can't take the direct route. Someone put a mountain range in the way. There's also the little obstacle of the new patrol ships."

"Ah yes, we came across one of those. It was Rufus."

Augustus grunted.

"He's always been a brown-nosed twonk. Not spoken to him for years, not since got himself embroiled with the politics of the New World, against the words of our father no less, wot wot!"

"But I thought you were all pro–New World?"

"Excuse me? Certainly not. We give the impression that we are, but deep down, we stick to our roots. It's something the naval side of

335

the family should remember now and then. Young Rufus made his choices, and now he has to stick by them. He and his cronies have been encroaching into the Old World regularly. They're all paranoid about the Elf King and his supposed attack that's coming. With them sniffing about, it'll make our flight in quite difficult."

"I can imagine. Where are we now?"

"Just north of Skellig-Krieg. I have a plan to get us in, but it's quite risky. We can't just rock up to our landing spot in broad daylight. We'll have to fake an emergency landing."

Hugh looked alarmed at the idea.

"It's alright, they're pretty used to it nowadays, especially when I'm involved. They leave me to it unless I request assistance. I always carry a crew with me, who always do a fantastic job at getting me out of any bother."

"As long as you know what you're doing, I'll leave you to it."

"Righto, I'll let you know when we are getting close to the manoeuvre. You will all need to be strapped down for the landing."

Hugh walked through to the others, wondering what sort of move Augustus was going to pull. Everyone was coming round, and someone had prepared some food and left it on the table for them.

"Are we there yet?" asked Barrington.

"No, but we aren't far off," said Hugh.

He sat to eat some breakfast, enjoying the taste of real food. He explained to the rest of them the reasons for their delay and the plan to get them on the ground.

"It all sounds a bit drastic if you ask me," said Barrington.

"Aye, I'll just have a wee chat with Augustus. We need to be sure this'll work. I didnae want to be caught again." Hamish had a swig of whisky, before getting up and heading to the bridge.

"Should he really be drinking that much?" said Hugh.

"He needs it," said Heather, "so that he can distance himself from the reality of this plane and the call of the sight. It's hard to explain, but it's what keeps him going."

"There has to be a better way than whisky."

"He'll nae hear a thing of it, so I widnae push the issue."

They all sat in silence, too hungry to face conversation. When they finished, they set to with the planning.

"I want to give the Orbis a try when we get out," said Hugh.

"We don't have enough time to play with it, Hugh," said Emily.

"Actually, it won't be playing. Barrington and I have been tasked with finding the book, remember. We can't go back empty-handed again. If we are not moving, we can get a fixed point to head for and hope that it won't involve too much travelling. I'm keen to get back to a comfy bed."

"Do you have a clue where the book is?"

"No, just that we have to find the missing book of lore."

"Two books," said Barrington.

Hugh looked across at him. "Sorry?"

"Two books. You just said one book, but we need to find two. We have yet to find the book of alchemy."

"That's a heavy task in itself," said Hugh, rubbing his eyes.

"Have you looked in your father's bag yet? There may be some sort of clue in there."

Hugh picked up a sodden bag and opened it up. There was a waft of the sea and some seaweed mixed in with the contents. He pulled out a wad of papers, all stuck together. The ink streaked across the many layers, rendering the writing illegible. He dropped them to the floor. They landed with a squelch, and Hugh searched deeper into the bag.

There was his father's old fountain pen, and Hugh was relieved to see that the lid was screwed on tightly and had survived its trip into the bay. He opened a flap closed with a toggle and discovered an old ring with the family crest on. He remembered his father wearing it, and he welled up at the lucky find and placed it on his right little finger, where it fitted perfectly.

"I'll keep it with me, always," he said, looking at Emily.

His mind went to the voice in the sight which always called out to him. He yearned to go after it, seek its owner. Emily watched him intently.

"Oh, Hugh. I know it's hard. But you have to trust me. That voice will only lead to trouble. If you go after it, I fear you'll be in mortal danger."

"But I think it's him, Emily. I really do. I know his bag in that room doesn't bode well, but I have to believe that he is there somewhere."

He wiped the tears from his eyes.

Looking further, they found an old pocket watch, which was jammed up with sea water, a comb, moustache brush and more seaweed. Hugh put the bag to one side to dry as Hamish appeared through the door.

"I'm sorry to break up the party folks, but we've to get ready for the landing."

They all stood, making their way to the bridge. Hugh noticed extra seats, enough to take all the passengers on-board. They sat down, strapped in and braced themselves for the landing to come.

"Just like the good old days, wot wot."

"Aye, it's been a while, old friend. This may be a different ship, but the layout's familiar. My Heather knows how to build a good ship."

He beamed with pride at his daughter, who blushed.

"Sorry, have you done this before?" asked Hugh.

"Once or twice," said Hamish. "It's been a few years since we faked an emergency landing, but I can remember my role like it was yesterday."

They all sat in silence, whilst Augustus and Hamish worked their magic. Hugh watched, as the captain leaned over and spoke into the mic.

"Mayday, Mayday, Mayday. This is Captain Augustus Volatus, requesting an emergency landing, over."

"*Reading you Captain Volatus. How can we be of assistance this time?*"

Hugh thought he heard people moaning in the background before someone shushed them.

"Unsure as yet. Please wait whilst we assess the situation."

"Will do. We can clear a path for your imminent arrival."

Hamish pressed a button on the console, sending the bridge into pandemonium with alarms, sound effects of cogs and springs swooshing through the air and people's voices shouting. Hugh looked on as the pair remained calm, even chatting to each other at points, sharing a joke or two.

"This is Volatus. The situation appears to have worsened up here. I'm unsure if we will make the airdock."

He nodded and Hamish pressed a button. Hugh looked out the window to his right, saw a pipe extend, which belched out black smoke.

"We see you. I take it landing safely is not an option. Do you require the catch net deployment?"

"Negative, will try to land her on Riddor's Pass. I can see somewhere to get her down."

"Roger that, we shall alert all craft ... This is a message to all craft currently in the vicinity of Riddor's Pass. Please vacate the area until further notice. We have an ongoing incident taking place. Please listen out for further updates. Over."

Hamish pressed another button and saw an orange ring appear around the smoke.

"This is Volatus, engine fire, engine fire, requesting jettison of the starboard side engine pod."

"Request granted. You are over water, no risk to civilians."

Hamish pressed another button, and he watched the pipe detach, doing a loop-the-loop before heading for the depths below, still smoking. Hugh could see the city ahead of them, the mountains holding back the clouds. They rounded the mountains, and the slopes of Riddor's Pass came into view.

"There she is," said Augustus, "the perfect landing spot. A nice blanket of snow to settle on too, by the looks of it, wot wot."

"Aye, absolutely perfect. Yese all just sit tight. We'll be down soon enough."

Hugh knew the alarm sounds were for show and the radio messages intended to confuse the ground control, but the chaos was putting him on edge. To his brain, everything signalled a crash landing, even though they were completely safe ... ish.

Augustus swung the airship around the rocky outcrops, all seeming far too close to the windows for comfort. Something buffeted the craft, a grinding noise making its way through to the bridge.

"Whoops," Augustus said, adjusting the course slightly.

Hugh gripped his seat for all he was worth. They were coming in fast and low now – too fast. The scenery passing the window was an indiscernible blur. Augustus pressed a button on the control panel. Nothing happened. He pressed it again. Still nothing. He repeatedly hit it, before looking round at his startled passengers and winked.

"Deploy land anchor," he said into the mic.

There was a jolt, and the whole craft shuddered continuously. Hugh saw there really was enough space to land, that's if you ignored the large wall of rock they were currently careering towards. He looked across at the others, who were also gripping their seats with eyes wide open. They were going to hit the wall. Augustus appeared not to notice the problem until Hamish eventually reached his limit.

"Do ye want to at least attempt to avoid the rock wall?"

Augustus looked to him, winked again and smiled and brought the mic up. "Release land anchor."

Nothing happened.

"Chaps? Release land anchor!"

The rock wall was looming rather large in the window.

"Release the bloody land anchor, wot wot!" There was another jolt, and the airship picked up speed. Augustus heaved back on the controls.

The rock wall disappeared quickly below the airship, then they heard a high-pitched scraping, which drastically slowed the ship, altering its course.

Augustus put the ship down heavily into a drift, submerging the windows deep into the snow, bringing the ship to a sudden halt. Hugh thought his eyes would pop out from the pressure of the forces being exerted on him. The lap belt held firm, preventing him from being catapulted towards the front window.

Hamish turned the fake noises and alarms off. All was quiet, apart from the sound of heavy breathing and the engines winding down.

"*This is ground control. Please confirm your status.*"

"This is Volatus. All good here, a few scratches, nothing a bit of polish can't resolve."

"*Do you need assistance, over?*"

"No, thank you. We can manage from here. Volatus over and out."

"*Glad to hear it. Have a safe day Captain Volatus.*"

Augustus stood up from his seat and brushed himself down. "Right, shall we get things underway then, wot wot?" He began making his way off the bridge, leaving everyone sitting open-mouthed.

"What the hell was that?" said Barrington, finally coming to his senses.

"What? wot wot!"

"What?"

"What?"

"Can you all stop saying *what!*" said Emily.

Hamish stood up, chuckling to himself. "I have to hand it to ye. Yer landings are still as fun as ever!" he said, patting Augustus on the back as he went past. "Aye, I dinnae ken, ye and yer crash landings ..."

They all made their way through the craft to the rear, which wasn't buried in the snow. From the outside, the damage to the craft looked atrocious and would need more than a bit of polish. The once protective metal of the gas sack now looked battered.

The crew assured Hugh that it would fly again, saying the sack was still intact and that the *Jewel* had been flown in much worse states. He was shocked but not surprised to hear this as the crew began the unenviable job of digging the airship out of the drift. He and Emily put their pins into the first hole of their firestones, which was just enough to keep the cold off the group, as long as they were moving.

"Alright, what now?" said Jeb.

Hugh pulled out the Orbis, ignoring Emily's glare.

"I want to try this out again, now that we're not moving."

"We need to *get* moving, Hugh," said Emily.

He ignored her and focused his energy on the Orbis. It instantly glowed and the needles swung round, the outer picking up the symbol for earth, and the hidden one appearing once more, before turning and holding its position with its outer counterpart, and the whole thing lit up.

"Thas it, laddie, it's locked in, well done. Now ask the Orbis to take you to the book."

Instinctively, Hugh asked the question in his head. The compass needle swung into action, getting its bearing, and the entire item pulsated in his hand. Everyone gathered round to see the results.

"What does it mean when it vibrates?" said Hugh, looking at Hamish.

"Well, it means yer near to the book. The more constant, the closer ye are to it."

They looked at each other, before looking back at the Orbis. The inner needle was pointing to beyond the rock in front of them. They made their way around it and saw the entrance to the Ranglestaff Mine further on down the slope.

"Now there's a place I ain't see for a while," said Gambi.

"Sorry, you've been here before?" said Emily.

"'Course, I have. I grew up round these parts though that was some time ago now."

"You never mentioned that to me before," said Jeb.

"You never asked. I spent a lot of time in that very mine, with a couple of ol' friends. One of them was called ... hrmmm, now lets me think ... Ranny, that was it."

"Ranny?" said Emily.

"Yeah, you knows him?"

"Of course, I do. He was very generous to my mother and me. He took us in, set us up as best he could, helped feed and clothe us. He even taught me a thing or two about the world of magic."

"Yer not talking about old Whimpold, are ye?"

Everyone turned to Hamish.

"Who's Whimpold?" asked Hugh.

"Whimpold Ranglestaff? Are ye joking? I told ye about the mine, the last time we were here. He was the largest landowner in the Krieg Valley at one point. Then he got mixed up with the wrong side in the Great War, had most of his land removed from him, I seem to remember."

"But you weren't around then. How would you know about that?"

"Technically, I wasn't around here, but it was a busy time for the family business. I was elsewhere mindin' me own business. Anyway, we've no need to delve into that one now. I saw him in Portis-Montis many years ago. He said he was there for business, talking about a job he had to do. He was on the lookout for someone, weavers' stuff, so I left him to it. It's not for me to get in the way of the weavers."

Hugh looked to Barrington.

"Are you thinking what I'm thinking?"

Barrington nodded back keenly.

"I certainly am. I have a good feeling about this."

"About what? Will you please enlighten me as to what's going on?" said Emily.

Hugh turned to her.

"Before we left, Balinas instructed us to find another book and the book finder. We have one piece of the puzzle which I have been carrying around since Barrington gave it to me in his shop, and we are both thinking that if this Orbis is correct, then the missing lore book of magic is not far away."

"But that means I will gain all the knowledge of my craft. All the missing lessons my mother never taught me will be in that book."

"Yes, but before you go running ahead of yourself, remember we have to take it back to the safety of Portis-Montis."

Emily looked at Hugh as if she had miss heard him.

"Sorry? This is the same book that links me to my world – and is possibly feet away from me – and you want to take it further away? That's not fair."

"Em, ye have to listen to these two," said Hamish. "They've been given a job of great responsibility. The lore books hold immense power, and they need to be somewhere safe. They must not fall into the wrong hands."

"I know that. But I'm sure I can look after it and keep it safe. Think of all the knowledge I could gain."

Hamish stood with a raised eyebrow.

"Fine!" she said. "We'll get the book, and it goes to Portis-Montis, but I want to come back with you."

"I see no problem with that," said Hugh.

"Good, then may I suggest we get a move on?" said Barrington. "We need to get out of this cold weather."

Augustus said he needed to stay with the airship, so the rest waded through the snow, watching the Orbis intently. Hugh and Emily attempted to intensify their firestones as much as they could, so the group wouldn't resemble blocks of ice by the time they reached the entrance of the old Ranglestaff Mine. They all looked into the ominous black hole.

"Is it safe to go in?" asked Jeb. "I don't fancy getting buried in a mine collapse."

Hugh looked down to the Orbis which was vibrating non-stop in his hand, the needle pointing towards the darkness.

"The Orbis seems pretty keen to enter. I also have a feeling that this is the right thing to do."

"It'll be fine to go in, I can assure you of that," said Gambi, joining them at the entrance.

"How can you be so sure?"

"'Cos I spent many happy years livin' up here."

They all turned to look at him.

"What?"

"You actually lived up here?" said Jeb.

"'Course I did, with Ranny and Don."

"You never told me that. And who's Don?"

"Again, you never asked, and never you mind. C'mon, let's get in from the cold. It's ruddy freezin' out here, even with them firestone things."

He marched into the tunnel – and the darkness. Hugh looked at the rest of them, who looked back encouragingly. He sighed, turned on his heel and walked into the abyss.

It was quite warm once they had rounded the first corner, so he and Emily reset their firestones. Hugh had expected it to remain dark, but the walls and roof seemed to glisten like a jewellery box.

He noticed the stones increased in intensity as they walked through, and he could see where Gambi was by watching the wave of illumination ahead of him. It wasn't long before they were stripping down the layers to compensate for the heat.

"What is this place?" asked Barrington, in awe of the bright colours.

"'Tis the old Ranglestaff Mine," said Hamish. "It made them a very rich family indeed."

"But what happened? Why did they stop?" asked Hugh.

"Well, some say that greed took over, and they dug too deep, unearthing some terrible beasts. I say that's poppycock."

"Why so?"

"Have ye seen any beasts wandering the plains below?" Hugh shook his head. "Exactly. The truth is, they backed the wrong side in the Great War and paid a terrible price for it. They were banished to live a life up here, with the other wizards that sided with them."

Up ahead, Gambi had come to a stop.

"If we had known what was goin' to be the outcome, and how bad the Elf King really was, then we may have made different choices. But we had to pick a side, and it split the wizarding world in two."

His voice echoed around the tunnel as the rest of the party caught up with him.

"Hang on," said Jeb, scratching his head. "Are you saying that you were here in the time of the Great War?"

They all looked to Gambi for an answer, but before he could speak, a voice called out from the darkness.

"What are *you* doing here, and who are they?"

Chapter 34

Hugh's skin tingled. It was as if the tunnel they were in sensed they were not welcome there, and he panicked that something bad was going to happen.

"I said, what are you doing here?" said the voice.

The air crackled around them.

"Now come on Don, thas no way to greet an old friend now, is it?"

"Huh, friend? Friends don't walk out one day and never come back. You deserted us, left us to face the wrath of the battle on our own."

"An' I told you at the time, I didn't think it was a good plan, and I was right."

There was a silence, as the voice known as Don processed what his old friend had said. The tunnel illuminated in a tumult of colour, causing the group to shield their eyes until they had adjusted to the sudden change in lighting.

"I knew you'd return, you old bastard."

Hugh saw Don was smiling. Even by the light of the tunnel, he could see he was a very pale man. He was tall, with greying hair, and wore the robes of a wizard, but Hugh had only ever seen these in books and only ever seen them in real life once before. They reminded him of the robes that Ranny had been wearing in Skellig-Krieg, as they too had seen too much life and not enough care.

"Come here," said Don, embracing his long-lost friend. "I told him you would return. I said, 'he'll be back, you mark my words' and here you are."

"Yeah, well, it was a little longer than I was expectin', but I'm here now."

"A little longer? You only went out to fetch a churn of milk and bread."

"I ended up walkin' a little further, but I has returned and brought us some visitors," he said, gesturing to the rest of the group standing behind him.

Hugh parted from the rest of them and walked up to Don, still wary of the man. "How do we know we can trust you?"

"Oh, one of those are you? Go on then, show me yours," said Don, rolling up his right sleeve (not even waiting for a response from Hugh, who did the same to reveal a matching tattoo). "Glad to see the family group is alive and well. I don't ever get the chance to use this." He held out a hand for Hugh to shake, and he saw it was grubby and calloused. "Donavan Bradnock, at your service. You can call me Don."

"Hugh Geber, nice to meet you," said Hugh.

"Geber? Are you any relation to the Jabir family, perchance?"

"Erm, nope. We are the Geber's of Portis-Montis, and always have been, as far as I know."

"Ah well, not to worry. I'm throwing out names from the days of old. There's been so much movement since then, and I don't get out much. The last time was to get this tattoo, and that was a long, long time ago."

"I didn't realise you were a member of the family," said Gambi, revealing his own tattoo.

"Yes, well, we've had some time to think. We decided mutually to change sides, and it was the best thing that we ever did. Anyway, let's not stand here chatting. I've a comfortable set up down in the caverns. Follow me."

He turned and headed off down the tunnel, which twinkled as he passed. It turned out Don had converted an old cavern into living quarters – and had made it quite homely. He had constructed rooms, panelled the walls and even gained some furniture.

The main room was lined with comfy wing-backed chairs and a chaise long. He had fashioned a chandelier, also made from the colourful stones, and it bathed the room in a colourful glow. Don went to a stove and filled a kettle from a flowing spring that poured from a wall, the excess water falling through a hole in the floor.

"It may not be much, but it's home."

"This is amazing," said Hugh, who was standing in awe. "Is that light really made from the stones?"

"Yes, orbs, to be precise. It's one of my own inventions. I like to call it an Orbelier ... you know ... orbs ... crossed with a chandelier ... oh never mind. Tea? The water is quite fresh, I can assure you."

He gestured for the group to take a seat and placed the kettle on the stove. Then he picked up a spherical stone from the shelf and placed it into the firebox. Instead of lighting it, he wiggled his fingers over the stone, and it illuminated. Hugh could feel the heat radiating out from where he was sitting.

"There we go. That should sort it," he said, taking a seat. "What?"

The rest of the group sat open-mouthed.

"The orbs are useful things when you gets used to how they work," said Gambi. "We used to use coal, and the soot was horrendous."

"Absolutely, my friend, and the orbs have looked after us all these years, I can assure you of that ... Oh, I wouldn't light that in here," he said, looking at Barrington, who was busy packing his pipe. "There's a room full of fulminate powder just over there."

He pointed over to a locked door across the other side of the room. Barrington huffed, stowing the pipe away in his pocket again.

Somewhere, off in the distance, there was the sound of a muffled boom. Hugh felt the slightest of vibrations in his seat, and some dust floated down from the ceiling.

"Are you still mining here?" he asked.

"Why, of course! We have to be ready for what is coming."

Emily looked at him.

"What's that exactly? You're not up to no good, I hope."

Don looked across at her in surprise.

"It's alright, dear, we're just talking about … men's things, nothing to worry about," he said, patting her on the leg.

Hugh sat with raised eyebrows, and Hamish spoke up from the chaise long he had collapsed into.

"Thas a ballsy move."

Emily was trying to remain calm.

"What? I just don't want to worry the poor women in the room."

Heather now glared at him.

"What did you say?" said Emily, her nostrils flared.

"Erm … I said … erm … well …" The ground shook slightly.

Hugh could hear debris bouncing off the wooden room. The chandelier was swinging on its mount, and Hugh noticed that his and Emily's firestones were glowing bright, along with all the stones in the surrounding mine. There was a popping and fizzing filling the surrounding space, as though the air itself were trying to ignite. Emily took a step towards Don, but Hamish was already on his feet, blocking her way towards the old wizard. She tried to push past him, but he stood like an immovable wall.

"Alright lassie, that's enough! Ye'll collapse the entire mine at this rate!" He was using all of his strength to hold her back, whilst the shaking around them eased.

"Goodness me," said Don, "they seem to have forgotten the rule about women not using wizards' magic …"

"Rule about women not using magic…? Why, you sexist pig!" said Heather, as she got to her feet.

Hugh heard a large chunk of roof collapse. Barrington was now

holding Heather back as she tried to claw her way towards the wizard.
"Have ye got a death wish? Shut up, will ye!"

The room had descended into chaos. Planks of the wooden ceiling
fell to the floor, as Hugh's hair stood up on end and he sensed he had to
do something, or they would all be buried in the mine forever.

"Enough of this madness!"

His voice seemed to boom around the cavern outside then back into
the room again, and it even took Hugh by surprise. As he spoke, the orb
chandelier and the stove illuminated so brightly it blinded all in the room.
They both exploded in a shower of sparks, the door of the stove blew
off, narrowly missing Hugh, and the room was plunged into darkness.
Silence swelled to fill the space, where chaos reigned moments before.
Hugh sat back down, feeling for the seat underneath him, surprised by
the power that he had released.

A small light showed in the doorway, appearing to swing around wildly
in the air. They heard numerous voices saying, "hup, hup, hup," as they
moved through the room. This was followed by clinking and the sound
of many people going to a lot of effort. Light came back to the room,
revealing a bizarre sight.

Nine small people, standing on each other's shoulders, had reinstalled
the chandelier and were now hopping back down to floor level.

Jeb stared at them, open-mouthed.

"What the devil are they?"

"Coblyns," said Don, "it's how we keep this place running."

"Goblins?"

"No, *coblyns*. We found them when we were excavating the deeper
shafts, useful little fellows."

As Hugh looked at the coblyns, he saw they were no larger than
two feet in height. They were the colour of polished copper from head
to toe and wore dungarees, also copper in colour. They had beards that
nearly touched the floor, and how on earth they could see was beyond

Hugh. Their hats came down to their noses, which were as round as their cheeks.

Everyone watched as the small people waddled back out of the room, the lead coblyn still carrying the lamp that Hugh saw in the darkness. They moved with a hobbling sort of motion, rocking from side to side.

"How curious," said Jeb.

"Right, I think ye owe these lassies an apology," said Hamish.

Don looked as though he were about to protest, but one look from Hamish told him this would be a very unwise idea indeed.

"I'm … sorry," said Don awkwardly. "I have been out of the loop for some time. Can you forgive me?"

He looked across at Emily and Heather, who just glared back.

"Erm, ladies, I believe the wee man just apologised?"

Heather mumbled something.

"A little louder for the room, please."

"Apology accepted," she said with a little more effort.

"That's better," said Hamish, turning to Don. "Right, seeing as the tea is off, shall we get down to business, but this time offending no one?"

"Erm, yes," said Don, (they all looked at him expectantly). "Not wishing to sound rude, but you were the ones that came in *here*, so what was it *you* were looking for?"

Everyone looked to Hugh to be designated spokesperson, and he tried to figure out a way to explain the situation.

"Well, we've been tasked with a job, and that is to find certain items which need to be returned to the university in Portis-Montis."

"Alright, so what makes you think they are down here?" said Don, not willing to give anything away.

"We have *this*," said Hugh, pulling out the Orbis, "and it guided us to the mine entrance."

Don stepped forward to look at it. "I've not seen that in many years. How did it come to be in your hands?"

352

"Sorry," said Emily, "but are you saying that you've seen this before?"

"Well, yes, but not for quite some time. You must remember it, Gambi?"

Gambi stood, scratching his head, attempting to kick start his brain into action.

"Come to think of it, I does 'ave a memory floatin' about in the ol' noggin of who had it. Wasn't it Trendle who first showed it to us?"

Don clicked his fingers. "That's the one, yeah."

"Sorry," said Hugh, "but who is Trendle?"

"Oh, he's Ranny's brother, used to run the wizard university up in Old Skellig. The New World name for the area is Naval Hill. He won the place after a battle with his older brother. Turbulent times back then, I can tell you. He'd returned from a trip from Portis-Montis, and he carried that weird compass. Apparently, it was something to do with the formation of the books of lore. He said he had to take it to a safe place. That was around the same time that we met Ranny, I believe? I remember like it was yesterday, though it was some time ago now."

"Yup, it certainly was," said Gambi. "Ranny was a young'un back then, of course, had a lot to learn. Shame about all that business with the war and losin' his land, but he seems to have grown into his boots now. Where is he anyways?"

"Oh, he's down in the lower cavern, probably muttering to himself as usual. He's not been the same since the war, caused him great shame, fuddled his mind somewhat."

Emily looked at Don in surprise.

"You mean to say that Ranny still lives up here?"

"Why, of course," said Don, "where else would you expect him to live? Since all the Old Worlders were ordered to leave the city, he returned to his home, at last. There was a time when he used to make the walk up and down here every day, but it was becoming hard for him, what with his bad leg, so in recent years, he stayed down in the city. I used to visit him regularly to make sure he was alright. When the order came to leave, he had no choice but to return up here."

"I remember when he used to trek up and down the hill with us," said Emily. "He was a real help when we first arrived here all those years ago."

"Hang on? Are you telling me you're the people he spent his time with, what was it, around twenty-five years ago?"

"Yes, about that. He was very helpful, set us up in a cave down the hill. He gave us some furniture and made sure we were safe."

"So it was you that had my furniture, was it? He refused to tell me what he was up to, and whenever I tried to follow him, he always went straight to town. He gave you my favourite lamp."

"Well, we were very grateful for your donations. I still have them in my place... well, did, until we had to leave. I'm not sure if I'm welcome there anymore. I just hope the greenhouses are staying open."

"Oh, they're still open. By the sounds of things, they're one of the few survivors of the great cull."

"So, what do you do up here?"

"We mine, mainly, for orbs."

"What are ye needing orbs for?" asked Hamish, now studying Don intently. "Yese wizards ain't up to no good again, I hope?"

Don puffed out his chest.

"No, no, nothing of the sort! I've already told you we changed sides. We have been planning and waiting, if you must know."

"For what?" said Hugh.

"My, we are an inquisitive bunch. We've been waiting for a particular point in time. Though I didn't think that this would be it." Hugh looked at him with confusion worn upon his face.

Don shook his head.

"I don't think I should reveal everything to you right now. Follow me."

The man marched off out of the door, and the others followed in silence. He led the group down into a tunnel, leading off from the cavern they were in. The floor was littered with round stones that had fallen from the wall. Emily kicked one with her foot, and it sparked and crackled.

Don stopped briefly, turning to face her.

"Please be careful where you walk. We wouldn't want to start a chain reaction off!"

He turned and continued off into the semi-dark tunnel, the orbs around them lighting up once more as they followed him along the route. Emily scowled at Don's back, and Hugh shook his head quickly, to prevent her taking it any further. After five minutes, the tunnel opened up into another large cavern. It was warm and humid, and somewhere in the distance, Hugh heard the muffled sound of an explosion. This was followed by a warm waft of air hitting his face, tainted with the smell of fulminate powder. If he closed his eyes, he would say the air was also tainted with a burnt metallic smell, so strong that he could taste it.

As they entered the new cavern, they all stopped in their steps and took in the surrounding room. The roof had to be nearly fifty feet high, and it was so long that Hugh couldn't make out the other end. The space was filled with row upon row of orbs of all sizes, sorted out in their separate colours. Small runes were inlaid into pieces of wood at the end of each row, indicating what lay in the piles beyond. There was a large metal cabinet set off to one side, with a sign which read:

DANGER CABINET: FOR EMERGENCY USE ONLY.

Hamish and Heather instantly started studying them. Then Hamish turned to Don. "And what the hell are ye planning to use all these for?"

"For the upcoming revolution," said a voice from behind them before Don could answer. They all turned around to see Ranny limping down an aisle towards them, using a staff for support.

Emily went to greet him with a hug.

"Ranny, how lovely to see you. I didn't know that you were living up here again. Don's been filling us in on all that's happened."

"Yes, well, there be many things that you don't know about me, Emily.

Now what brings you 'ere?"

He sounded disgruntled, like someone who had been pulled away mid-work to deal with an unpleasant issue.

"They're here for the book, Ranny."

Don's words took a moment to sink in, then Ranny's eyes opened wide.

"I asked you before if you were after me books," he said to Hugh and Barrington (who both looked as confused as each other). "Back in Skellig-Krieg? Well anyway, if I'd known it were goin' to be you two ... what, Don?"

Don leaned in to whisper into Ranny's ear, before standing back and smiling at Emily once more.

"What? ... Emily?"

Ranny looking across to her, as she stood, tight-lipped.

"But she's a — *Ow!* What you go an' do that for?" He looked at Emily and saw the look she was giving him. He cleared his throat, and shifted uneasily on the spot. "No offence, I was jus' expectin' ... the person who'd come to collect the book ... well, you know?"

Emily Flared her nostrils.

"No, Ranny, why don't you enlighten me?"

"Well ... what I means to say is ... it's not that you aren't capable an' that ... but we was expectin' ..."

Emily stood, tapping her foot and chewing the inside of her cheek.

"... well, someone more ... manly?"

As soon as the words slipped out to the old man's mouth, Hugh knew he had said the wrong thing.

"What? You taught me magic when I was younger. You helped me to control my powers."

"Ah, well now, that was basic stuff. This is more ... serious."

"So, you thought that just because I have a pair of mammary glands and no balls, that I wouldn't be capable of collecting a book?"

"Well, I means to say … it's not what I was intendin' to say as such … but in a roundabout way. Well, yes, I suppose."

The surrounding ground shook, and a waft of warm air blew across the room.

"Emily, stop!" said Hugh in desperation.

"It's not me, for your information."

"Then what's causing this?"

"It's the damn coblyns again," said Don. "They've started to head closer to this chamber, and I specifically told them not to." He ran off through the pile of orbs, which were all rattling against each other, leaving the rest of the group to look for cover.

"Quick, in 'ere," said Ranny, hobbling over to the danger cabinet and opening the door. They all ran for the opening, as parts of the ceiling caved in further down their aisle. "Well budge up then!"

"It's not like there's a lot of room in here, old chap," said Barrington, trying to squeeze in as tight as he could.

"It ain't made for guests," Ranny replied brusquely.

Outside, they heard more of the ceiling caving in, and bits were now hitting the top of the cabinet. It was loud and uncomfortable, as they were all squashed in like sardines. Eventually, the noise and shaking subsided, and everyone let out a sigh of relief. Ranny went to open the door, but found it blocked shut.

"Ruddy coblyns," he said, as he attempted to raise his staff. "A bit of space please."

With much huffing and awkward manoeuvring, they created a small pocket of space for Ranny to work his magic. He raised the staff and dropped it to the floor. The front of the cabinet was blasted off, and the pressure change made Hugh's ears pop. The dust and debris settled to reveal a scene of carnage.

"What the bloody hell was that? Why did you blow the door off?" said Don, running over the mounds to get to them.

"We was stuck in the danger box. I worked me magic, and now we ain't stuck no more."

"Ranny! How many times do I have to remind you? Protocol dictates that you wait to be rescued from the box and that you *don't* blast your way out. It may be unsafe, and you keep destroying our stock on a monthly basis. We are running out of danger boxes."

Hugh and the rest of the group were stepping back out from the now destroyed danger box and looking around them, whilst the pair continued to fight.

"Well, we're all safe, ain't we?"

"Yes, but that's not the point" – a noise from above made them both look up – "Look out!"

Don shoved Ranny off to one side as a lump of ceiling detached, but Hugh looked up to see he was still in danger.

—*POP*—

'Oh, bugger it, not again!'

He was back in the sight once more. His panic had saved his life as he saw he had brought his body with him again.

'Hugh ... Hugh ... is that you?'

'Father? Where are you?'

He turned around, trying to locate the direction of the voice. His surroundings appeared slightly lighter than they had been on previous occasions, but there was an area to his left that compelled him to draw closer. He didn't know why, but he sensed it was the right thing to do.

'And where do you think you are going, Hugh Geber?'

Hugh turned around to face Emily.

'Oh, hello. Didn't expect to see you here. You got out of the way then?'

'Well, obviously! And don't play innocent with me,' she said, busy weaving runes around her life-link. *'What are you doing? This isn't some sort of toy*

you can just mess around with.'

Hugh felt a tingling on his chest where the firestone was. *'Look, Emily, it's not like that. I can't control when I step in and out at the moment. It just happens.'*

'Hmm, likely story. Are you not going to protect yourself then?'

'Ah yes, I always forget about that bit.'

'Again, you need to be quicker with these things. Are you sure that you were not distracted by something else? Where were you off to?' She folded her arms.

'I … well … erm … funny story there, you see—'

'You were off to find that voice again, weren't you?'

Hugh hung his head in silence, looking down to where the ground would be if there were any.

'I specifically told you not to follow that voice, and yet here I am, catching you in the act. This has to stop Hugh. You don't know what dangers lurk behind the voice, what demons are waiting to attack you. Right, come on, we need to get back.'

'I don't know how.'

'Then it's about time you learned.'

She connected to him by the hand, her tone now changing from irate to more relaxed. As they connected, a wave of warmth and emotion flowed into Hugh.

'I'm sorry,' he said, turning to her.

She let out a sigh

'Me too. I apologise for being short with you. I just care for you so much and don't want to lose you. Right, concentrate on the location where you left, then, in theory, you will end up back there.'

Hugh could already feel Emily heading back, and he turned his mind back to the cavern.

−POP−

He was back in the vast chamber, and he took in the surrounding view. The parts of the roof which had caved in were being fixed by Don,

Ranny and Gambi, who were patching it up with magic. They were using staffs with glowing orbs on top, with the power channelling through them, flowing upwards to the roof. The air was tinged with the strong smell of burnt metal, and debris littered the floor. Hugh sniffed at the air.

"What is that smell?"

"Used magic, the aftereffects of using so much power," said Emily.

Barrington and Jeb were still cowering in the danger cabinet, awaiting the all-clear that all was safe. Heather and Hamish were already out and studying the colourful rocks, playing around and making them glow. The piles of orbs lay
semi-collapsed by their feet.

"Oh good, you're back," said Barrington. "Is it safe to come out?"

"Yes, it's safe," said Emily, before turning to Hamish and Heather, "and you two, watch what you are doing with those. We want no more explosions … leave them."

They turned to look at her, ready to protest.

"Now!"

They put the orbs down, and they ceased glowing. The three wizards finished their repairs to the ceiling. They made their way back to the main group, all looking suitably shocked. Ranny stood shaking his head, looking at Don.

"What?"

"I told you them coblyns would be more trouble than they're worth."

"Ah, but look at all the good work they have done." He waved his arm around towards the collapsed piles of orbs.

"Yeah, an' how much work is it gonna take us to puts it all right again, eh?" He turned to Emily. "Well, I s'pose we'd better get you this book that you've come for, but before we do that, there is something else that you will require. Call it a rite of passage sort of thing."

He disappeared, only to return moments later with a book and another stick, the same as the ones Hugh saw them using to fix the roof.

"This staff is for you. It's had your name on it since birth, though we were unaware it was gonna be yours. Had I known all those years ago that you were the one chosen for this job, then I would have been able to give you this then, but these things have a way of happening at the right time."

He passed her the staff, and the ground briefly trembled beneath their feet, followed by another warm breeze. Barrington and Jeb turned to head back for the cabinet, fearing another explosion.

"S'all right, you two. That's the confirmation that I needed. This staff is now bonded to you, Emily. It has accepted you as its master and will only answer to you. You must look after it, as it's part of you now. There is one more task you must do to complete the ritual. Walk amongst the orbs, feel, link, find your way."

"What, why? What will happen?" she asked.

"You'll see."

Everyone watched Emily enter the orb mountains. Hugh lost sight of her, and she seemed to be gone for an immeasurable amount of time. He was about to ask if they should go in find her when it happened.

Whoosh. Zip. Pop.

A flash within the piles was followed by another warm breeze which hit Hugh's face, and the ground briefly trembled once more. Emily appeared from the pile, looking amazed, with a turquoise stone embedded in the end of the staff. The wood was still softly glowing from the action that had just taken place.

Ranny bowed out of respect for her.

"Congratulations. You're now fully initiated into the world of wizardry, though this doesn't mean that your learning's over. This is a task which will never end."

Emily bowed in return, and her firestone swung outwards, causing Ranny to gasp.

"Where d'you get that?" he said, glaring at the triangular stone.

"This?" said Emily. "I inherited it from my mother."

"I always wondered where that ended up."

"You've seen this before?"

"Why, of course. It was in my possession for many years. I thought it lost, but it seems to have found a new allegiance."

"But how did you gain possession of it?"

"A story which now saddens me, but we cannot change the past," said Ranny.

"I'm sure whatever it was, it cannot have been that serious."

"I'll tell you, but you has to remember I was a different man then to the one I am today. It comes from a long time ago before the original uprising and the days of the Great War. I was a rich landowner back then. I'd inherited the land from me pa, well, the person I knew as pa at any rate. I'd lost all those I knew as me family, as well as an old friend called Billy, in the battle of the Krieg. We was farmers back then, but after the battle, I realised I had me powers, see, and I didn't want to return to the old ways. I let others farm the fields for me, and rebuilt meself a place which is now known as the Rangles Inn. I even named a lane next to the house after Billy, out of respect like."

"So, how did you make your money and get the firestone?"

"I'm gettin' to that bit. It turns out that the land I'd inherited was rich in orbs. There were thousands of 'em, scattered across the area. Well, if there's one thing a wizard needs more than anything else, it's orbs. It got me thinkin', and I says to meself, 'Ranny, you could make a lot of money out of this,' and knows what? I did."

"So how did the firestone come into play?"

"Well, I lets the money go to me head, didn't I? It turned out that I was needed to help create one of the books of law. We was called to a meetin' at Portum Castle in Portis-Montis," he shivered at the mention of this. "Ruddy hate that place. The Weavers had decreed that these books be made, and had already made Orbis, which had their powers imbued within it. It was our job, as the different races, to create the books and to link each of our powers to Orbis.

"Anyway, turns out the elves were much further ahead of the game than the rest of us like, bloody showing off, weren't they? They'd created this new-fangled 'firestone' and were wavin' it about like a new toy. I offered 'em money for it, but they refused point blank to sell it.

"I couldn't believe they would dare to refuse me, a wizard of all the people, the one chosen to bring together our information for the book of lore. So I decided there an' then to gets it for meself. Besides, silly buggers had left it on the side in their tinkerin' shop, ain't they? Not only that, they also left the instructions on how to make it too. It was an opportunity not to be missed, wa'nt it?"

"Sorry," said Barrington. "Are you saying that the person who stole the stone from Balinas was you? I hardly think that's possible. That would make you ridiculously old?"

"Abouts five 'undred and eighty summit, but I ain't countin'."

"But how's that even possible?" said Hugh.

"Tha's wizards' business," said Ranny. He put his hand to his own chest where the firestone would have once been, but not before Hugh glimpsed a deep red, solid triangle of stone, probably a carved orb. The old wizard caught his gaze, and Hugh looked away quickly.

Ranny turned to the book, which was wrapped in cloth, and passed it to Emily.

"Keep the protective cloth around it. I designed it to protect the book from almost anything, from water to fire. You never knows what you'll get in a mine. This book will teach you all that we knows so far about magic. Take it to Portis-Montis. Take it and learn it, for you will need it for the journey that is to come. I feel this is the start of a whole new road for you."

"What do you mean? I'll have to return to the greenhouses at some point, surely?"

"If I'm not mistaken, you are long overdue a break from that place. You must return this to the Chamber of Prophecy, for that is where it belongs, then follow the path that is being laid out for you."

Emily looked at him, took in a deep breath, and released it slowly.

"Alright, I will do this, but only because it's you, Ranny." She took the large book, looking surprised at how something so big, could be so light.

"Don't be so surprised. Be grateful. We's enchanted it some time ago to make it easier to carry."

"Thank you. I really can't tell you how much this means to me."

"Oh, I know. Now away with you all, we have tasks we must be getting on with."

Barrington stopped and refused to move.

"Alright, so we have one of the books of lore, which we shall deliver back to Balinas, but what are *you* going to do?"

Ranny wore a look of false confusion that wouldn't convince anyone.

"What do you mean?"

"Well, there's a huge pile of orbs there, and from what I can tell, they hold a lot of power. In the wrong hands … well, what exactly are they for, and what are you up to? Not being funny, but your track record isn't the best."

"Ah, yes, those are hard to ignore," said Don. "We've been planning for some time now, getting ready for the uprising. We've heard the news that the Elf King is on the move once more, and this time we intend to be on the winning side. Our plans are to—"

"Tha's enough!" growled Ranny, taking the group aback. "We's not to reveal anything to anyone, yer blabbermouth. I want this lot outta here, now."

Gambi now looked at him. Ranny let out a sigh of annoyance.

"What?"

"Well, I was wonderin', if it's alright with the two of yer, if I could stay here?"

Ranny looked at him as if he were assessing his old friend.

"Fine, but don't go walkin' out on us again and … What now?"

Jeb was standing with a hand in the air.

"I was also wondering if I could stay here, too. I have no wish to return to the New World right now, not that I'd be welcomed with open arms as it is."

He looked imploringly at Ranny.

"This ain't a ruddy bed-and-breakfast!"

"Now, come on, Ranny," said Don. "You were only saying yesterday that we needed more help around here. Plus, there are a lot of orbs to tidy up." He looked at the old wizard with raised eyebrows.

Ranny huffed. "Fine. But the rest of yous can ruddy well bugger off."

"Aye, it's alright," said Hamish. "We need to be getting home anyway, but thank ye for your kind hospitality."

Hugh, Barrington and Emily looked at him with uncertainty and even disappointment.

"Heather and I have things we need to do," said Hamish by way of an explanation, "and ye know we've Betsie to tend to."

Barrington looked longingly at Heather.

"Well, maybe I could assist you?"

"No, Barrington," said Emily, "we need you."

"Yes," said Hugh, "other things will have to wait."

"Easy for you to say," he muttered under his breath.

They bid Ranny, Jeb and Gambi goodbye, and Don helped them find their way back out of the tunnels. Emily begrudgingly let Hugh put the book into his bag for safekeeping but only after a lot of heavy persuasion. Don left them at the exit tunnel, saying he had no wish to get cold again.

They followed the icy breeze hitting their faces, so Hugh and Emily activated their firestones once more. Augustus was pacing outside the entrance, wrapped in a large fur coat and mittens to match. His eyes were covered in a pair of goggles to protect them from the weather, and a large fluffy aviators hat covered his head.

"Ah ha. I thought you may have gone in here, wot wot. Did you achieve all you needed?"

"Yes, thank you," said Hugh.

"I was wondering if you were caught in a rockfall, what with all the ground movements happening within the area. I thought I heard some explosions too. Damn things sent more snow down from the mountain. Thought it was going to hit the *Jewel*, but I deflected it."

He gave a little demonstration by blowing into his gloved hands and releasing a small glow of light into the falling snow. It ploughed a path through it with ease.

"A lot has happened, and it's a lot to explain," said Hugh. "Can you get us down into the city, and we can tell you on the way?"

"I'm afraid not. I'll be a few hours away yet before the old girl is ready to fly."

"What about Heather and the rune wing?" said Barrington.

Heather shook her head.

"Och, I'm afraid not. The downdraught alone would cause suspicion. It's not as subtle as an airship, which can land at the dock without too many questions." Barrington looked downhearted once more.

Augustus cleared his throat, and the group regained their composure and were ready to move forward with the conversation.

"Right, I have a ship to dig out, wot wot."

"Thank you, Augustus," said Hugh. "Are you sure that we cannot help you any further?"

"No, no, I think my lads and I have it all well in hand. You head down to the city now, before you all freeze to death."

"Thank you, Augustus. I think the firestones will keep us warm enough."

"Right you are. One more thing, if ever you need the help in the future, you only have to ask for the great Captain Augustus, and I'll be there for you. Stay safe."

They watched as he disappeared into the falling snow. The rest of the group began bidding each other farewell, with Hugh and Emily having to distract Hamish, whilst Barrington and Heather said their own personal goodbye.

"Well, I'd best let ye get on with yer walk. It'll take a while to get down in this weather."

He went to turn, but Hugh stopped him.

"Hamish," he said, swallowing hard, "erm, which path is the best to get down from here?"

"What ye talkin' about, laddie? There's only one path, and yer on it now."

He went to turn again, and this time it was Emily who stopped him.

"Och, what is it now?"

"Well, erm, didn't you want to say goodbye to me?" she said.

"Well, yiv changed yer tune? What's the matter with yese two?"

The unmistakable sound of lip slurping met Hamish's ears. His eyes went wide, his nostrils flared.

"Hamish, don't..." said Emily, but it was too late.

His kilt flapped outwards as he spun on his heel. He took in the frame of Barrington, devouring Heather's face. His eye twitched, and his nostrils flared to an enormous size, and he charged like an angry bull.

Barrington didn't stand a chance.

He released the vacuum hold on Heather's face, in time to see Hamish's fist coming towards him.

"Get yer hands off me daughter, ye wee bastard!"

Barrington flew in one direction.

Some gold teeth went the other.

Barrington face-planted the snow and slid across the floor, leaving a red trail in his wake whilst Hugh, Emily and Heather all tried to restrain Hamish.

"Aww Dad! Will ye pack it in!"

"Ye dare to touch me daughter, ye wee bawbag, ye never asked me!"

"I'm not yer property, Dad. Ye don't own me. I have to live my own life!" Hamish stopped struggling, thrown off his stride by Heather's comments.

"But yer all I've got, lassie. Without ye, I've to go back to my old life."

He looked into his daughter's eyes, and Hugh saw the pain the situation was causing him.

"I'm still yer daughter, Dad, but ye have to let me live me life at some point. I cannae be shut in the marsh my whole life."

"She's right," said Emily. "Anyway, we still need you to help us find the other books. You're not going anywhere just yet."

Hamish had calmed down, so Hugh went to tend to Barrington, who was collecting and re-inserting his teeth.

"Are you alright?"

"I've been better, dear Hugh, but it's nothing I can't handle."

He rubbed his tongue around his mouth, wincing with pain when he found the gap. He spat some blood into the freshly fallen snow, its red a stark contrast to the white background. He placed another tooth into his mouth.

"Please, don't do or say anything you will regret down the line."

"Oh please, do you really think I would go in all guns blazing?"

Hugh looked at him with raised eyebrows.

"Alright, I'll go easy, but let me do it my way."

"Fine, but no fisticuffs."

Barrington replaced the last of his teeth, took in a deep breath, before going to face Hamish.

"Hamish, would you care to take a quick walk down the path with me?"

Hamish glared at Barrington, before deciding.

"Aye, I'll go for a wee walk with ye," and they walked a little way down the track to be out of earshot.

It was cold, and the remaining three huddled together, all lapping up the warmth now radiating out from the firestones. A tense quarter of an hour passed, whilst Hugh watched on with the others. He thought that he heard raised voices at one point, but it could have been a lull in the wind.

"All sorted?" he asked hopefully, as they returned.

"Aye, we've settled our differences. Heather, I'm sorry for reacting the way I did. I know ye can perfectly look after yer own affairs. I'll try to be more easy-going in the future."

Hugh looked to Emily, Heather and Augustus, who were just as shocked as he was.

"Well, I'm glad that you have sorted things out. Now, can we please get off this mountain? I'm freezing."

They all agreed and said their final farewells, this time without raising fists. Hugh promised to keep in contact with Hamish, and Barrington with Heather. She turned to de-cloak the ship, and Hamish gasped.

"What happened to me wing?" He rubbed his hand along the Barrington-sized head dent.

Barrington rubbed the spot where his head hit the wing, the memory all too clear in his mind.

"Och, it's alright Dad, it'll buff out. Besides, I thought it was *our* wing? Come on, Betsie will need to be fed; she needs a reward after helping us out in the sight."

Hamish looked from Heather to the wing, and back. "I s'pose it'll get us home, but it'll take many weeks to get her back into a decent state again."

"Thas the spirit, c'mon, let's shake a leg."

Heather and Hamish said one more farewell to the group before climbing aboard. Hugh noticed the old guide had far less of a problem getting through the door than Barrington. They stood back and shielded their eyes as they watched the RW1 take to the sky, re-cloak and disappear. Hugh thought he saw a ripple in the snow as it powered off, but any sign of it was hidden by the amount of snow now falling.

The weather was closing in, so Hugh, Barrington, and Emily headed down from the mountain, which was tough going at first, as the snow was falling heavily.

They reached the gorge and saw it was mid freeze, its waters partially held within the winter's grip. Though they couldn't see the water moving, they could still hear its rumble from deep below the ice. They carried on their descent, relying on the cairns used to mark out the track.

As they descended, the snow thinned and turned into rain, with fat, cold drops that hit Hugh's face before rolling off the end of his nose. By the time they reached the tree line, the afternoon was already drawing to a close. Hugh and Emily moved their firestone pins to position two, illuminating the path ahead.

It was slow going, for the track at this level had turned into mud, leaving the ground underfoot unstable. Emily was putting her new staff to good use, though Hugh wondered if she really should show more care to something so precious. As they approached the main track to the valley run, they dimmed their stones.

They could hear people up ahead, and they saw torches moving up and down the tree-lined path. They headed into the cover of the trees and walked as quietly as they could towards the moving people.

"How many do you think there are?" said Hugh. He spoke in such a quiet whisper he was unsure if anyone had heard him.

"I don't know," said Barrington, his breath fogging in the cold evening air. "There's certainly a fair few of them. I wonder what they're doing down there?"

They all craned to listen out for any discernible noises. It sounded like many people digging, and metallic sounds reached their ears.

"Whatever it is, it doesn't sound good," said Emily. "Come on, let's see if we can get any closer."

Hugh and Emily moved the pins from their stones back to hole one so as not to be seen by those down on the track. They crept as close as they dared, and the sight that greeted them chilled Hugh to his core.

The old track was unrecognisable, for the trees to either side had been cleared. Great trenches had been dug into the ground, and the remnants now appeared to be in large jute bags. The workers were well underway to constructing some sort of outpost. Strange, coiled wire covered in spikes had been laid all around, forcing anyone coming towards the city to pass through the narrow gap, just wide enough for a horse and cart.

"They're definitely worried about something," said Barrington.

Emily nodded.

"Yeah, well, whatever it is, I don't think this way is an option for us to get back into the city anymore. Come on, let's see if we can get across the track, any further up."

It was tough going, trying to beat through the sodden undergrowth, whilst attempting not to be heard by those on the track below. Things were made difficult by the steep terrain they were encountering until eventually they had no choice but to get across to the river side of the track.

They were two tree depths in when a small patrol marched past. Hugh was about to set off when Emily grabbed him by the arm, nearly making him cry out in shock. She stood with a finger to her lips and pointed toward Dallum. Hugh looked and saw a lone runner coming towards the armed guards.

"Halt! Who goes there?"

"Don't shoot! I'm part of the scouting team."

The man was out of breath, and the guard that shouted the order turned back to the other men.

"Stand down lads, he's one of ours." He turned back to the scout. "What news do you bring us?"

"Convoy, sir, from Kings Seat," he said, out of breath, "passed through Dallum this evening. They are headed this way."

"Was it a big convoy?"

"Fairly, sir."

The guard mulled the message over before coming to some sort of decision.

"Right, this could be the start of it. Well done," he said to the scout.

"Head back to the city and get refreshed. We will need your team tonight."

The scout didn't move.

"Was there something else?"

The scout nodded and handed over two letters. The guard read the first one.

"Hmm, it appears Smithson is to return to us."

Hugh looked at Emily and Barrington, then back to the guard and the second letter. It was sealed with a wax seal. The guard opened it up, read it quickly, then looked to the scout.

"Who gave you this?" he said, his tone now urgent.

"One of the convoy drivers, sir. He didn't say who he was."

"I'm afraid you'll have no time to rest. Take this letter to Ceremony House, on my orders."

He whipped out a piece of paper, ordered one of the other guards to bend over, so he could use his back to write a note.

"Take this and don't let anyone take it from you. It gives you clearance to get to the right place. Do you know where to go?"

The scout nodded and took the paper and letter.

"Good, now run, as fast as you can." The scout took one last look at the guard, before running off down the road at full pelt.

"What was it, sarge?" asked one of the other guards.

"It would appear things are moving at quite a pace. He is on the move."

"Who, sarge?"

"The Elf King."

Chapter 35

Hugh, Barrington and Emily walked in silence, all digesting what they had just heard. They kept to the tree line until they found a safe place to cross the track. They passed a danger of death sign, and Emily warned them not to step on the fresh mounds of earth, saying it would be the last step they would ever take. They dodged and weaved into the thicket on the opposite side. Eventually Hugh couldn't keep the questions he had to himself.

"Is it just me, or is anyone else wondering what Smithson was doing in Kings Seat?"

"Yes, that is strange," said Barrington, out of breath from walking through the dense undergrowth.

Emily stopped and turned around to the pair.

"Will you two try to keep the noise down? It's pretty obvious what Smithson was doing there."

She stared at them, and they looked back with blank faces.

"Oh, for goodness sakes! Hamish told us that two people ambushed him at his cottage, so it stands to reason that it was Smithson and Collins."

Hugh pondered this.

"But Smithson doesn't like the Old World or anything to do with it."

"What's that got to do with anything?"

"Well, everything really. I can't see him being willing to use a rune net, even if it was to catch Hamish. I wonder what he wanted him for?"

"Really?"

"What now?"

Emily let out a sigh.

"Again, it's the most obvious answer that's staring you in the face. Hamish is the most famous guide in the Old World. If you were searching for something and found out the location of said person who could find the object, then surely you'd want to get hold of him by any means possible. I'm sure finding Heather was probably not part of the plan, hence the bungled attempt to get rid of her."

"Oh ..." said Hugh and Barrington, finally joining up the dots.

"You two really are going to have to use your brains more if we are to get through this in one piece... What are you doing now?"

Hugh was sniffing the air.

"Don't you smell it?"

"What's that, old bean?" said Barrington, as he and Emily began taking in long, purposeful sniffs.

There was the unmistakable smell of freshly cut vegetation. Hugh carefully walked forwards, following the scent as it became stronger, and it wasn't long before they found the source of the aroma. What they saw left them chilled to the core.

"Well, this may cause us a little issue," said Barrington.

Hugh looked at him.

"You think?"

"How did they manage to clear all of this so quickly?"

"Foresting machines," said Emily.

Hugh and Barrington stared back, nonplussed, and Emily let out a large sigh.

"We have machines at the greenhouses, designed to clear areas of unwanted vegetation. They have flailing chains on them, and we push them into the vegetation. Those in charge of the city liked the idea, so scaled it up to take out larger objects, like trees."

"Oh…" said Hugh and Barrington said collectively.

If this was the place they had climbed out of the new tunnel from the greenhouses, it had changed from all recognition and now resembled a massacre on nature. Where once stood forest and dense under-story of foliage, there remained only a wasteland of cleared space.

The first fifty yards were filled with sharpened stumps to impede any approaching forces. Beyond that, was a wide, open run up to the wall. It would be impossible to get anywhere near it without being seen.

"How on earth are we going to find the tree stump amongst this lot?" said Barrington.

Emily looked across the desolation towards the river. She walked towards the bank, as if she were getting her bearings.

"The bend in the river is where the tunnel came out, which means …" She moved closer to the edge of the undergrowth but remained protected by its cover. She blew into her hands, risking a small glow, and released it in the direction she thought it would be. Hugh felt a warmth inside of him, and it wasn't coming from the firestone.

They watched as the small glowing dot, which looked no larger than a firefly, made its way across the desolate vegetation and stopped over a lone stump. Behind it, the area warmed up and moisture rose into the air. Hugh feared it would give away their position.

"There," she said, pointing to a gnarled stump.

"But how can you be sure?"

"It's protected by runes. I used a locator rune set to find it, and it's stopped on the correct stump. If I hadn't had protected the exit, those clearing the area would have found it."

Hugh now looked to where Emily was pointing.

"Are you sure?"

"I'm certain of it."

"Do you think they broke the cover when they cleared the area?"

Emily shook her head.

"No, there are enough enchantments covering that old lump of wood to protect a small fortress. The other end is protected by the vipera fronde. The likelihood of anyone discovering the tunnel is minimal."

"Hrmm," said Barrington, now stroking his chin. "So, how do we get to said entrance? We can't just stroll up to it, or we'll be caught within a matter of moments, and I don't think we'll escape the cells a second time round."

"How did you all get into the city before?"

"We had Heather with us, and she used some runes to make us invisible," said Hugh.

"Did she really? And how did she know it wouldn't have any adverse effects on you?"

"She and Hamish use them on each other all the time. Plus, Barrington and I don't appear to have grown any extra limbs."

"Well, not yet," said Barrington.

Emily glared at him.

They stood in an awkward silence, with Emily looking pensive.

"Right, here's what we are going to do. Hugh, you have links with Heather inside you, which we can use. We will need you to draw upon the runes needed to make us all invisible."

"Emily, I've barely begun using runes. I hardly think I am the right choice to be using complicated magic."

"Hugh, you are the only one that stands half a chance of making this happen. You must look within yourself, find the correct runes and use them as Heather would. I believe in you, and I know you can do this. All you have to do is trust yourself, call to the runes, and they will appear ... yes, Barrington?"

"Well, it's not that I don't have faith in my friend here. I mean to say, you have my fullest confidence Hugh, but—"

"Good, then that's the last issue resolved. Right, Hugh, when you are ready."

Barrington let out a little squeak as Hugh delved inside himself and tried to latch onto the part of Heather that resided within him.

It seemed to want to play hide and seek, as each time he got close to it, the bit he was chasing disappeared.

'What are you doing?' said Emily, inside his head.

'Well, I'm trying to latch onto the part of Heather. It keeps getting away from me.'

'That's because you are not showing enough command over the runes. You have to become a master at this, Hugh, the same as when we are in the sight. If you don't learn to control the power, it will begin to control you, and that is a very dangerous road to go down. Many people have been driven to madness and led to do things they wouldn't normally do when not in control.'

'But I am concentrating as hard as I can. I am thinking of being invisible.'

'That's not enough. You need to command them with all of your will. Try again,' she said. 'Make them submit to your power.'

Hugh moved his mind back to the job at hand. It was difficult, made more so by the knowledge that his every move was being assessed by Emily. Not wanting to let her down – or face another lecture – he used all of his will to find the runes and force them into his control. He saw them, a mass of moving balls of light. He moved in closer, seeing they were composed of many runes, all swirling around each other.

'Very good,' said Emily, almost making him lose his bond on the ball of light.

'Call the runes to you, Hugh. Don't go after them; make them come to you.'

It was as if someone else had temporarily taken control of his mind – as though he was at one with the greater universe. He didn't know where the words were coming from, but come they did.

'I call forth the runes of invisibility. Come to me now and do my bidding.'

The moving balls of light separated, and runes floated towards him. He cupped them in his hands. Instinctively, he knew what he had to do.

Out in the plane of the living, Barrington watched on in amazement as Hugh closed his eyes and gently blew into his hands, cupping a small glow of energy.

"Would you look at that." Hugh opened his eyes and moved towards him with outstretched hands.

"Now, uh now, now hang on a minute ..."

But it was too late. Hugh winked at his friend, then opened his hands, the energy flowing over Barrington.

"Oh, my!"

Barrington slowly disappeared before their very eyes from the head down, leaving Emily in awe.

"That's amazing!"

"Has it worked?" said Barrington's voice, from where he disappeared.

"Oh yes," said Hugh, in total shock from what he had just done to his friend.

"Well, don't hang about then. Summon the power again and cover me and you," said Emily.

Hugh repeated the process and watched as Emily slowly faded away, before repeating the process on himself. The strange sensation fell over him, as though someone had cracked an egg over his head. It continued all the way down to his feet.

"Am I gone?" he asked.

"Yes, and me?"

"I can confirm that you are both gone" said Barrington. "Ow! What did you do that for? That was my eye!"

"Just checking where you are," said Emily, sounding smug. "Ow! Oh, you missed, that was my shoulder."

"Hmph."

"If you two have both finished, I think we ought to get to that stump, before these runes wear off," said Hugh. "Oh…"

The light Emily had sent out to the stump was now joined by many other small moving lights. Her small act had caused the local fireflies to come out of hiding, and the area was a mass of moving dots, clinging to the radiating heat. There were four stumps to choose from.

"It's alright," said Emily, "it's that one just in from the river."

"I think I have it, what about you, Barrington?"

"Yes, I see it, old bean. Come on, let's get there, before we are revealed again."

They all carefully made their way out into the open, unseen by the guards off in the distance high up on the wall.

"Right, here we are," said Emily.

"Where?" said Barrington.

"Well, here? Where are you?"

"I'm here, next to Hugh."

"No, you're not, I'm next to Emily."

"Are you?"

"Yes … no … urgh!"

"Hugh, keep your voice down," said Emily.

"Sorry, but I just put my hand on a dead badger!"

"Err, how did you get me confused with a dead badger?"

"I didn't think you were a dead badger, it's just that … oh, forget it. Everyone, back to that tree."

"Which tree, old bean?"

Emily huffed. "Oh, for goodness sakes, Barrington. The tree we were all stood next to."

They all regrouped back under the cover in the undergrowth. "Right, let's link hands," said Hugh.

"I'm not linking hands with you. It's been near a dead badger."

"Barrington."

"Fine."

With a bit of effort, they got themselves to the right stump. There was a glow, and Hugh watched as the pile of sticks and mud moved to reveal the trapdoor to the tunnel, which lifted in the eerie light.

Barrington opted to go down first, then Emily, but she had to get her staff down before she descended.

"Drop it down, and I will catch it," said Barrington's voice echoed from the bottom of the shaft.

"How will you see it?" said Emily.

"Never fear, my dear, I still have my naval train — OW!"

The sound of the staff clattered at the bottom of the shaft.

"You were saying?"

"Will you two pack it in! Emily, you really need to look after the staff. We need to get a move on. I can already see you your outline coming through."

She hurried to get into the tunnel, and Hugh followed behind her, knowing he too would reappear at any moment. By the time they reached the bottom of the rock wall, they were all back to normal and visible once more.

Emily sent another glowing ball upwards, and the entrance sealed itself up again. As they headed down the tunnel, Hugh noticed that part of the roof had dropped in, probably disturbed from the removal of the vegetation above them.

"I'll need to get someone to shore up this ceiling if we are to keep this tunnel open," said Emily.

Barrington looked up cautiously.

"Are you sure it's safe enough to keep going on?"

"It should be. We are deep enough here. Besides, there is no other way to get back into the city."

Unable to think of a better reason not to use the tunnel, Barrington kept quiet. The walk back seemed to take an age, and Hugh constantly feared being trapped underground by a cave in. It was a relief to them all when they finally reached the ladder to the greenhouses. Hugh could still remember his trip down the ladder and stood rubbing his arm.

Emily passed them both a protective suit.

"Get these on, and make sure they are tight this time," she said, looking at Hugh.

He looked back, tight-lipped, eyebrows raised. Emily picked up the spare suit, folding it up carefully into itself, ending up with a tight package. Hugh noted she had forgotten to tuck in the arms and legs, then watched as she used them to turn the bundle into a backpack and tied her staff in with it. She finished putting on her own suit, then donned the newly formed straps before climbing the ladder.

The climb was slow going, partly due to fatigue, but also because of the staff getting caught at regular intervals. Hugh's own bag was also making life difficult, and as it was so full, he barely had room to move. They eventually arrived at the top of the ladder, and Hugh made sure to not look down, as he pulled himself out of the hole in the floor.

Emily replaced the trapdoor, then covered it with soil and vegetation. Hugh and Barrington were busy fighting the vipera fronde, which was attempting to wrap itself around them. As if out of nowhere, a machete swiped through their bindings, and they turned to see Emily now clearing a path for them to get out. It was tough going, but they eventually made it to the safety of the clearing.

"Right, put the suits away in the lockers, and we can see about getting out of here."

"Who's there?" called a voice.

They all stopped dead, no-one dared to move. This was it. They were done for. They had come all this way to be caught at the last hurdle, and now they had to face what was coming their way.

Chapter 36

Smithson was back in the lobby of the Hotel Alpine and had found his favourite bell, ringing the thing for all it was worth. He had insisted that the caravan of people moving from Kings Seat stopped, if only for him to get some food and away from the awful ride he was having.

"Hotelier, where are you?"

Eric appeared, nightcap on, doing up his dressing gown.

"Alright, I'm coming. Gettin' me out of bed at all hours of the day … oh surprise, surprise, it's the bell ringer. What do you want?" he said, moving the bell once more from Smithson's reach.

"Less of that tone from you, Hotelier. I'm hungry and everywhere else is shut."

"You mind your tone, talkin' to me like that. We're shut too. It's the middle of the night!"

"Not according to the night watchman."

"Bleedin' idiot. Well, I'm up now. What do you want?"

Smithson placed a handful of krunes onto the desk in front of him.

"A sandwich will do. Make it quick. I want to be back on the road."

"Right, I'll see what I can find." Eric scooped the money up, then went off muttering to himself. He returned five minutes later with the end of a bread loaf, some cheese and water. "You can serve yourself. Make sure you don't make a mess." He went to leave, before Smithson stopped him.

"Thank you, Hotelier, for your welcomed hospitality."

Eric looked at him.

"Well, if you want conversation as well—"

"No, I'll be fine," said Smithson, "Though I can say, you won't be seeing many people from Portis-Montis for a while."

"What are you takin' about?"

"Oh, nothing really. Only the news that Mr Geber and Mr Delphin met their untimely demise out in Kraken Bay," he said, ripping off some bread.

Eric took a hand to his mouth and stared at the desk in front of him.

"So it's true then?"

"What did you say?"

"Sorry," said Eric, looking up from the desk. "Oh, nothing … nothing …"

"Hmm, well thank you for your information."

"What information?"

"The information you passed to our people. They were caught after breaking the curfew, then tried to get away after escaping the cells at the King's Seat. Terrible way to behave if you ask me."

"I didn't pass any information on. I would never do such a thing. To betray customer privacy is to break the hoteliers' code."

"If you didn't pass on the information, who did?"

"How am I supposed to know? All I can say is, it certainly wasn't me. I would never dream of breaking the hoteliers' code like that."

"Anyway, they got their just desserts, so that's not significant anymore."

"May I remind you to show some respect to the dead. Those poor, poor people."

"Poor people? They were criminals on the run; they deserved all they got."

"Right, that's it. Out!"

"What?"

"I said *out*! You're not welcome in this fine establishment any longer." Smithson stood open-mouthed.

"Well, I have never been treated so poorly in all my life. Out, indeed. You're too late to throw me out, Hotelier, I was already leaving."

He shoved the board with bread and cheese onto the floor, scattering cheese and crumbs across the expanse of polished marble in front of the desk. He turned on his heel, the sound of crumbs crunching under his foot and marched out of the hotel, leaving Eric to stand agog, listening to the sound of the clatter echoing around the empty lobby.

Chapter 37

The trio were standing in silence in the middle of greenhouse nine, nobody daring to move.

"I said, who's there?" the unknown voice asked again.

Hugh's stomach felt as though a lead weight had been dropped into it. They all looked around for the mystery voice which was yet to reveal itself.

"It's Miss Le Fey, deputy botanist in charge of these greenhouses." She stood, pointing her staff in the general direction of the voice. "Who and where are you?"

"Ah, Miss le Fey, you had me worried there for a minute," and Jones, one of Emily's students, stepped out from the undergrowth. "What's that?" he said, eyeing up the staff wearily.

"None of your business, Jones. What are you doing here at this time of night?"

"Well, I might ask you the same thing?"

"Jones, I'm not I the mood for games."

"Sorry. Alfred called us all to a meeting and told us what was going on. He was the one who posted me here, told me to look out for anything out of the ordinary. He also said he was hoping some people might turn up, sounded quite desperate about it."

"Alfred called you to a meeting?" she said. "What are you talking about?"

"Well, he inducted us into this club," he said, rooting through his pocket, pulling out a card. "Then he gave us all one of these. All a bit odd if you ask me. He was all cloak and dagger about it."

Emily took the card and looked at it. Expecting to see the EGF logo, she was surprised to see a scythe and hoe crossed over in the centre, encircled in a wreath of holly.

"What's this?"

"Greenhouse Watch, first division, at your service, miss." He stood to attention and saluted.

Emily rolled her eyes.

"Can I take a stab in the dark and guess that Alfred told you not to reveal this card to anyone, unless one of your fellow watch members reveals theirs first?"

"Oh yeah, I always forget about that. How did you know about that? Are you part of the club too? You know it's pretty confusing all of this. You ask me, I ask you, then we reveal, and we're good to talk, otherwise, hold your tongue ... Oh, yeah, forgot that bit too."

"I don't want a running commentary, Jones. What are you doing here?"

"Oh, right, well, Alfred told us we were to stand guard here, until someone came out from the vipera fronde. We had bets on who it would be. Looks like I'm down ten krunes. I got the night shift 'cos I was late to the meeting."

Emily looked at him disapprovingly.

"Anyway, we is to report back to him when someone appears. Who'd have thought it would be you?"

"Jones ... oh, never mind," she said, shaking her head. "Let's get to Alfred's shop. We can talk more there ... what now, Jones?"

He dropped the hand he had up.

"Sorry Miss, but they have set up in a room at the Old Rangles Inn. A great place if you ask me, lots of ale."

"Oh, how very organised of him. Have we also put up a big sign saying Local Greenhouse Watch Office yet?"

Jones looked at her, confused for a moment.

"Nah, why would we do that? It would give us away. Cor, you're proper silly Miss Le Fey. GW sign, I dunno?"

"Jones, just get to the point already."

"Oh, sorry. We got a great place sorted out. Just you wait and see," he said, tapping the side of his nose. "Now you're to follow me, nice and quietly please." Emily rolled her eyes.

They headed out the greenhouses and carefully made their way across the front yard to the gates. They had to hold back, ducking behind the wall, as a group of guards walked past.

Hugh was worried the fog from their heavy breathing would give them away, but it appeared the guards had spent too long in the pub in the wall and were into deep conversations about the current goings on to notice anything out of the ordinary.

They stalked the guards all the way to the back door of the Old Rangles Inn, having to wait for the guards to relieve their bladders down an alley. Hugh was happy to be in from the cold night air, as they closed the door behind them. They followed Jones down the corridor, until he stopped, winked at them and knocked a tuneful rap on the wall.

The door in the wall cracked open, then swung into the room, to reveal a group of people around the table.

"Oh, it's you Jones. I've told you before, just a simple knock will suffice ... Emily, Hugh, Barrington!" Alfred set his drink onto the table, making his way over to the new arrivals. "I'm so pleased to see you're safe and well. We feared the worst, after the latest update from Kings Seat."

"What update was that?" said Hugh.

"We had word from one of our Kings Seat contacts. You sailed across Kraken Bay, of all places? Why on earth would you put yourself in such danger like that? Everyone knows to keep to the outer side of the markers. What made you do such a thing?"

Hugh and Emily looked to Barrington, who flushed and looked away.

"We were attempting to run from the King's Seat guards," said Hugh, "and someone didn't read the charts properly. Let's not get into it now."

"Well, it was certainly a foolhardy move. Anyway, it's great to see you all here, safe and sound."

He gave Emily and Hugh a big hug before shaking Barrington's hand. He dispatched Jones to the bar to get them some drinks, whilst the trio took a seat around the table. Jones soon returned carrying a tray, drinks slopping about the place, and some of Trevor's legendary bar snacks.

"Thank you, Jones," said Emily, staring at the solid treats.

Barrington took great gulps of ale, then wiped his mouth on the back of his sleeve.

"Indeed, dear boy, thank you very much."

"So, tell us what happened?" said Alfred, unable to wait any longer. "It looks like you've been through the wars a bit." Hugh set to filling Alfred and the rest of the room in on their adventures.

It was met with gasps and faces of shock and wonder. Alfred looked at Hugh, then spoke to the rest of the people in the room.

"Alright team, thank you for all of your help tonight. I'll be in touch when we next need you. Remember, not a word of this to anyone, and don't reveal yourself to the enemy. Secrecy at all costs. Jones, is there something you wanted to say?"

There were some audible tuts from those around him.

"I was just going to say, I hope you were okay with me bringing them back here, rather than fetching you?"

"Ah, I see. Well, they have known of the room's existence for a long time, so you've broken no rules, if that is what you are worried about."

"Oh good, that's what I thought, just wanted to check." He joined the rest of the group, heading towards the door.

"And don't forget, leave here in ones or twos, leaving large gaps between you," said Alfred. "We don't want anyone getting caught."

They all nodded to him and shuffled out of the door. Once they had all dispersed, Alfred turned back to the trio.

"So tell me, which parts of the story did you omit?"

"Well, Augustus didn't just happen to find us, like I said. He was in the area, but nowhere near the incident."

"Right, go on."

"I was on the brink of being wiped out by a tentacle, then I entered the sight."

"But … your body? Surely that would have been wiped out, leaving you stranded?"

"Not quite. When I said I entered the sight, I was referring to all of me." He gestured up and down his body.

"So, are you saying that you can enter the sight, full body, at any point?" said Alfred, in awe.

"Yes and no. I can enter full body. The only issue is, I have no control over when it happens."

Alfred looked as though he was about to say something, but Emily beat him to it.

"I've told him he has to gain control over this, Alfred, but it seems Hugh cannot do it."

"Though it has saved my life, more than once, I might add," said Hugh.

Alfred sat with his arms crossed, taking it all in.

"Hmm, well, you cannot rely on luck all of the time, Hugh. Emily is right.
You'll need to gain some control over this, otherwise you could end up entering the sight at the wrong time."

Hugh was cornered, aware that all the eyes in the room were now on him.

"It's not that easy. You make it sound like it's the simplest of things, but it's not. I am trying to get control over this. There's just so much to learn, and everyone keeps having a go at me." He blinked and tried to stifle a yawn. "We've been through so much these last few days, my body is still trying to catch up."

Hugh rummaged into his bag, pulling out his father's own, slightly damp bag, and placing it on the table.

"This is what we retrieved from the library of lost souls of past prisoners at the King's Seat."

"The what?"

"Terrible place," said Barrington. "Morbid and as grim as it sounds. Shelves full of the dead prisoners' belongings." He caught Hugh's eye, who looked saddened. "Sorry, dear Hugh, but we have to tell it as it is."

Alfred stayed quiet, letting his fingers fall over the leather satchel. Hugh pulled off the ring from his right little finger.

"This was in there. I was hoping, if it's alright with you, that I could keep it."

Alfred cleared his throat with a cough.

"Of course, yes. It was my father's, then Fredrick's. It only makes sense for it to pass to you."

They all sat in silence, and Alfred wiped a stray tear from his eye.

"We also found this."

Hugh pulled out the lore book of magic from his bag and unwrapped it from its protective covering. He could sense the power held within its many pages trying to get out.

Alfred looked at it with reverence.

"It's beautiful. I can't believe you have found one of the missing books of lore. How and where did you find it?"

"With the help of this," said Hugh.

"What's that? A broken compass?"

"No, this is the Orbis, the book finder. With this, we can now search for the book of alchemy and return it to its rightful home."

Hugh explained all the events that took place in the caverns and how they discovered the missing law book.

"Well, that explains where Ranny ended up. I'm glad to hear that he is safe. So do you now have a bearing to follow so that you can find the lore book of alchemy?"

"Sadly, it wavers about too much to get a fixed location. But when I gain proper control over this thing, I'll be able to locate the missing book. I just need more time to practice."

Alfred's eyes appeared to light up. "You realise, with this, we will be ahead of the Elf King, and it will gain us all the missing knowledge from the world of alchemy, and more besides?"

"Yes," he said. "Then we take the lore book back to the Chamber of Prophecy, like we are supposed to do. This isn't something that one person alone can, or should, hold."

"Of course, we wouldn't dream of doing anything else, but it would be nice."

"No, Alfred. No buts." Hugh took a deep breath in, then realised that the others had a similar look in their faces. "I think, before we go any further, we all need to agree on something. These books come with a lot of power, and in the wrong hands, they could cause absolute devastation for the world. We need to make a pact, and I think I know how."

He pulled out a piece of paper and the fountain pen that belonged to his father, pleased to see the screw-top lid had kept the water out, and began writing quickly.

We, the undersigned, agree to return the books of power to their rightful place. We will not use them for our own personal gain over the other books and will help guide the one who is destined to control them to the right place at the right time. We may use the book of our own lore to become better practiced in our art and jobs.

The punishment for breaking this promise shall be death. Signed,

Hugh signed the note, then passed it to the others to sign.

Barrington looked at the paper, then laughed out loud.

"You seriously don't expect us to sign this, do you? And the last time I knew, you weren't up to speed on magical contracts."

"That's why Emily is going to help."

"I am?" she looked at him in shock.

"Yes, you are. You cannot disagree with me; it's too dangerous for one person to hold all the knowledge. We must work together on this, and for this to be a magical contract, you'll have to help me find the right runes to use. That way, nobody will be tempted to break the rules."

He gave Emily a long, hard stare until she finally gave in.

"Alright. I agree, nobody should hold that much power, and yes, if we all become skilled in our own art, we'll be able to help the one when the time comes."

She took the pen and paper from Barrington and signed it, before passing it to Alfred.

"I suppose you're correct," he said, putting pen to paper.

He pushed the paper towards Barrington, holding the pen in mid-air for him to take. They all stared at him, waiting for him to capitulate.

He sighed. "Fine, but I still think this is all over the top," he said, signing the sheet, then screwing the lid back on tightly. "Now what?"

"Well," said Emily, "I am going to have to join energy with Hugh, and we will have to look into ourselves. I don't think we need to enter the sight. We'll need to step across to you two and take something from you for the contract."

"When you say you need to *take* something, what do you mean?" asked Barrington.

"It won't hurt. It just needs to be something from within you. I'll know what it is when I find it."

Hugh looked to Emily, and they both went quiet and closed their eyes, with Barrington and Alfred looking on.

They both jumped, as unspoken words appeared in their heads. Hugh and Emily opened their eyes, cupped their hands together and formed a large ball of energy, before letting it fall upon the paper. Hugh watched the mass of runes spread out across the sheet, as they interwove together, forming an unbreakable bond.

Hugh looked back up to the rest of them.

"Well, that's settled then. Shall we move forward?"

The rest nodded in agreement. They decided that there was nothing else that they could do for now and that what they needed now was sleep.

"We've blacked out the windows," said Alfred, "so there's no need to worry about light showing through to the street. I will go now, but I'll see you in the morning. You can help yourself to food from the kitchens. I'm sure Trevor won't mind."

It was only now that Hugh remembered the fix they had put Trevor in.

"Where is he?"

"Who, Trevor? He's still in the cells. We are yet to get a full update on his wellbeing, as he was still in questioning the last time I enquired, but Bernie assured me he will be alright. As soon as he is out, I will know."

Emily's eyes went wide. "He's still not out yet?"

"I'm afraid not. The new chap in charge is being overly cautious and keeping hold of anyone he thinks is working for the other side. With this place being as well-known as it is for underhand dealings, it was only a matter of time before he was brought in for questioning, and that's without the added worry of the extended family. We can only hope he is alright."

The rest of them looked back at Alfred, open-mouthed, unable to process what they'd heard.

"Listen, he knew what he was undertaking when your father gave him that card, and he was known for being very lenient with his customers. He always offered a place of safety in return for their loyalty and trade. I'm sure he will be out soon enough. Now, why don't you three head upstairs. You all look exhausted and in need of a good rest."

Too tired to put up a fight or to ask any more questions, they bid

Alfred a good night and headed upstairs. Barrington went to the room he was in before, and Emily went with Hugh. There was no conversation as they took their boots off and fell into the bed. It was only moments later that the corridors of the Old Rangles Inn were filled with the sound of snoring.

Chapter 38

The next day was bright and crisp. Hugh, Emily and Barrington were awoken by a cheery call from Alfred at the bottom of the stairs. As Hugh stretched out in the bed, the smell of dust and toast filled the air, quickly followed by freshly cooked bacon. He didn't need the groan from his stomach to know that he was hungry, and gauging by the speed Emily was getting her shoes on and Barrington was already heading down the corridor, they were more than ready for breakfast as well.

They made it down to the dimly lit bar area in time to sit down to the freshly cooked breakfast prepared by Alfred.

"Good morning, you three, I hope you slept well. I thought I would take the opportunity to cook some food for you. I hope you don't mind."

Nobody complained as they dug into a hearty breakfast of toast, bacon, eggs, tomatoes, sausage and mushroom. It was a welcomed feast after their recent culinary experience in the cells of the King's Seat. Hugh's mouth watered as he ate. Food had never tasted so good. Once they had finished eating and topped up on some tea from the pot, Alfred got down to business.

"Alright, so we need to figure out how to get you three out of here without being caught by the authorities."

"Sorry, us *three*?" said Emily.

"I'm afraid so. Since your escape from Kings Seat, many posters have been erected, bringing the news that you are no longer with us. Rumour has it that Smithson sent word that you have all died. If you were to be seen out and about now, it would cause great confusion, let alone jeopardise the entire operation we are working on."

"What operation might that be?" asked Barrington.

"It's in the early stages, and I was only brought into it in the last two days. There is talk of an uprising, and I have been tasked with the important mission of recruiting people to the cause, hence me talking to those in charge at the Greenhouses. I know they are already aware of the uprising that's coming, and they were keen to help in any way possible. As you know, they have been appalled at the way the Old-Worlders were expelled from the city. They are expecting the powers to attempt to take control any day now. They were saddened to hear the news of your untimely demise but were overjoyed to hear you made to back unscathed. I paid them a visit on my way here to update them on the situation, before any keen students did it on my behalf."

"That's nice to hear they were concerned, but if the greenhouses are to be taken over, I wish to be there to fight."

"That's very admirable, Emily, but like I say, if the powers that be realise you are, indeed, not dead, then it will spark a massive manhunt for Hugh and Barrington. I dare say it won't be long before someone connects the dots. It will only take one person to spot you, or a loose mouth somewhere for the whole story to come crashing down around us. No, I think you will be much safer if we get you away from here to Portis-Montis with Balinas. We can put the students to good use, and like I say, I have the full backing from the rest of the greenhouse team."

"Really?"

"It was they who suggested we induct the students into a new security guard, sprites know, we need all the help we can get right now."

"Seriously?" said Emily. "I would be careful which students you use for the cause, Alfred. Some of them have a reputation for being, well, unreliable."

"I know who you are thinking of, Emily, and I have already covered those issues."

"But what is to happen with my job and my students?"

"Your colleagues are fully aware of the situation and that you will be needed for the cause. Your students are well trained, naturally, and any extra training needed will be covered by others. Your job now is to assist Hugh and Barrington get hold of these books. I had a long chat with Balinas last night and he agrees with me."

"Balinas was here?" said Hugh, looking around, expecting him to appear at any moment.

"Calm yourself, Hugh. We had a conversation via the sight. Balinas is not allowed to leave the university, either in person or via the sight. He has filled me in with more information regarding your task, and I could update him on the progress happening this end. He didn't seem too surprised you were still with us, but then he would know these things. It's important now that you get the lore book of magic back to Portis-Montis. It will mean one less book that the Elf King can get his hands on."

"But how are we to do that when we cannot walk outside? I can't imagine what will happen if we were to walk up to the security in the airdock," said Barrington.

"Well, now that you mention it, I have that one covered." Alfred stood and walked to the bar, retrieved some papers, then came back to the group, handing them a package each. "Here you go. These are your new papers with all the details that you need."

Hugh looked at his papers. He was to be known as Reginald Pirbright, husband to Dierdre, both in their sixties. Emily was to play the part of Dierdre, and Barrington was to be Reginald's brother, Bob. Hugh looked upon from the papers to Alfred.

"I hate to break the news to you, but I don't look like a sixty-year-old and neither do Emily nor Barrington. I can't see us passing off as these people, so we will have to come up with a different plan."

Alfred raised his hands. "Bear with me here, Hugh. For this to work, you will need to change into someone new."

"But we can't do that either. I think you have overestimated our skills."

"You can do it with help. We need to take a trip into the sight. Emily, can you take Hugh, and Barrington you can come with me."

Barrington looked back, confused. "Where are we going?"

"We need to pay another trip to Balinas. He is expecting us and has woken early especially for this, so let's not keep the poor chap waiting."

He went to the bar and returned with a jug and four glasses.

"Hugh won't need one of those," said Emily.

"He won't?" said Alfred in surprise.

"No, he can step in without the aid of water."

"How very interesting. Tell me, Hugh, how is that even possible?"

"Not now, Alfred. We need to get a move on."

Barrington looked as if he was pondering a large thought.

"If Hugh can enter the sight with his whole body, why not give him the book? He can take it to the Chamber of Prophecy, and we can meet him there?"

Alfred shook his head. "I'm afraid it's not as simple as that. You cannot cross over into the library, or the Chamber of Prophecy. It's one protection put in place to protect the books and the rooms from unwanted visitors. Balinas cannot leave the university in person nor via the sight. The only privilege he has is to enter the sight in spirit."

"Alright, then send him outside the university. Then he can make his way from there."

"Again, you are not thinking about the complexities of the situation. What if Hugh popped out of thin air in front of someone? It's hard enough to explain to someone who understands the sight, let alone to an outsider. Then there is the book. We don't know what happens when you take something like that into the sight. It could cause a universal shift of massive proportions, or something within there may desire the object. Also, we don't know where the Elf King is. Hugh may pop out in front of him, and he would soon cotton on to what is happening. It's all too risky."

"Well, when you put it like that ..."

"Please, can we get on with this now?" said Emily.

Alfred didn't answer her, as he passed them each a glass each. They filled them with water and stuck a finger in. Hugh watched as they all went still, then felt himself crossing over.

–POP–

As soon as he was in, he began protecting himself, calling on the runes needed to prevent others from attacking him.

'Well, I must say, this is very impressive, Hugh. To see you here full body is something to behold. There are few that have managed it.'

'Don't go too gushy on him. He will get a big head, and we wouldn't want that,' said Emily, finishing working on her own runes before helping Alfred to protect Barrington and his life-link. Hugh was busy calling on his own runes for protection.

'Alright, let me see. Ah yes, this way if you will.'

Alfred headed off in a direction – of sorts – though it all looked the same, apart from the darker patch to Hugh's left. He was drawn to it, before Emily stopped him once more.

'Hugh!'

'What's wrong?' said Alfred. Hugh saw his outline turn to face them.

'Hugh is always drawn to the voices that call to him whilst he is here. I've warned him not to go after them, but he insists on following them each time he's here.'

'Actually, for you information, I haven't heard them today,' said Hugh.

'Then where were you going this time?'

'It's that dark area over there. I think that's got something to do with my father.'

'*What dark area? Hugh, you must try harder to avoid things like this. Dark areas are not to be explored, along with strange voices.*'

'*Emily is right, Hugh. You cannot head towards these impulses. They will only lead to disaster. Look at where it got your father.*'

'*What's that supposed mean?*'

'*Oh, well uh, nothing, forget I mentioned it.*'

'*But ...*'

It was too late. Alfred had already turned to head off, with Barrington trailing behind him.

'*Come on then, let's get a move on,*' said Emily. '*I'll stay behind you. We wouldn't want you wandering off.*'

Up ahead, Hugh saw a ball of light growing, and soon enough, Balinas came into view.

'*Well, hello everyone. You are, if I may say so, a lovely sight, so to speak, or perhaps a sight for sore eyes.*' The elf gave them a bemused smile, then continued. '*And Hugh, would you look at you, in here, full body already. Emily has taught you well, hasn't she?*'

'*We'll explain all that later, Balinas. For now, we must work on changing these three into sixty-year-olds.*'

'*Ah yes, I do love a bit of shape shifting.*'

'*I'm sorry,*' said Barrington, '*did you say shape shifting?*'

'*Well, yes? How else are we to get you to resemble older people?*'

'*Perhaps masks, wigs and whatnot?*'

'*Oh Barrington, how very human of you. No, we must call upon the runes which are inside all of us Old Worlders, and before you start asking questions, Barrington, they will have to wait for another day. Now, if you will all just stay still, this won't take a moment.*'

'*But …*'

It was too late. Being the closest to Balinas, Barrington was the first one to receive the shape shifting experience, though as Hugh couldn't see his outline clearly, he didn't know if it had worked. Balinas wasted no time in moving onto Emily, and this time Hugh could see her outline visibly changing. He was shocked to see how effective it was.

Now it was Hugh's turn – being the only one to be there in person, the change was more dramatic for all to see. It was the strangest sensation. Hugh sensed his entire body structure changing from the inside out. and being stretched and squeezed all over.

He looked at his hands, which were changing shape and now covered in sunspots. His frame felt heavy and all of his skin felt looser. And to top it all off, he ached in most of his joints. Balinas stood back to admire his work.

'*Am I supposed to ache all over?*' asked Hugh, holding his elbows.

'*I thought it better to make it more realistic. That way, you won't be tempted to do the things you can normally do. Never fear, I can change you back when you arrive here … I hope. Anyway, must dash. I can hopefully get some shuteye before the sun rises. Bye for now …*'

'*Balinas, what do you mean by hope?*' said Barrington to the disappearing form of Balinas, but it was too late. He was gone. '*He can turn us back, can't he?*' said Barrington's ball of light.

'*I'm sure it will all be fine,*' said Alfred, though he didn't sound too confident. '*You know what Balinas can be like. He has a warped sense of humour at the best of times. Anyway, shall we get back?*'

Before Barrington could protest his concerns any further, Alfred had encompassed the group, and began pulling them all back towards the bar at the Wrangles.

–POP–

Hugh dropped back into reality and took in the rest of the group. Emily and Barrington were now completely unrecognisable to him, as he was to them. He touched his face, feeling the crevasses of old age replacing his once smooth skin. He was also shocked to find a beard upon his usually clean-shaven face. He had gained some stubble on his trip beyond the wall, but that was nothing compared to the rug that was now attached to his face.

Alfred looked at them all in amazement. "Oh my, I've heard of shape shifting before, but to see it in action is really something." He had walked around to look at Hugh and poked his face. "That's truly amazing."

"Yes, and that skin is attached to my body, so please don't poke it."

"Sorry, it's just that you're all unrecognisable."

"Well, that is the idea," said Barrington. "It would be an awful disguise if we still looked the same. Ha! He couldn't remove the tattoo, I see."

"And that's a good thing?" said Emily, as she rooted through her pockets and pulled out her EGF card.

"Please, let's not go down this road right now," said Hugh. "I'm sure there are more important things to focus on."

"Yeah, alright. Has anyone considered that we may need different clothes to wear?" said Emily, holding up a baggy sleeve.

"Oh, yes, of course. Excuse me for just a minute." Alfred disappeared through the back, then returned carrying an assorted range of clothing. "Sorry, it's all I could get at short notice."

They searched through the pile, looking for items that might fit. Eventually, they all found something that might work and took it in turns to get changed out the back. After ten minutes, now fully transformed, they were ready to get moving. Alfred led them to the back door, then turned to address them.

"Well, this is where I leave you for now."

"What? Are you sure you can't come with us?" asked Hugh. "The shop must be awfully quiet now."

"No, I'm afraid I too am being watched. It is quieter than I would prefer, but I have things I must tend to here. Besides, it will be safer for you three to go on without me. I'm sure you'll be fine. You have your new papers with you?" They all nodded. "Good. Here's some money for the flight home. It's more than enough for a standard ticket. Sorry I can't get enough for a higher class. It's getting harder to earn a crust around here."

"Don't be silly," said Barrington. "We're more than grateful for any help that can get us home."

Emily nodded.

"Yes, Alfred, you've done so much for us so far. Thank you."

"Thank you, Alfred," said Hugh, going to give his uncle a hug.

"This feels weird," he said, before releasing him. "Give me time to get a head start. You never know who will come around the corner, and I don't want to try and explain anything if we are seen together."

Hugh looked let down, but he understood.

Alfred said, "I advise you to steer clear of all public transport, at least until you reach the bridge to the airdock. There are more guards on-board the transit system, and the longer you are on there, the greater the likelihood you'll be questioned."

"But it will take us ages to get to the airdock from here," said Barrington.

"I know, but it's better to be safe. Keep well away from all the stations, and you'll be fine. So ... goodbye then. Take care of yourselves, as always, and see you soon ... I hope."

They watched him turn on his heel and walk out of the door with sunken shoulders. Hugh thought he saw him wipe a tear off his face as he rounded the corner out of sight.

"Alright, looks like we have a bit of a walk to get across the city then," said Barrington.

The other two nodded but said nothing. It was all Hugh could do to hold back his emotions, not knowing when he would see Alfred again.

He was all the family that he had right now.

They walked through the streets of Skellig-Krieg, which were uncharacteristically quiet, now that half the population had left the city. Some shops were boarded up with BUSINESS CLOSED plastered across the front. Hugh saw where the shops were open, the shopkeepers were attempting to entice people in, with signs in windows offering cut price goods. Frequently, they saw guards on patrol, but their disguises worked well, and they were left to go about their business.

They walked for at least three quarters of an hour before they came across anything that resembled a crowd. They were now heading towards the centre of the city, where more of the New World population worked and lived. People seemed to be gathered around a building at the end of the street they were on.

"What the devil is going on?" said Barrington, as they approached the growing crowd.

They nudged their way to the front, to see what everyone was looking at. What they saw, chilled Hugh to his core. There on the wall, was the EGF symbol, as bright as day for all to see.

Hugh swallowed hard, and he could hear the breathing of the other two quicken. He felt exposed, out in the open, and expected someone to arrest them at any moment. His heart was pounding in his chest, and he struggled to keep his cool. They quickly pushed their way out of the crowd, causing people to tut and look their way.

They kept their heads down, not making eye contact with anyone. Hugh suddenly realised, to his horror, that they were right next to a train station. It was too late. There were guards now making their way down the stairs from the station above. Some were already making their way through the crowd, shouting orders. Emily stopped to fuss with something in her pocket.

"What are you doing now?" Hugh hissed at her, but she didn't answer. She pulled out her EGF card, put it into her mouth, and started chewing vigorously. Hugh and Barrington instinctively went to their right arms, pulling at their sleeves.

"Nobody move! Who is responsible for this? Somebody answer me now, or you will all be brought in for questioning."

The harder the trio tried to push their way out, the more attention they drew to themselves, and the more the crowd attempted to stop them. They were so close to the edge now Hugh could see the open space beyond the last row. A train rattled into a station overhead, and Hugh decided to go for it. He sensed the others had also had the same idea, and they all pushed with all their might.

"You three … yes, you there, stop moving this instant. Somebody stop those three from leaving!" said a guard, overlooking the scene from the steps.

Now panicking like cornered animals, the small group of three pushed their way out. They were free, but several hands tried to stop them, pulling at anything they could grab a hold of. They broke free, only to see several guards coming towards them. Hugh wanted to run, but his joints now ached so much, he didn't know if he could walk, let alone flee the situation.

It was then that something caught his eye. Something yellow, and round, rolling down the street toward a pillar supporting the train line. He froze with fear, as the other two bumped into him. They were about to berate him, when they too saw the object rolling past and bump into a supporting stanchion for the tracks above. Barrington's eyes widened.

"Is that what I think it is …?"

But Hugh had already turned to run, the other two right behind him, trying to get away from the orb and the train track above them. He made for a side street, as the adrenalin coursed through his body. The pain momentarily dissipated, as the three attempted to put as much space between themselves and the situation as they could, but it was no use. With the guards hot on their heels, Hugh's eyes were filled with a bright flash of light.

The world went into slow motion. He was flying through the air along with the old figures of Emily and Barrington, with glass and debris flying past him. He was robbed of all sound. He was spinning and he saw a train in mid derailment before it was blocked from sight by a wall. He had now done a full three sixty and saw the ground coming towards him. Time sped back up to real speed, as Hugh headed towards the road.

—POP—

He was back in the sight, but something was wrong. Everything was resonating around him, his ears in pain. Before he had time to get his bearings…

—POP—

His ears were ringing as he looked skyward, his head thumping with pain.

Dust filled the air, with bits of glass and debris landing around him, yet he heard none of it. He rolled over, and looked over to Emily and Barrington, who were trying to roll over and get to their feet, but failing. Hugh felt numb all over, as he tried to right himself and get up from the floor, and he saw numerous pairs of feet running past him to get away from the danger.

The blast had thrown them further into the side street, and as Hugh looked out in front of him, all he could see was the blown-out shop fronts, their windows now scattered across the ground in pieces. People were pointing and shouting, covered in blood, but he couldn't make out what they were saying. Some people hunched over bodies, screaming for help, whilst others lay lifeless in the street.

His hearing was slowly returning, but the ringing persisted. Slowly, some formation of words came through.

"It was them. It was them! They did it! I saw them running away!"

"Guards, get those three, stop them from running away again!"

All around him, he heard the screams of people panicking, crying and fearful of a second blast. Irate onlookers now turned their anger to

Hugh, Barrington and Emily, all wishing to dispense their own justice on the would-be bombers.

Hugh felt feet landing in his chest and stomach. People were clawing at Emily's hair, as she lay on the floor screaming, defenceless. They grabbed her staff and repeatedly landed blows onto her. Further across, he saw others throwing punches onto Barrington's elderly frame.

It turned out most of their pursuers were protected from the majority of the blast – as they themselves had been – by the crowd that had gathered moments before, and the side street they were originally on. The guard that spotted them first was nowhere to be seen.

Though battered, bruised and covered in cuts, the remaining guards ran towards the trio. Hands grabbed Hugh under his arms, dragging him to his feet. He saw his friends being roughly pulled up from the ground. The next thing he saw was a baton coming towards him.

Then everything went dark.

Chapter 39

Hugh came around in a cell, this time with windows and bars. His struggled to focus, and the back of his head was throbbing once more. The rest of his body felt as though it had done ten rounds in a wrestling ring. He looked around bleary-eyed, taking in the surrounding scene. He was on the floor of the cell, and he could see Emily and Barrington were in there with him and not looking in any better state than he was. And there was someone else, too.

"Trevor?"

The innkeeper was black and blue and looked as though he, too, had been through the wars.

"Who are you? And how do you know me name?"

"You can trust us," Hugh looked around, and winced and yelped with the pain.

"How do I know that? You could be one of them, sent in to get information out of me."

"You could try the *other* method," Hugh suggested.

"Dunno what you are talkin' about? I ain't speakin' and you ain't gonna get nothing from me."

Hugh let out a painful sigh. Trevor looked like a beaten man that wasn't going to open up anytime soon. Hugh looked around again, checking that nobody else was with them. He chanced it.

"It's me Trevor, Hugh," he said in a hushed voice.

"You don't look like Mr Hugh. You look like a bunch of elderly terrorists to me."

"What are you talking about?"

"The explosion. It *was* you, wasn't it? That's what they're all sayin'. You killed hundreds, injured more and derailed a train. That's not what any of this was supposed to be about, but now you've put us all in terrible danger. And what you go an' leave that graffiti on the wall for. Hardly subtle, was it?"

"We had nothing to do with that, you must believe me. We would never do anything to harm people, let alone kill them. But it's definitely me, Trevor. You can trust me."

"How do I know that?"

Hugh thought quickly, remembering his tattoo. Pulling up his right sleeve, he was relieved to see that the mark was still intact. Trevor eyed him with suspicion. Emily and Barrington were now fully conscious again.

"Oh, that proves nothing, except that you've gone and dropped us all in it. Why? Why did you have to kill all them innocent people? You don't deserve to have them marks on your arms. Anyway, Mr Hugh had a card, not one of them stupid tattoos."

"It's alright, Trevor, you know me."

"Trevor?" said Emily.

She tried to move, but found she was too stiff, and Hugh saw she was also covered in cuts and bruises.

"I'm sorry, but I don't have the faintest idea who you all are?"

Barrington, who was also sporting many bruises and cuts, including a large gash above his left eye, which was still oozing, was attempting to sit himself upright.

"Why it's us, dear man," he said with a grunt. "The ones who stayed at your inn not three months before. I even paid for you to keep our belongings to be kept safe whilst we went back to Portis-Montis."

Trevor sat himself up, wincing with the pain, and ran through things in his head. "It can't be. Mr Barrington, sir?"

"Yes, that's it, old bean. We're in here, I can assure you of that."

Barrington also rolled up his sleeve to reveal his own tattoo.

"I'm still unsure it's you. The Barrington I knew also carried a card. No wonder they knew you were with the EGF. It all makes sense now."

Emily looked to Hugh and Barrington.

"Well done, you two, that's our cover blown! I told you, did I not? I told you the tattoos were a bad idea."

"To be fair, they will have your card as well. If you are Emily, that is?"

Emily shook her head.

"Nope, I had the foresight to dispose of my card. Something that's impossible to do with a tattoo." She looked at Hugh, who refused to meet her gaze.

Suddenly, she started, let out a yelp of pain, then began patting her chest.

"What?" asked Hugh, concerned that he wouldn't want to know the answer.

"My firestone, it's gone! And the staff too!"

Hugh did the same, also realising that he had been stripped of his precious amulet. They also had his bag with all the information in and the lore book for magic.

Emily sighed.

"That'll be why we are in more pain. The firestones would be helping to ease it."

"They'll have taken them from you when you came in. So, it's really you, is it?" said Trevor.

Hugh nodded.

"It certainly is. We have been altered somewhat by Balinas though."

"Balinas is here? I thought he never left the university. I can see he did a good job on you all."

Hugh explained all that had happened to Trevor from the point where they had last seen him. He shook his head in disbelief that many members of the EGF were hiding out in the caves in the mountains.

"That explains a lot," he said, once Hugh had finished.

"What's that?"

"Old Ranny, he used to come in regularly. He always said the inn was his, and I was occupying his land. Funny really. We're related on me mum's side, distant cousins, or something like that. She never knew what happened to that side of the family, only that they disappeared after the war, got banished for two hundred years and went into hiding. We only knew him as Whimpold."

The rest of the group looked on in amazement.

"But I thought the land was removed from the family," said Emily.

"Well, it was, but his daughter, she wasn't involved in the war like, anyway, she fought to keep the house, sayin' it wasn't her fault her dad went loopy. It seemed to work, as they let her keep the building, well, the shell that remained, but not the rest of the land or the money. She converted it over time into the inn it is today. Quite amazing really."

"Yeah, absolutely," said Hugh. "So does that make you a ... wizard?"

"Of sorts, though we don't tend to use magic that often. Look at all the trouble it's got us into in the past. It's good with injuries like."

He shuffled over to Hugh, and moved his hands over his chest, and he felt a warm glow, and a few bones clicked back into place. Trevor moved up to his head, and the pain disappeared.

"I'll not sort the outer injuries for now, might cause a few questions."

He moved to Emily and Barrington and repeated the same manoeuvre on them. Now more able to move, they readjusted themselves into a more comfortable position. They sat in silence, mulling over the situation they were now in and the news they had just heard. Hugh was just beginning to wonder who might be behind the atrocities, when Barrington broke the silence.

"So, what are we to do now?"

"We'll need to get out of this place for a start," said Hugh.

"I don't want to break the news to you, old bean, but not only are we behind lock and key, but we are also locked in bodies that are not as nimble as our own. Even if we do get out of here, I doubt we could run far. I, for one, still ache all over, and the rest of you don't look in any state to run. No offence, Trevor."

"None taken. It ain't going to fix old age."

Hugh had to agree. He, too, was tired and ached from head to toe.

"So escaping with the manual methods is out the question," said Emily. "That only means we'll have to use alternative methods."

Hugh looked back at Emily, totally perplexed.

"Alternative methods? Barrington's just said there is no way out of here. I cannot think of any way we can get out of here alive."

"The sight, Hugh? You are too quick to forget these things. We can contact someone to get the message that we're in trouble. I'm sure they can organise something."

"But you are not near any water. How will you jump in?"

"I'm not talking about me. You are the one with the ability to enter without having to be near water."

"I can't enter freely," said Hugh. "I don't know how."

"Can't means won't, and we don't want that sort of attitude. You need to think over everything we've been through and bring it all together. Think about how you feel as you enter, any sensations you experience as you enter. Focus in on that, and the rest should just take over."

"You make it sound so simple."

Barrington let out a deep, wheezy sigh.

"Hugh, you have to believe you can do this, otherwise it won't happen. The other option is we wait and see what happens when we're hauled in front of a judge?"

"A judge?"

"You must not forget the reason that we're in here in the first place.

We're the ones that are under suspicion for the explosion, and I doubt we'll be able to get out of this one. The scenes we witnessed before being brought here will stay with me for life."

Hugh sat, knowing what the answer was but not wanting to face the reality. He knew it was down to him to get them all out, but he had to figure out the first step.

"Alright, let me see. So, I feel this strange feeling inside ..."

Hugh focussed on the sensation of tugging on his navel and closed his eyes. He could sense the invisible line between the planes and tried to step over, then took in a deep breath and opened his eyes.

"Nope, still here," said Barrington, his temporary old face looking back at Hugh.

Emily shuffled over to him.

"Listen, I know you can do this. I believe in you, we all do." She held his hand. "Try again, please. We need this to work."

Hugh nodded, closing his eyes once more. He sensed Emily's warmth next to him, which comforted him, and he found the sensation again, then searched for the line. This time, the line wasn't invisible. He could see it plain as day. He stepped over, feeling a gentler tug than usual, and dared not open his eyes.

'Open your eyes Hugh,' said Emily next to him.

'I'm sorry. I just don't think I can do it. I'm so tired. I get close, but it always seems to be just out of reach.'

'Hugh, just open your eyes.'

He did as Emily said and was taken aback as to how dark everything had become. The room had disappeared, and he was surrounded by the coolness of the sight. It was darker compared to more recent trips in. He looked to his left and saw Emily as clear as day, already protecting herself with runes.

'Well, get a move on then, you need to get your runes in place.'

Hugh began pulling the required runes into existence, still in shock.

'*But, how?*'

'*You pulled me in with you.*'

'*I can see that, but I can see all of you.*'

'*It was a surprise to me too, I can assure you of that. It's the first time that I've been in here full body.*'

Hugh had finished sorting out his body protection. '*So, what now?*'

'*We need to find someone, maybe Alfred, as he's local, and we can be sure that he has access to the sight, but we must be quick. We don't want to be caught outside of the room.*'

'*That's something I can never grasp. I never know how fast time moves in here. I always spend longer but arrive back on the living plane moments later.*'

'*Hmm, that's interesting to know. We can look into that later, but for now, let just get on with finding Alfred.*'

She held out her hand, and Hugh instinctively took it, feeling the wave of warmth flow through his body. It made his chest tingle. Together, they began looking around.

'*I wonder how we go about this,*' said Emily.

'*Think of Alfred, I suppose. That worked for Hamish.*'

Hugh thought back to the strongest memory he had of his uncle, back to the time they hugged for the first time in the shop. He could sense that Emily was also thinking of the apothecary. Other images flashed before his eyes, things he couldn't make out. Before he could think about what was happening, they were moving through the sight. A light appeared, and before he knew it, they were standing in Alfred's shop. It was hazy, as though he were only partially there.

Emily was still stood next to him, and appeared whole, but when she attempted to pick up a jar off the shelf, her hand passed through it.

'Our bodies are still in the sight. We must be quick.'

Alfred jumped up from behind the counter, startled. "Who's that? Emily, Hugh, is that you?"

'It's us,' said Hugh, *'but we still look old.'*

"Goodness me, you made me jump. What are you doing here? What's wrong?"

Emily quickly explained the situation, whilst Hugh stood feeling out of sorts. The colour slowly drained from Alfred's face.

"Dear me, what have we done? I told you, didn't I? Did I not specifically say to stay away from the public transport system?"

'Yes, but what's that got to do with all of this?' said Hugh.

He was swaying gently on the spot.

Alfred looked at him. "Never you mind now. Where's your body?"

'What do you mean?'

"You both physically travelled by the sight to get here? But I can only see you clearly, Emily. Hugh seems distant … dear me, you need to get him out of there, *now!*"

'Yes, Hugh dragged me with him. What are you talking about, and what is going on, Alfred?'

Then she looked at Hugh and gasped.

"I cannot tell you," he said, already getting his cloak on, grabbing some bottles from under the counter and placing them into his pocket. He shot a worried look at Hugh. "You need to get him back, right away! Leave the rest to me."

He blew briefly into his hand, and something glowed.

'But I don't understand?'

Before Emily could say anymore, Alfred sent the glowing ball towards them, and they were heading back into the sight. They were greeted there by Aeolus.

'*What are you doing here?*' asked Emily.

'*I sensed you were here so came to your aid mistress. He needs to get back. He won't last long. I shall help you return.*'

Emily looked to Hugh. '*What's wrong?*'

'*I don't know, but I feel weak.*'

'*Right, we need to get you back.*'

Hugh was aware of becoming drained from all the effort he was putting in to stay in the sight, as Aeolus knelt down next to the pair, and Emily helped Hugh up, before nimbly climbing on herself, and the beast was up and off.

Hugh could sense himself faltering. He didn't know what was going on. Emily caught him as he nearly slid off and looked at him with great concern. Aeolus sensed her worry, picking up his pace. A light appeared in front of them, and he bolted towards it.

–POP–

The unicorn skidded across the cell floor, narrowly missing the other two occupants, taking them by surprise. Emily dragged Hugh from the unicorn's back, and within an instant, the beast was gone, leaving the cell in a state of chaos. Barrington was on his feet, trying to get a grip on the fast-changing events.

"Emily, Hugh … what's going on? What the hell was that? What's wrong with Hugh?"

Emily ignored his questions, running straight to the cell door, pounding on it hard.

"Help! Please, somebody help!"

The sound came of someone running to the door, with keys jangling. They seemed to fumble, dropping the keys, more than once. The cell door swung open, revealing Bernie looking panicked and out of breath, and several other guards.

"Help him, Bernie, *Please!*"

"It's alright, Emily ... yes, I know it's you." He turned to the other guards. "You two, get me water here, quick. You, stand outside, monitor things in the corridor, and you, get to the front door. Alfred will be here any minute. I don't care how you do it, but get him up here."

The guards stood to attention before leaving the cell.

Barrington looked to his old friend, anxiety written across his face.

"Bernie, what's going on?"

Bernie ignored Barrington's question and immediately began tending to Hugh.

"I was already on me way over here when Alfred ran into me. How much time has he spent in the sight?"

"Well, we were briefly there just now," said Emily.

Barrington shook his head.

"It was longer than you think. We were worried you wouldn't be back in time for the security check."

"That wouldn't matter. We're all part of the extended family here. Has Hugh been into the sight any other times today?"

"Well, yes," said Emily, "we were in there with Balinas this morning."

"Have you been teaching him the runes of protection?"

"Yes ... no ... kind of. I taught him to look within himself. He seemed to pick it up from there, so I wasn't worried."

"Did you show him the energy rune?"

"Well ... it was all so rushed ..."

"Yes or no, Emily?"

She clutched and squeezed at her hands.

"No, I didn't remember."

At that point, Alfred burst into the room. "

We need water, quick ... ah good, thank you."

Alfred pulled a sponge from within his cloak, dipped it into the jug of water and carefully soaked Hugh's mouth. He pulled out the bottles he had in his cloak, pulled the stoppers with his teeth and poured the glowing liquid within down Hugh's throat.

"Come on boy, come on, pull round, come to papa," he said.

They all knelt around Hugh, waiting with bated breath for any signs of life from Hugh's limp body. The time ebbed away painfully slowly, as Emily sobbed into Barrington's shoulder.

"Come on, Hugh!"

Alfred hit the floor next to him. Hugh took in a great gasp of air, and everyone fell about with relief. Emily threw her arms around him, still sobbing.

Barrington wiped a tear from his eye and swallowed hard.

"Sprites be praised," he said, looking upwards.

"Give him some room, Emily," said Alfred, who was still out of breath.

Emily pulled back, wiping her lined face on her sleeve.

Alfred smiled, looking deeply into Hugh's eyes.

"It's good to have you back."

"Wha ... what happened?"

"You caught us off guard a little there. Your energy was being drained, improper protection within the sight. I should have spotted it earlier, I'm sorry."

Emily began sobbing again.

"It's my fault. I should have shown him how to do it properly ... I should have seen ... such a foolish error! I'm so sorry, Hugh!"

"Emily, you mustn't blame yourself," said Alfred. "I too should have spotted that his protection wasn't up to scratch. The others too. It's a simple mistake, one which can be remedied with an easy lesson."

He looked to Hugh, picked up the jug and passed it to him.

"Here you need this."

Hugh took the jug, taking big gulps of water.

"Thank you, all of you," he said, looking to Emily. "You brought me back here. I wouldn't have made it without you. What happened back there?"

"You had a chink in ya armour, me old mate," said Bernie. "In essence, your energy was being sapped from your body each time you entered the sight. Any longer, and we wouldn't have got you back."

Hugh let out a big sigh, the reality hitting him in the chest.

"Gosh, well, the more grateful I am for your help, then. How did you get here so quickly Alfred?"

"I wasn't that quick Hugh. Time in the sight moves at a different rate. I bumped into Bernie, who ran ahead of me. He's much fitter than I will ever be."

"I was on me way here. I'd not long left Alfred's shop. We were discussing the explosion and the fact we had you in the cells, though I didn't know it was you at the time. He explained to me what had happened earlier, and I pieced it all together. I was on me way back when Alfred caught up with me. I had to bolt it here as fast as I could. Good thing too. Oh, Trevor, you can work ya magic on ya face now. We know they're safe. I have also secured your release."

"Oh good, I'd forgotten about that," he said, waving his hands over his face. When he pulled them down, he looked like the old Trevor once more. "Sorry, we had to make it look like I had been thoroughly questioned. That way I would get out quicker. Thanks Bernie, I owe you a drink later."

"No worries matey, all in a day's work for the city guard. Should've seen the governor's face, fuming he was." He winked at Trevor.

"You are good, Bernie. If you will excuse me, I have an inn to get back to." He stood up and headed towards the door. "Will you be alright, Mr Hugh sir?"

Hugh nodded.

"I think so, Trevor. I'm already feeling a lot better. Thank you for all you've done so far. Do you think you could work your magic on our outer injuries before you go?"

"Of course. Hugh, stay where you are. You two, sit in front of me –

one at a time, if you will please."

He rubbed his hands together, and Hugh felt the familiar warmth radiate through his body, and as he looked down, all the cuts and bruises he had gained disappeared. He turned to one side and helped the others get cleaned up.

"Thank you, Trevor. You really are an amazing man," said Hugh, sitting up and shaking his hand.

"No worries, Mr Hugh, sir. You take care of yourself. Emily, that is definitely you, is it? I still can't believe it. Will you be in for a drink later?"

"I'm afraid not. I have to help take one of the books of lore back to Portis-Montis."

"You found one of the books?" he said, his face lighting up.

"Later, Trevor," said Alfred. "I will fill you in when I've had time to see these three off."

Trevor's face dropped, but he could tell he wouldn't get any more news. "Righto, see you later then," and he walked out the door, whistling a tune to himself.

"Alright," said Bernie, "we need to get you three out of the city."

"But how?" said Barrington.

"Oh yeah, that was the other reason I was comin' down 'ere. I also convinced the powers that be you were no threat to the state. It also helps that we have one of our own higher up, if you catch me drift. Gov's face went the colour of beetroot when I told him that one."

"Well, we're all very grateful for that. How are we to get back home?"

"Don't you worry, Barrington. We've got it all covered!"

Half an hour later, the trio had been reunited with their belongings, firestones and Orbis, and were on the move once more. Hugh was walking with everyone else through the airdock, under the protection of the city guards, with people staring at them as the group walked by.

They had bypassed all the usual security protocols and were now heading to the outside world. Hugh took in a deep breath, before heading out to the ship. They were met with an empty space.

"Oh no," said Hugh, who had just caught a sight of the large drop.

'It's alright Hugh,' Emily's voice said inside his head. She held his hand, and he felt the firestone glow warmly upon his chest.

Barrington's old form walked up to his friend. "Bernie, my dear friend, did you buy us any tickets for a flight?"

"Well, no, but I arranged you a ... ah here it is."

They heard it before they saw it. A battered ship, belching out thick black smoke, rounded the end of the airdock.

Barrington stood open-mouthed.

"You have to be joking."

"Nah, he said he was passing and was more than pleased to help."

The airship was banking round then, to all their surprise, Augustus appeared out of an open window with a megaphone.

"Hello, wot wot!"

Hugh leaned into Emily.

"If he's waving, who's flying the ship?"

Someone called "Look out!" and there was a good deal of screaming.

Augustus looked momentarily flummoxed, then clued in to the distress and disappeared from the window. The engines ramped up, fogging out the entire western side of the airdock, as he pulled up to avoid hitting another airship. Barrington stood, shaking his head into his hands.

Before they had time to recover, a whipping sound came from above Hugh, and he jumped to the side. A landing line dropped between himself and Emily, narrowly missing them both.

It bounced off the edge, only to hit one of the awaiting ground crew. Bernie looked over the edge, then up at the incoming ship.

"Yup, that's definitely him alright."

The sound of the engines being wound down, clattering to a stop before backfiring, was followed by the sound of the winch kicking into action. From out of the dispersing fumes, came the battered hulk of the

Jewel of Ranthina. Augustus came level with them, waving madly from behind the cracked front screen, smiling proudly.

Part of the nose dropped off, as the ship came to a stop, bouncing off the ledge next to the waiting group, making them jump. They heard someone yell down below, and Augustus attempted to peer over the edge of the bridge, then returned to looking out of the broken window and shrugged.

Lines were thrown out of a door on the port-side, and a ramp was pulled into position. Augustus stepped out onto it before the crew had finished tying it on, causing a moment of chaos and a lot of shouting. He turned back to greet the weary travellers.

"Hello," he said far louder and slower than need be, "I am your captain, and I will take you to Portis-Montis today. Never mind the old girl here, she's been in far worse states than this, I can assure you of that." In the background, Hugh saw a crew member nodding in agreement.

"Augustus, it's us, Hugh, Emily and Barrington," Hugh said in a hushed voice.

"Really? Is that really you, Hugh, wot wot? Why are you flapping your hands, Emily?"

A few heads turned in their direction.

"Will you shut up!" said Barrington.

"Well, that's not a way to greet your cousin now is it? Oi, what are you doing?" Bernie and Alfred had taken an arm each and dragged Augustus back onto the ship.

"Will you get your ruddy hands of me!"

"Augustus, you blitherin' fool," said Bernie. "You'll blow the entire operation shoutin' their names out like that!"

"What? Oh, sorry."

They let go of him, and he brushed himself down. Hugh, Emily and Barrington made their way quickly onto the ship.

Emily rounded on the captain, not giving him time to draw breath.

"Augustus! What the hell?"

"Emily, that's enough," said Alfred, raising his eyebrows. "He's apologised to us, and we wouldn't want to lose your lift home, would we?"

"Sorry, but a bit of subtlety wouldn't go amiss."

"I thought you would be grateful for the lift, wot wot! It took me ages to dig this thing out."

A crew member stood open-mouthed next to Augustus, shaking his head. He cleared his throat.

"What? Oh yes, these lads helped too." The crew member shook his head, muttering something indistinguishable.

"I only got you this pier for fifteen minutes, so I'm afraid you will have to make this quick," said Bernie.

Alfred turned to the old frame that housed Hugh.

"Well, at least we get to say goodbye properly, weird as this is." He embraced Hugh, who returned with as tight a hug as he could muster.

"Thank you, Alfred. Let's hope it's not too long before we see each other again."

"Let's hope not," he said, letting go of Hugh. "Goodbye, Emily. Look after him for me."

"I will, and look after my place. I'll be back for it soon enough."

"I certainly shall. I'll also fill in the rest of the team at the greenhouses with the latest updates. They will be pleased to hear that you made it back to Portis-Montis alright."

Emily turned to Bernie.

"Thank you, Bernie, for everything," she said, hugging him, taking him by surprise.

"No worries, Emily," he said, turning to Barrington. "Take care, old friend, we'll see each other soon, I'm sure of it."

"That we will," said Barrington, grasping his outstretched hand, pulling him in and patting Bernie on the back. Bernie bid farewell to the rest of the group, and he and Alfred disembarked, ready for the ship's take off.

Everyone else took a seat up front whilst Augustus got to work.

The gangway was dropped, and they rose into the air. Augustus fired up the engines, which spluttered into life, filling the air with smoke once more. It sounded as though they might fall off for real this time.

"Are you sure this thing is airworthy?" said Barrington.

"I've taken her back in worse states than this."

"I bet," Barrington replied under his breath.

"Wot wot! Speak up."

"Oh, nothing."

The others held back sniggers, whilst Augustus muttered his annoyance. With another loud backfire, they were off.

Hugh would have thought that given the ship's state, the captain may have flown her with a bit more care. Two near misses and a couple of nosedives later, one of which caused the port-side door to drop out, he was pleased to see the coastline of Ranthina come into sight.

They had spent most of the flight resting their aching bodies in the lounge whilst the crew sought to fill them up with food and wine. It was just what they needed after the experience they had been through. He may have been bonkers, but Augustus didn't scrimp on the hospitality for his guests.

Augustus came through from the bridge.

"Right chaps, I've been in contact with Balinas, and he has arranged for one of his fellows to meet you at the end of the secret tunnel."

"You're not taking us into the airdock?" said Hugh.

"I'm afraid not. Bit of an issue to sort out involving a derailed train, but nothing for you to worry about though. I'm sure it'll all come out in the wash ... eventually."

"Ah, I think you'll be alright there. Alfred mentioned something about the track being blown up."

"Really? I hope they're not trying to pin that on me?"

"You're in luck. We were being blamed for it, but seeing as we are supposed to be dead, I think you're off the hook. Just remember the last part about our non-existence, and it'll be fine."

"But you're not dead, you're here."

"Yes, but people haven't found that out yet, and we would like it to stay that way for as long as possible."

"Alright," he said, in a way that made Hugh think he wasn't really sure.

"So are you dropping us near the tunnel," said Barrington. "I don't dare chance the rope ladder with this body."

"Erm, sort of, wot wot."

"What do you mean by sort of?" said Emily.

Augustus disappeared into the draughty corridor and returned with three backpacks.

"Ah, good, some provisions," said Hugh. "Are we to walk a little way?"

"Nope. Parachutes, wot wot!"

"What?"

"There's nothing to worry about. Lads, can you help them into them please?"

The crewmen gathered around the trio, who tried to fight back, but their old frames let them down once again. They came out of the experience looking like bread loaves gone wrong, with body parts bulging out all over the place. They strapped any spare baggage to their fronts, Emily clutching her staff for all it was worth. They all scowled at Augustus, who smiled back.

"See, perfect fit. Right, if we're all ready, let's get moving. Balinas's chap will be waiting for you in the tunnel."

"But what about the trains? We don't know when they will be due, and I, for one, don't fancy landing on the mail train," said Barrington, whilst the crew edged them slowly into the corridor. They were hit with an icy blast of wind.

"They're not running, little issue with a train still blocking the tracks, again, nothing to worry about. Alright, if we're ready, let's get this show on the road."

Hugh was offered up to the doorway. He resisted all the way, refusing to look down.

"No, no, I really don't want to. I don't even know how to do this."

"You'll be fine. I'll guide you down to the right place. Just don't forget to pull the chord to release the parachute, preferably before the ground. Oh, and make sure you don't pull the detach chute chord until you are safe, wot wot!"

Augustus gave Hugh a shove out the door with his foot, and he fell out backwards.

"Wait, what…" Hugh's voice became a scream that tailed off into the distance.

"Did he just scream like a girl?" said Augustus, turning to the other two. "Right, who's next?"

Chapter 40

Hugh was dropping like a stone. He had rolled over and was now looking towards the ground below. The air was hitting him so fast, he couldn't even scream. Each time he opened his mouth, the oncoming air rushed in, leaving him to force it out again before the next breath rushed back in. His eyes were streaming, but as fast as the tears came, the air whipped them from his face.

He searched for the straps of the parachute, looking for a chord to pull. To his horror, he saw three, none of which were marked. Augustus mentioned nothing about a third option. Hugh had so much adrenaline coursing through his veins, he thought he would explode. He frantically scrabbled at the chords, not knowing which to pull. There was a red one, a yellow one and a green one. He grabbed hold of the green one, hoping it was correct.

A sharp yank later, and something whipped out of his pack, and his descent jolted to a slower pace. Everything was serene until it was broken by a wail dropping past him at speed. He looked down, seeing another parachute unfolding below him, showing that Barrington had found the right strap. Above him, he heard someone jolting, and he hoped it was Emily.

They were now at the will of the winds. Hugh saw the train line below, but he was more concerned about the incoming mountains. Numb with fear, he had absolutely no control over his descent and knew that if they ended up in the mountains, they would all be split up for sure.

Barrington was shouting something grim below him, but he couldn't hear what he said, only that the tone was urgent. He looked up to his right and saw Emily drifting off. She was frantically kicking her legs, trying to alter the course she was on, but it was no use. The further down the trio descended, the further apart they got, and the closer the sheer rock face came.

Hugh attempted Emily's tactic, but to no avail, and he prepared himself for impact.

Then, from out of nowhere, a wind picked up. It was coming from the mountains, and Hugh wondered if it was luck that the downdraft caught them all. He noticed a white haze coming towards them, and it almost felt like he was being scooped up and guided towards the ground. He seemed to level off with the others, and he saw they were slowly spiralling to the rocky terrain below, next to the train track.

It was only now that he realised he didn't know how to land a parachute, and the ground was coming up faster than he realised. He lifted his legs together and hoped for the best. He landed, expecting to feel pain, but at the last moment he had slowed right down, landing on a large mound of moss. He heard the canopy flapping behind him and relaxed.

He was down.

On either side of him, Emily and Barrington were already detaching themselves from their parachutes. Hugh pulled the yellow strap, expecting his pack to fall off him, but nothing happened.

At that moment, a gust of wind hit him in the face. He was pulled backwards off his feet, then dragged across the ground.

"Detach, Hugh, detach!" said Barrington, who was disappearing at a fast rate.

Hugh scrabbled for the last chord, whilst being thrown around by the out-of-control parachute. One moment he was on the floor, the next he was in the air, then thrown to the floor again. He found the red chord and yanked as hard as he could. He was moments away from being fully airborne once again as he dropped painfully to the ground, his parachute flapping off into the mountainside above.

He laid for a moment, dazed from the experience. Eventually he sat up, then stood, to be taken out by another rogue, semi-inflated dome. This time, he was floored and wrapped up. He panicked, fearing he would be suffocated. Hands began grabbing at him, and he was eventually pulled free by Barrington and Emily.

Hugh sat out of breath.

"Never again. Ever!"

"My dear friend, we couldn't agree with you more."

"What's wrong?" said Hugh, turning to look at a crowd of people now watching them. "What are they all doing here?"

Hugh, Emily and Barrington began climbing the steep railway embankment, to the shocked gaze of the onlookers. With much effort they reached the top, and what they saw chilled Hugh right down to his aching bones. A crane was being assembled next to the wreckage of a silver star locomotive and carriages.

Hugh was lost for words as he looked on at the mangled remains in front of them.

Nobody moved.

Nobody spoke.

Slowly, Barrington edged forward. They were only a short distance from the tunnel. The onlookers parted, as the trio advanced forward.

"Afternoon … hello … hi …" said Barrington to the amazed faces. "Don't mind us, we just need to, erm, yes, well anyway."

They picked up their pace, running into the tunnel, avoiding a large piece of twisted metal that used to be track. Hugh ignored the calls of the crowd as they came to their senses.

The tunnel was dark, but the trio did not stop running, as they heard those behind them getting into action and heading in their direction. It hurt to run so fast, but Hugh knew they had to get away. A voice called to them from the darkness.

"This way, *quick!*"

They followed the barely audible voice, finding the entrance to the hidden tunnel with outstretched hands. Hugh couldn't see where he was going, when he bumped into someone.

"Ow!"

"Shhh."

The sound of those chasing them ran past then tailed off before doubling back as a lost cause. Hugh heard them discussing the fate of those they were after.

"They looked really old."

"Yeah, what were they doing all the way out here?"

"And why were they attached to those sheets."

"Parachutes, Bill."

"What?"

"They call 'em parachutes. It's what all the posh people do for fun."

"Will, you two shut up? We won't hear them with you two blabbering on. What do you think, guv?"

"They won't last long in these tunnels," said an authoritative voice. "They'll have to come out at some point. We'll send a message down the line, get some people to wait at the other end. We'll get them either way."

There were sounds of the others agreeing with him, with a few of them chuckling. They listened to the party turn back towards the light, discussing the complexities of surviving unprotected in the winter weather before the voices tailed off.

"This way, Mr Geber."

They followed the mysterious, hushed voice, and now Hugh's eyes were adjusting, he saw the outline of a figure ahead of him. The smell of soot faded into that of damp, and torches flickered into life. They shielded their eyes as they adjusted, and Hugh saw their Collins guide.

"Thank you, I thought we were going to be caught then."

"It's not a problem, Mr Geber. We'll be back in the library soon enough. We're all expecting you."

"What do you mean? Who's waiting for us?"

"Not to worry, sir. You're perfectly safe now. Follow me, please." He set off down the steps, away from the confused trio. "Come along, please. I have work to be getting on with."

Hugh looked back to Emily and Barrington, who shrugged. Torches flickered to life once again, showing the path ahead. The walk seemed to go on forever, with Hugh wondering why he was struggling through obstacles that were much easier on their outward passage. Now he was calming down, his body had finally reminded him of how old its current frame was. He ached from head to toe and was extremely relieved to reach the entrance to the Great Library.

The door swung open, to reveal a crowd of the Collins family there to welcome them. Hugh's ears were met with a round of applause, and he was overwhelmed by the greeting and the familiar smell of inks and old leather, parchment and bindings from the innumerable books which filled the room. A wave of relief washed through Hugh, and he was glad to be back home again.

There, at the front of the welcome committee, was Balinas.

"Welcome back Hugh, Barrington, and young Emily. What a lovely surprise to have you with us too."

After everything they had been through, Hugh was happy to be back in the safety of the library. Many pats fell upon his back, each feeling heavy and painful, as Balinas dismissed the crowd and guided the trio towards the Chamber of Prophecy. Hugh had forgotten the number of stairs that needed to be descended, and his knees were thoroughly warm by the time they finally reached the great room.

Balinas led them towards a screen. "I took the liberty of ordering you all some fresh clothes. You look like you could do with them. Take it in turns to go behind here, and I will transform you back to your usual selves."

Emily went in first, leaning her staff on the wall as she disappeared from view. Hugh and Barrington watched Balinas raise his arms into the air, and the area behind the screen glowed. A few minutes later, the usual Emily that Hugh knew came out, looking fresh and relieved to be out of her ageing disguise. Barrington, keen to go through the transformation, went up next. He came out looking relieved, and then it was Hugh's turn.

He went behind the screen, seeing a pile of neatly folded clothes with his name on them. His hair stood on end, before the surrounding air crackled and glowed. He felt the clothes on him go tight as his frame return to its normal stance, and his posture straightened up once again.

Hugh pulled off the old clothes, which were now pulling apart at the seams, and replaced them with the ones from the pile provided for him. He had more movement, and most of the aches and pains were left behind with his old body form.

He came out from behind the screen a new man.

"Thank you, Balinas. That's much better."

"You're welcome. Come this way. I have some food for you, and you can show me the goods you have found."

They made their way over to a table where food and drink had been laid out. They wasted no time tucking in, and Balinas looked on happily. Hugh talked him through their adventures, how they had found out about orbs and the lore book of magic. He went into detail about Orbis, and how they had it with them the whole time.

It was exhausting reliving the experience, and he felt like a stuck record repeating it all again. Balinas made a good audience, gasping and looking suitably shocked at the right places. When they had had their fill, he clapped his hands twice, and their plates melted away into nonexistence.

Balinas clapped his hands together.

"Right, shall we get down to business."

Hugh took his bag and pulled out the lore book for magic. He sensed its eagerness to be out into the room once more, as he unfolded its protective wrapping.

Hugh passed the book over to Balinas, who looked on with warmth and seemed to go all gooey over it.

"Hello, we haven't seen you for a long time, have we? No, we haven't."

The others looked on as he seemed to go soft eyed over the book.

"Are you alright?" said Barrington. "It's just a book."

Balinas looked at Barrington in great offence.

"Just a book? How very dare you! Don't you listen to him, he knows nothing about the universe," he said to the book.

He hugged it to his chest, before rounding on Barrington.

"My dear man, this isn't a mere book. It's one of *the* books of lore. A relic from the Old World! Just a book indeed. Now you come with me, and we'll put you back in your rightful place ... yes you are the first one ... don't worry, we'll dispatch them to find the rest, never you fear... I'm sorry for letting you go."

"The man's bonkers," Barrington muttered to Hugh.

"Not bonkers, Mr Delphin," Balinas called out. "Just more open-minded, something that you could do with learning."

Barrington went red in the face and scowled back at Balinas, who placed the book into its position on the pyramid under the light. It momentarily glowed, and a warm wind blew through the chamber.

"That's better. One book down. Congratulations you three. Now we must focus on the next task, finding the remaining books."

"I beg your pardon?" said Barrington.

"The other books. There are three more to get."

"But we've only just got back!"

"Well, you can rest here for a week or two, figure out your next steps."

"But what about my shop?"

Balinas let out a chuckle.

"You and your shop," he shook his head, still laughing gently to himself.

"Yes, I'll need to know how it's doing without me at the helm."

"It's fine. In fact, business has never been so busy."

"Really? Oh, well, erm, I guess it will be alright for a little longer then."

"That's the spirit ... Ah, it seems we have a visitor."

The sound of footsteps came from the stairwell from the great library.

Hugh and Barrington ran to get some heavy books, before Balinas stopped them.

"I sense there is no need for those today, gentlemen."

Hugh and Barrington looked back, confused, before turning back to look at the stairwell. With each step, Hugh's breathing increased. The torches on the wall flickered into life, as the person finally made to into the room. Hugh stood staring, open-mouthed, dropping his book with a thud, filling the air with a cloud of dust. His heart fluttered briefly like a moth coming to rest as he looked from the person to Emily then back the newcomer again.

Barrington went over to Balinas.

"Well, this should be interesting."

They both looked at the unfolding scene.

"Hello, Hugh."

"Who's this?" said Emily, standing to face the newcomer.

"Hugh? Who is this?" said the mystery person.

"I think you'll find, I asked first," said Emily.

The pair rounded on Hugh, who swallowed hard.

"Adelia, what a lovely surprise!"

Acknowledgements

Well, here we are at the end of another book, and if you are reading this, thank you. It takes a lot of people and support to write a book, especially from those closest to you. None of this would be possible without the help and support of my wife, Kay and my two children, Seb and Josie. Thank you for putting up with the endless hours of typing that go into these books and for supporting me through the good times and the bad. I would also like to take the time to say thank you to all of my friends who have helped me along the way, from words of encouragement to numerous cups of coffee.

When it comes to the book itself, I have a large team backing me up, and it would be rude of me not to mention them. Thank you to Warren Layberry for all of your help and support, with numerous emails, calls and editing throughout the entire creative process.

Thank you also to Lynn Godson – The Digital Wordsmith for proofreading expertise and the many messages, coffees, chats and support.

That you to Patrick, Kim, Benjamin and the rest of the team at Publishing Push for all of the work and support you have provided, guiding me once more through the choppy waters of self-publishing. Thank you to the team at Reedsy for making it possible to find professionals and link up with them. It goes without saying that everyone has gone the extra mile to help make this book become a reality, and I am eternally grateful for all of your support along the way.

On a slightly different tack, I would like to say thank you to Steve Cawte for helping me with the book launch of Firestone, along with Rob Bushnell, Cheryl Page and Rob Purle, for reading excerpts from the book itself.

Last and by no means least, thank you to you, the reader, for not only buying the book and reading it, but for your continued support and messages. Without you taking a chance on me and joining me for the adventure, this wouldn't be possible. So now I must go and dig Hugh out of the hole he has dug for himself. You can keep up to date with the announcements about *Tempus, Book Three in the Lore of Tellus Series* by following me on social media and signing up to the mailing list.

Coming soon: Tempus

Hugh Geber, Barrington Delphin and Emily Le Fey are in hiding under the protection of the Collins family at the University for Science and Progression, after returning to Portis-Montis with the lore book for magic. The unexpected arrival of Adelia Geber, Hugh's sister in law, has only added to the complicated mix.

Three books of lore still remain out in the open, and tensions are rising across the New World, with reports that the battle for Skellig-Krieg against forces loyal to the Elf King, is expected to happen within within days.

When their cover is blown, the group must decide whether to leave Portis-Montis unprepared to look for the next book of lore, or to join those readying for the battle of Skellig-Krieg — a decision which threatens to pull the group of friends apart. When the news reaches them that the Elf King, and Robert Smithson are already on the trail for the next book of lore, the group must face their woes head on. The situation couldn't be more dire.

Now they must decide between joining a battle that threatens to destroy not only the world in which they live, but also harm those they hold close, or to go after the books, which in the wrong hands will spell disaster for the world at large.

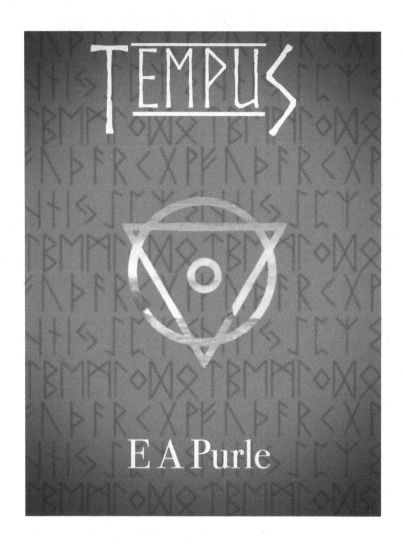

TEMPUS

E A Purle

Previous books in the series

LORE OF TELLUS
BOOK ONE

On the world of Tellus there are two ways of doing things: the Old Way and the New Way. In the city of Portis-Montis, these two ways and their worlds collide.

Hugh Geber is the alchemist at the University of Science and Progression. In a world where everyone follows the family career, he has found himself the last in line to carry the torch.

When a meeting with Chancellor Robert James Smithson leaves him with an impossible deadline and a mysterious package, Hugh is left with no choice but to try and save the family name along with his job. Fate, however, is not on his side, and his world is turned upside-down.

Now Hugh must not only fight for his place within the university, but also find out what lies behind the mysterious package before time runs out.

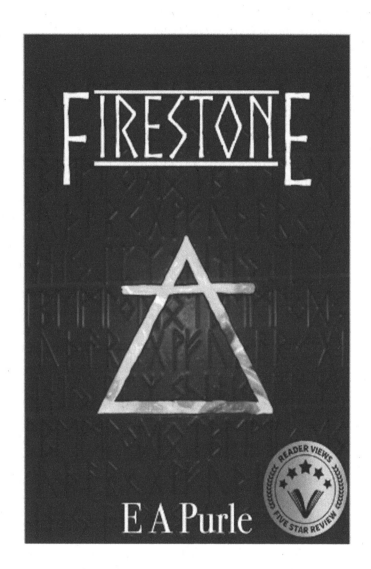

Firestone: (Lore of Tellus, Book One)

E.A. Purle Alicorn Books (2021) ISBN 91802270566

Reviewed by Tammy Ruggles for Reader Views (12/2021)

Talk about a YA steampunk lover's dream! What happens when the old way meets the new way? Tellus is a world where the old and the new clash on a daily basis, and main character, Hugh Geber, is the alchemist at the heart of the story.

At the University of Science and Progression, Hugh feels obligated to follow in his family's footsteps, but Chancellor Smithson throws a wrench into his plans by handing Hugh a challenging deadline and a strange package. Hugh now has to attempt to salvage his family name and his position, but it is a near-impossible task. His life is thrust into a whirlwind, which sets the stage for an amazing journey of suspense, conflict, drama, and steampunk.

Purle sets up this drama with intriguing, well-developed characters that you want to follow throughout the story. In fact, you get so immersed in their lives that you care about every single thing that happens to them. Add the mystery of the package, and the old-versus-new mentality, and you have a compelling story on your hands. Hugh is fighting for more than his job. He's battling for something bigger—his family name, his integrity, and tradition, but time is the enemy. How can he keep one world in the old, and one in the new? It comes down to pure survival.

This author has created a world in which you can easily become absorbed. Each scene opens up new possibilities, exploration, and descriptions which pique the senses and imagination. I love the author's use of vivid imagery and creative engineering. The unexpected events add spice to the story, and you really don't know what lies around the corner. The alchemy aspect is intriguing, of course, and the characters are easy to like — especially Hugh, as a heavy burden rests on his shoulders. I love the contrast of the old and the new, and there are parts of the book that will stay with you even after you've finished the tale.

There is a sweet quirkiness to some of the story that I enjoy, which adds a lot of personality to a book that's already overflowing with it, and so much more. "Firestone" could very well be the next "must-read" YA steampunk/fantasy series.

See below for the different ways to keep up to date
with E A Purle.

You can subscribe to the
mailing list here:
http://eepurl.com/hol2A5

 @ EAPurle

 @ EAPurle

 @ EAPurle

 @ Author.EAPurle

EAPURLE

 @ EAPurle

🎵 TikTok @ Author.EAPurle